EYES OF EMBER

THE IMDALIND SERIES, BOOK TWO

REBECCA ETHINGTON

IMDALIND PRESS

Copyediting by, Another View Editing; C&D Editing
Cover Design @ Sarah Hansen, Okay Creations
Formatting by Inkstain Interior Book Designing

Production Management by Imdalind Press

ISBN (print) 978-1-949725-01-8
ISBN (e-book) 978-0-9884837-2-9

Printed in USA
This Edition, April 2013

ISBN: 978-0-9884837-2-9

❀ Created with Vellum

THE IMDALIND SERIES

CONTENTS

To My Mom
Who has stayed with this story from the beginning.

1
———

I AM GOING to kill Edmund LaRue.

I repeated the words to myself as a reminder that the thought was still there; that my conviction was still true.

The thought had started as an ember of possibility when I had seen Edmund wipe the last of Ryland's memories three nights ago, and with them went all the memories of me. If it had been more than an ember, or if I had been more powerful, I would have killed him then. As it was, Ilyan had grabbed me and dragged me away.

Being forced to leave the one person in the world that I loved had snapped something deep inside of me, which caused the thought to grow; the ember growing into a spark.

That spark promised me that I would be the one to kill Edmund. He had destroyed my best friend, the one person left for me to love. I owed him for that.

The spark became a flame when I went back and visited Ryland in our space between dream and reality for the last time. Inside of our Tòuha I had seen him as a little boy who looked at me and told me my eyes looked like diamonds. I could feel the flame in me then; an inferno of hatred, desire and power.

Although my mind was set on its course and my chosen path was clear, my heart and body had not gotten the message. I spent the next three days trapped in overwhelming heartbreak that I could not escape, try as I might. My body ached with emotional pain and erased any desire that I had to move.

I knew it was not a natural reaction. Something else was wrong. Somehow I knew that this was affecting me far more than a normal heartbreak should, but I still accepted it. In turn, I accepted my lack of determination to fight it. In the back of my mind, burning with a heat that seared deeply into my soul, the desire to strike Edmund from the earth still reigned.

So I lay still, an emotionless mask in place as my soul battled with itself. My mind planned Edmund's demise while I ached for what it could not have; what had been taken from me.

I could have stayed locked in my torment forever if Ilyan had not been so persistent.

"Silný, it's time to wake up."

His voice was soft in my ear, his hand resting against the side of my face. His fore finger rested softly on the mark below my ear; the mark that had destroyed my life. I pushed his hand away and covered my head with the thick comforter in an attempt to ignore him.

"You have to get out of bed sometime, prosím Joclyn." He placed his hand over the blanket, the weight of it pushing into my shoulder. I wished he would move away. I didn't want his comfort.

"Leave me alone," I said, my voice harsh.

"I can't do that, Silnÿ. You know I won't." Ilyan's Slavic accent grew deeper as he spoke.

I knew he wouldn't leave me alone. He had been trying to get me out of this bed for the last three days.

From under my comforter, I had watched him as he moved around the tiny studio apartment we had been trapped in. My eyes followed him as he made bowl after bowl of vegetable soup, forcing me to eat and drink when I wouldn't even bother talking to him. I watched him as he sat at the table working on some project or another. He had made a nest of blankets in the small space of floor near the bed, content to give me space and privacy but also too scared to go far. I had listened as he had spoken on the phone with Ovailia every hour on the hour, getting updates of who had arrived in Prague. Part of me wanted to be there with Wyn and all the others like me, but the other part reminded me how much danger I was in and how important it was that I stay hidden.

Ilyan had even called Wyn and prompted me to talk to her about what I was feeling, but nothing Wyn said had helped either. I ignored it all.

I wasn't sure what I wanted, or what I needed. The desire to seek Edmund out right then was strong, but I still couldn't dig that desire out from behind the oppressive wall of despair and pain that I had built.

The pressure of Ilyan's hand increased as he moved it around to rub my back. I shied away from the contact even more; it made me uncomfortable. He wasn't supposed to be the one to comfort me. The one who should be was gone forever, though.

I didn't want Ilyan to touch me.

"Joclyn."

I pulled down the blanket enough to look out at him.

His straggly blonde hair was longer than usual, hanging down to his shoulder blades, and his face was full of worry.

"Ahoj," he whispered as I emerged from underneath the blankets. "How are you feeling?"

I closed my eyes, unsure of how to answer him. I was angry, desperate, lost, broken, in pain, and sad. It shouldn't be possible for one person to feel so many emotions at the same time.

"I hurt," I said, my voice cracking with uncertainty.

"Where?" he asked, alarmed.

"In my heart." It was the best response I could come up with. While my heart did hurt, it was more than that. Everything inside me was shattered. Rather than a broken heart, this felt more like I had broken everything. My heart was constricted, but around it, my whole body felt tight and as though it was bound together with hot wire.

Underneath the lethargy the desire for revenge burned steadily.

"I know how you feel." I reeled and swelled with anger. I knew he meant well—that he was trying to connect with me —but it felt like he was invalidating my feelings.

"How could you possibly know how I feel?" I snapped. Ilyan didn't back away from my harsh words. He continued rubbing his hand against my spine, the pressure somewhat dulled through the blankets.

"Edmund has taken something away from me, too, Silnỳ. Ryland was my brother as much as he was your other half; your mate. I can't help but feel that I failed you as much as I failed him."

I wanted to yell at him for not teaching me to use my magic better, for not training me the right way. I wanted to blame him for taking me into a battle unprepared, but that wasn't right. It wasn't *entirely* his fault, and he didn't deserve all the blame. It was my fault, too. It was my fault we had lost Ryland.

"I failed him, too. I failed you. I failed everyone." I pushed the blanket away from myself as the frustration of what I was saying hit me. "All you asked me to do was get him out, and I couldn't even do that."

I cringed at how bitter my voice sounded; how angry each syllable tasted against my tongue.

I shifted my weight as I repositioned myself to sit, the pressure in my unwilling joints building as I moved. Ilyan reached out to help me as he came to sit next to me. My back seized and I swayed, my body torn between crying, yelling, and finding some way to disappear.

"You didn't fail, Silnỳ," Ilyan's hand moved from mine to rest against the skin of my cheek. His touch was hot with the warmth of his powerful magic that pulsed underneath his skin. Ilyan kept his ability restrained inside of him, just the opposite of Ryland who had comforted and healed me with every touch.

Ilyan caressed my cheek, letting his fingers trail behind my ear to rest on my mark. He kept his hand there, his eyes wide as he looked into mine. I could tell he was trying to understand what was going on inside me and I wished I could tell him, but even I didn't know.

"I did fail," I spoke harshly, "and now I am alone."

I wasn't sure if I had spoken out of loss or in anger at the new reality Edmund had made for me. Both thoughts occupied the forefront of my mind, each vying for my attention.

"You have me, Silnỳ, and you have Wyn. We are both here to help you through this." I stiffened away from his touch. I knew he was right, but I was still scared to let anyone else in. My heart hurt too much. I was broken now more than ever.

"I know," I whispered, trying to find the strength to explain. "I want him back, Ilyan. I wish..."

"I know," Ilyan said, cutting me off softly. "I want him back, too. But he is gone, Joclyn. There is no finding him. His mind has been erased."

"Please, don't..." I begged. I didn't want to hear it.

I moved away from him, my body leaning against the wall.

"Why did we have to fail?"

"Everything happens for a reason, Silnỳ," he said. "Perhaps we must move through this trial to meet our true purpose." His voice had taken on the regal air that was so fitting for him as the ruler of the protectors of magic, the Skřítek. I cringed against his tone.

"True purpose," I repeated, shocked to feel the flame within me grow stronger.

Ilyan ran his fingers through the stubble of hair on the back of my head then down to my back and over the skin that had been revealed by the shredded club clothes I still wore. I pulled away from his touch, my stomach twisting at his intimacy.

"What do you want to do, Joclyn? What is your true purpose?" Ilyan asked softly.

His words were like gasoline on an open flame. They burned and smoldered inside of me, igniting the need for revenge, making it stronger. The web of heartbreak and confusion shattered, the remaining fragments swallowed up by my growing determination. I could see everything before me, my true path as it had been laid out.

"I want to avenge Ryland. I want to be the one to destroy Edmund LaRue." My voice rang clear through the apartment, the power behind it causing Ilyan's eyes to widen in shock.

"You want to fight?" Ilyan asked.

"Yes."

"Then I will teach you everything you need to know," Ilyan replied as my nerves jumped in anticipation. I could feel my soul piecing itself back together with the thought.

"Everything?" Before, Ilyan had only taught me the basics and it had ended badly for everyone.

"Yes, Silný. This time you need to know everything. I had hoped that by bringing you two together that I would be able to unlock your true ability. That's why I taught you so little. I wanted to see what you could do, and it was very foolish of me. But now, Ryland has lost his memories of you and become his father's puppet. He is now only a weapon at Edmund's disposal. Ryland as he is now will stop at nothing to hunt you down and kill you Joclyn. If you wish to be the one to avenge your mate, you must prepare."

I nodded once and attempted to cast aside the last of my self-pity, pain, and heartbreak. Though it didn't leave, it became another fragment of the broken person I had become.

Ilyan squared his jaw and stood to face me, his hand extended toward me.

"Then come; it's time to begin."

I widened my eyes. He didn't mean now, did he? But it was obvious that he did. His jaw was clenched and his eyes held that maniacal power I had seen in him so many times before.

I breathed deeply, preparing myself before I took his hand. Ilyan pulled me to standing, my joints swelling in subtle pain as I moved. I stood facing him, defying the agony of my long-inactive body. I had only been standing for a moment before I knew something was wrong. My head swam and my body felt like it was turning on the spot, even though I knew I wasn't moving. My balance left from the crazy motion, and I shifted sideways as my body fell. Ilyan's arms reaching out to catch me just in time.

"Are you all right?" Ilyan asked. The alarm in his voice surprised me. I nodded my head, the room spinning less and less.

"You haven't stood in a few days; I suppose it is to be expected." His voice was low, as if even he didn't believe his words. His grip on my elbow tightened a bit as we began to move, obviously worried I would fall again.

When he looked at me, his forehead crinkled before grabbing one of the half-filled glasses of water that he had been forcing me to drink from for days.

After I drank, Ilyan walked me toward the small bathroom. I looked behind me reluctantly to where the small double bed was pushed up against the side wall and the bathroom wall. A sliding glass door was at the foot of the bed and the tiny kitchen was on the other wall. The only floor space to speak of was between the bed and kitchen, but most of that had been taken up by Ilyan's makeshift bed.

It was a tissue box that someone had mistaken for a studio apartment. The idea of spending any amount of time in this claustrophobic space was nauseating; sharing it with another person was terrifying.

"I want you to take a shower. There are clothes in the bathroom for you."

Sure enough, sitting on the counter in the bathroom was a small pile of clothes, including a black hoodie I had never seen before.

"Where is Ryland's hoodie?" I asked, unsurprised by my alarm.

8

"It's gone, Joclyn. When we failed, many of our number fled to the Motel. They were followed. Anything that was left there was destroyed out of necessity."

My heart sunk and my head swam again, Ilyan's hold on my elbow increased as my body swayed to one side.

"Maybe now is not the time for a shower," he said.

I looked down. My shirt consisted of merely scraps of fabric and my stomach was covered by dried blood and ash. My mind flashed back to memories of that night; to Ryland digging a tiny blade into my chest. I swallowed hard, willing the tears to stay away.

"Now is fine," I said.

"Good, but first..."

Ilyan placed his hand against my face, his eyes boring into mine as he pushed his magic into me. I wondered what he was doing, but he only smiled at me, his blue eyes twinkling. My head began to prickle as his magic congregated there, causing my hair to grow back to how it had been before.

Ilyan removed his hand. I turned to look at myself in the mirror. Dark black make-up was smeared all over my face, my bright silver eyes twinkling among the smudges, but my hair was black, straight, and long again—maybe even a bit longer than it had been originally.

"Thank you."

"Of course," he said as he turned on the steaming water before moving toward the door. "Enjoy your shower. I'll have a surprise waiting for you when you get out."

The door clicked shut behind him. I didn't look at it for long before turning toward the sink that I had leaned against. My reflection was staring at me through the mirror, my mouth opening in shock at the haggard face that looked back. All my battle wounds were still visible and much of my body was covered with dried blood. I ripped off what was left of my shirt and followed the trail of dried blood up to a small scar that now lay over my heart.

A small line of raised skin stood out where Ryland had stabbed me in his attempt to kill me. The scar was rough from the quick healing he had done in the brief time that he had regained control of his body. That had been the last time he was himself; before his mind had been erased forever.

I ripped my eyes away from the scar and they landed on the ruby necklace that hung around my neck; another gift from him. I reached up and grabbed it, removing the chain from around my neck, and scraped off the blood that had dried to the beautiful ruby to reveal the bright stone underneath.

I hadn't touched the stone since I had used it to see an adorable five year old boy who had promised to take my pain away and who said he loved my eyes. It had been the final proof that Ryland as I knew him was gone.

I threw the necklace into the sink, the stone clinking loudly against the porcelain. I didn't want to enter the Tõuha ever again, yet seeing it there in the sink made me want to snatch it back up and keep it safe. I hadn't felt the beat of Ryland's heart emanate from it for days, though. The connection had died.

The bathroom had filled with the steam from the shower and I was surrounded by the sweet smelling fog. It smelled vaguely of plant life, making me wonder what Ilyan had placed in here to react to the steam that way. Something to help settle my nerves, I was sure. The hot mist seemed to fill my head and I swayed again, my hands clenching the sink in an effort to steady myself.

I turned the cold water tap of the sink on with one quick

movement then brought my hand back to its position against the counter to keep myself upright. The water flowed over the ruby, removing bits of blood that swirled down the drain. I let it flow for a minute before shutting it off, leaving the necklace to sit in the bottom of the sink with some blood still attached to the smooth surface.

I slunk out of my pants and stumbled into the shower. My stomach shifted, the lack of contents adding to my swirling world.

The hot water scalded my skin, but I didn't care. I let the water run over me as it burned the heavy makeup off of my face, washed the ash and blood from my body, and singed away the dirt and rubble from what had been Ryland's home. The heat moved into me as if it was trying to thaw the emotion out.

I leaned against the side of the shower, breathing deeply in an effort to regain some stability.

It wasn't working.

The spinning was only increasing as I looked at the faucet of the shower, trying to focus on it to steady myself. The silver fixture moved, spun, and duplicated itself, even though I was certain I was holding still.

My eyes closed as I breathed in the steam, hoping that somehow the dizziness would leave, yet it got worse. I was forced to stumble out of the shower, hair unwashed, only to have my foot catch on the shower curtain and send me slamming into the ground.

My shoulder impacted hard on the tiles while a jolt of pain seared down my spine. I yelled out on impact and frantically tried to right myself, however the dizziness expanded, and I collapsed back onto the floor where the cool tiles under my skin seemed to clear my mind a bit, so I focused on them.

"Joclyn!" Ilyan yelled through the door, his voice panicked. "Are you okay?"

"Yes." My voice was muffled by the tile. I wasn't sure Ilyan had heard me because he continued to pound on the door. I tried again, but his panicked yelling drowned out my voice. Great, he was going to barge in and I was lying naked in the middle of the bathroom floor.

I forced myself up and grabbed the hoodie and pajama pants from the counter, pulling them on over my damp body. Right at the moment that I pulled the hoodie down, my body collapsed again as the door was flung open, allowing Ilyan to tumble into the room with his blonde hair swinging.

"Joclyn!" he yelled.

"I'm here."

I was surprised by how weak my voice was. I knew I wasn't feeling well, but I didn't think it was that bad. I shook my head hoping that the dizziness would leave, but it only got worse.

Ilyan kneeled down next to me. His hands flew to my cheeks, his magic plunging into me as he checked for any injuries.

"I'm fine, Ilyan." I batted his hand away from me, breaking the connection.

"Are you sure?" His accent was so thick, I barely understood him.

I nodded, but I was starting to wonder if I really was. This was beginning to feel more like I was being drained than a dehydrated dizziness. It was as if someone was reaching inside me and scrambling everything together.

Ilyan wrapped his arm around my waist and pulled me to standing, his body supporting me as my head continued to spin. I didn't dare say anything, so I let him lead me out of the bathroom.

"Bacon?" I asked, surprised at the smell of bacon and eggs that had filled the small living space. Ilyan was a vegan and had eaten no more than fruit or vegetables for the last few centuries. The fact that he would even attempt to make bacon and eggs was humorous as well as heartening.

"Yes," he grimaced, "I just hope I did it right. I think the influx of protein might help you."

Ilyan placed me at one of the chairs at the tiny table where what was surely a full pack of perfectly crisp, browned bacon sat in all its greasy goodness before me. I hadn't eaten meat in what felt like months and just the smell was making my mouth water.

"Thank you, Ilyan." I smiled brightly at him, ignoring the swelling and swimming that was going on inside my brain.

His eyes were shining joyfully, but it wasn't only happiness I saw behind his eyes, there was something there I couldn't quite place. I was trying to figure out what it might be when the swelling in my head grew into something more painful and I called out, clutching my hands to my head.

I could barely make out Ilyan rushing towards me from the kitchenette; calling to me, yelling for me. The pain continued to grow as my vision blacked out, and the air swirled past me as I fell from the chair.

I never felt the impact, but on my way down I could have sworn I heard someone laughing.

2

———

"SAKRA, Ovailia! I don't know how it happened!"

Ilyan's voice woke me up from a deep sleep, and I immediately regretted it. My body hurt and my bones creaked and ached as if they were swelling. My chest fought with every breath, a heavy weight restricting my movements.

Ilyan yelled something in Czech and I reluctantly opened my eyes. Even my eye lids hurt.

It was night. The only light in the room came from a small lamp near the balcony that lit up the room eerily with a heavy, yellow glow. The bacon still sat on the table, and the chair I had been sitting in was knocked over. A large, dark stain spread over the carpet nearby. I moved to try and get a better look, but a pressurized pain spread over my skull. I closed my eyes tightly against the threatening migraine.

"That's just it, Ovailia, it's as if her magic has been drained. Normally it's a suffocating torrent when I try to heal her, but now there is nothing there. Nothing is fighting me."

My magic was gone? I reached inside of me and pulled it up as I had been taught to do, but it didn't respond as usual. It was slow and heavy, like when you move your hand through sludge. Even the attempt to work it up and push it outside of me caused pain.

"You are asking me questions I do not know the answers to," Ilyan spoke harshly before transitioning into Czech again. I shifted my weight again and my back seized up in the exact places I had broken it a few weeks before.

"Ilyan!" I called out to him. My spine curled, arching itself out in a fan before freezing me in place.

"I have to go." I heard the phone click shut, and a moment later Ilyan's hands pressed against my skin. His magic filled me instantly. It raced through my skin faster than lightning and with more strength than I had ever experienced.

My eyes opened wide in surprise at his power filling me so aggressively. If the way Ilyan's magic burned into my body at that moment was any indication as to how powerful he was, I was beginning to understand why he was revered.

Moments after his hands had touched my skin, my back relaxed and straightened. Some of the bone pain had also left, and I was feeling blissfully relaxed.

"Are you alright?" he asked, his voice strained.

"I think so," I said. I shifted a bit, but decided against any larger movements as my body protested again.

"What happened, Joclyn?" Ilyan asked, "Do you remember anything?"

"Not really. I remember my head swelling, and then I was falling, and someone was laughing..." I looked to Ilyan, concerned that I sounded like a mad man. He moved aside the thick braid he had obviously placed in my hair and pushed his hand against my neck. My nerves jumped a bit in confusion about what had happened.

"Someone was laughing? Do you know who?"

"No," I whispered.

Ilyan's hand still rested against my neck, his magic reaching into every part of me. It was warm and comforting, and though it was not the magic I wished for, it still helped.

"Are you going to heal me, Ilyan?"

"I've been trying, Silnỳ. I am not sure I can." My eyes grew wide and my heart raced until his magic surged again and my nerves calmed.

"Trying?" I repeated, my eyes falling to the dark spot on the carpet. "What happened, Ilyan?"

Ilyan's line of sight traced mine, and I saw him stiffen at the sight of the large, dark splotch. "You fell, and then you began to bleed a dark fluid. It wasn't blood, but it was foul. Your whole body was shaking. I thought..." He lowered his head, hiding his glistening eyes. "I thought I had lost you."

"I was bleeding?" I asked, confused.

"It's the only way I know how to explain it. Something formed on your skin then poured out of your eyes and ears." Ilyan looked away and closed his eyes. I could feel the stress rolling off of his body in waves. It added to my fear and I grabbed his wrist, needing some form of connection.

"It's okay, Joclyn. You're going to be okay." His voice was strong, yet I could hear the lie. He didn't really know if I would be alright, and it scared me.

"I guess you never should have forced me to get out of bed," I joked, trying to lighten the mood. Ilyan's head snapped up to look deeply into me, the intensity of his gaze like a pressure against my soul.

"I guess not," he said, his hand moving to trace the lines of the braid.

"I heard what you said to Ovailia," I said. Ilyan's body stiffened as if I had caught him saying something he shouldn't. "About how my magic isn't fighting you anymore," I clarified. He relaxed a bit, surging his powerful tendrils through me again.

"You are the only one I have ever met who actively fights me, or is strong enough to do so."

"What?" I let my question trail away, not knowing what to ask, however I needed clarification.

"My magic is stronger than most, Joclyn. Most of the time it floods into another person and at times I have trouble controlling my own strength. But you have always fought me. You are as powerful as I am it seems."

My eyes opened wide as I tried to process what he had said. I wasn't sure if he was kidding or not, his tone could go either way. Regardless of whether I was normally powerful or not, though, I still couldn't reach my magic right then.

"I tried... I tried to use my magic, but it didn't respond." Ilyan's eyes grew wide and my heart thumped again in fear. "What's happening to me, Ilyan?"

"I don't know," he said. "But, I have ideas."

"What?"

"Do you remember at the party?" he asked, and my body stiffened automatically. "When Ryland sealed himself to you, completing the Zělství?"

I didn't respond. I only stared at him, waiting for him to continue.

"When magic is sealed together it is a permanent union. If Edmund has made Ryland break the connection between the two of you, your magic would be separated from half of itself. When one of our kind who has mated dies, they take half of their partner's magic but leave half of their own behind. Yet, if Ryland has broken that connection..." Ilyan paused and dragged his hand heavily through his hair while his eyes darted away from me.

"He's broken..." My voice caught as the air sucked itself out of my lungs. The Ryland I had known was gone, but breaking our bond would mean there was no hope of getting him back. The thought terrified me.

"So what makes you think that this could be caused by a broken bond?"

Ilyan looked away, making me nervous about what he was about to say.

"Ilyan?"

"I have seen it once before, when my mother died. With half of her own magic gone, and none of my father's to replace it, her body began to shut down. It would be akin to what happens to humans when an organ in their body does not work. They fade and suffer until they die."

"So I am dying," I cut him off.

"I believe so."

"And you can't save me this time?" Panic clenched my stomach, spreading pain deep into my legs. I ignored it. "Ilyan?"

"I am trying, Silnỳ. There are normally ways around this, but nothing is working."

His eyes were shining with tears and boring into me with that same pained look he had before. He moved his hand from my head to rest his fingers against my mark.

"I can't let you die, Silnỳ. I will do everything in my power to stop it."

I couldn't look at him anymore. I couldn't cope with seeing him cry over me. I didn't want to.

I rolled away from him, calling out as the pain engulfed my body again. Ilyan helped to move me and lifted the blanket over me.

"Sleep, Joclyn. You need your strength."

I barely registered that the flow of his magic had changed before I was plunged into the black abyss of sleep.

I HAD BEEN HERE BEFORE.

I had stood in the center of this clearing a hundred times. I had looked up into these trees and watched their long arms stretch to the sky in hopeful longing. I watched them now, and although they were the same, something was terrifyingly different. Perhaps it was the color, or the way the branches cut a jagged edge into the night sky. Whatever it was, it made my heart stutter.

A thick mist swirled around my legs, picking up the light-weight cotton of my pajama pants. It crept over the forest floor in a dense cloud that wet my bare feet and made the forest floor look like a living thing with its rise and flow.

I heard a deep growl behind me and my body tensed, although I didn't dare to turn. There was a pause as the mist continued to roll and swell before the growl returned accompanied by a warm, putrid breath against my ear. The deep sound rumbled through me as the fog swelled at the same time that the owner's hard chest rippled against my back.

"Hello, Joclyn."

Cail.

The fog took on substance, the sound of his breathing freezing me for a second. I could almost feel his warmth, his excitement, rippling off of him and increasing my fear. I felt his magic pulse, one influx of energy reverberating through the heavy sludge of magic inside of me. It was enough to serve as a warning. So I ran.

My feet carried me out of the clearing, plunging me into the pitch dark of the forest. I ran as my eyes adjusted to the black and starless night. The trees flew by me as I picked up speed, what was left of my own magic attempting to carry me faster. I could still hear his foot falls behind me from the crunch of the dying plant life as he passed, marking his progress.

He was getting closer, his breathing louder; he was almost right behind me.

"Run Joclyn, run to my master!" he yelled from behind me, but I barely heard him. I picked up my pace and ran faster, only to sense the world around me shift and change. As I slowed in confusion, I could feel carpet under my dirty feet and the air no longer smelled so crisp and vibrant. Everything here was dying.

I looked down the hall. Once again I was in a place I knew, but nothing about it was quite right. The cream colored walls were dirty and covered with black spider webs of soot and flame. The carpet had been burned away in giant patches and part of the wall to my right had been blown away, leaving a gaping hole straight into the night sky.

I walked along the burnt fragments of carpet toward the door, a door I had entered almost every day of my life— Ryland's. My heart thudded angrily in my chest as I moved closer, the slab of wood dangling by one hinge.

I ducked underneath it into his room, a room that was gutted by flame. Embers still glowed in the corner where fragments of his bed were scattered. I stepped cautiously around the partition to where his big, squishy couch sat.

The sofa had been torn into pieces that lay haphazardly around the space, exposed stuffing melted into the carpet and walls.

"Jos," Ryland's tender voice spoke from behind the battered couch. "You came."

I stepped around the couch, my feet guiding me to him.

"Ryland!" I almost threw myself into him. He was broken and bruised, the way I had last seen him. His body crumpled in on itself as he fought for control over his mind.

Burrowed into a bit of the broken couch and sections of his collapsed closet, embers of a still burning fire glowed near him, the light shimmering in his hair. I sat next to him, careful to avoid the smoldering and broken bits of the room around him.

"What did you do to your hair, Jos? I always loved your hair."

"My hair is long again, Ryland. See." I pulled the braid Ilyan had given me around so he could see, but his eyes were focused somewhere off in the distance, his arms lifted slightly as if he was reaching for something.

"...Steal the car..." His voice faded in and out before he slumped even further. His body gave out as his arms fell, I grabbed at him, summoning the sludge inside of me, determined to get him out of there. My hands shook as I looked around, my heart pulsing frantically. Ultimately, however, I knew there was nothing I could do.

"What? Not going to save your love?" I froze at Edmund's voice, my body tensing.

"Edmund," I gasped, moving closer to Ryland in fear.

"Go on," he taunted, his voice deep and menacing. "Save him. Let me see how powerful you are."

I refused to take my eyes off Edmund. He was right there; right in front of me. My magic may have been useless, thick and stagnant inside of me, but my heart beat heavier and my desire for revenge grew. I looked away from him to grab a small, burning stick and hurl it at him, hoping that my weak attack would at least let him know that I was willing to fight.

"Now, now," Edmund said, "none of that. After all, what's the point of your useless weapons when I possess the most powerful weapon of all?"

"Miss me beautiful?" Ryland's twisted voice whispered beside me and I spun to face him. My stomach plummeted as I came face to face with the pitch black eyes of a new Ryland. The Ryland who had lost his fight with his father, whose memory had been erased.

"No!" True terror filled me at seeing him.

"I believe you have something that belongs to me." Ryland's hands pulled me to him and lifted the back of my sweater, letting his hand come in contact with my skin. I began to scream in fear as his magic rushed into me the second I felt his cold touch. It flowed in an angry wave that spread to the very tips of my toes and lasted a moment before it began to sweep out again. As the heat left, so did my magic.

The thick, useless, almost dead bits of magic that had hidden inside of me seeped away and into Ryland. My screams died down as the pain left with my magic while I was left weak and helpless from the lack of power. I slipped out of Ryland's arms and onto the ash covered floor.

"Dispose of it," I heard Edmund say.

Ryland's hands encompassed my head, placing pressure against my skull. His hands grew hot and his magic filled my skull with fire as he attempted to burn away my brain.

My own scream jostled me awake, my eyes adjusting to the dark studio apartment. My legs fought against the heavy comforters Ilyan had covered me with. I kicked and screamed to get away from them, to make it back to Ryland at the same time that my body called out in pain from each shift of weight sending agony through me. I ignored it all, my focus only on finding Ryland.

"Ryland!" I yelled out loudly. I was sure he was right there; sure he was going to answer me.

Strong arms encircled me, and for one fleeting moment I was certain it was Ryland. But the arms were wrong. They were leaner, stronger. I pushed away from Ilyan's arms, screaming out as the pain from my aching body became too much.

"Joclyn! What's wrong?" Ilyan yelled above my screams, his eyes as wide as mine in his panic at being awoken.

"Ryland!" I yelled out again, not giving Ilyan an answer. I continued to scream and yell for Ryland as I scrambled across the floor, my legs giving out a few steps in. I tumbled down to the ground as another wave of pain shot through my spine, crippling me.

"Joclyn!" Ilyan was at my side immediately, his hands moving to press against me.

"Don't!" I yelled, pushing him away. I didn't need his magic to calm or heal me. I didn't need him. I needed Ryland. "I have to find Ryland!"

I clawed my way toward the window, desperate to get out, to see if I could sense him. To see if I could save him. He had been in my dream; he remembered me in the dream. No, it hadn't been a dream, it was a Tŏuha. A shared consciousness. I still had a chance at saving him.

"Ryland?" Ilyan said.

"Yes!" I yelled, continuing to claw my way toward the glass. "He was there. In the Tŏuha. I saw him, he... he remembered me... I can save him..." I reached the glass as my spine clenched again. I screamed as my body threw me to the ground, the pain incapacitating me.

Ilyan was there a moment later, his magic rushing into me in a wave of power. My body relaxed as the pain seeped away despite its attempt to possess me.

"He's gone, Silnỳ. He's gone," Ilyan said.

"No! I saw him, in the Tǒuha. He remembered me. He…"

"It wasn't a Tǒuha, Silnỳ…" Ilyan moved me toward him, my pain-filled body unable to resist the unwanted contact.

"It was… I saw him." I was becoming desperate. I needed him to understand. I was running out of time.

"No. Your necklace still lies in the bathroom and your magic… Silnỳ, the bond is not strong enough to connect with him without it." I tried to push away from him, but it was useless. My body was too weak.

"I saw him, Ilyan… I saw him." I needed to get to him; I needed to open the window and find him.

"It was a dream, Silnỳ. He's gone."

"No!" I sobbed, attempting to move away from Ilyan again, yet he held me in place. "No, I saw him."

"He's gone."

Slowly I gave in, the tears of my pain and my broken heart too much for me to fight. I cried into Ilyan's bare chest, his hair falling around both of us as he cradled me and began to sing. I leaned into him as he sang the same song he had comforted me with the night he had flown me away from Ryland.

The rough Czech words surrounded me as he sang over and over, soothing me back to sleep.

3

———

"Jos! Jos! Did you fall asleep again?" Wyn's voice was loud over the speaker phone. I startled awake from my doze, my head swimming with the pain.

"Sorry," I looked toward Ilyan who had obviously begun standing in alarm at Wyn's exclamation. Seeing me awake, he settled back into his seat, returning to the leatherwork he had been working on since we had first gotten here.

"What were you saying?" I prompted. I heard her exhale on the other end of the line. I knew it was irritating talking to me like this, but I was finding it hard to stay awake for long.

I had been haunted by the same dream every night since it had first awakened me in a panic five days ago. While I had given up on my foolish attempt to track Ryland down, the lack of sleep mixed with the screaming panic I awoke in had made me exceptionally weak. I wasn't awake for much of the day anymore. If it wasn't for Ilyan—calming me, protecting me, and healing me several times throughout the day—I knew I might have passed away already.

I cringed at the thought.

I looked up to Ilyan again, unsurprised to find him watching me, his eyes lifted from his work.

"I was saying," Wyn replied and I was sure she was rolling her eyes, "I have finished your room in Prague for whenever Ilyan lets you out of that jail he's trying to pass off as a living space. Nice white bed, a huge loft you can fly up and down from all day long. Talon insisted that I make it brown, though."

"No I didn't!" I heard Talons voice break through the speaker phone, having obviously grabbed the phone from Wyn. "Don't you dare listen to her, little girl. She wouldn't even give me a say in the matter." I heard Ilyan laugh from across our small living space. I couldn't help laughing along with them, but the action sent a sharp pain through my chest and I winced.

Ilyan set down his work and moved over to me, his hand pressing against the skin on my hands the second he was within distance.

"We don't need your lungs to collapse today, do we?" he said low enough that the phone couldn't pick it up. He smiled sadly, a look I returned. I didn't like the reminders that I was going to die, however putting a light spin on it seemed to take the edge off. At least I wouldn't die alone. I reached out, grabbed his hand, and held on. I needed contact, and I was learning to accept Ilyan. It was odd how the advanced knowledge of my death had made me desperate to know I wasn't alone. That I wouldn't die alone.

"Anyway, as I was saying," Wyn continued after having wrestled the phone away from Talon. "It is brown, but there is no orange. It looks nice. You're going to love it."

I smiled a bit and turned to Ilyan who shook his head. We hadn't told Wyn what was going on, mostly because we didn't want her to worry or run back to the United States. She was safe in Prague. She needed to stay there.

"I bet I will," I agreed. "Unless it's too brown, then I may never talk to you again."

Wyn laughed and I tried to follow along, but my chest hurt too much even with the magical crutch that Ilyan's magic had given me. He let go of my hand and reached up to touch my cheek.

"Wynifred," Ilyan interrupted, his eyes focused on mine while his hand remained resting against my face.

"Yes, My Lord." I smiled at how her demeanor changed at Ilyan's one word.

"Joclyn needs to work on her magic now. We are going to have to continue this conversation at another time."

"Goodbye, Wyn," I said softly, cringing as my chest pulsed with pain.

"Later, Jos. My Lord." Ilyan didn't give me a chance to respond. He simply pressed the button to end the call and let his magic surge a bit more.

"They do seem to come in waves don't they?" Ilyan said. I nodded in agreement, my head spinning as I did so.

"So, tell me," Ilyan began, and I knew what was coming.

At my insistence, Ilyan had begun mentally training me the morning after my first nightmare. He recited different ways to use defensive magic, the process of building shields, and every other bit of magic he hoped could help me defeat Edmund. Once he recited it, I would recite it back. I'm not sure who held out more hope for my survival, me or Ilyan, but I couldn't deny the burning desire to defeat Edmund that still glowed brightly inside of me. After all, on the slim chance I survived this; I still needed to be ready. Either way it was still a good way to get my mind off of what was happening inside of me.

"What happens when two fire-based, water-bound orbs collide?"

"A fire wall." I said, giving him the simplest answer.

"Good. And redirection of objects without the use of wind?"

I cringed as I felt his magic snake its way up my spine, the warmth wrapping around my bones like a blanket.

"Is based in the thoughts of the mind and the second tier of energy storage. Both must work in succession for the task to be successful."

"Good," he said with a smile. "And the magic of the Vilỳ?"

"It awakens that hidden magic that humans possess. They can manipulate that magic for the human's benefit. Magic is only awoken in mortals by the bite of a Vilỳ or from bonding with a magical being." My voice caught as something shifted inside of me. Ilyan froze for a moment before asking another question, his deflection weakly covering up his worry.

"What else is based in the mind?" He didn't look at me, and my fear increased.

"Internal sight, movement of thoughts and images from one person to another..." I stopped at the look on his face. He wasn't overly concerned or angry, he simply looked heartbroken. The misery in his eyes took my breath away.

"Ilyan?" I whispered, and his head turned toward me. "How much longer do I have?"

When Ilyan hesitated, I squeezed his hand, hoping to prompt him to tell me. He returned the gesture, looking away from me.

"Your kidneys have failed; your lungs attempt to collapse every time you are pained there. You also have what I can only relate to a tumor snaking its way up your spine. So, not long." I cringed and clung to his hand tightly. Hearing him actually say what was going on inside my body made it more real.

"I can survive a broken back, but being separated from my mate is what kills me." I tried to smile. "Go figure."

"Go figure," Ilyan repeated, the American saying sounding awkward with his accent. He smiled slightly and reached out, running his fingers along the mark below my ear.

"I had an idea," he said. "I think you need to say goodbye to Ryland, too."

"I can't, Ilyan. You know I can't."

Ilyan moved his fingers away from my neck then opened the palm of his hand as the ruby necklace flew through the air to land gracefully in his outstretched fingers.

"You can." He let the necklace fall so he was only holding it by the chain. The ruby sparkled, taunting me.

"I can't control my magic, Ilyan. You..."

"I will do it for you," he cut me off, "and I will be here the whole time, keeping you alive. Safe."

I hesitated, my eyes unwilling to leave the glistening surface of the ruby.

"Don't you want to say goodbye to Ryland?" I looked away from the ruby and up to Ilyan. I did want to see Ryland again, but not the little boy in the Tòuha. I wanted *my* Ryland. I suppose, given the chance to say goodbye to either, though, I would take it.

I nodded once in agreement.

"Good, and when you come back, I want to talk to you about one last thing. I may have a way to save you; it's a long shot, but it might work."

"What is it?" I asked.

"We will talk after you return. Are you ready?"

I wasn't, yet what else could I say. I didn't have the time to prepare myself, and I was aware that I would talk myself out of it if I waited too long. I nodded again before I lost my confidence.

"Good." I felt Ilyan's magic bubble and boil inside of me as it worked to move the dying sludge that was poisoning my body. He pushed, pulled, and prodded it until it reached the surface. I could feel the thick acid burning underneath the skin of my hand, the rancid magic eating me away.

Ilyan dropped the necklace into my hand and began to work again as he pushed my magic out of me.

My hand began to fill with a fluid that seeped out of my skin as Ilyan pushed. Thick like mud, but smooth and the color of congealed blood, it bubbled out of my skin slow and hot. In that moment I knew why Ilyan had said I was bleeding when I had collapsed. It looked like I was holding a giant blood clot in the palm of my hand. I would almost believe it was, too, if it hadn't been for the smell. The second it had appeared in my hand a foul smelling stench had filled the air and my stomach heaved in response.

I squirmed and attempted to pull my hand away to get the foul smelling stuff off me, but Ilyan held onto me, keeping my hand in one place.

"It's okay, Silný. It's okay."

"Is that really..."

"Your magic?" Ilyan finished for me. "Yes."

"What's wrong with it?" I said. I couldn't tear my eyes away from the warm goo that was now seeping around the necklace.

"The best explanation I have is that it has rotted and died within you and in turn is poisoning you." His magic continued to push mine through my skin, the color becoming almost purple as more moved to join the growing mass.

"Can't we remove it, then?" I asked, wondering if that was what he had in mind.

"I've tried, but it did not work."

"You've tried?" I asked, affronted.

"Yes," he spoke simply, as though this odd invasion of privacy was nothing more than a handshake. "I tried it after you had the first nightmare while you slept. I hoped that draining what was inside of you would heal you. Unfortunately, it keeps coming back."

"You've done it more than once?"

"Every night. I will try everything to save you, to protect you, Joclyn. Until the day you die. I promise you all that and more."

Ilyan looked at me for a moment, but all I could do was smile. Ilyan had saved me so many times, and he expected nothing in return. I had never wanted him to get too close, but now I was glad he was here.

"Thank you."

He nodded.

"Are you ready?" His question tore my mind back to the dying magic in my hand. He had stopped forcing the rancid power out of me, leaving the necklace in a small pool of the stuff in my hand.

"I will be with you the entire time, Joclyn. Don't worry. And when you come back, we will talk." His eyes lit up for a moment before his determination took over, his jaw set.

"Don't leave me," I begged.

"I promise; I won't."

Reluctantly, I closed my eyes and let myself step into the white space that I shared with Ryland. Except now it was full of color.

I stood in the middle of the space and spun around. I was surrounded by thousands of crude drawings that covered the walls and floor in a rainbow of color. What once had been an undefined space was now enclosed by four walls. There were no windows or doors, so someone had taken the liberty to draw them in.

"Joclyn?" I spun around at the small voice to see Ryland standing in the middle of the room. His petite, five year old frame seemed to be glowing as I faced him, his blue eyes shining at seeing me there. Ryland as I had known him, as I was bound to him, was not this boy. He was not this age. This boy was only a subconscious projection, the last of the memories that his father had left him with.

"You came back!" He squealed and barreled into my legs, almost knocking me over onto the hard ground. He hugged me tightly, chalk and crayon dust wiping off onto my pants. I leaned down and ruffled his shaggy black curls.

"I take it you missed me then?" I asked softly.

"Of course I did! You were gone so long that I thought I would be alone forever."

"You haven't left?" I asked as Ryland enthusiastically shook his head in answer. I arched my brow in confusion; that didn't make sense. Ryland had always been able to leave before. He had left me alone in our space a number of times, and yet this time he was trapped.

"Nope, so I drew you a gift!" He motioned around him, his wide smile returning. "Do you like it?" He spun his fingers, and a bright red crayon appeared in-between them.

"You drew all this for me?" Ryland's face lit up at my response.

"I even drew a really, really special one for you. Do you want to see?"

"Umm... yeah." I smiled at him and he skipped away, excited to be showing me one of his many masterpieces.

I followed him until he stopped near a wide expanse of blue that I assumed to be a swimming pool.

"What is it, Ry?" I asked, coming to stand next to him and still not quite sure which of the surrounding images I should be looking at.

"It's you," he said quietly.

I followed his line of sight to a crayon drawing that was obviously meant to be life size. The portrait Ryland had drawn was of me with long, dark hair, big eyes that were actually crude sketches of diamonds, and stick hands and legs.

The figure wore a purple robe and had a pink crown on her head. I wanted to laugh, but instead I smiled, feeling exceptionally happy.

I kneeled down next to him, wrapping my arms around his tiny shoulders.

"You drew this for me?"

"Yeah," he said.

"It's beautiful, Ry. Thank you."

"You like it?" he asked, his little voice bursting with pride. I squeezed him against me, his frame so small against mine. I was overcome by a memory of Ryland, the way he should be; large, older than me, muscles, and scars.

"I love it." I said.

"Good! Now, you can draw one of me." He pushed a blue crayon into my hand and struck a pose in expectation.

"Actually," I said, feeling guilty as Ryland's face fell. "I came to say goodbye."

"Goodbye?" he asked, and my face fell more.

"Yeah, I may not come back. I'm not sure. I'm... I'm very sick. My friend is trying to help me, but I am not sure it is going to work... I wanted to say goodbye, in case." I felt the tears come and I cursed silently. I didn't want to cry. I didn't want to be weak anymore.

"You don't look sick," Ryland said.

"Not here, but where I come from I am very sick."

Ryland screwed up his face like he didn't believe me, but then seemed to think better of it. His face brightened a bit, but I could tell his smile was forced. I felt bad leaving him here alone. I didn't have a choice, though. I was quite literally lying in Ilyan's arms as he kept me alive long enough to say goodbye.

"You'll be back," Ryland said. "I know you will."

"I hope you're right, Ry." I ran my fingers through his curls, the way I always used to, and he smiled a bit.

I couldn't bring myself to say any more. I turned away from him and walked determinedly to a black door that was set into the endless space. I wasn't sure if it was the right way to exit because I had always been forced out before, but the door seemed right, so I grabbed the knob.

"Goodbye, Jossy," Ryland whispered, using a nickname I hadn't heard since I was six.

"Goodbye, Ry," I whispered softly to myself, not daring to turn back to face him again. I bit my lip and turned the knob, grateful when my eyes opened to Ilyan's worried face leaning over me.

I could tell right away that something was off; Ilyan's face was relieved but also... disappointed. Then I felt it; the strong buzzing under my skin. I could feel my perfectly healed body, the energy, the power. I hadn't felt this strong since I had flown into the LaRue mansion.

I sat up, sending blankets tumbling around me. Nothing hurt. My magic had restored itself, and in turn, healed my body. I stared at my hand numbly; I was going to be okay. I could have danced and sang, but everything in me was frozen in shocked relief. I stood and spun to face Ilyan, his face as stunned as I felt.

"It healed me." I wasn't sure if it was a statement or a question. I was awed. I still couldn't believe it. Relief washed down my spine and I exhaled shakily.

Minutes ago I had been accepting my death, yet I had been healed. I fought the urge to call Wyn and scream into the telephone receiver about what had happened, or storm out the door right now to track down Edmund. Instead I stared at my hand in disbelief, the tingling warmth that occupied me taking over. I looked at my hand that had held my liquid magic not long before; the slime had dried into a film that coated my palm, but otherwise, nothing remained.

"Did you know it would do that?" I asked.

"I can honestly say I had no idea. I had assumed the bond was broken, but to have a connection strong enough for it to repair the bond within a Tǒuha... I didn't think that was possible."

My skin prickled and pulsed as I flexed my fingers and toes. I had been lying down for the last week, mourning, and pining, and dying. I had almost given up hope of seeking my revenge on Edmund. I had tried to find comfort in the possibility of seeing Ryland in whatever life was after this. After that, however, I could find him, fight him. Now Ryland's sacrifice could be worth something. I smiled brighter and threw myself at Ilyan, wrapping my hands around his neck only to get a face full of hair.

"Thank you," I whispered. Slowly, his arms came around to encompass me.

"Of course, this means Ryland can track you easily now." Ilyan had spoken offhand, though the few words had been enough to shatter my celebration.

"What do you mean?" I untangled myself from Ilyan to stand in front of him.

"If your bond is strong enough to reseal your magic during a Tòuha, then it is strong enough to track you over large distances. If he can do that, I do not know where—if any place—you would be safe. I can shield you as long we stay together and in one location, but for now, it limits you to the interior of this apartment."

My jaw dropped, all my hopes at a celebration of good health dashed. Part of me wanted to yell at Ilyan for spoiling my joy, but he still had that devastated look on his face.

"So, are we trapped here?" I asked, finally able to process all that Ilyan was saying.

"Until I know how far he can track you, and until you are strong enough to fight him if he does." I couldn't help noticing that Ilyan's jaw was set into a hard line. He didn't seem to be celebrating my miraculous recovery at all. It worried me.

"Which will be how long?" I asked, my frustration rising.

"I do not know, Joclyn. Perhaps a year, maybe more."

4

I could hear the feet behind me; slow, steady, loud.

Edmund.

I turned a corner in the dilapidated house and squished myself against the burnt wainscoting, knowing full well it would not hide me. It would, perhaps, only allow me to be caught faster.

I dreaded being caught; I dreaded the pain I would feel, the terror that would encompass me. I also relished the pain, though. It was the only way I could be released from the nightmares that had haunted me every night for months.

They were always different, although the general theme of them stayed the same. Cail would chase me from the forest to the house where I would die at the hands of Edmund, Ryland, Timothy, or Cail.

I felt a heavy thud in my chest as the sound of the shoes grew louder, Edmund's gait easily decipherable to me now.

Thump, whack, thump.

I pushed myself into the wall as he came around the corner, Cail following him like an injured dog.

I pushed my hands toward him, sending a stream of light, but the attack bounced off of him, causing him to smile more. I pressed myself against the wall, eyes wide as I sought escape, knowing it was useless.

"Ah! There you are!" Edmund said joyfully like an old grandfather welcoming home a prodigal son, but it held no relief for me. My spine froze in terror and I hesitated a moment too long, allowing Cail to come up beside me and pin me to the wall.

I cringed away from the contact, away from what was coming, but it was no use. I could already hear the footsteps approaching.

A soft step on the left, a slight drag on the right. My mind must have been paying much more attention than I gave it credit for to have pulled this little detail of Ryland into my nightly terrors.

"We were worried you didn't want to play," Edmund continued lightly, as if I wasn't being restrained. "We were worried we would have to chase you down all night."

Edmund smiled and leaned toward me, I recoiled away from him automatically. With nowhere to go, I turned my head into the wall. A large lump blocked my throat at seeing Ryland slinking toward me, his eyes black, his beautiful face covered in a sheen of sweat.

"We didn't want to chase you down, did we Cail?" I couldn't pull my eyes away from Ryland as Edmund spoke. I stared at him as I tried to control the beating of my heart, the frantic mixture of panic and need making me dizzy.

"No, Master," Cail's voice was right in my ear, the putrid smell of his breath washing over me.

"Hold her," Edmund instructed and Cail complied quickly.

I had yet to understand the relationship my subconscious had created between Edmund and Cail. Edmund used him as a puppet, and every time Cail would obey without question. Sometimes his face would be screwed up in maniacal joy at what he was asked to do, and other times I could have sworn he was disgusted by it. It was as if my mind didn't know what to do with him.

I gasped at the pressure Cail put me under as I turned toward Edmund. Ryland now stood in between us, Edmund's hand resting lightly on his son's shoulder. It was the same image that had been burned into my head right before Ilyan had flown me away from them.

Edmund smiled at the panic on my face; his joy at seeing my torture evident. I heard Cail laugh in my ear as he prepared for his part in some sort of performance.

"Tsk. Tsk. Tsk. Running away were we?" Ryland's light voice was laced with a venom I had grown used to hearing in these dreams, whether I liked it or not. I began to fight against Cail's restraint, my hands growing warm against him. It was no use, he ignored the attack and his hold only grew.

"What should I do with her, Father?"

Ryland's eyes never left mine as he smiled while Edmund's wicked grin joined his in perfect synchronization.

This was the only part of the dream I couldn't bat away, the only part I couldn't blame on my subconscious. I couldn't ignore it because the pain was real. It never followed me as I woke, but I couldn't shake all the pain that Ryland caused me. I couldn't wipe it from my mind.

"Pull her through."

It was a command I had never heard before and so I cried out in anticipation of the unknown. Seconds later, I

39

felt Ryland's hand make contact with my stomach for a moment before the pain hit and the contact changed to something deeper. My stomach burned as his hand began to move through me, pulling my insides apart. I screamed louder.

I was still screaming as the dream faded away and the grey room that had been my prison for the last three months drifted into view. The comforter shifted as Ilyan came to my rescue. He moved to lay behind me and pulled me against his bare chest, his magic flowing into me and calming my frayed nerves. His arms were tight, pulling me against him before they caressed the skin on my arms lightly. My screaming died down, but the tears remained. They flowed freely down my cheeks and onto the pillowcase, wetting a spot so soaked every night that it had been stained with the salt water from my tears. It was the only time I cried anymore; the only time my emotions were raw enough to let the dratted things escape.

"Shhh... Silný, it's okay. To je v pořádku."

I leaned into Ilyan as he began to sing his song, the words whispered gently in my ear. As Ilyan sang, I sang with him, my voice shaky against my tears, the Czech words flowing roughly off of my tongue.

"Hush now, child. Be still, be calm. The world will change at the new dawn, and when it does, you will see how you and I were meant to be."

I sang it over and over again, long after Ilyan had fallen asleep, his arms still wrapped around me.

I wasn't going to get any more sleep tonight. Ilyan's arm around me had become a dead weight over my side. I wiggled a bit, the close contact making my nerves jump around.

When I could no longer stay locked in that position, I lifted his arm off me and slid from the bed and onto the floor, my knees coming up to press against my chest. I pulled my black hoodie over my knees, trapping the warmth against my body. I sat like that with my fuzzy pink socks poking out, my eyes focused on the carpet that once had held the dark stain of my rotten magic.

Ever since I had survived the attack of my own magic on my body three months ago, I had been confined to the claustrophobic depths of the studio apartment. I knew it was the only way to keep my magic hidden from Ryland and his father, but that didn't help the 'prisoner for life' vibe it had given me. I was restrained inside of this space with Ilyan's strong, immovable shield around me at all times.

I had been trapped here with nothing to do other than perfect, expand, and stretch my magic. I had thrown myself into preparing to fight; to keep myself alive for when I came face to face with Edmund. Even though I had such a strong desire to focus on, I still felt like I was dying inside; trapped between the tiny apartment of my reality and the undefined space that Ryland and I shared within our Tŏuha.

I couldn't survive for very long without renewing my connection to Ryland through the Tŏuha. We found that out the hard way. More than a day and my body began to ache, my energy exhausted.

I reached down into my hoodie to pull out the ruby necklace Ryland had given me, knowing I needed to go visit him. As I pulled the necklace free, my finger rubbed against the scar that rested over my heart, the skin raised and jagged.

I hated that scar as much as I hated the mark below my ear, each one a painful reminder of what I had lost, but sadly, I could handle my mark better. The mark had just appeared there, it hadn't been carved into my skin by someone I loved. Whether or not he was in his right mind at the time, it was still Ryland's body, his face, that I had seen hurt me. I sighed and moved my hand away, my fingers shaking slightly as I looked down at the glistening ruby. It had continued to be as dead as the day I had passed out over a plate of bacon; no warmth, no heartbeat, nothing. The stone remained quiet, even though I used the connection every day.

Ilyan was sure that Edmund was not using the necklace to hinder the connection between us, but he had still taught me to place a weak shield in between the stone and myself.

Preparing for the Tòuha, I filled the necklace—my only connection to Ryland—with my magic. My body grew warm and filled me with the heat of Ryland's power as his latent magic that lived inside of me awakened. It was the same comforting warmth I had grown up with, the same feeling my body constantly craved. I wished I could feel the sensation all the time, but the magic wasn't mine and Ryland was too far away. Besides, his magic was being used for other purposes now. It was a miracle Edmund hadn't been able to fully break the bond between us in the first place, so I would have to accept the fragments I had been left with.

My magic pulsed and grew alongside Ryland's as I pushed more and more of it into the beautiful stone. Even though I loved the sensation Ryland's magic gave me, even though I longed to see him, I still dreaded going into the Tòuha. Every time I saw Ryland inside, it was the equivalent of seeing someone through glass, never being able to truly touch them. Never knowing if you would ever be able to break the glass and get them back. It was painful, but I had to go. If I didn't my body would waste away to nothing again.

My eyes closed and I wandered into the colorful world that lived beyond my eyelids. I had spent every morning of the last few months coming in here and coloring with Ryland, sharing our dreams, talking about stories and making up our own.

It was a place where we created new memories while our old ones lay forgotten.

Well, at least his did.

"Jossy!" I turned at his voice, a wide smile spreading across my face at his appearance. Ry bolted across the space toward me, running headlong into me so that we both fell backwards onto the hard floor.

Ryland sat up from where we landed, his pointy elbows digging into my stomach. He smiled his large grin that I loved so much, his blue eyes twinkling.

"Hey Ry, did you miss me?" I asked, pushing his long, black curls out of his eyes.

"You know I did, Jossy, you're so funny." He chuckled and rolled off of me.

"Funny ha ha, or funny hee hee?"

"Definitely hee hee." he said as he continued to giggle.

"You sure about that?" I asked, poking him in the ribs.

He could hear the mischief in my voice so he jumped up and away from me before I could grab and tickle him.

"Don't, Jossy," Ryland squealed.

"Why not?" I asked, moving up on all fours in an attempt to look like I was going to lunge at him.

"Because, if you do, I can't show you my new drawing,"

"A new one?" I asked, my curiosity peaking.

Without being able to leave, Ryland had continued to spend all of his time coloring new masterpieces to fill the white void. Every time I came he had a new drawing to share or a new story that he wanted to tell me.

He grabbed my hand and towed me behind him toward the swimming pool. I willingly followed; his joy at sharing his new creation infectious.

"Just wait until you see it," he called back to me, "I want to play 'Princess and the Dragon of Delagn' after you see it, 'kay? It looks just like a dragon."

"Okay, but can I be the dragon this time? I'm tired of being the... princess," I stammered as Ryland signaled toward the wall where he had drawn his masterpiece. I froze, my head flopping curiously to the side.

On the wall before me Ryland had drawn a giant cage, which stood as tall as I did and was drawn with heavy black lines. Inside the cage unintelligible figures had been drawn in hundreds of colors. The door to the cage stood open, Ryland standing next to it, and on his finger perched Ryland's 'dragon'. It was small and scaled like a dragon or a dinosaur, but it wasn't a dragon at all. Its scales were a bright jewel blue and on his back were large, feathered wings. The face of the creature was somewhat feminine yet distorted somehow. Its cheek bones were high, eyes large and wide, and its nose was almost nonexistent. Even though I had only fleetingly seen one before, I knew what it was immediately.

Ryland had drawn a Vilỳ.

The little creature that had given me my mark, his poisonous bite awakening my magic. My hand moved to cover the mark that lay on my skin instinctively.

"Do you like him?" Ryland asked, "I am going to name him Opal because he kind of looks like a woman, but I really think it's a man."

I only half heard what Ryland had said. I couldn't rip my eyes from the intricate drawing before me. This picture was much more detailed than Ryland had drawn before, more than a child his age should be able to.

"When did you draw this, Ryland?" I asked.

"Last night, it took some time, but it was worth it. See, this is me, holding Opal. I am about to let him loose and he's going to grow big and strong and destroy an evil wizard. You can be Opal, and I'll be myself and the wizard, cuz I always wanted to be a wizard..."

"Did you see this somewhere before?" I interrupted him, panicking a bit. "Why did you draw this?"

Ryland screwed up his face and squared his shoulders, upset I wasn't going to play his game. "I just drew it, Jossy. It didn't come from anywhere. I thought it would be a fun game."

"A game." I ran my fingers over the delicate chalk of the Vilÿ's face, careful not to smudge the marks. "Do you know what this means?"

"If you want to be the wizard that's fine, I just thought it would be cool if..."

"You remember me," I spun to him and grabbed his tiny little shoulders.

I looked deep into his eyes, expecting him to smile and be his old self right away, but nothing happened. He gazed at me like I had gone mad.

"Of course I remember you, you're right here."

I stood and wheeled away from him, back to the black door that served as my exit.

"I have to go."

"You have to go?" he called after me, his little voice upset. "But, you just got here! We have to play the game. Don't you want to be Opal?"

I turned back to him when I had reached the door, my gut wrenching to see tears in his eyes. "I'll be back, Ry.

Okay? I need to go tell Ilyan something and then I'll be right back."

"You promise you'll come back today?"

"Of course I do." I ruffled his hair before turning the knob of my door, my eyes opening instantaneously to the brightening apartment.

"Ilyan!" I noticed the empty mass of blankets on the floor and turned to the bed to find it empty as well. I hadn't been gone long—less than twenty minutes in the Tŏuha, meaning it would only have been a matter of minutes in the real world. I stood up and ran to the bathroom door, hearing water running behind it. Steam seeped underneath the door, filling the room with a warm, musty smell.

"Ilyan!" I called through the door, knowing he would ignore me the first few times. Ilyan needed his morning showers to wake him up or he was grumpy all day.

"Ilyan!" I called again, this time letting my magic flow through the door to turn off the water. I heard Ilyan swear loudly in Czech before turning it back on. I knew I shouldn't bug him, doing this would only make him more upset, but I didn't care. My heart beat uncomfortably, the drawing still visible in my mind's eye. I knew I shouldn't dare to hope—dare to dream—but I couldn't stop myself.

"Ilyan, it's important!" I tried again.

"Is someone dying?" he yelled back. "Are *you* dying? Because I think I have reached my quota for saving your life this year!" Yep. Definitely surly.

I kicked my toe against the door and offered up my own brand of cussing. Fine. If he wasn't going to come out, then I would send the drawing to him. I pressed my palm against the door and sent the image right into Ilyan's mind. I waited a moment, and then I heard it, a sharp intake of breath. The water shut off and a moment later the door opened to reveal

Ilyan; wet, soapy, and only covered by a towel from the waist down. His wet hair fell over his shoulders, dripping down the skin of his chest, which was zigzagged with scars. I gulped and looked away. This wasn't the first time I had seen him like this, but it always made me uncomfortable.

"Where did you get that?" he said, ignoring my reaction to him.

"Ryland. He drew it," I said, my face breaking out into a wide smile.

"He drew it?" His eyes narrowed as though he didn't believe me. I folded my arms and stared him down.

"Yes, he drew it. He wanted to play a game about it. He didn't understand what it was."

"Show me." Ilyan grabbed my hand and placed it against his forehead. I sighed as his magic pulsed and flowed into me, pulling the memory out of my head.

I watched the Tõuha play before me; the speed picked up and slowed down, at times portions repeated, as Ilyan gleaned the information he wanted. The second he was done, I pulled my hand away. Ilyan had done that to me once before, when he was trying to teach me how to do it myself, and it had given me a headache then, too. He could only perform that particular magic with certain people, and seeing as I was one of them, I guess he figured he had permission to do it whenever he wanted to without asking.

"See?" I asked, still bouncing on my toes in excitement. "He remembers, doesn't he?"

"I am not sure. He could, or it could simply be a desire he had at that age."

I stopped bouncing immediately, my hope falling to my toes. "What do you mean, a 'desire'?"

Ilyan shifted his towel and ran his fingers through his wet hair, his tell for when he didn't want to share something with me. I folded my arms over my chest, refusing to look away from him.

"Ilyan," I said, "tell me." He hesitated a moment longer.

"Edmund kept the Vilỳ prisoners in that cage for hundreds of years. Ryland must have known about their existence from the day he was born. He is not without a heart; he can't look at a trapped creature and not wish to release them. The drawing could very easily be a projection of his desire to let them go at the time. I didn't even know it was Ryland who had let the Vilỳ out until you told me last spring, and besides that, who knows how he let them out, or how many, or even what color." He finished, his eyes never leaving mine.

"But the Vilỳ was blue, just like the Vilỳ who bit me." I said, my resolve weakening as I clung to my last bit of hope, however Ilyan's irritating logic was drowning it far too fast.

"It could be a coincidence."

"So, you are saying he doesn't remember me at all?" I snapped.

"You know where I stand on this, Joclyn. He's gone." Ilyan reached out to put a wet hand on my shoulder, but I moved away from him. He had ruined the little bit of hope I had found, dashed it into a million pieces.

"But, I saw it. He can't... He has to..." I stumbled around, my chest heaving angrily.

"I am sorry, Silnỳ. I didn't know you were still holding out hope." I snapped my head up to him, the magic in my fingers prickling angrily.

"You should be holding out hope, too, Ilyan. Even if you don't think it could ever happen, you should still believe there is a chance. He's your brother. You can't turn your back on that."

Ilyan opened his mouth to rebut yet said nothing. His lack of response making me more upset.

"Enjoy your shower," I spat, and with one thought, I sent him flying away from me. He hit the shower curtain and crumpled into the shower as I turned the hot water on over him. I looked at his startled face for a moment before slamming the door between us, my hands still in balls by my sides.

5
———

I SAT with my back against the sliding glass door that led out to the tiny balcony. The balcony I wasn't allowed to enter that was filled with fresh air I wasn't allowed to breathe. I sat this way so I didn't have to look out onto the city of Santa Fe and dream of leaving my prison. With my back toward the world, I couldn't be reminded of all I was being forced to sacrifice. Of course, it couldn't take away the thoughts, but it didn't make them quite so sharp.

My head leaned against the cool glass, my eyes closed in concentration. My hands sat on my folded knees, fingers extended. I allowed my magic to pulse and flow into the air and used my mind to control the objects that littered the ground in front of me.

A top spun gracefully on its point, a block changed color in a rainbow of hues, the carpet they sat on grew in length while fluxing and bending around the other two objects. All the while, a flurry of conjured snowflakes danced and spun around me as I sat cross-legged against the glass.

It was probably a little excessive, but I needed to keep my mind off of my fight with Ilyan.

Ryland's drawing had dug up my passionate hope that he was trapped instead of erased. Then Ilyan's offhand comments had just as quickly dashed them. I was trying so hard not be mad at him, but I was fighting a losing battle.

I closed my eyes tighter as the water from Ilyan's shower stopped. My anxiety increased the speed of the top, the influxes of color, and the movement of the carpet. Without opening my eyes I could still see the objects moving in front of me. It was just as Ilyan had taught me while I had lain dying. My magic served as my second eye, the whole room visible within my mind.

The door to the bathroom creaked open and my mind glanced away from its work to see Ilyan exit the bathroom. His blonde hair was wet and hanging down to his shoulder blades, soaking the top of his yellow, button up shirt. I returned my sight back to the objects in front of me, increasing my workload to include the carpet in the color changing cacophony. I accelerated the snowflakes that danced around my head until they were a white blur.

The distorted mass of white and color all became too much and I shut off my internal sight to sit in the blackness, the cool glass pressing against the back of my head, until Ilyan's soft hands wrapped around my fingers, distracting the flow of my magic.

His touch was gentle against my skin, his hands held tightly to mine. I felt the top fall to the side and the snowflakes melted back into the air as my magic disconnected from them.

I looked up at him, ready to bicker or battle or whatever he had in mind after I had thrown him into the shower, but instead his eyes were closed. His face was calm as he sat before me, his tall frame folded gently.

"I was thirty-two when Ovailia was born, an old man by

human standards at the time. I remember running to Prague to see my parents, leaving the monastery I lived at in the middle of the night. There had been some complications with the birth, but I was told my mother was healing fine. I was still worried, which is why I didn't wait to go to them. I ran into her room expecting healers and burning oils, but my mother was alone. She looked so fragile in her giant bed, her small frame swallowed up by blankets. She placed this tiny baby in my arms; a girl with hair that looked like sunlight. That's what Ovailia means, 'light of the sun'."

Ilyan looked at me, his face blotchy enough that I knew he had been crying in the shower. His grip tightened on my hands, keeping me close to him. He knew me well enough now that he could tell when I began to shy away from contact, but this time even I was fighting that impulse. I had never heard Ilyan open up before, and I desperately wanted to know more. His voice was so soft that I leaned in to hear him better.

"She had blue eyes, like me, like my father. He was so proud." It was weird to hear such a normal memory of Edmund; my brain almost fought the image of him as a normal, loving father to Ilyan.

"He clapped me on the back and said soon it would be my turn." Ilyan smiled, but it was a sad smile. For the first time I wondered why he wasn't married, why he had never bonded. I opened my mouth to ask, yet thought better of it. It wasn't my place, and besides, I really wanted to hear what he had to say.

"I held this little baby in my arms and promised to protect her. To keep her safe. I guarded her as she grew, taught her, and played with her. She could beat me in a flying race before she was ten... and then my father turned.

Ovailia had always been closer to him than I was. They had gone everywhere together; had secrets I would never understand. I didn't know what had happened until it was too late. Until I couldn't protect her anymore. She had seen one hundred and twenty years when she came to the small chapel in France where I lived, covered in blood and begging for help. I wasn't even sure then that I could trust her. I am still not sure."

I squeezed his hands, not knowing any other way to comfort him. Without thinking, I reached up to touch his face, but my hand stopped halfway there and fell to my lap. Ilyan dropped my other hand and stood, turning his back to me as he dragged his fingers through his hair in frustration.

"He has done it to all my siblings, Joclyn. Destroyed them. Hurt them. Ovailia was the first of many. He's destroyed all of them, leaving me only one shattered sister that's willing to side with me. That's why I don't hold out hope. Because I know what he is capable of. But, please, I don't want to dash your hope. It was never my intention to hurt you; I never wanted to break your heart. If you believe, then I will believe, too. Can you forgive me for dashing your hope before? For being so rude?"

I stared at him for much longer than necessary, my brain still processing this little bit of his past. For the past few months I had gotten to know Ilyan better than I had anyone else. Anyone other than Ryland. I had thought I understood Ilyan, but hearing this part of his history made me realize how little I knew. There were a thousand years of him I did not know.

Even with all of that, I knew the face he had when he was truly sorry. I knew of his goodness. And I saw both of those now.

"Yes, Ilyan, of course." His face lit up at my words.

"Thank you," he replied softly before his eyes gleamed with the maniacal energy I had seen too many times before. I cringed at what I assumed was coming. In the last few months it had usually accompanied our training sessions. "I have a little proposition for you."

"Do I need to be worried?" I asked, sliding my hand through the air in front of me to send the block and the top back to their places on the table.

"Perhaps." Ilyan lifted his hands and the table and the nightstand moved themselves into the kitchen at the same time that the bed stood on end in order to give us the most space possible. I groaned and leaned my head back against the glass.

"Sparring... really? This is how you make it up to me?" I hated sparring. I hated holding weapons that were only meant to kill. I hated hitting him with power and magical attacks, but most of all I hated being hit with them. This was punishment, not a reward. Ilyan seemed to find my response humorous; he laughed and slid his hands down in front of him, a large sword appearing from nothing.

I groaned. The use of swords was so archaic, but when battling ancients I guess it was a necessary skill to learn, even though they were rarely used anymore. Magic alone was more effective to use fatally against another magic user and guns were of no use because bullets would be easily disintegrated by a simple shield.

"Oh, trust me, this is half reward and half punishment for throwing me into the shower." His eyes twinkled as I moved to stand. I could stubbornly sit on the floor and refuse to participate, but he would attack anyway. I had tried it before and the results were not positive.

"I am sorry about that," I pleaded, even though I knew it

was no good. "Can you at least tell me the reward portion of this?"

I slid my hand through the air to produce my own sword for the battle I was about to endure. My weapon was nowhere near the caliber of Ilyan's. His was engraved with jewels, the metal twisting beautifully. Mine was a boring, solid metal t-shape; the kind that I had used in theatre class for years. I needed to work on creating something a bit better, but I wasn't sure I cared enough. I could attack Edmund with magic, after all, if I ever became strong enough to fight him, right? I groaned and swung the sword, the metal feeling awkward in my hands.

"Well, you have decided that Ryland's mind might still be intact."

"We," I corrected him, rolling my eyes.

"Yes, well if he is in fact 'there' I know someone who can help us, but he is a bit too far away at the moment. Which means, we will have to go to him." Ilyan began swinging his sword around in preparation while mine clattered to the floor.

"We're leaving the apartment?" I said.

"Yes, but...."

I didn't let him finish, I squealed and ran to him, wrapping my arms around his neck tightly.

"Thank you, thank you, thank you," I sang as I danced around on his toes.

"You are welcome, but you do need to let me finish." He pried me away from him and I stepped away, suddenly very uncomfortable for having rushed at him.

"We will leave the apartment once you can beat me in a sparring match." Ilyan concluded.

My energy dropped, my jaw falling agape.

"Not fair! I'm never getting out of this hell hole." I kicked my sword in frustration, the heavy metal popping my toe out of joint. My magic quickly repaired it and I stomped around a bit, cursing the tiny apartment and its lack of hiding options. I gave up after a minute and pulled my hood down lower over my head.

"I'll make you a deal," Ilyan said from behind me, and I rounded on him.

"If it's anything like your last deal, I don't think I am interested." I folded my arms and glared at him. Ilyan took two steps forward and tugged on some of my hair that stuck out of my hood.

"If you can mark me once, right now, I will take you out on a date tonight."

"A date," I scoffed, grossed out a bit. I stepped away from him, and he laughed darkly.

"Alright, well not a date. A non-committal dinner and movie outing with a friend." He winked and I felt my insides shift.

"I just have to mark you once?" I was very skeptical. Marking Ilyan once was usually still the equivalent of winning a match against him, only slightly more attainable.

"Just once," he assured me. I nodded and reached my hand out, the sword flying into my grasp.

"Just once," I repeated. "Right; I can do this."

I moved my sword in front of me as Ilyan had taught, the point looking him right in the eye. Ilyan did the same, but his face held a curious little smirk, not the terrified expression I was sure I displayed. I held still, clenching my jaw and silently begging him to make the first move, though when it became obvious he wouldn't, I lunged at him. He smoothly moved from one position to another, his sword clanging loudly as it hit mine. The impact sent me off balance and I stumbled to the side, ramming my shoulder into the wall.

"My point." Ilyan announced. I scowled and turned around to see him shifting his sword from side to side, spinning the blade. I didn't wait. I lunged again. Ilyan moved quickly and the clashing of our blades reverberated through the small space as we fought.

I continued to try to mark him, to hit him, or throw him off balance with no success.

"Ugh!" I yelled. I had to be able to do something. Ilyan merely smiled at me in response and continued his attacks.

While I wasn't bad at this by any means, Ilyan was that much better. I swung wide and aimed for his blind side only to be pushed away by his swift movements. Then, as he arced wide for another attack, I stumbled again and flailed around in an attempt to block him, my sword barely meeting his.

"Come on, Silnỳ!" he yelled, his accent deep and rumbling. "Play hard, fight hard."

"I hate swords," I growled under my breath.

"I heard that." He smiled.

"Why do we even have to use them? You told me no one does anymore." I said, letting a little whine escape into my voice. Ilyan simply smiled at me once more.

I shook my head and came at him again, this time trying for his legs. Ilyan saw my move and jumped away, his sword sweeping out to tap against my shoulder.

"My point," he announced, his cocky undertone grinding on me.

I jumped up, instantly going for another attack. I almost had him when an invisible barrier blocked my path. I always forgot how quick he was until he used his magic against me.

"Not fair! Foul Play!"

Ilyan smiled at my outburst.

"You can do it, too, Silnỳ. In fact, I ask that you do. In battle you will not be constrained to weapons, if you use them at all." He bowed deeply to me, his sword disappearing back into the air it had come from. I swallowed and let my sword fall to the floor, clanging loudly. Now I was in trouble, our sparring matches always led to this, and I always failed miserably.

'Attack me with magic.' he would say... *'Why don't I stand still so you can land all your attacks on me without hassle?'* I would rebut.

Well, not really. I wouldn't dare say that to him. That was how it always went, though. There was no glory in this for me, only pain and more broken toes.

Ilyan spread his hands once in a high arch and the walls shimmered as he trapped us in another protective shield. This one guaranteed that we wouldn't destroy the tiny prison we called home.

But it wouldn't be prison for long. I just had to mark him once and I could leave for the night. Win the match, and I could leave forever. I jumped to my feet, I could do this.

I didn't hesitate this time. I needed the upper hand if I was going to have any chance of marking him. I sliced my hand through the air, sending a long chain of magical energy soaring to him like a javelin with the intent to wrap him in it like a vice. Ilyan jumped back as he diminished the flow of my attack, but not before the end of the chain sliced through his shirt.

"Very nice, Silnỳ. But not good enough." I saw his motion a moment too late and dove to the side as a ripple of energy impacted with the shield that surrounded us, sending a wave of colors vibrating through the protective layer.

"Try harder," he yelled as he sent a line of freezing water above my head. I winced when it hit the shield above me, showering me with droplets of ice.

I threw my hand out, shooting a pulse of light and fire toward him, which breezed through the bright colors that fluxed around us. I didn't stop to see if it made contact, instead I scrambled to my feet hoping to gain my bearings. I faced him and instantly threw a handful of conjured metal beads in his direction. The pellets disintegrated against Ilyan's personal shield as he streamed electricity toward me. I threw a shield up just in time, the powerful magic crashing into my barrier instead.

"Fight back, Joclyn." He yelled. "You would have won in the bathroom. You had it all, emotional force, surprise..."

"The fact that you were only wearing a towel didn't hurt, either," I countered, throwing another attack in his direction only to have him dodge it. Ilyan laughed boisterously at me.

"Yes, but how often are you going to be fighting someone in a towel?" He shot another surge in my direction, which I countered, and the two streams collided in the center surrounding us with brightly colored sparks.

"Not often enough," I said under my breath.

"That is why Ryland will always defeat you. He can play on your emotions, and he knows it."

"Don't remind me." I shoved wind in his direction, smiling when he skidded away from me again.

Ilyan brought this up every day. I was perfectly aware that he was right. I just didn't like the reminders. This time, however, I realized that he had given me a weapon, too. I could play on Ilyan's emotions.

I waited for his next attack only to dodge it. I embraced

my speed, moving as quickly as I could to sidle right up to him. I grabbed his shirt and pulled his tall body into me, his face millimeters away from mine.

"Don't hurt me." I said softly as I placed my hand gently against the skin of his neck. I let my hand grow warm with power for a moment to signal to him that I had won. His eyes changed from soft and concerned to a smoldering pride so fast I might have missed the change had I not been looking directly at him.

"I win."

"That is dirty, Joclyn." I stepped away from him, not liking the look that he was giving me. "I am not sure if I can accept that as a win."

"You better!" I snapped, "It had all the elements of a successful attack plus surprise and a play on emotions, just like you said. Although why it worked on you, I will never know."

"I'm your protector, Silnỳ. I am hard-wired not to hurt you." He released the barrier and put the room back together with one swipe of his hand, but I stayed still, my brain clicking together.

"My protector?" I asked. "What do you mean, *my* protector?"

Ilyan stopped and turned to face me, his hand dragging heavily through his hair again. "I protect everyone, Joclyn. You included."

I just stared at him in disbelief. He had said it before and I had taken it to mean just that, but this time his inflection had been different. Something had been off in the way he said it, as though it was a job he took pride in. It didn't mean wandering around and saving people to him. He was still dragging his hand through his hair, making it obvious he was keeping something from me.

"Get a better poker face, Ilyan. What aren't you telling me?" Ilyan smiled at me before returning from the kitchen, a small box in his hands.

"Až jednou pochopíš všechno a přijmeš, kdo jsi, poté, a teprve poté, ti povím všechno, má lásko. Ale ani o vteřinu dřív." I glared at him. He knew my Czech consisted of 'pass the leaves' and 'where is the bathroom'.

"Understand? Accept what? Love what? What did you say, Ilyan? You know I don't understand most of what you said. My Czech is not very good." He smiled at me and placed the small box in my hands.

"Exactly."

I jerked the box away from him angrily. I hated cryptic answers, and Ilyan was full of them.

"I made those for you, for Prague, but wear them tonight. They will look nice in the city. I am going to go get you something besides pajama pants to wear. Stay inside." He smiled at me once before leaving, the door locking behind him.

I looked down to box, a small pink ribbon tied around the top. It never ended well when a man made anything for a woman to wear, and the thought of what could be inside this package worried me.

I slipped the bow from the box and tipped it, letting the contents fall out into my hands.

The most intricate red leather shoes rolled onto my palms. I could tell right away they would fit. The toes of the shoes were folded into a fan shape that gave the impression of a blossoming rose. A tiny pearl was nestled in the middle of each one. Surrounding the sole of the shoe was a five part leather braid that circled seamlessly around. I couldn't find the beginning or the end. The stitching around the sole and around the top was small and intricate, each one done with precision. I stared at the shoes in awe. That these could be made by a person, let alone Ilyan, was impossible. I lay the sturdy shoes on the floor and slipped my bare feet into them. They were beautiful.

Of course, I recognized them as what he had been working on while I had lain dying months before. While he had been nursing me, healing me, he had also been working on these shoes. Even then, he hadn't thought I was going to die.

I hadn't considered it in three months, but now I couldn't help wondering what Ilyan's backup plan could have been. I had known he had something else in mind if joining Ryland in the Tŏuha hadn't cured me. Something deep inside told me these shoes were meant for that, not for a night on the town.

6

———

IT TOOK a minute after Ilyan had left for reality to click in. Ilyan was getting me clothes, and I was going to get to leave. Of course, this would mean being around people again— something I really wasn't fond of—but I would be outside my current prison and that was all that mattered.

I bounced on my toes and took the few steps to retrieve Ilyan's cell phone from the kitchen counter. I flipped the phone open and speed dialed to call Wyn. As the phone rang, I paced the floor in anticipation. It was surprising how soft the shoes were. The leather clung to my feet with the few steps I took. I could tell I was going to love them.

"Hello?" She sounded groggy. Odd, it was only nine at night in Prague right now.

"Wyn!" I almost screamed, my excitement exploding out of me. "I get to leave!"

It didn't even take her a moment for what I had said to sink in. She squealed and repeated it, presumably to Talon who was always nearby.

"When are you leaving? Are you coming home? Please

tell me you are coming right home," she rattled on, Talon chuckling in the background.

"I'm not sure yet. Ilyan is taking me out for dinner tonight. Then we get to leave soon."

"But you don't know where to yet?" Her voice had dropped, and my heart sunk a bit with it. I was so excited to be leaving the apartment, I hadn't thought about where we would end up, yet the thought of not getting to see Wyn again soon was depressing. As much as I was getting used to Ilyan's company and beginning to enjoy being around him, I needed Wyn.

"Don't rain on my parade, Wyn." I grumbled.

"I'm sorry," she said. "It's just that I miss you. It's been months, and with everything that's happening, I worry."

"What do you mean with everything that's happening?" I asked.

I plopped down on the bed, curling my toes in the beautiful shoes, and waited. There was a much longer pause than I was used to as Talon whispered something in the background. It wasn't like Wyn to hesitate. She usually said what was on her mind whether it would offend someone or not.

"Wyn," I prompted. "What's going on?" My stomach tightened a bit in anticipation.

"Just with everyone looking for you, people being able to track your magic, and all that."

I knew Ryland could track my magic, and would presumably be looking for me, however Wyn made it sound like something more active.

"*Everyone's* looking for me?" I said quietly. "Everyone like Ryland everyone, or everyone-everyone? I don't suppose you and Talon were planning a rescue mission to get me out of my studio-sized prison?"

"Ryland everyone, Jos." She paused, and my shoulders knit together in frustration.

Twice in one day I wasn't being told exactly what was going on. Worst of all, people were keeping things from me that directly pertained *to* me. 'People' being Wyn and Ilyan to be specific, and Wyn was probably just following orders. While Ilyan had a right not to tell me everything, I trusted him with my life, my secrets. He had become more than a friend. Hearing that he was keeping something from me for the second time in under an hour made my head hurt.

"He can't track my magic behind Ilyan's shield, Wyn," I said, a little perturbed that my good news had been smashed.

"I think it's a little bit more than that. I think it's more of an active searching." Active searching? Wyn made it sound like someone was hovering on the balcony waiting for me to absent-mindedly walk out.

"Why wouldn't Ilyan tell me?"

"I am not sure Ilyan knows, Jos." Her voice was quiet.

"What?" I asked, my back straightening in alarm. "What do you mean he doesn't know?"

There was a scuffling and more whispering on the other end of the line. I held the phone to my ear tightly, desperate to hear anything.

Ilyan always knew what was going on. He had spies and contacts everywhere who reported back to him. His phone rang off the hook most of the day with reports on Edmund and Ryland, Prague, and who knew what else. The fact that he could possibly not be aware of something scared me.

"Wyn?" I asked when I couldn't wait anymore. There was a bit more of a whispered fight and then Talon took the line, his deep voice booming through the long distance connection.

"Hey, Jos. It's Talon, how're you doin', little girl?"

"I'm fine, Talon. Can you please tell me what's going on?" I was practically begging, but I needed someone to pull me back from the edge of my growing fear.

"Sure kid," he exhaled deeply, and for a moment I was worried he was going to lead me on, too. "Last week I was harvesting in the orchard when I overheard someone crying and whimpering, though I'm not sure who. They were begging for help and pleading with someone. I heard them give whoever they were pleading with your location. I ran to find out what was going on, but nothing was there. No one was in the trees."

"A few other people have heard it, too," Wyn broke in, having obviously put me on speaker phone, "someone whimpering and crying. But no one can figure out who."

"What are you saying; that there is a spy in our midst?" I said, purposefully making my words sound like a spy movie in an attempt to break the tension. It didn't work.

"That's exactly what we are saying, Jos," Talon said.

I threw myself back on my bed. I should be happy. I was finally getting out of the house, we had decided Ryland might still be able to be saved, and soon I was going to leave this prison forever, yet at that moment, I was stressed and uncomfortable.

"And Ilyan doesn't know?"

"Ovailia is looking into it, but I don't know if she has told him yet. I would assume not if he is planning on taking you out to dinner tonight," Wyn replied. Afterward, I could hear Talon whisper something behind her again.

"Why didn't you call and tell me or Ilyan?"

More whispering, I waited for a minute, my impatience growing.

"Jos," Wyn sighed, "Ovailia is looking into it. If she had found something, she would have told him, right?"

Ovailia should have told him even if she didn't think she had 'found something.' Something wasn't right. My heart ached and beat uncomfortably. I didn't like things being kept from me, and these were the worst types of things; things that affected me. To make it worse, not only were things being kept from me, but from Ilyan as well. I needed answers, and being stuck in this apartment was limiting my resources.

"Can I..." I was going to regret this. "Can I speak to Ovailia?"

"Why?" Wyn asked, worried. I didn't blame her, being around Ovailia was uncomfortable enough, asking about something like this was sure to be an unpleasant experience.

"Because I need to hear it from her, and I have something else to ask her anyway." I said, quickly stringing together one worry with another.

"Ilyan will be very upset if you go behind his back," Talon warned, his voice deeper than usual.

"Nah, if he is, he'll just torture me by making me spar with him again."

Talon chuckled softly, his voice making the phone's microphone vibrate. Talon and Wyn had warned me about Ilyan's temper, but I had never seen it. Maybe it had something to do with this protector nonsense he had been throwing around, which was the other thing I wanted to ask Ovailia about. My stomach tightened as I began to second guess myself. Ovailia on the phone. What was I thinking?

"Alright, but it's your funeral."

I heard a knock on a heavy door and then Talon said something, his voice muffled. Ovailia snapped something back. I instantly regretted this decision, and she wasn't even on the phone yet.

"Hello, Joclyn, what a pleasant surprise." Ovailia's voice was as sweet as acid, as usual. It didn't sound like she was pleasantly surprised, it sounded like I was asking her to pluck all her hair out strand by strand.

"Hello, Ovailia." I tried to sound chipper.

"What can I do for you?" I almost lost my nerve, but decided to plow through. If for nothing more than to be off the phone with her. Trying to explain why I wanted to talk to her without asking my questions would have been worse.

"Wyn tells me there is a spy in Prague, and I know Ilyan doesn't know." It wasn't a question, it was a statement. I hoped my bluntness would prompt her to tell me what I needed.

"How could you possibly know if I have told Ilyan or not?" I could almost see her eyebrows arch and rise delicately on her perfect face.

"Because, if he knew, he wouldn't be taking me out to dinner tonight." There was a pause, but it wasn't the pause of someone who was contemplating how much information to tell you. This was Ovailia, and her pauses ended with her decision of how much to scold you.

"He's taking you out? Out of the apartment?" I was surprised by the alarm in her voice, she obviously hadn't told him.

"Yes, and I am concerned that as 'My Protector' he doesn't know that Edmund might already know where I am hiding." I placed it well, hoping the words were heavy enough that she would either give away what Ilyan had meant or verify that the words meant nothing.

There was a pause, and I waited. I didn't dare say

anything, worried I wouldn't get any of the answers I needed, however instead of answers, Ovailia began to laugh.

"Your protector?" she said through her wicked laugh.

"Your *protector*. Oh, you stupid little girl, don't make me laugh. If he had told you that, you wouldn't be saying the words with such pride. You would be terrified." She laughed harder and my stomach dropped. "I will tell Ilyan when I am ready. Don't you ever come prying for information from me again, or I can assure you, you will get more than you bargained for."

The phone went dead, and I dropped it to the floor like it was poison.

That hadn't gone at all as I had planned. Not only did Wyn dash my joy at getting to leave the apartment, but my impromptu espionage for answers had blown up in my face. The only positive information that I had gleaned was that it was obvious that the news of the spy was being kept from Ilyan, and that Ilyan was in fact 'my protector'—whatever that meant. Worst of all, my chat with Ovailia left me feeling dirty and even more stressed.

Secrets, lies, spies. I didn't like it at all.

I stood and stumbled around the apartment for a minute, waiting for my brain to tell me what I should do next. Ilyan wouldn't be home for an hour at least, and who knew how much trouble I had just gotten Talon and Wyn into—I cringed at the thought.

I needed to talk to someone, and there was only ever one person I could really talk to.

Without thinking, I grabbed my necklace and pushed my magic into it. This Ryland wouldn't hold my hand and talk me through my problems like he used to, but I could at least talk without him judging me.

I opened my eyes to the Tõuha and gasped. Everything

had been destroyed in the few short hours since I had left him. Every single drawing, every one of Ryland's masterpieces, were smudged and smeared, some erased completely. I looked around me in shock, my mouth hanging wide open in horror. Could this day get any worse?

"Ryland?" I asked softly. Normally he was right here waiting for me. But no one was here. No running feet. No happy, smiling face; just months of masterpieces, destroyed.

"Ry?"

I ran through the room filled with smudged and destroyed dreams until I heard him. His little whimper was soft and broken. I ran toward the sound until I found him hunched against the wall, crying into what had once been the drawing of him holding the Vilÿ. He rubbed his fist into the face of the creature, his body shaking with sobs.

"Ryland?" He spun at my question, his face screwed up in anger.

"Go away!" He yelled, throwing broken bits of chalk and crayon at me. "I don't need you anymore!"

"Ryland? Wha... what happened?"

"Go away!" he yelled again, his words cutting through me.

"You don't mean that, Ry."

"Go Away!" He turned away from me, rubbing harder into the blue smudge and turning it into a blur.

I rushed to him, wrapping my arms around his tiny frame. He fought me off, but I fought back harder while he cried and continued to push away from me. I held on as he battled, his cry getting louder rather than softer as I had been hoping for. His pushing turned to punching and finally I was forced to let him go. He skidded away from me, both of us panting hard. I couldn't stop looking at him. I didn't know what had happened; where this had come from.

"Ryland?"

"Leave me alone! Go back to wherever you come from and never come back here again!" he screamed at the top of his lungs and backed himself into the wall. I wanted to reach for him, but was scared as to how he would react.

"I can't do that, Ryland, you know I can't do that. I'll die." I spoke softly, partly in the hope of calming him down, but mostly because I was scared. I didn't know how to react or what to say.

"Then die!"

"Ryland!" His words cut through me; he couldn't possibly mean that.

"You don't care what happens to me, you don't care that I am here alone, and you don't care about me. You just want that other guy!"

"What other guy?" I asked, confused.

"The one you are waiting for, the one you lost. You think I'm him, but I'm not. I am just me, and you don't care!"

"Ryland, I do care... I—" I pleaded with him quietly as I tried to piece together the puzzle of his outburst. He interrupted me, his next words like lemon against an open wound.

"No, you don't! I hate you!"

"You don't mean that." My voice was almost a whisper.

"Yes, yes I do," Ryland was losing momentum as his tears took over. "I have to."

"You have to? Ry, you don't have to do anything. I know you don't hate me, so please don't say that." I carefully moved closer to him, watching his movements to see how far I could get. He stayed leaning against the wall, crying and eyeing me as I got closer.

"You don't hate me," I said as I carefully placed my hand on his knee to comfort him, but he only cried harder.

"I have to, Jossy. He said… you don't…" He stuttered a bit until his voice disappeared.

"He?"

"You don't love me anymore, you love the other guy." His shoulders shook, and my heart shattered.

"Of course I love you, Ry. You are my *everything*."

He stared at me, I could see something click together in his mind, and a weak light began to return to his eyes. I took the opportunity and moved closer to him.

"Really?" His face brightened with hope. I returned the smile and wrapped my arms around him, pulling him to me.

"Yes, really. I couldn't live without you, and I never want to hear you say you hate me because I know it's not true."

He nodded against me and I squeezed him tighter, grateful when he returned the hug. I held him for much longer than necessary, but I wanted him to calm down; to know the truth of what I had said. I wasn't sure how to communicate that to a child. A hug seemed the simplest way.

"Now, about this 'other guy' I don't think you are the other guy. I think you are you. I loved your drawing, and I am sorry I didn't say so. I shouldn't have said those things before, and I am sorry I did."

"Thanks, Jossy."

"No problem, little man. Now, I did come bearing good news."

"You did?"

"I did. I get to go to the city tonight." I smiled brightly, hoping at least one person would be excited for me. Instead, his face fell a little bit.

"But I'm still stuck here."

I sighed. Obviously this was not the best timing to have told him, given the outburst he just had.

"How about tomorrow, after I get back, we get rid of our white room and make the city. Then we can have our own adventures; pretend to be superheroes and magicians and anything you want. I'll spend all day with you if you want."

"Really?"

"I would love to."

Ryland's face lit up like a million fireworks and he crashed against me in a big hug. Giggling like crazy, I reached for him as he jumped up, his face serious again.

"You've gotta go! That way you can bring the city back with you." He grabbed my hand and heaved until he pulled me to a stand, dragging me toward the door. "I'll make super hero capes, and villains, and all sorts of stuff." He jumped up and down a bit before running away, presumably back to where his chalk lay scattered.

"Bye, Jossy!" he yelled behind him, his focus on his new tasks.

"Bye, Ry," I said softly before turning the knob on my exit door, my eyes opening to Ilyan staring right at me.

7

"Been busy have we?" Ilyan said, his lips pulled up in a half smile.

"I wouldn't call it busy." I pulled myself to standing and stretched my joints out a bit. My body was supercharged after the Tŏuha, though strangely stiff from sitting. I glanced toward the digital clock on the floor. I had been sitting for twenty minutes which meant I had been with Ryland for a little over two hours. We had done the math when I first started having to visit the Tŏuha every day. Two hours in the Tŏuha was equal to about twenty minutes of real time, and it was a good thing it wasn't the other way around because I needed about forty minutes of real time in the Tŏuha for my body to stay perfectly strong.

"More like stressful and confusing."

"Hmmmm, yes," Ilyan said, moving away from me. "Ovailia called me."

"Great," I grumbled, dreading his response to my foolish phone call, however instead of yelling, Ilyan only smiled.

"Don't worry, Silnỳ, despite Ovailia's best efforts, I am not upset with you. I have decided that the one who kept things from me in the first place should be the one to gain the punishments."

"So Ovailia's in trouble?" I said.

"I don't know what *you* qualify as being 'in trouble', but she is no longer acting in my stead, that role has been taken over by Talon."

"Talon?" While he seemed the obvious choice, something about changing leadership in Prague made me worried.

"Yes, Silný. This would not be the first time he acted in my name. Many years ago, before Ovailia returned to us, it was expected that Talon would take my place if I was to pass."

Ilyan cocked his head to the side and looked at me heavily, his eyes digging into my soul.

"Why are you worried?" he asked.

I sighed and joined Ilyan in the kitchen. "I don't know. Something feels off, like a snake has wound itself up my spine." Ilyan raised an eyebrow at me, or perhaps at my odd description.

"Shouldn't we be running back to Prague right about now? I mean someone is 'crying' information about us all over the city."

"You mean the bunker?" he asked, his eyebrow still raised.

"Excuse me?"

Ilyan narrowed his eyes and pulled out our two juice glasses. "Everyone is confined underground, in the side of a mountain near the city of Prague. When we say Prague we mean our bunker. So someone is going around our underground bunker—not the city—crying and doing who knows what."

Everyone had made Prague sound like this wonderful

place, but if it was really just hiding under a mountain, it sounded just as terrible as the tiny room I had been trapped in.

"Shouldn't we go back, though? Make sure everything is okay?"

When Ilyan came over to stand next to me, I craned my head to look up at him, his face soft and concerned. He reached out and placed his hand against the side of my face, his fingertips tracing the rough lines of my mark as always. I didn't move away from him; I didn't flinch. I only stood there, my heart thumping a bit at the contact.

"I would if I thought something was wrong, but I am not sure if I do, yet. Talon will be looking into it for me. I will keep you safe, Silnỳ, that I promise you."

"My Protector." I had barely spoken above a whisper, but he still heard me, making me regret my words. His face darkened as his hand dropped from my face to a tight hold against my elbow.

"Ah, yes." He said softly before moving away from me. "That is another thing, please don't go to Ovailia for answers. I keep things from you because you are not ready to hear them. You will not receive the truths you are looking for from Ovailia. She will only paint a canvas with lies to manipulate you."

"If she is going to manipulate me, then why do you trust her?" I had expected him to be angry at my impolite question, instead he only spoke quietly to me.

"I trust her because of what she has done to redeem herself. I trust her because, out of all of my siblings, she is the one who has stood by me. She may not be the best in character, but she is the best on word. So, for now, I will trust her."

Ilyan's voice had strengthened into that commanding

tone I had grown so used to. I fought the urge to sink into my sweater and hide from him. Instead, I took a deep breath and looked at him firmly.

"So you will trust her with every bit of information about me, but you will not give me the same information?" I tried to keep my voice level, yet I wasn't sure it had worked. My anger flared with each word. The darkness in Ilyan's face faded away, but I barely noticed.

"I have not told her everything about you, only enough so that she understands my position."

"Which is...?" I prompted, but Ilyan only raised an eyebrow at me.

"I will tell you when you are ready, Silnỳ." Ilyan said simply, which only added to my frustration.

"Why can't I be ready now?"

"Because I am not the one to tell you."

"Then who is?" I spat, my hands slamming hard against the countertop.

"You will know him when you meet him." Ilyan's voice raised to match mine, and I cowered, slinking away from him. I was fuming a bit too much, even for my taste.

I hated that he was keeping something from me. I hated that he treated me like an all-important piece of his life but wouldn't tell me why. I hated that he didn't trust me. I slammed down into one of the chairs around our tiny table, burying my head in my arms.

"Silnỳ, do not be upset with me." I felt his hand rest on the back of my head, his fingers moving through my hair. I ignored the contact, holding as still as I possibly could. "You will know all soon enough, and then the weight of the world will be on your shoulders."

When I turned my head to look at him, his tall frame crumpled a bit so he could meet me at eye level.

"Is that why you are keeping things from me, Ilyan, because of 'the weight of the world?'"

"You already have so much pain in your heart, Silnỳ. I do not want to add to that. I only wish to see happiness in your soul, and when the time comes for your knowledge to change, I will be there to help you carry it." I didn't know whether to be grateful or scared, but I smiled all the same. Ilyan's hand moved from my hair to trace my mark, his sad smile melting me.

"You are beginning to sound like Ovailia when I removed her from her post."

Ovailia being stripped of her power did not sound like a party I wanted to be invited to. Knowing how much Ovailia felt she was entitled to, taking away the power she had scraped into her possession would mean trouble.

"I'm glad I'm not in Prague. I don't know what would be worse, Ovailia in charge, or Ovailia mad because she is not in charge."

Ilyan smiled as he poured me a glass of orange juice from a jug. Ilyan never ate anything processed, which meant I never ate anything processed, which meant pulp-free orange juice and fruit loops were a casualty of my predicament. I sighed at the memory.

"Ovailia not in charge is worse. She tends to snap and act out when she doesn't feel respected."

"As opposed to...?" I opened my hands in question. Ovailia was always snapping and acting out.

"My point exactly."

I grimaced, suddenly glad I was safe and hidden in our little apartment since I was the one responsible for her dethroning.

"Poor Wyn." I said

"Poor Talon." Ilyan agreed. "I wouldn't worry. If anyone

can rein in Ovailia's temperament when I am not there, it's Talon. Although, he may be calling a bit more than Ovailia does."

Ilyan set three bowls on the table filled with honey covered strawberries, boiled greens, and berries wrapped in dandelion leaves. When I grabbed a blackberry and began to untangle it from the leaf it had been wrapped in, Ilyan looked at me as though I had brought Fruit Loops into the house, but I ignored him. I could eat the leaf separately, however with the berry it made my stomach spin.

"You're never going to gain enough strength to defeat Edmund if you don't eat the food I give you." He was using that voice again. Ugh.

"You sound like my mother." I said without thinking. My heart thumped uncontrollably when a flash of her crumpled body on the kitchen floor raced to the forefront of my memory. Ilyan didn't seem to notice the pain in my face, which was probably for the better.

"Well someone has to look out for your well-being." He was dead serious and pushed the sickly looking bowl of boiled greens in my direction. I always steered clear of his boiled greens. They looked like cat vomit.

"Might as well be 'My Protector' then," I said a bit acidly, sliding the bowl back to him.

Ilyan froze and leaned over the table toward me. I didn't raise my head to acknowledge him. I just shrunk into in my oversized hoodie.

"Don't," I said, "I'm sorry I said anything." I didn't like the feeling his stare was giving me. I looked up, unsurprised to see his gaze still boring into me.

He paused, contemplating what to say while his penetrating stare froze me in place. His eyes never left mine as he grabbed the bowl of strawberries and placed it in front of me. Ilyan reached for my hands and wrapped them around the cold bowl. I could feel the warmth of his magic pulsing and flowing under his skin.

"I will always protect you, Joclyn." My breath caught and I pulled my hands away from his, the bowl dragging along the table with them. Ilyan only smiled.

"Go get ready, Silnỳ. There are clothes for you in the bathroom. I want to leave in about an hour, so we can get some sight-seeing in before dinner."

"Leave?" I was confused. He couldn't possibly mean we were still going to go out. Especially with some super spy giving away information about us to who knows who in some bunker in Prague. It sounded like the plot to a B-grade movie. "We aren't still going into town. You can't be serious?"

"You marked me. A bit dishonestly, but you marked me," he said with a smile. "A deal is a deal."

"But what if they find us?" I could hear the panic in my own voice; obviously I was bit more freaked out about this than I had been admitting to myself.

"Then they find us, Silnỳ. It has always been a risk."

"But..." Ilyan stood up so fast my words fell from my mind in shock. In one swift movement he had come around the counter and was kneeling down before me, his hands wrapped around mine, his skin warm.

"Vždycky budu tě chránit, drahá moje." I froze at the words, my heart thumping uncontrollably.

"Protect." I said softly, repeating the only word I recognized.

"Yes, protect." He smiled brightly and pulled me to standing. "Now, go get ready, please."

Without another word, Ilyan placed the bowl of strawberries in my hands and shooed me off to the bathroom.

I shut the door behind me, my stomach swimming with eager anticipation. One hour. In one hour I would be escorted from my prison and into the world outside. Even though I was nervous about leaving given the current state of things, my excitement was stronger. I grinned at myself in the mirror and plopped a strawberry into my mouth, my face twisting a bit at the raw honey flavor.

I wrapped my hair up in a high bun on top of my head and jumped in the shower. My mind buzzed in expectation of getting out of the apartment, and I spent the majority of the time dreaming of what I would see and how I would recreate the city for Ryland. His little heart had seemed so broken by what had happened before that I needed to do something to help him cheer him up. He needed to know how much I cared for him. If I had learned one thing, it was to never bring up who he used to be.

What if he never remembered? What if I was doomed to visit the Tŏuha every day for the rest of my life? Or worse yet, what if the possessed form of Ryland died, taking my Ryland and the Tŏuha with him. If that happened, I knew I would die, too. Maybe then Ilyan could save me with whatever mystery procedure he had planned to try before.

I shook the thought from my head and stepped out of the shower, thinking again of magical cities and already planning games we could play in a newly built realm within the Tŏuha.

I had dressed without thinking and now that I was looking at myself in the mirror, I wanted to scream. What had Ilyan been thinking? Tight, bright turquoise jeans, and a bright white t-shirt? I gaped at myself in the mirror, horrified. Colors? Tight fitting clothes? I wanted to throw up. I grabbed for the hoodie, desperate for something to cover up with. It was bright red, to match my shoes I guessed, and fit as tight as everything else while the fabric was so thin it was almost non-existent. I yelled out in a panic, and stormed from the bathroom, determined to make Ilyan go out and purchase something more reasonable.

I had made it a few steps out of the bathroom when I froze. Ilyan was leaning against the kitchen counter speaking in Czech, his focus on the phone he had pressed against his ear. My jaw dropped; he looked so different. I had never seen his hair braided before. The long, blonde strands were perfectly woven together in a golden weave that trailed down the back of his head to fall halfway down his back. The absence of sheets of hair framing his face defined his facial features. He looked more distinct, stronger somehow, and his light hair contrasted starkly with his tight black polo shirt. For the first time he wasn't wearing torn jeans, either, instead he had opted for dark-washed skinny jeans. I cursed his style sense. He looked good.

Ilyan looked up at my entrance, and his line of sight trailed to the precarious bun on top of my head before he laughed. I pulled the hair tie out, having forgotten the silly thing was still up there. When he clicked his phone shut and moved toward me, I finally closed my mouth after realizing it was still hanging open.

"What?" he asked, his accent rolling around the word.

"You look..." I paused, unsure of what to say or even how to phrase it. The only word that came to mind was sexy, and saying that aloud to Ilyan was wrong on a very deep level.

"Did I do it wrong?" Ilyan asked, alarmed. He jumped away from me and ran to the nightstand where a magazine was folded. He unrolled it and flipped through it looking for a specific page. Having found what he was looking for, he rushed back over, shoving a picture right under my nose.

The magazine picture was a Louis Vuitton ad featuring a

man dressed in exactly what Ilyan was wearing. I looked from the ad to Ilyan a few times in shock before I began to laugh. So much for style sense, Ilyan had just been copying ads he had found in fashion magazines. My laugh continued to grow as I snatched the magazine from him, flipping the pages until I found a similar ad, this time with a girl wearing what Ilyan had provided for me.

"Vat?" Ilyan asked, his agitation accentuating his accent. He shifted his shirt, obviously worried he had done something wrong.

"Nothing," I managed through my laughter. "It's nothing, I thought..."

"What?" Ilyan asked again, his face screwed up in alarmed confusion. I dampened my laughter and placed my hand on his arm.

"Have you really been taking style hints from magazines all this time?" Okay it was more than hints, it was downright plagiarism, but I wasn't going to tell him that.

"Yes! How else do you expect me to fit in? Your clothing styles make no sense to me." He shook his head and walked away from me, ignoring my returning laughter.

"Well, I am going to need new clothes; I can't go outside in this."

"Why not?" Ilyan rushed back to look at the magazine, obviously not understanding.

"Well they are tight, and have colors, and... and..." Ilyan hiked an eyebrow at me like I was crazy. "This hoodie has no fabric what-so-ever."

I threw both the magazine and the offending hoodie at him. He caught the sweater and the magazine floated before him for a minute before settling itself on the counter. His face broke into a wide smile, happy his clothes weren't really the issue.

"Pants I will replace, the hoodie you are going to want to keep."

"I can't wear this out, Ilyan. There isn't anything to it." He laughed at me again, and I fumed a little bit.

"It's one hundred and ten degrees out there today, Silnỳ. If you wear any other hoodie, you will pass out from heat stroke."

"One hundred and ten degrees?" It never got that hot back home, ever. I would be surprised if it had even gotten to ninety in the summer. I cringed. That extra twenty degrees sounded miserable. I couldn't go out without a hoodie, I couldn't. I grumbled and grabbed the hoodie back from him, trying to ignore the way his face lit up as well as the joy behind his eyes.

8

THE CITY of Santa Fe was full of life. From what I had seen from the confines of my tiny prison, I never would have thought that city streets could have so much energy.

Ilyan had walked me out of the apartment and into the boiling heat of the city, his hand wrapped firmly around mine with his shield protecting me, keeping me hidden.

I had not been very happy with the idea of holding his hand, but the skin connection was needed to keep the shield in place. Besides, Ilyan had promised me it would only be for an hour, and then he would release me, taking the shield with him. I wasn't strong enough to hold my own shield yet.

The idea of being unshielded in the middle of the city scared me. The thought of Ryland finding me—scratch that, hunting me—sent an uncomfortable mix of jitters and nerves through my already bristling stomach. I tried to settle it with the knowledge that Ilyan would be there. No matter how much this 'Protector' nonsense gave me the heebie-jeebies, I knew Ilyan would in fact protect me, and that made me feel more comfortable. Whether or not he would tell me why he was my Protector, I still felt safe with him being around.

Ilyan took me out of the apartment and onto the street below where a green taxi was already waiting for us. He held my hand tightly as he helped me into the car then slid in to sit right up against me even though there was plenty of room in the backseat.

The car had barely begun to move before my nose was plastered against the window. I watched in wonder as the driver sped us downtown at Ilyan's instruction. It had been almost four months since I had been outside. Three months since I had been able to feel the wind or the sun. I felt it briefly before we got in the cab, but now it was right outside the vehicle, taunting me. Without permission, I rolled down the window and stretched away from Ilyan to get as close to the hot breeze as possible.

I felt the warm air move into the car where it swirled around and made the air conditioned space uncomfortable, but I didn't care. I could feel it. I could feel the energy in the wind and the pulse of the sun. My magic began to buzz at the sensation the wind gave me, the feeling of earth energy —or whatever it was—filling me up.

"Maybe sightseeing wasn't such a good idea," Ilyan laughed behind me. "Perhaps I should have taken you into the mountains and let you roam free for a few hours."

"You make it sound like I'm a caged animal, Ilyan." I didn't look away from the window. I leaned closer to the moving air, letting it pick up the strands of my black hair and move them around.

"If you get your head any further out that window, you are going to look like a dog. A caged dog."

I could hear the chuckle behind his voice, the happiness infectious. I looked back at him briefly before leaning away from him, pulling his arm and torso with me as I stuck my head and shoulders out the window. The driver began to yell as I stretched my face to the sky, the sun and the wind warming my face, but I didn't hear what he said, I didn't care. I smiled at the way the sun warmed my nose, the shiver of energy flowing down my spine, and the way my shoulders seized as if I had been tickled. Ilyan said something back to the driver a moment before his hand tugged me into the car, his arm wrapping me against him.

"You are going to upset our driver, Silnỳ." Ilyan spoke against my temple, the latent smile evident in his voice.

"I didn't even get to stick out my tongue."

"Next time, little puppy, next time." Ilyan patted my head condescendingly and I laughed a bit, moving away from him with a joking snarl.

"Caged animal, remember," I said. Ilyan smiled widely at me, his shoulders shaking as he held in a laugh.

"Yes, I remember." His smile broadened as the car pulled to a stop, the driver announcing our arrival and the charge, which Ilyan promptly paid. "How would you like to be free?"

"You gonna let me fly?" I asked, although I already knew the answer.

"Not today." Ilyan pulled me from the car, lifting our intertwined hands to eye level. He moved my hand close to him until his lips pressed against the back of it. His eyes met mine over the top of our hands, giving me that look I couldn't quite understand.

My stomach flipped and I cringed away from him. I didn't like the contact and I really did not like the way my body reacted because of it. I fought the need to pull my hand away, knowing I needed the connection, so instead I held on tighter and walked down the busy street, towing Ilyan after me.

After a few steps, I slowed to a stop. This part of Santa Fe was nothing like I would have expected it to be. Instead of tall, glass skyscrapers, there were perfect rows of adobe buildings, each carefully built to replicate the old style of the Native Americans and Spanish Settlers. The burnt orange color of the buildings contrasted with the blue sky beautifully. At the head of the street there was a large, sandstone cathedral. It was a graceful box of ancient architecture with its elegant stone arches and circular stained glass windows. It was beautiful even though it didn't look complete without the tall stone towers that are common in cathedrals.

"Wow." I said, a bit more awed than I had intended, however the way the street was designed kind of deserved it.

"I take it you like it then?" Ilyan said and began leading me down the street, his hand tightly wound around mine.

"Honestly, I would like anything as long as it had moving air, but this has a unique charm. It's kind of... unexpected."

"Santa Fe has a long, drawn out history. The buildings are designed this way as a reminder and a link to the past. It's one of the reasons they don't have a larger downtown."

"I don't think they need it," I countered. My eyes dragged over one of the buildings as we passed. Its interior was an upbeat teen clothing store which had a window filled with graphic t-shirts and feather accessories—clothing that Wyn would wear. The contrast between the old and the new was somewhat silly, but it didn't take away from the nostalgia of the architecture.

"Prague is mostly the same. There is the old town and the new town. The new never mixes with the old."

"And is there a cathedral there as well?"

"A few," Ilyan said. I could tell there was more to his answer, yet part of me didn't care at the moment. I wanted to focus on this city and my current freedom.

I let Ilyan take the lead, his embrace gently pulling me along as we walked by small boutiques and larger restaurants. I finally had to pull him to a stop when we came to a row of street vendors under the overhangs of the buildings. Each person had a blanket set in front of them with jewelry, watches, and other handmade objects laid out, each with a tiny paper price tag. I slowly walked by them, taking in the large amounts of turquoise and silver.

My feet stopped when I saw it. The simplicity of my need making my legs week.

A long board.

It wasn't even for sale. It was simply someone's possession that was being used as a different way to showcase the intricate turquoise jewelry that lined its top. Still, I needed it.

Mine had been lost forever when Ilyan had picked up my broken body from behind that dumpster and brought me into this crazy world I now lived in. I missed it. I hadn't longed for it in that deep, pining way I had seen other teenagers do; I simply missed it. I missed what it represented; the part of me that had disappeared when it had. I missed being normal.

I kneeled down next to the street vendor's blanket without letting go of Ilyan's hand. When I looked up at the old wizened woman, her legs covered with a beautifully woven blanket, she looked down at me happily.

"Which one do you like?" Ilyan's voice was soft in my ear. It took me a second to grasp that he thought I was ogling the jewelry.

"I don't wear jewelry, Ilyan," I answered honestly, suddenly worried that he would buy me something.

"Which one?"

I scowled at him, unsurprised to find him smiling at me expectantly. I sighed before pointing absentmindedly at the board. Ilyan raised an eyebrow still trying to figure out which piece I was referring to.

"I like the long board, Ilyan," I clarified, looking away uncomfortably. "It reminds me of mine."

"Sometimes I forget how much you have lost. People, loved ones, even objects. It's all part of you." Ilyan squeezed my hand, and I turned back to him as his fingers trailed over the jewelry lightly. They fluttered around the bracelets and necklaces before stopping on a small, turquoise bracelet with stones flat against one another; it wasn't jagged like the others.

Ilyan picked it up and held it in his hands, his eyes closed as if he was measuring something.

"Turquoise," Ilyan began, "can draw out negativity. Did you know that?"

"No." I was a little surly, I didn't like the idea of Ilyan buying me jewelry, and I had a bad feeling that was exactly what was going to happen.

"And this particular turquoise will help bring up feelings of love and of family." Ilyan looked up at the old woman who nodded her head in agreement, her beautiful face breaking into a smile.

"Your young man is right," she said, her voice shaky and warm. I almost wanted to laugh right out at her comment. Ilyan was neither young nor mine. "That is Navajo turquoise, it will bind you to your family and to the ones you love."

The old woman smiled knowingly at Ilyan, her face

lighting up. I turned to bat her assumptions away but was stopped by Ilyan's smile. My eyes instantly widened in surprise; Ilyan rarely smiled like that. I must have looked ridiculous because Ilyan continued to grin happily at me.

"We will take it." Ilyan held the bracelet underneath my wrist, his magic unclasping it and snaking it around me. I looked away nervously from his obvious use of magic to the old woman who was busy counting the money Ilyan had paid her with.

"Ilyan... I..." Ilyan pulled me away from the seller before I could argue more.

"I think it will help you, Joclyn. Trapped in rooms, hunted, people trying to betray you, running for your life," he smiled, but it was sad, "I think you could use a little bit of a negativity release. With all that's going on, you could use a stronger connection with those who care about you. It's no long board, but I will replace what you have lost—as much of it as I can—when all this is over." I could only nod at his words and the sincerity behind them.

I lifted my wrist up to look at the stones, which were pretty, though part of me wanted to take it off and give it back to the old woman. As much as I didn't like the message of the stones, I could already feel my magic collecting around my wrist, seeping through them and then back into me. It did it of its own accord, whether I wanted it to or not. I smiled a bit before shrugging my sleeve over the bracelet, letting it disappear from view.

Ilyan continued to move down the street at a slow pace, but somehow it was more focused than it had been before.

When we reached the end of the street with the large cathedral now towering over us, Ilyan dragged me over to where another street vendor was selling empanadas, but my eyes never left where the large church rose up above the street level. Smoothly cut stone formed delicate arches that surrounded the beautiful stained glass window that sat directly above the door. It was breathtaking.

"The Cathedral Basilica of St. Francis of Assisi," Ilyan said as he placed a hot pastry in my free hand.

"It was built in the late 1860s. Back then, this city was made up of the Palace of the Governors and a handful of adobe homes. Seeing it like this makes me long for the old."

I knew I shouldn't be surprised, but I still was. Ilyan was being more open about his past than usual and it disturbed me to be reminded of how old he was.

"So you lived here then?" I tried to keep my voice level.

"No, not here. But I did live in the church that was here before they built the cathedral. La Parroquia. It resembled a fortress more than a church, but I still loved it."

I turned and looked at him, his gaze never deviating from the large building in front of us. The picture of him in some religious get up did not fit in my eyes, but he had now mentioned living in a monastery when Ovailia was born, a church in France, and a cathedral in New Mexico.

"You and churches, I am beginning to see a theme. I wouldn't have pegged you for the religious type." I had seen the look in his eyes when he had faced a fight; I doubted he could live without that for long.

"I'm not." His answer was firm as he turned his head a bit to look at me.

"Then why all the churches?"

Ilyan looked away. He wasn't happy or sad, simply distant.

"Have you ever been around very pious people, Joclyn?" I almost laughed at the thought, but kept it inside. The tone of his voice was far too serious for laughter.

"We stopped going to church after my dad left. He

always insisted we go together. After he was gone, my mom didn't want to go anymore, so we didn't."

Ilyan turned back to face me and smiled a bit. His expression was almost understanding.

"I don't remember a lot," I finished, wishing he would look away from me.

"Pious people, those who are truly spiritual, are amazing creatures. I am almost convinced they are humans at their best. Now, mind you, I have seen some terrible things happen in the name of a God—wars, conquests, sacrifices— but on the whole—at its very base—religion makes people better."

"So, you believe in God then?" I asked.

"I believe in something. I am not sure if it's God, though. The stories of where I come from differ from yours. There are no Adam and Eve in my past."

I turned toward Ilyan, taking a bite of the pastry he had given me. I hadn't heard this story before and I was content to hear him tell it from the beginning. I gestured my pastry hand toward him, prompting him to continue.

"My kind, the Skřítek, guard the wells of magic. There is a place deep inside the earth under Prague where magic bubbles up in what can only be described as mud. We call these the wells of Imdalind."

"Wait, what?" I asked, interrupting him. "That's the name of Ryland's family's company."

"Now you know where Edmund got the name," he smiled. "It is Edmunds greatest desire to take control of the wells of Imdalind again."

"Why? What would he do with them?" I asked, although I already knew it would be nothing good.

"Create a new race, destroy the world, or stop the existence of magic. The possibilities within Imdalind are endless, which is why those that are left of my kind are sworn to protect the wells of mud with our lives."

"What has the mud done before? Besides hold magic I mean?"

"It was through this mud that the first of every kind was bred. We do not know where they came from, only that they woke with their legs in the mud, their lungs stinging with their first breath. They walked out of the mountain, and as each bonded with a mortal it awoke something inside of the mortals, their own magic. It is from the wells of Imdalind that all magic begins and ends."

"How do you know that that's what really happened?" I asked, holding in a laugh. The story sounded more like a legend than a history.

"Because we know who was there. The first of each of the holders of magic. The first of the Drak, the first of the Vilÿs, the first of the Trpaslíks and the first of the Skříteks—my grandmother, Frain."

"Your grandmother?" Would there ever be anything about Ilyan that wouldn't surprise me?

"Yes, I have heard this story since the day I was born. My mother and grandmother would tell it to me at nights when our home was lit by candlelight. My mother also told me as she lay dying from the loss of my father's magic."

Ilyan turned away from me, looking toward the church, but I could tell he wasn't seeing anything. I knew that look. I had been trapped in that look for months. It was the look of one trapped in their memories. I reached up and placed my hand on his shoulder. At my touch, he turned to face me.

"Which is how you knew what was happening to me all those months ago?" He nodded once.

"But you would let me help you while my mother let

herself waste away." He sighed heavily and my heart tensed. I knew exactly how he felt.

"I'm sorry." I let my hand fall from his shoulder, not knowing what else to do.

"It was a very long time ago, Silnỳ."

"I am still sorry."

The silence between us stretched uncomfortably. I willed myself to look away from him, to ignore his warm hand wrapped around mine. I finished my food, shoving the wrapper in my pocket, and turned to him, unsurprised to see his unfocused gaze on something beyond me.

"So," I began, desperate to end the silence and break Ilyan's intense gaze. "If you believe that your kind came from this mud, do you believe there is a god, too?"

"Not particularly," he said, coming back to himself.

"If you don't believe in a god, then why do you spend so much time in churches?"

"Because of how humans act when their souls are so close to God. They care for one another beyond how they would normally. They help, and support, and love one another. It's amazing to watch."

"You must think me an uncaring, hateful person then." I shifted my weight, wishing I could remove my hand from his. He must have sensed my discomfort because the heat from his hand around mine increased as his magic pulsed.

"Not in the least. You are one of the most caring, brave people I have met in quite some time. You willingly risked everything to save Ryland, handled ultimate losses with grace, and—"

I snorted and Ilyan stopped to look at me, his forehead furled in confusion.

"I wasn't graceful, Ilyan. I refused to move and then practically let my body kill me."

"But you didn't," Ilyan said.

"Because you're stubborn," I said, shoving our entwined hands into his chest. When Ilyan smiled, I glowed assuming I had won.

"Not as stubborn as you." My mouth dropped, odd clicking noises coming from my throat. Ilyan laughed deeply, the happy sound ricocheting off the people around us. Several people looked toward us, smiling at the exchange. I could only guess what was on their minds. First date, young love, newly married, and it got worse from there. I instinctively sunk into my sweater, pulling the hood up around my face with my free hand. Ilyan's laugh stopped, but his smile remained.

"When are you going to stop hiding?"

"As soon as people stop looking at me," I said, affronted. Ilyan raised an eyebrow at me and I crinkled my noise at him in frustration.

"I don't see that happening any time soon, Silnỳ."

"Then don't count on me coming out of hiding anytime soon," I spat, grumbling a bit.

"And you say you are not stubborn." Ilyan grinned, his eyes shining. I shied away from him, my reaction increasing his smile and causing me to fume a bit more. Ilyan dropped my hand then, his warm magic and the protective shield leaving my body. Now it wasn't a question of *if* Ryland would find me but how fast. Suddenly I felt unprepared to be attacked, to fight; unsure if I could come out of a fight still standing.

I stiffened in fear, my eyes darting around the street as if Ryland was simply going to step out from behind a garbage can. My panic softened when Ilyan placed his hands on either side of my face, forcing me to look at him.

"Calm down, Joclyn."

"What if they find me, Ilyan?" I said, struggling to keep the stress out of my voice.

"Then they find you. You are brave enough to fight them now. You are strong enough to face him." He didn't need to elaborate. I knew who he was talking about.

"Ilyan, I—"

"I know you are," he cut me off, not letting me give voice to my fears. His words were so soft—his eyes so gentle—that against my better judgment I felt my anxiety dissipate, replaced by a heavy confidence I wasn't used to.

Ilyan moved his hands from my face to move the hood down from around my head, releasing my hair to fall down my back. "And then we will know if they can track you and how fast."

I cringed. Being unshielded made me uncomfortable. This was worse than having people looking at me. I couldn't hide under a hoodie to escape. I wasn't even sure what would happen if they did find me, or if I really wanted to know if they could. Having that knowledge didn't seem like something desirable to me.

"I need to know so that I can keep you safe, and if they do come, I will be here to protect you."

"My Protector?" I said.

"Yes," he spoke softly, his hands trailing around my neck to rest on my shoulders, the soft touch of his forefinger grazing my mark. "Now, let's go have some fun."

9

I SAT underneath the twinkling lights that had been draped around the large outdoor patio of the cantina, listening to the fast paced salsa music that filled the air. Couples danced and swirled on the floor in front of me with their bodies meshed together in a seamless blur of color.

I sat back in my wicker chair, pressing my strawberry lemonade to my lips. The sun was setting behind the mountains that surrounded the city, giving a soft yellow glow to the sky. It touched the facades of the buildings and kissed them into a honey color that glowed from the inside out. I had never seen a city that was so unique and beautiful; I was in love.

Even though the sun was setting, the temperature hadn't dropped. My hoodie felt heavy and hot against my skin while a thin layer of sweat had built up on my neck. I was contemplating taking it off, but didn't want to be the recipient of the told-you-so look from Ilyan, though the thought of dying from heat stroke due to my own stubbornness scared me. I took another sip of lemonade; at least I could keep myself hydrated.

I shifted my hoodie a bit to help the airflow, but I was still uncomfortable. I glanced to Ilyan hoping he hadn't seen me fidget. Luckily he was still intently watching the dancers.

He looked completely out of place in this melee of noise and color. The rugged lines of his face caught in the lights, giving him an ethereal hue almost as if he himself was glowing while he sat in his chair, smiling serenely. It was a stark contrast to the drunken, boisterous group we were surrounded by.

He turned and caught me staring at him, so I smiled brightly and turned back to the dancers, feeling strangely odd about being caught looking at him. I heard him chuckle and he returned to his glass of wine.

The waitress had looked at him like he had lost it when we ordered and he requested wine instead of the obligatory tequila. Ilyan had only raised an eyebrow, sending the girl to retrieve wine I was sure hadn't been in their stock before then.

"Come on, Silnÿ." Ilyan's hand jutted into the space in front of me. "Let's dance."

"Oh, no," I said, sinking into the chair. "I don't dance."

Ilyan bent down slightly, bringing his eyes closer to my eye level. "Don't dance, or don't know how?"

"Both, considering the last time I was on a dance floor didn't end so well." My insides scrambled together at the thought of Ryland's graduation party, my first and only kiss, and then the disastrous failed rescue mission that had followed.

"Yes, I know. I was there."

"Then you know why I don't want to participate," I said smugly, hoping he would walk away.

He didn't.

His lips pulled up into a half smile, his eyes twinkling.

"Would it help if I told you I invented the Salsa?"

"You did not," I said, trying to restrain a smile. His eyes lit up as he laughed, his hand still jutting toward me unwavering.

"Well, no, but I have been dancing it since it was invented. Come, let me show you." Ilyan wrapped his hand under my arm and pulled me up.

"I'd rather not." I stepped away from him, but he mirrored my movements.

"I won't hurt you, Joclyn," he promised. "And if you don't dance with me, I'll be forced to take away your win and we will have to stay in the apartment for an additional week."

My jaw dropped a bit at that, but Ilyan only smiled more. Although I would normally have guessed it to be an empty threat, I didn't want to take the chance. I plopped my hand down in his and rolled my eyes, trying to ignore the grin that lit up his face.

Ilyan led me onto the dance floor, and I tried to ignore the stabbing pain that being there was giving me. The swirling and moving couples made way for us as we weaved through them until Ilyan had placed us directly in the middle where the cobweb of lights zigzagged over our heads.

Ilyan took my hand in his and brought our joined hands up to eye level. His other hand brought mine up to his arm before moving to rest lightly on my back. He looked at me intently as the music flowed around us. I could have sworn he was waiting for me to move first, but there was no way that was going to happen. I rolled my eyes at him and went to drop my hands, yet he held onto me tighter.

"Follow the way my feet move," he began. "Mine move forward. Yours move back. Watch."

I looked down, nerves rising as I watched his feet move

smoothly across the floor. I tried to follow, but it was harder than I thought it would be. Ilyan made it look easy.

I missed my long board. I could control that perfectly, and I was sure Ilyan would fall off after about ten feet. I smiled at the thought and missed a beat. My supporting foot rolled and my other one kicked him in the ankle. I was no good at this. I swore loudly and tried to pull away, but Ilyan increased his grip and pulled me back, crashing my body into his.

"Don't think so much, Silnỳ," he whispered in my ear. "Feel the music and move with the beat."

I could feel Ilyan's hand grow warm against mine, his magic bubbling right under the surface, but it never crossed the barrier of our skin. I had been left to my own devices without a shield to protect me or magic to calm me. I groaned and pushed my lacking self-confidence to the side in an attempt to move with him in the right way. Ilyan's hand increased pressure on my back, pulling me against him as he began to push and pull me in the right direction. While still not perfect, at least I wasn't stepping into anyone anymore.

"Now, you move your hips a bit more..."

"Did you say 'move your hips' to me?" I interrupted trying to keep the laugh out of my voice. "That's not going to happen."

"It is part of the Salsa, Joclyn, you must try it." At that, Ilyan began to move his hips in the way that all the other men on the floor were. It looked absolutely ridiculous.

I laughed loudly at him, but he didn't stop the movement. He continued stepping and swaying and shaking as he took my giggling, stumbling form along with him. He spun me once, and I over spun, crashing into him. I felt a laugh build in his chest as he continued to move. I had never seen him laugh like this before. This was natural and carefree; Ilyan was having fun. His emotion enraptured me and I began to awkwardly sway my hips along with him. Ilyan's laughter increased as I moved ineptly around his perfected movements.

We moved as the band played. Ilyan's movements were flawless while I stumbled along with him as we both laughed aloud. Ilyan smiled at me with the same confusing look in his eyes before spinning me under his arm. I turned around awkwardly in front of him, my eyes tracking the crowd as I became dizzier and dizzier.

That was when I noticed that others were watching. For one fleeting moment I hadn't noticed, I hadn't cared. Not until I saw a beautiful Hispanic woman looking at me. She was laughing, possibly finding joy in the happiness that Ilyan and I shared, but even her notice cut into me. I stopped spinning and sunk into myself. Moving instinctively, Ilyan's arms came up to wrap around me, pulling me into his chest. I wished he wouldn't touch me, but I didn't want to make more of a scene. Right now I wanted to run from the dance floor. Coming out here had been a mistake.

"Others will notice you, Joclyn," Ilyan whispered in my ear, his chin resting on my shoulder. "But you can not let it change who you are deep inside. Have fun for you, not for the people around you."

He spun me away from him, my eyes scanning the crowd. Everyone was laughing, joking, and playing; all of them were happy, and none of them were looking at me.

Ilyan came up behind me, his arm wrapping around my waist as he returned me to the dance with my back against his chest.

"See, no one else is even noticing you. No one else

matters. Only you. Only me. Only the Salsa!" I could hear his smile as he pushed me away from him causing me to spin around to face him again. His feet continued to move and his hips to sway as I poorly mimicked his movements.

I couldn't say I got better, but I did actually begin to enjoy myself again. Before long Ilyan was laughing just as loud as I was while we danced our way through the endless Salsa music.

Ilyan had pulled me out of another turn when his face fell. He never missed a beat, but his eyes had turned from joyous to serious far faster than I had thought possible.

"Well, that was fast," he said, his voice hard.

"What was fast?" I asked, trying to follow his line of sight, but he had returned to staring back at me.

"Go for a walk with me?" he asked.

"Umm... okay."

Ilyan had barely waited for a response before winding his fingers through mine and taking me with him as he turned and began to swerve through the crowded cantina. We passed by our table and Ilyan held out his hand, letting his drink fly into his open palm. He drained the glass before lowering it to another table on our way out.

"Ilyan?" I whispered, sure I wasn't going to get a response.

Ilyan was about to plow us into a large group of people when my body grew warm with his magic. It didn't flood me as fast as it had when my magic was killing me, but the speed was still startling. Something was obviously wrong.

The warmth filled me just as a large breeze came and lifted us off of the ground. Ilyan held onto my hand tightly as he flew us out of the crowded restaurant and onto the golden tin roof of the building. I looked down at the confused people below who all seemed to be commenting on the wind, but no one had noticed our odd departure.

"Ilyan, what—" Ilyan clapped his hand over my mouth as he held me still, his eyes focused on the lively party below us. My body felt stifled as his magic pulsed stronger within me before turning into a low, simmering heat that siphoned away to form a shield around me again.

"Two hours, Joclyn. That's all it took for them to track your magic." His face lit up in a wicked grin that I knew a bit too well, and my heart beat erratically. I looked down to the dance floor as a short man with broad shoulders and dark red hair walked into the space followed by a hulking mass in black leather. Cail and what I could easily recognize as Edmund had found me. Their movements were slow and focused. Their static figures standing out in the torrent of activity.

"He's come himself, I see," Ilyan smiled with a wicked joy. "Well, I suppose he needs a challenge every once in a while."

Only one person could track my magic. I swung my head toward Ilyan, my eyes wide. Finally he removed his hand from over my mouth.

"Is *he* here?" I whispered. Ilyan's fingers moved up to touch my mark, his touch light on my neck.

"Yes, but don't go looking for him." My heart fell at his words.

"I need you to stay here. If anyone approaches you, fly right to me. Don't hesitate. Don't try to fight them."

He looked away from me, his eyes scanning the party below us.

"I can fight, Ilyan," I said. Suddenly finding my confidence, after all I had been pushing and preparing for this day for the last three months.

"Not well enough, Silnỳ. Not well enough to face Edmund, not yet." He turned toward me and wrapped his hands around my forearms. "Not. Yet."

"But you said earlier..." I began, remembering the softness of his voice, the strength of his earlier confidence in me. I felt like he was suddenly taking it all back. I didn't disagree with him, yet the seemingly abrupt change of his mind still stung.

"I know, I—"

"Stop treating me like a child!" I pulled my arms away from his touch and tried to move away from him. I regretted it instantly. The simmering heat of the shield left, and within moments, Cail's face turned up to the roof of the cantina where Ilyan and I stood.

Ilyan grabbed my hand and took off into the air, dragging me behind him. His magic swelled inside me as he shielded me again, flying us down the street to land near a large white statue that adorned the façade of the main cathedral.

"I'm not treating you like a child, Joclyn," he hissed icily.

"Then why won't you let me fight, Ilyan?" I wasn't sure why I was fighting this. I didn't even think I was ready to face Ryland. I certainly didn't know if I would be able to fight him.

"I need to protect you, Joclyn. I have to keep you safe and this is the only way I can do that."

"By hiding me?" Ilyan stopped me with one look, the desperation in his eyes deepening the blue hue.

"Yes, until you are strong enough to fight."

I didn't respond. I knew Ilyan was right. I couldn't seek Ryland out. He would kill me. Even though I wanted to believe I was ready to fight, I was not sure I could, or if I was strong enough.

"Stay here. Don't do anything stupid, Silnỳ."

"Why would I do anything...?"

"*Please.*" Ilyan removed his hands and waved both over me once like he was framing my body. The heat of the shield stayed with me even without his contact. I stared at him wide eyed. I hadn't known he could shield me without touching me.

"This shield is unmovable, Joclyn. If you move even a step out of the way, it will shatter. It is as strong as the one I placed around the apartment, but it is fickle. I can control it when I am away from you, but it is around you, not inside you. It cannot move like you can." His eyes were a combination of fear and excitement as he kept glancing behind him, an eagerness to fight battling with his need to stay with me.

"So, if Ryland finds me?"

"It should hold, but if you move..."

"Then it's gone," I finished for him, my heart beating wildly.

"And you fly right to me."

I nodded once in understanding and Ilyan took a step away from me before moving back, his internal conflict still raging.

"Stay," he commanded me like a dog and I fumed a bit, but pushed it away to nod at him.

Ilyan looked at me one last time before flying away, directly toward his father who stood in the middle of the busy street.

10

ILYAN SHOT through the air like a bullet to land gracefully a few steps away from Cail, who stood protectively around Edmund in the middle of the main road.

As the three faced each other in anticipation, I could feel the pressure of the situation even from a distance. While I watched, their words flowed up to me much louder than I would have expected.

"Hello, son," Edmund crooned, and I cringed at how happy and normal he sounded. The impending battle didn't seem to bother him at all.

"Father." Ilyan's voice was tense and I could tell he was gauging what he should do. Part of me hoped he would fly back to gather me up and fly away.

Cail silently paced in front of Edmund, his body tense and ready at the same time his eyes moved from Ilyan to the street around him as he searched for me. I instinctively held my breath and controlled my jitters.

"I hear you stole something that belongs to your brother," Edmund continued as if Ilyan's tense voice had been nothing other than a casual greeting.

"I stole nothing. I am simply holding it for safe keeping." Ilyan ground his foot into the road, and for one ridiculous moment, I was reminded of an old-time gun fight. I shook my head at the thought. This was no ordinary gun fight, this was much more serious.

"Hmmm, that is not what I hear," I saw Ilyan flinch a bit at Edmund's words, his back tensing. "Stop that, Cail, you're going to wear me out."

Edmund gave one casual swipe of his hand and Cail stopped pacing immediately. Moving himself to stand in front of Edmund, he never let his dark eyes leave Ilyan.

"Yes, Master."

This time I flinched.

At the Rugby game, and even in the ballroom of the mansion, I had never seen Cail respond that way to Edmund. It might have been that I hadn't been paying close enough attention, but he had never struck me as the subservient type. I had only seen Cail act that way around Edmund in my dreams, and the fact that my subconscious rendering of him could have been that precise made me uncomfortable.

"Don't move," I said to myself, as if my own voice would be able to help me keep still.

"Well, job well done I'd say. She's safe. You're safe. Everyone's happy, and we are here to collect." Even though his words were still upbeat, Edmund's voice had begun to darken.

"I don't think so," Ilyan said just as darkly, as if Edmund's words had been some great joke. The sound reverberated up to me, making the whole street sound as if it was haunted.

"I was afraid of that," Edmund sighed, his feet stepping back as he moved himself out of the way.

"Cail." Cail stepped forward at Edmund's words. His

anticipation was palpable as his eyes never left Ilyan's. "Restrain him."

"With pleasure."

Ilyan bowed his back slightly in preparation for Cail's assault.

Cail turned to face Ilyan with a stream of power and light shooting out of his fingers. Ilyan didn't dodge. He simply stepped gracefully out of the way. The energy, however, continued on and slammed into a supporting beam of the cantina's outdoor overhang.

The Salsa music was replaced by screams as the roof to the patio collapsed. Without hesitation, Ilyan lifted his hand and detached the entire roof, sending it flying toward Cail. The screams from the people in the cantina increased as the air seemed to explode around them.

The roof made contact, sending Cail to the ground. The pile of wood, fabric, and fairy lights sat in a crumpled heap in the middle of the street.

Edmund clapped his hands as if he was enjoying the show, and I knew why the second I looked down to the street.

With the roof to the cantina gone, a stationary dark figure stood alone in the center of the once crowded restaurant.

My heart beat was disconnected at seeing Ryland there. As Ilyan turned to face him, I took a step forward without thinking, the shield wavering at my movement. I hesitated. I didn't know what I wanted. Did I want to be near him? Did I want to fight him? Or did I want to save him? What did I actually think I could do?

My whole body shook as I struggled through my options. My mind called for one action and my heart for another.

"Ryland," I whispered.

I stepped back, hoping my movement hadn't broken Ilyan's shield. My magic pulsed and flowed with more heat and power than I had ever felt, but still I knew it wasn't enough. I couldn't even mark Ilyan without playing dirty, and tricks like that with the possessed Ryland would get me killed. I clenched my fists and focused on Ilyan's slow movements toward Ryland, trying to keep my thoughts off of my inability to help.

Before Ilyan could move too far toward Ryland, the shattered remains of the cantina roof exploded into fragmented bits, leaving Cail standing in the rubble. Distracted by the commotion, my eyes flew back to where the now empty dining area was devoid of any dark-haired men.

Raw fear rippled through me, taking my breath and logic away. Ryland was coming to find me. I stood still, listening to the beat of my heart, expecting Ryland to come around a corner at any moment.

Ilyan must have jumped to the same conclusion because he began to battle Cail, his eyes scanning around for Ryland while also keeping tabs on his father, who seemed content to let Cail do his dirty work.

"Hello, little pony, have you come to be broken?" I froze at the words, my whole body going rigid as my pulse skyrocketed. I felt Ryland's hand trail down my scalp, his fingers running through my hair. I didn't dare turn. I didn't know if I could manage it.

"I like your hair better this way; it's beautiful. I think— seeing you like this—I *would* like to keep you as a pet." As Ryland came around to face me, his black eyes were the only things I could look at. Not for the first time, I had to remind myself that his mind was gone.

He wasn't there.

It isn't him.

It isn't him. I reminded myself over and over, trying to ignore the heavy thump of my heart against my chest.

Then Ryland reached up and placed a cold hand against my skin. I felt the warm buzzing of Ilyan's shield evaporate. Ilyan must have felt his magic surge as his power returned, but I couldn't look away from the black depths of Ryland's eyes to see if Ilyan had noticed.

"What? Not going to say hello?" My eyes ran down his face to his lips to the lips I had only gotten to kiss once. Even though my face burned with happiness, I had to tell myself again that it wasn't him.

It isn't him.

My head was buzzing with internal yells, many prompting me to run.

It isn't him

"Goodbye, Ry." I whispered the words before slamming my hand into his stomach. I filled my hand with all the abnormal buzzing I felt and lunged it at him, sending him spinning through the air to land on the street twenty feet away.

I didn't dare look. I took off into the air, needing to get to Ilyan.

At some point in my brief contact with Ryland, Ilyan had begun fighting with Edmund, leaving Cail to take a supporting role; the scene before me was terrifying. I landed further away from Ilyan than I wanted to, scared to get too close.

Ilyan's and Edmund's hands moved seamlessly as they fought. Tables, daggers, swords—objects both real and conjured—everything flew across the space between them. Physical weapons to magical attacks, they blended into one another. The energy fields and magic that they fought with sent flashes of color through the darkened street.

I watched for a moment, stunned into a stupor. I needed to get to Ilyan, but more importantly, I needed to help him.

My hand flexed in preparation for an attack when I was struck across my back by a long strand of white-hot heat. I fell to the ground as the burning pain seeped into me before dissipating. I scrambled to flip around on the asphalt only to get tangled up in the remains of my hoodie, which had been shredded by the whip-like attack. I yelled as I pulled at it, frantic to remove it and get away. My efforts were halted by Ryland's legs straddling me and holding me in place.

"Now, where were you going?" he sneered. "I told you that I need to break you."

He sat down on my legs, the pressure inverting my knees painfully. I moved to place my hands against his skin, ready to attack him, but Ryland grabbed my wrists before I could make contact. He transferred both of them into one hand and leaned towards me, pushing my arms above my head. His searing magic moved into me and blended with my own, his negative energy stopping the flow of magic and blood to my arms. I attempted to pull my hands away—to kick him off of my legs—but he was too strong and his weight too much for me. I could feel my body weakening the more I fought him.

"Do you know how they break a horse?" He increased the weight on my legs and against my wrists as I fought him. "You have to whip it."

Ryland sliced his free hand through the air in front of me sending the same burning sensation, this time through my chest, and I screamed out at the centralized pain. He swiped his magic across me again and again, the pain surging with each new impact. I continued to fight him as I screamed and writhed, my hands still bound as he pinned me down.

I was desperate to escape the agony, but I also knew I should be hurting more. With each painful swipe of his hand the pain grew only to be swallowed up by my body as I absorbed his energy, the Zělství forming a loop between us.

I waited until his next strike and grabbed the burning energy before my body dissipated it within me then combined it with my own magic and shot it back at him through my hands, directly into his face.

Ryland yelled in pain as he fell off me, freeing my legs. I scrambled up, the now shredded fabric of my hoodie falling to the ground. I didn't wait to see if Ryland was still down. I did the only logical thing that I could think of, I ran and hid.

I bolted into a dark alley, the large adobe buildings towering over me and enclosing me in the dark space. A few steps in and the darkness engulfed me, leaving me alone with my pounding heart as I felt my way along the rough wall, waiting until I was far enough into the alley not to be seen, then I jumped into the air. The wind caught me and hoisted me onto the nearest roof.

I knew it was pointless to run. I could already feel my own magic pulse toward Ryland; the heavy weight of the pull increasing the closer he got. It was part of the magic of the Zělství, the bonding. The connection that was supposed to have been such a joyous occasion had turned into my own personal hell. I was, at that moment, being hunted by my mate.

I ran and hid behind a large air conditioning unit, knowing it was hopeless. I attempted to convince myself of my need to fight him, no matter how much I hurt at the thought. The pulse of my magic continued to grow as he moved closer while the sounds of Ilyan's battle with

Edmund and Cail from the street below echoed in my ears. The air was becoming thick with the smell of dust and burning wood. I had only vaguely begun wondering what had caught fire when Ryland suddenly pulled me up by my hair.

I controlled my breathing, squaring my jaw to face him. His gaze was so full of hatred that my stomach tightened and churned in warning. I fought against his hold, my arms swinging wildly at him when it became obvious he wasn't going to let me go.

"If whipping doesn't work, make the horse submit." he stated blandly, as if reciting the words from a book just before his hand flew through the air and made contact with my stomach. I gasped as the air left my lungs and was replaced with the pain of the impact.

I reached up and cupped my hands around his face, letting my magic flow into him in a boiling heat. He should have screamed in pain, but instead he smiled before slapping me hard across the face. Ryland released the hold on my hair, sending me tumbling to the roof's surface. I reached up and touched my swelling face, unsurprised by the trickle of blood flowing from my nose.

I moved myself up onto my hands and knees as his leg swung forward, his heavy shoe making contact with my stomach. Pain jolted up my spine and stayed there, centering in the tender bones and tissues of my back.

I fell to the ground, my stomach landing hard on the gravel of the roof. I tried to sit up, but was stopped as Ryland once again came to sit on my legs. I cringed in pain as he leaned over me, the weight of his body adding to my agony.

"Stupid girl," he said, pushing me further into the gravel; the large ruby of his necklace pushing hard and cold into my skin. "Haven't you noticed? Our magic doesn't have any effect on each other. If I wish to break you, I'll have to do so literally. One. Bone. At. A. Time." With each word he ground my wrist into the gravel, pressing the delicate bones into a dangerously compacted state. I felt the snap as my bones broke, the turquoise bracelet Ilyan had given me also shattering under the pressure. I screamed at the pain that shot up my arms as each bone cracked.

My magic pulsed, attempting to heal me even as he broke me, and then I realized, magic didn't work on him, but it could still work against him. I pressed my hand into the gravel beneath me and pulsed the panicked flow of my magic into it, sending thousands of pieces of gravel off the roof and into Ryland's face. He jumped away from me, unable to breathe or see through the arsenal that I had propelled at him. I spun around, ignoring the pain that still shot through my body, to magically reach for the air unit and rip it off the roof and right into Ryland.

The large metal box smashed into him and sent him flying into the street below. I crawled to the edge of the roof and peeked over. Ryland had landed with the air conditioner on top of him, right in the middle of the brutal battle that Ilyan had been fighting.

At first all I saw was his hand sticking out from underneath the large unit. It was like the Wizard of Oz. I expected the fingers to curl away into a lifeless form, but instead they flexed and moved with strength. We didn't have much time.

The whole area lay in ruins. Most of the cantina was on fire, the street had been ripped apart and was full of giant pot holes, and pieces of asphalt were littered around like odd pieces of modern art. In the middle of it all, Ilyan stood straight and tall with his braid remaining sleek as it fell down his back. Cail was gasping and clutching his side while Edmund stood next to him laughing. When the air conditioning unit had hit the ground, the fighting had stopped and Cail had fallen to his knees, thankful for the chance to heal. Edmund, however, seemed uninterested in the interruption and had squared his shoulders, his hands moving swiftly through the air, a wave of energy falling behind. Color and energy built as he gathered his magic together. It was obviously meant to be a death blow.

ILYAN SEEMED TO SENSE THAT AS WELL, AND WITHOUT EVEN A word, he took off into the air. Edmund's explosion lit up the air behind us as Ilyan scooped me up and continued his flight. I felt his magic grow fast and strong inside of me as the shield returned thanks to our physical contact.

Almost immediately, the glow of Edmund's useless attack faded, and I could hear him yelling angrily at his apparent loss.

Ilyan soared through the night sky, the hot wind whipping at our clothes while I looked back to the destroyed city street, relieved to see Ryland standing. My heart began thumping all the more at the possibility of being followed, though. They had proven once already how quickly they could find me.

"Are you alright?" Ilyan's panicked voice broke through my thoughts and I turned to face him.

"A little beat up, but what's new?" I tried to laugh, but my lungs ached from the large bruises I was sure I had.

"I'm sorry," he said.

I didn't give him a response. I wasn't sure what needed to be said.

Ilyan's magic flowed stronger through me as he checked over my injuries, his face growing hard at what he found.

Part of me wanted to push him away, yet I was grateful for the comfort his warmth provided me. His arms around me were a reminder that at least there I was safe.

I leaned into him as he held me, healed me, and flew us away from the man I loved.

The man who hunted me.

11

———

WE FLEW in silence for almost an hour as I drifted in and out of sleep while Ilyan held me, and each time I awoke my body felt better. The bones in my wrist had begun to fuse themselves together when I woke the last time, the pain masked by Ilyan's magic. I was still very tired, but the temperature was dropping the longer we flew, and without my hoodie, my teeth had begun to chatter a bit.

"We are almost there, Silný." Ilyan pressed me closer to his warm torso, my own magic surging in an effort to keep me warm.

I placed my head against his chest and listened to his heart thump for a minute. The rhythm never changed; the comforting beat was steady and strong as it echoed through my head. I felt myself falling asleep again but shook it off. It was too cold for me to sleep without risking hypothermia.

"I'm sorry, Ilyan," I whispered into him, sure he could hear me.

"For what?"

"For ruining our noncommittal night out to dinner."

Ilyan laughed and I couldn't help grinning a little. "I wish Ryland couldn't track me so easily. I wish he..."

I stopped myself. We had been over this before.

Ilyan sighed heavily and ran his hand over my bare arm.

"At least we know how fast he can track you now."

"Which is?" I didn't want to hear the answer, but my curiosity had won me over.

"Too fast for me to be comfortable." He said and I knit my shoulders together, that didn't sound promising. I was going to be locked away in hiding forever.

"I am sorry you got hurt. I should be there to protect you at all times. I shouldn't have to fight them every time they come after you. I didn't know how many there would be, or how well Ryland could track you. I failed you." He ran his fingertips over the tender skin of my wrist, his magic flowing through my skin to check the healing bones.

"Does it hurt much?" Ilyan asked.

"No." I watched as he traced over the bones, his touch soft against my skin.

Ilyan didn't respond, he only wrapped his hand around my wrist as his magic surged. I watched as the rush of power began turning into something tangible. A sturdy cast formed over the broken bones, immobilizing my wrist.

"You should heal faster than before, now that your own magic flows through your veins, but this will help to speed up the process."

I looked at the cast Ilyan had placed over my wrist, the heavy plaster still pulsing with Ilyan's magic. It was odd to think that something so simple and rudimentary was still needed, even with the magical possibilities that were available to us.

"Thank you."

"Why did he do this to you anyway?"

I looked at my wrist where his long fingers were running over the skin that peeked out above the cast. It didn't hurt anymore, but just like when Ryland had dug the knife into my chest, I wasn't sure I would ever forget it. Every time Ryland hurt me physically, he scarred me internally, too.

"His magic didn't work against me," I said. "I only absorbed it. He never actually did any damage."

"What?" His voice was alarmed, putting me on edge.

"I felt the pain initially, but it would disappear. The same thing happened at the... the... party." I struggled to say the word, surprised at the fresh wounds the memories still held. "Every time he attacked me, nothing happened."

"And what about him, does the same thing happen to him?" Ilyan asked, his voice hard and controlled.

"Yes. In the end he didn't even react, that's why I pushed him off the roof with the air conditioner."

"This is bad," he said, his arms tightening around me.

"What? Why?" I tried to twist around to look at him, but his arms held me in place.

"First and foremost, it is limiting you. Ryland will always go after you. He will never choose to fight me. He will seek you out until he kills you, and if your magic will not work against each other, you are even more limited in your ability to fight him. Ryland would gladly enclose you in a fiery building or drop a semi-truck on your head, but would you do the same to him?"

"I threw an air conditioner at him. Isn't that enough?" I was offended, I had pushed myself way beyond my comfort level, and he was refusing to recognize it.

"And the second you did, you worried for him." His statement was a little too true to life. I felt my chest stiffen against it. "I can guarantee you, he did not do the same for you. If I had not taken you away, he would have crumbled the building underneath you, hurled a fiery car toward you, or flung your body into a telephone pole. What would you have done in return?"

I didn't know what to say, I knew every word that Ilyan had spoken was true. I had worried about Ryland every time I attacked him. I had watched for signs of life after I had launched him off the roof. If we had not escaped, I would have done the same thing I had always done; acted in desperation to save him, even as he attempted to kill me.

I needed to be stronger, but I didn't know how to be. Saving him was one thing, fighting him was another one entirely

"I can't do this,"

"You can, Joclyn." Ilyan gently moved my head up to look at him, my body still tight against his as we cut through the air. "We just have to change our game plan."

"And, how do you suggest we do that?"

"Oh, I have ideas." Ilyan smiled the powerful grin that was so natural for him and I fought a shiver from moving up my spine. I don't know if it was from the icy air or worry about what he had planned, but either way, I was uncomfortable.

I pulled away from his gaze to move back against his chest where I fought to keep the 'ideas' that Ilyan had floating around inside his head from occupying my thoughts. Ilyan stayed silent, which helped me to keep my mind clear.

We flew until I could see the sliver of dawn's first light peek over the horizon. The dim light crept into my brain and I yawned, hating the reminder of how little sleep I had been able to sneak in. I was glad for Ilyan's supportive arms; without them I wasn't sure I would have been able to keep myself airborne.

Just as the sun peeked out over a river that lay down to our right, Ilyan began a quick descent to a small community surrounded by farmland.

"Are we going to be farmers, Ilyan?" I asked my voice stretched out as I yawned again.

"No, I have had more than enough of that to last me a lifetime," he replied.

I couldn't think of why Ilyan would choose to be a farmer. The work seemed far too slow and monotonous, but then he had also lived in at least three churches that I knew of. They were both odd choices.

"Do you see that house in the middle of the main street, the one with a green roof?"

I looked eagerly toward the center of the town, easily picking out the green roof amongst the brightening buildings. The house was huge. Daydreams of my own bed and bathroom filled my mind. I had lived in close proximity to Ilyan for far too long.

"It's not much," Ilyan said, but I scoffed at him.

"As long as there is a giant bed in my own bedroom that I can sleep in for the next two days, I will be happy." I grinned and bobbed happily, careful to keep Ilyan's hands against my skin, and therefore the shield Ilyan was protecting me with intact.

"There is a bed, of that much you can be sure."

"A bed?" I asked, terrified. "What do you mean *a* bed?" I craned my neck to look at him.

Ilyan looked down on me for a minute, his lips turned up at the corners, before looking away.

"I mean, there is one bed where we are going." I didn't miss the hint of sarcasm in his voice.

"Not two?"

"Not two." He didn't seem too torn up about this.

"But the house is huge..." I looked toward it aimlessly, my excitement dashed.

"We call it the haunted house. We haven't used this safe house for decades, so I am hoping that if there is a spy they won't be able to find us here."

"The haunted house? Why would you call it a haunted...?" We were close enough to the house now that I could see large portrait windows and the family inside having breakfast.

"Someone lives here?" I yelled in a panic.

Ilyan clasped his hand over my mouth as we landed on the roof right against a window that obviously led to the attic. The glass was so old and grungy I couldn't see inside. Ilyan's hand moved down my arm to wrap tightly around my unbroken hand, keeping contact with my skin. The motion reminded me that we were nowhere near safe.

"Someone lives here?" I asked in a whisper the second Ilyan had removed his hand.

He looked to me with an exasperated face that I knew all too well, our feet securing us precariously on the steep roof.

"Yes, Silný, someone lives here. The safe house is in the attic. We will be confined to a very small space for a week, and only a week," he added hastily as my mouth fell open in panic. "We call it the haunted house because while they can't see us, they will be able to hear us moving around and talking."

"So we are like ghosts?" My panic was steadily increasing.

"Ano, and thanks to your nightmares, we are going to be very loud, scary ghosts." I blushed and turned away.

My nightmares. I still needed Ilyan every night when I woke up from my tormented dreams. No wonder he hadn't been worried by the one bed thing. He was turning into an over-protective older brother. I shook my head and turned to Ilyan who had opened the window to pull me inside.

'We stay in the attic' had been an exaggeration. Ilyan pulled me into a tiny alcove that was partitioned off from the attic by wood paneled walls. Each wall had a window that looked into the family's cluttered attic. I could see them having been installed for security purposes, but my guess would be that they were actually to prevent someone from going crazy in the eight by eight box I had been led into. The windows mirrored the one we had come from, magic shimmering over the glass to keep the family from knowing we were here.

I plopped down onto the bed that took up the whole room, and a plume of dust filled the air around me. I pulled Ilyan's hand that was still wrapped firmly around mine and forced him to sit next to me, causing more dust to fly into the air.

"Please tell me this is a nightmare, Ilyan. Tell me I am going to wake up any minute." I couldn't keep the whine out of my voice. I had gone from a studio apartment with a kitchen and a bathroom to a room with a bed in the attic of someone else's house.

"It's only for a week, Silný." He squeezed my hand and I fought the desperate urge to pull away.

"And then where; a Murphy bed in a bowling alley?" I was mad, and Ilyan's laughter at my comment only made me more upset.

"No, somewhere much better than this. I promise you."

"Where?" I asked.

"I have a little house in the south of France. It's right on the beach and has a few bedrooms and bathrooms. It is mine. It is not a safe house. No one except Ovailia and Talon know it's there. After a week here I am going to take you there until we figure out who has betrayed us and you are ready to kill Edmund with your own hands."

"A beach house?" My spirits were soaring already. I had never been to a beach in my life, let alone one in France.

"Yes." Ilyan said. "With your own bed."

I bounced a bit, sending more dust in the air, as I wrapped my free arm around his neck, bringing his tall torso down to my level.

"Thank you, Ilyan," I said. "For everything."

"I am proud to do it, Joclyn." When Ilyan returned the hug with his hand strong against my back, I let him hold me against him, my body leaning heavily into him. His arms were so comforting and the wildflower smell of his hair was so relaxing that I found myself slipping into sleep right then. He must have known it, too. I felt his magic pulse against my hand, the heat of his energy growing strong for a moment before receding.

"Don't fall asleep yet, Joclyn. I have a surprise for you." I pulled away, his smiling face greeting me. I stifled a yawn, but he only smiled more.

"Look, Silný." I looked away from his intense glance and into the rest of the tiny room.

In that one pulse of energy Ilyan had completely changed the room. The bed was clean and covered with a new comforter. The carpet on the floor was new, and the walls were white instead of the gross brown wood paneling. My mouth dropped as I looked at it. It would have taken me hours to create such a change, but Ilyan had done it in less time than it took to breathe. There was even a dark blue, black-out curtain over the window.

"I take it you like it then?" Ilyan smiled from beside me. I quickly snapped my jaw shut, worried he had noticed.

"I can't believe you did this..." I let the sentence trail

away, unsure of what else to say. He had done it all in the blink of an eye, and all while he still kept his powerful shield centered around me.

"I can take it back if you prefer to sleep on dust..." I only laughed at him.

"No, no. This is fine. Thank you, Ilyan."

"Anything. Now, unless you want to hold my hand for the next week..." Ilyan held our hands up to eye level and squeezed a bit. I didn't feel awkward holding his hand or being near him anymore, yet being obligated to have him touch my skin for the next week sounded miserable.

"Uh, no. Shield me please." I sat down on the new squishy bed, expecting Ilyan to place an immovable shield around the house, which would mean I was trapped again, but I knew there was no other option. I steeled my mind against the thought of being confined here for the next week and allowed myself to dream about being in a beach house.

Instead of shielding us, however, Ilyan froze for a minute before coming to kneel in front of me.

"I want to try something new if you don't mind." His voice was soft, but this unknown suggestion somehow made me uncomfortable. I scooted away from him out of habit.

"What?"

"I want to create a Štít inside of you that will hold some of my magic. It will never infiltrate your body, and I will always have control over it, but this way I can keep a stronger barrier around you as well as be able to track you if we ever get separated."

Ilyan had spoken very fast, his voice strained like he was having a hard time breathing. I raised an eyebrow at him in confusion.

"A Štít?" I repeated. Just when I thought I was getting a

decent hold on our abilities, he threw something else at me that I had never heard of.

"Yes. Think of it like a bubble inside of you that holds my magic. It will help me to keep you safe as well as allow you to leave this tiny room from time to time." I jumped in excitement, and Ilyan smiled broadly at my response.

"I can leave?"

"If you let me do this." He wasn't as excited as me. My hope deflated like a punctured balloon.

"What's the downside?" I didn't want to hear it, however I could tell from Ilyan's tone that there was one. I knew I was right when he sighed and looked away, his classic hesitation. I reached out with my free hand and pulled his chin back to face me.

"Ilyan. What's the downside?" He sighed again and ran my finger along his hairline out of habit; it was something I would do to Ryland. I regretted it instantly. His face went blank as he stared at me. I pulled my hand away, screwing up my face like I had eaten moldy cheese, which was actually how I felt inside.

"I have only done this to someone who has undergone the Zělství a few times before. I am not sure how it will work. It could upset the balance between you and Ryland in some way, or it could upset your magic and you could fight against me even more when I try to heal or calm you. It's a risk."

My heart plunged down like a lead weight. Hearing him talk about the connection between Ryland and I breaking made me uncomfortable. Silly, considering that the connection was the reason I was being tracked, the reason I was bound to enter the Tõuha on a daily basis, and a probable cause of my nightmares. I wouldn't have to have a Štít if it hadn't been for my bond with Ry. The only good part about my bond was Ryland, and he didn't even remember me anymore.

"What if it does break the connection between us? Will my body turn against me like before?"

"It's a risk," Ilyan said, his other hand joining to mine. I could still feel his magic surging through me, his shield keeping me hidden from Ryland, keeping me safe.

"And if it does? Do you still have your mysterious back-up plan?" Ilyan smiled, that odd look back in his eyes.

"Yes."

"And what is this mysterious back-up plan?" I asked, hoping to get some more information out of him.

"Something a good friend told me about eight centuries ago." He smiled coyly and I could tell that was all I was going to get out of him.

"I hate cryptic answers, Ilyan! Why do you always have to be so mysterious? It doesn't add to the good-guy persona very well." I groaned and threw myself back on the bed in frustration, pulling Ilyan with me.

"Strangely, I am only cryptic with you," he said as he pulled me back to sitting. "And I only do it to protect you."

"My Protector." The words cut into me a little too heavily this time, and fear sunk into the pit of my stomach at what it could mean. It all felt a bit more real after having been attacked.

"Yes, Silnỳ, and as your Protector, I need to be able to keep you safe." He paused and looked away from me, the pained look back in his eyes. "Will you let me place the Štít?"

I groaned and dropped my head to my legs. I understood Ilyan's warnings, but part of me—a very selfish part—desired the freedom that a Štít might give me. Ilyan ran his free hand over my back, his other still attached to my palm. I wished I had the strength and the ability to cast my own shield—to keep myself safe—but I wasn't there yet. And even if I was, I knew I didn't have the focus to keep it up 24 hours a day. Reluctantly, I nodded my head.

"Okay,"

"Lie down, Joclyn." Ilyan whispered. I could still hear his trepidation even though I had given him the okay.

After I had laid down slowly, Ilyan's hand slid up my arm to rest on my shoulder, his fingers never losing contact with my skin. His other hand moved to my other shoulder, leaving his head to hang over me.

We looked at each other, nerves and a heavy sense of personal-space invasion creeping through me. I wanted to push him away, or at the very least, stop him from looking at me.

"Try to push your magic into one place, Joclyn. Move it all to your toes, or your stomach. Focus it somewhere. I am going to have to battle through the barrier you have against me. It may hurt a bit, but the less you fight me, the less it will hurt."

"You didn't say anything about pain, Ilyan." I choked out, second guessing myself.

"It may not hurt at all, Joclyn. I have never known anyone to be able to fight my magic before, so I don't know what's going to happen." I could feel the warmth in his hands build as his magic congregated right under his skin.

"But you have done this before?"

"Many times, Silný. You have nothing to fear."

I nodded and pushed my magic down to my toes as he had asked, nodding my head once it was done.

"Brace yourself."

I cringed at his words. I didn't know how to react or what to prepare myself for. I closed my eyes and felt the muscles in my face tighten in expectation. At first it felt as it always did when Ilyan pushed his magic into me—warm tendrils circling through my body—but then they began to grow. It reminded me of when I had been sick; when his magic had whooshed into me with a speed I had never expected. This time I could feel not only his power, but also a wall inside of me; the force of his magic building against the barrier I unwillingly kept within myself.

"Ilyan," I gasped when the pressure began to build into a pain.

"Let me in, Joclyn. You have to break your barrier down."

I tried to focus through the pain—tried to find a way to break the barrier I wasn't even sure I controlled—as I felt the pressure grow, Ilyan's intent to break the barrier obvious. That was when I felt it; what could only be described as a tear inside of me. I focused on it, trying to force it to get bigger. The pressure within me grew and I did the only thing that made sense to me; I relaxed my body, starting at the tiny tear in my barrier.

As soon as I did, I felt the wall fall away; the tense shield inside of me disappearing. With the disappearance of the barrier, the pressure of Ilyan's magic flooded into me stronger than anything I had ever felt. I arched my back in an attempt to escape the pressure and heat which leapt into me. I howled as it continued to build, Ilyan yelling and swearing in a panic as he sat over me.

Before it became too much, before I felt I would be torn apart by the intensity, it slowed. The heat swelled in a spot inside of my left shoulder and seeped away from the rest of me—the pressure leaving—and my body relaxed.

I wasn't sore. I wasn't hurt. My body merely felt heavy and tired, my lack of sleep from the night before and the exertion of the last few minutes draining me. I sunk into the blankets, letting my body fall like a dead weight.

"Joclyn." Ilyan shook my shoulders, but my body didn't want to respond. I could hear him. I could feel the desire to answer or reach out and touch him, but I couldn't make myself do it.

"Joclyn! Please be alright!"

I felt heat from the spot in my shoulder seep away from the whole while magic that was unmistakably Ilyan's crawled through me. I opened my eyes to him, surprised to see his face so lined with worry.

"Oh, God! Thank you!" He grabbed my shoulders and lifted me into him, my body collapsing against him. "Are you alright?"

When he pulled me away—his eyes dragging over me— I could still feel his magic seeping through me.

"Did I hurt you at all?"

"I'm fine, Ilyan." I was surprised at how weak my voice was.

His face lit up at my words, relief washing over him. The tendrils of his magic returned to my shoulder, but the all-encompassing warmth remained, his shield around me already in place.

"I'm so glad. You have no idea..." Ilyan shook his head, abruptly ending his thought.

I leaned forward into his chest; my body too tired to support my weight. "Was that supposed to make me so tired?"

"No, but I may have exhausted your body a bit more than usual. Having to break down your barrier caused an added toll. I can't normally push that much magic into a person."

"Why not?"

He hesitated.

"Because I kill them, Silnỳ." My body tensed, and I felt Ilyan's magic instantly move into me, relaxing me. It was odd to have him so willing to calm me; he had never used his magic on me so freely before.

"But I thought you said that the Štít was safe?" I asked, alarmed.

"It is Joclyn. I could never hurt you. I was just scared," he pulled me to him, his arms wrapping heavily around me. "So scared."

"How do you know you wouldn't have hurt me, Ilyan?" I tried to ignore the fear that was growing inside of me.

"I know, Joclyn."

"But you said you killed someone?" I questioned, my voice breaking.

"I was very young at the time. You asked me why I was in the monastery, and that is why. Repentance for my sins I guess you could say. It was an accident and I have since learned to control it."

"An accident?" Despite being so tired, my mind was now wide awake. Fear at what had almost happened, along with curiosity at a piece of Ilyan's past, woke me right up. I felt Ilyan's arms stiffen around me, his unwillingness to let me go evident.

"I was fifteen. I went hiking with my two best friends, Talon who was only eight, and Sarin who was eighteen at the time. We were trying to scale a cliff when Sarin was bitten by a snake. A combination of fear and the snake's venom froze his magic and he fell about twenty feet."

I listened to his voice through his chest. He was speaking so quietly that he was barely audible to me, though I could hear the sadness he still held at the memory as well as the pain and regret that still occupied him, which was surprising because it had happened more than a thousand years ago.

"Talon went for help, but I knew I could heal him. My father had taught me how, and besides, I was the King's son. I could do anything... or so I thought."

He paused, and I couldn't help smiling since thinking of him as cocky was quite humorous. Ilyan didn't like it when people used his formal titles even now. I had done it once in the last month when I had been mad at him, and the glare he had given me would forever be forged into my memory.

"I pushed my magic into him as I had been taught, looking for his injury. I kept pushing as I continued looking, and the more I pushed, the more his body began to shake, the wider his eyes grew, the less he could breathe..."

"And you killed him?" I wrapped my arms tightly around him, keeping my head firmly against his chest. His heart was beating erratically now, the panicked beats echoing through my skull. I wished I knew how to calm him or help him to feel better, however I wasn't sure I knew how, so I moved closer, holding him.

"Yes."

"But it was an accident. It didn't mean you had to hide in monasteries for hundreds of years."

"I know. But when my father found out what had happened, he wasn't mad. He was overjoyed to think that his son possessed so much magic that he could kill a man with one thought. I could see then that he wanted my power for his own use, but I only thought it was for a simpler cause. I was so young, so naive."

"Everyone makes mistakes, Ilyan." I pulled away from him, and wrapped my hand firmly around his, wishing I could comfort him more.

"I make more than my fair share." He said stiffly "But no

more. I have been careful with my magic ever since, Joclyn. I am very sorry if I hurt you."

"I'm fine, Ilyan," I said, shaking him off. "Does everyone hurt when too much magic is used? Could I have..." I had fruitlessly attempted to push my magic into others before—into Ryland. What if I had hurt him?

"No, Silnỳ, it is my weight to bear on my own," Ilyan said, his eyes digging into mine. "Since then, I have perfected my control over it in the last eight hundred years. I will never hurt you, and now, I can always keep you safe."

I felt the pulse of his magic in my shoulder and was suddenly very worried about what this new connection could mean. I knew I had acted rashly. I hadn't thought it through, and then, after it had already been put in place, I was scared. Ilyan's words reminded me so much of Ryland's promise to me right before he had been erased. There was a chance that Ryland could still be there, though, and the Štít with Ilyan could hinder my connection with him. My mind continued to spin in confusing circles until I flopped to the side, groaning and regretting my hasty choice.

"What happens if it breaks my connection with Ryland, Ilyan? Besides my not being hunted as easily, I mean." I heard Ilyan laugh behind me, and my back stiffened in irritation.

"You can't feel it can you?"

"Feel what?" I asked, turning enough to be able to see him.

"You let your barrier down long enough to let me break in, but now it is as strong as it was before. The Štít may be here," he said, placing his hand on my left shoulder, right above my heart, "but I still have to fight your barrier to go anywhere else. Your connection with Ryland, and you, should be fine."

I couldn't help the smile that spread over my face. I probably shouldn't have been so happy considering all that the connection between Ryland and myself meant, but I couldn't lose Ryland, not yet anyway.

My eyelids closed a bit longer than usual, and Ilyan chuckled before lifting and moving my body gently to the inside of the bed against the wall.

My head sunk into the pillow and my body was swallowed by the soft comforter he covered me with. I missed the fabric of a hoodie against my skin, however I was exhausted enough not to let it bother me too much. Ilyan tucked me in, his hands sliding over the blankets and flattening the fabric against me.

"Sleep, Joclyn. I will be here when you wake to take all the bad dreams away." I smiled up at him—my eyes hooded and groggy—he ran his finger along my jaw line, but my eyes had closed before his finger made contact with my mark.

12

THE DREAMS NEVER CAME, yet I still awoke that evening to Ilyan's arms wrapped round me, his deep breathing in my ear. I wiggled away from the contact. While I had become comfortable with Ilyan in a lot of ways, that wasn't one of them. I don't know what made it okay with the dreams as opposed to without them, but there was a line there. I moved as far away from him as possible—which, unfortunately, wasn't very far—while shrugging off his proximity as being an effect of the cramped quarters. After all, where else was he going to sleep?

I pressed my back against the wall to gaze at the dim light of dusk seeping in a bit through the heavy blackout curtains. We had slept all day, and thanks to the absence of the dreams, I felt more refreshed than I had in months. Of course, I still didn't feel perfect. It had been over twenty four hours since I had last visited Ryland in the Tŏuha, and I was already beginning to feel the effects of that.

Rested in one way and exhausted in another. I yawned widely and pulled the necklace out from underneath my dirty white shirt. I sincerely hoped a shower would be in my future today.

I looked at Ilyan, sleeping with his mouth slightly ajar, before turning away with my head against the wall and plunging my magic into the necklace. I smiled in excitement, looking forward to building a city with Ryland this morning, before closing my eyes and opening them on a disaster zone.

I didn't know how else to explain it. Ryland had destroyed all of his masterpieces before the last Tòuha I had shared with him, but now our white space held even more destruction. What had once been perfectly smooth, white walls were crumbling and cracking to reveal dark grey veining and what I could only describe as slime. The entire place looked like it was rotting.

I turned on the spot, but the space was empty as far as I could see. I couldn't even hear any crying like I had before. This time, everything was filled with silence.

I began to walk, making sure not to step on any of the dangerous looking fissures that were lining the space, my footsteps echoing around me ominously. I couldn't help the fear that crept up my spine. The air was filled with tension, and my heart was screaming at me in warning. Everything here reminded me of the nightmares I had been plagued with, not the sweet moments I had shared with Ryland.

This deterioration didn't make sense. Ryland's behavior in our last visit might suggest a connection to my dreams, but I didn't know something like this was possible.

"Ryland?" I didn't dare talk too loud, scared I would find him in the same disgruntled state I had found him in before. There was no answer, though, so I continued walking, my panic growing as the destruction increased.

I had made it about halfway across the silent space

when a smell of intense rotting reached my nose. It was sweet and pungent like rotting fruit yet with the terrible undertone of death. It reminded me of the dumpster in the alley behind our apartment complex; the dumpster I had almost died behind. The smell continued to grow as I moved until I could go no further.

I pressed my hand against my face trying to disrupt the smell, but it kept coming in waves of intensity. My vision began to blur as my brain was deprived of oxygen, so I moved back a bit to escape it while my eyes continued scanning the space where the smell was emanating from. The veins of deterioration increased the further you moved in that direction until the floor became a black mass. Not the gentle black of velvet, but a deep, pulsing mass of oil and dirt.

I felt a pull toward the darkest area. I didn't need to be told what was over there, I knew it had to be Ryland. The thought of my little friend trapped in that mess made my heart clench. I took a few steps forward only to be pushed back again by the smell.

"What are you doing here?" I spun at Ryland's small voice, his tiny frame standing behind me.

I looked down on him, surprised to see his face twisted in fear and anger. I had seen that look on him once before, but he had been much older then. Seeing it again made my stomach flip.

"I came to see you, Ryland," I tried to say as normally as I could. "What happened here?"

"You shouldn't have come," he replied, ignoring my question.

He wasn't even looking at me, he was looking behind me at the black mass as if he expected something to jump out at him. I followed his gaze, freezing when I saw that it had moved closer.

"What is it, Ryland?"

He didn't answer, he simply grabbed my hand and began dragging me away, his little body putting as much of his strength into it as he could. Even with that, he barely moved me. I could still feel the pull toward the darkness, something calling me toward it, however my feet stayed planted as he pulled.

"You have to get out of here, Jossy," he pleaded, his fear growing even more.

"Ryland? What's going on?"

He shifted his feet at the question, his eyes still not meeting mine. I could tell he was crying. I kneeled down to him, gently placing my hands on his shoulders.

"Ryland?" I whispered.

"You have to go," he looked at me with pain and fear and anger—everything meshed together in a face that only said heartbreak to me—and then, he firmly placed his palm against my forehead and pushed me away from him.

My eyes opened to the tiny room where Ilyan slept next to me, his mouth still agape. I looked around wildly, trying to place what had happened or how much time had passed. The light had almost fully left the sky and the first few stars were now visible from the gap in the curtain. I hadn't been gone for too long, maybe only ten minutes. An hour in the Tŏuha wasn't long enough for me to fully recover.

I blinked furiously before dropping the necklace; the cold, lifeless stone becoming more of a dead weight than ever. I wasn't exactly sure what had happened.

"Ilyan?" I spoke his name far too softly. I knew I wouldn't be able to wake him that way. Besides, part of me knew I didn't want to. I could still feel my heart call to the black pit of rot in the Tòuha, still screaming that that was where Ryland was stuck. I knew it was foolish, but I also knew that his memories weren't completely gone. I needed to get him out.

I grabbed the necklace again and pushed my magic into it, the moldy room flying into view the moment I closed my eyes. I got a glimpse of the black wall, my feet turning toward it when I felt a heavy weight against my back.

"Get out!" The words ricocheted around my head and followed me back to the small attic room, my breathing becoming a frantic pant.

I dropped the necklace again and leaned forward, shaking Ilyan's shoulder roughly. I hoped he woke up in a good mood. I wasn't sure how prevalent showers were going to be, and we still had a whole week until we went to France.

"Ilyan?" I spoke louder this time. I needed him to wake up. I was scared and confused about what had just happened.

He inhaled sharply as my voice startled him awake, his body jolting upright. Ilyan grumbled and yelled something in Czech before his brain caught up to his body. His hair waved down his back as he shook his head.

"Ilyan?" I whispered, not wanting to disrupt his waking routine and make him even surlier than I was expecting.

"Joclyn?" He turned slowly, his eyes widening to see me sitting there, awake and not screaming.

"You didn't have any nightmares?" I shook my head in confirmation. Ilyan's magic flared in my shoulder, his excitement surging his energy.

"Do you think it has anything to do with..." he stopped himself abruptly, shaking his head.

"With what?" I asked, leaning away from the wall.

Ilyan paused, his eyes looking anywhere except at me.

His lack of response brought back the real reason why I had woken him in the first place. I hoped Ilyan had the answers I wanted.

I didn't beat around the bush, I just asked him right out.

"Can a Tòuha rot?"

"What do you mean?" Ilyan's nervous mannerisms stopped and he swung his legs around to sit cross legged in front of me. "Did something happen?"

"I'm not sure." Now I hesitated. I didn't know how to explain it and I didn't want Ilyan to do his crazy, headache inducing, mind reading thing on me again. My head was already pounding enough from trying to figure out what was going on.

"I went to see Ryland, and everything had been destroyed more. It looked like it was dying, and then there was this smell..." I cringed at the memory of the stench, my face crinkling.

I shook it off only to see Ilyan staring at me, his eyebrow raised in confusion.

"When you say 'destroyed more' what exactly do you mean? Was it destroyed prior to this?"

I sunk into myself, wishing I had a hoodie I could hide in. I had forgotten that I hadn't told him about Ryland's destroyed artwork, about his outburst or anything that had happened in the last Tòuha. I had been too wound up in all that had happened with Ovailia that I hadn't even mentioned it.

I pulled the blanket up around me in a desperate attempt to hide in any way possible as I told him about what had happened the last time. His face grew more and more concerned.

"But this time it wasn't something that he had caused, Ilyan," I said, "It was almost like everything was rotting."

"What do you mean *rotting*?" he asked.

I sunk away from him. His tone was making me uncomfortable.

"I don't know," I said. "It almost looked like everything was crumbling away, as though it were a piece of molding bread."

Ilyan looked at me. I could feel his magic pulse and swell in my shoulder. The feeling was comfortable and yet...

"It's the Štít, isn't it?" My voice was soft.

"I don't think so," Ilyan replied hesitantly, but I could hear the strained undertones that had weeded their way through his voice.

"Then what?"

Ilyan stood, his motions making it clear he was going to pace. The small amount of space hindered him, though, so he stood still, fidgeting uncomfortably.

"Ryland reacted negatively in the last Tŏuha before the Štít was placed, so it can't be that. It has to be something else."

"What?" I repeated, but Ilyan only chuckled darkly.

"If I knew, I would tell you, Joclyn." I could tell he was trying to make his voice soft, but he was irritated. Whether that was because he had just woken up or because of what was happening, I wasn't sure. But I was irritated, too.

"When are things going to get better, Ilyan?" I asked as I slammed my back against the wall. "Ryland can track me faster than either of us thought possible. He is pushing me out of the Tŏuha, but if I don't go, I'll die."

I groaned and sunk sideways into the bed, dragging the blanket along with me.

"You still sound like a surly a teenager," Ilyan said, his usual morning grumble sneaking into his voice and mixing with regret.

"I am a surly teenager," I spat. Had he forgotten so soon?

Ilyan intertwined his fingers through mine, his magic swelling through me from the Štít as he relaxed my body. I peeked out at him from underneath the blanket at the same time his magic surged again, removing the cast from around my wrist, his finger gently running over the skin of the now healed hand.

"Come on, Joclyn," he said as he gently pulled me to a sitting position.

"Come where?"

Ilyan smiled and pulled me up, the door leading into the attic and the house creaked as his magic opened it.

"Ilyan?" I was worried. I didn't feel comfortable going into someone else's house, although it did feel an awful lot like the crazy adventures I used to go on with Ryland. My heart thumped, more out of excitement than nerves.

Ilyan didn't respond. He simply smiled at me and dragged me out of the little room, weaving us through cluttered walkways lined with boxes before stopping in front of the hatch and fold out ladder that led below.

"Ilyan," I tried again, "what are we doing?"

"You're hungry, aren't you?" he asked as he rolled his eyes. "Well, they have food and bathrooms down there and I don't feel comfortable leaving the house yet, so..." He turned toward the hatch as it opened to the dark house below.

"What if they see us?" I asked, but Ilyan only smirked and pulled me down the ladder.

Ilyan hit the bottom and turned, grabbing me around the waist and helping me down.

"Don't worry, Joclyn, everyone is asleep, and even if they were awake, I'd make sure they couldn't see you." Ilyan smiled as his magic flared in my shoulder to send warm ripples through my body.

He then took off down the hall, his feet silent as he moved. I moved after him, but I felt like every step I took caused louder and louder squeaks around the quiet space. Finally I gave up trying to be quiet and took off down the hall to catch up with Ilyan.

He led us to the kitchen, stopping at a large, ornate bathroom on the way. It wasn't as nice as Ilyan's bathroom at the motel, but it was five star after the tiny bathroom at the apartment.

"I want to take a shower later," I said as we entered the dark granite kitchen.

"Later," Ilyan whispered back before placing his finger to his lips in a reminder to be quiet.

I rolled my eyes at him then turned to rummage through the cabinets. I could tell after looking through the first cabinet that we had walked into Ilyan's own personal hell. I carefully picked up a box of 'Chicken and Dumpling' dinner, displaying it for him like Vanna White. Ilyan stuck out his tongue in disgust before he moved to the cabinet next to me. I leaned around to peek over his shoulder before having to press my hand against my mouth to stop laughing. The cabinet was absolutely stuffed with mac and cheese, ramen noodles, and Vienna sausages.

Ilyan made another disgusted sound and moved away with a look on his face of what I would have expected if he had unwillingly walked into a butcher's shop. I grabbed a box of mac and a small can of Vienna sausages and shoved them in his face.

"They go good together," I said, unable to keep the smile off my face.

"If you're human," he countered. I rolled my eyes at his not-so-subtle reminder of his differing species.

"You're half-human. You could at least try." I shoved the

box into his hands, and he held onto them like they were poison.

"No, I am half-Chosen." He tried to place them back in my hands, but I side-stepped him, failing to restrain a laugh.

"I'm all Chosen and I love them. Besides, the mac and cheese has milk in it." Ilyan's scowl deepened further, making my laugh grow more.

He attempted to get me to take the box back, but I side-stepped him again only to run into the counter. I spun around and grabbed a container of flour off the counter, ripping the top off in a threatening manner. Ilyan rolled his eyes at me.

"Come one step closer and I'll get you," I said as menacingly as I could.

Ilyan placed the mac and cheese on the counter before over-dramatically stepping toward me. I froze, the look in his eyes stopping all thought. I let one nervous chuckle escape me as he continued to come closer.

"I'm sorry," he said, his voice laced with honey, "you will do what, now?"

I opened my mouth to retort, my rebuttal paused when the light to the kitchen flashed on.

"What's going on in here?" The old man's voice was loud and stern, shaking just enough to show that he was scared.

His yell combined with the sudden appearance of the light startled me. My magic surged through my hands and into the flour, causing the whole thing to explode in my face. The old man took one look in my direction, froze, and turned down the hall screaming and swearing as he went.

"He could see me, couldn't he?" I asked.

"Well, not you," Ilyan said through a smile as he moved to wipe the flour from my face with the palm of his hand.

"But he could see the flour. So you were essentially a floating face."

I stared at Ilyan for a minute before joining in with his laughter, the ridiculousness of what had happened hitting me.

"So much for getting a shower tonight," I said through my giggles.

"True, but you do make one great ghost," Ilyan said lightly before pressing his lips against my forehead.

My laughter stopped. I hadn't been prepared for the gentle swoop my stomach experienced at his touch.

13

ONE NIGHT without the dreams had changed something about them. The trees were taller, darker, and more sinister. The singular growling I had previously heard was all around me, the one voice changing to many. Each new tone warned me of their impending arrival.

I stayed glued to the spot in the middle of the large clearing, waiting to know what else had changed, what I should do, which way to run. I spun in place as I tried to find the culprits of the noise, trying to figure out if I should attack or if I should run. The dreams had never felt so real before, the change was frightening.

My chest heaved as I breathed in and out, my nerves coursing wildly as the growling grew and figures formed amongst the trees. Their black shapes shifted around the tall trunks of the forest. They melded into the grey night only to disappear a moment later. They shifted and moved around me until they took on real substance, forming a wide circle, trapping me.

The growls deepened, and the shifting of the shapes increased. I stood still, waiting for the dream to tell me what to do. I felt my magic moving under my skin, but it wasn't a normal surge of energy It was preparing me for an attack. This was the surge of a pull; the same pull I had felt in Santa Fe when Ryland had been around. Ryland was close. My mind reeled in a desperate attempt to figure out what was going on.

I knew this was a dream, but something was different, something was off. I stood still, showing feigned strength, even though I was desperate to hide.

All at once the growling stopped, the shapes disappeared, and I was alone. I stopped spinning. I stopped searching. I felt the pull of my magic again and tried to ignore the desperation my heart felt at its call.

I closed my eyes and tried to wipe the feeling, preparing myself for the battle I knew was coming. It wasn't fair for my haunted dreams to make me fight Ryland again so soon.

And then I heard it, the one growl that had always begun the dreams. I listened intently, trying to decide if it would be Cail, Ryland, or Timothy. It was always one of the three.

"So, I bet you thought you were free. Free of these nightly terrors." I spun at the voice, my insides tensing at seeing Edmund standing at the edge of the tree line with Cail standing next to him protectively.

Edmund moved out of the trees, Cail following, as the dark shapes that I thought had vanished materialized again; dozens of Trpaslíks emerging from the woods. Cail stood apart from those around him, his dark eyes dancing with menacing joy. I shrunk away from him instinctively, waiting for him to pounce at Edmund's command.

"Do you really think you are safe?" Edmund asked again, my insides freezing over at the wicked sound. He didn't sound as if he was enjoying himself anymore, he was simply angry now.

"I am safe." I pushed my voice out as strong as I could make it, the sound bouncing around us. Cail smiled at my response while Edmund seemed to fume more, his large frame becoming even more menacing.

"Safe with your Protector? Safe with Ilyan?" Edmund spoke his name like acid. It was the polar opposite to how he spoke to Ilyan. The two-faced nature of this man was unsurprising, but still unsettling.

I didn't challenge him with a response. I simply faced him, my eyes never daring to move away.

"He would rather hide you than face us," Edmund sneered. "Hide like a coward. Is that what you are, a coward?"

I straightened my shoulders and met him straight on. "No more of a coward than you are."

Edmund laughed, the sound deep and joyful, making the hairs on my head prickle.

"Really? How am I a coward, Joclyn; can you tell me that? I never hesitate and I fight when needed. Not like some newly awakened half-breed I know."

I flinched inwardly at his verbal assault, but didn't let it show.

"At least I don't kill people for sport." The bitter taste of loss and revenge coated my tongue.

Edmund sneered at me, his lips turned up in a joyous smile.

"You're right. You simply choose not to kill anyone." His eyes flashed and I took a step back out of habit. I had seen that look enough in these dreams to know when to be scared of it.

This time my reaction was visible, and my movement

did not go unnoticed. Cail stepped toward me, his body coming precariously close as he came between me and Edmund. I moved away only to find a wall of henchmen behind me.

"You are scaring her, Cail." I couldn't miss the wicked joy in Edmund's voice.

"Let me do it now," Cail said as his eyes dug into me.

"Be gentle with her, Cail. I am enjoying this little game. I want to see how it pans out."

"Oh, but sir, she seems to think that her dear Protector is innocent," Cail said, his eyes never leaving mine.

"Even Ilyan has killed, Joclyn. He has killed hundreds of times. He even killed Wyn's mother. Your best friend's mother, and yet, you still trust him?"

My hands flexed at Edmund's words, strangely I didn't doubt for a moment that they were true. It bothered me, but not as much as it should have.

"Ilyan doesn't kill for pleasure unlike you." I tried to keep my jaw strong as I faced Edmund, but it was hard. I was so scared that my insides felt as if they were quivering.

"You know this for a fact do you?" Edmund continued. "Ilyan sure does seem to enjoy a battle, doesn't he, Cail? He just can't walk away from a fight. From a possible kill."

When Edmund smiled—his blue eyes flashing—I froze; I knew what he was referring to and it scared me. It was the face of power Ilyan always got; the look of pure, crazy joy.

"You're wrong." My voice caught as I spoke, causing Cail to laugh. The deep sounds made his youthful frame rattle. I turned my head to face Cail, my angry glare directed at his dark eyes.

"Oh, really?" Cail said, his tone making me cringe. "You know this for a fact?"

"Yes." I tried to sound confident, however I knew my voice had begun to waiver and my hands to shake.

"Trust him, do you?" He moved closer.

"Yes." I kept my voice strong even though Cail's responses felt like ice down my spine.

"Trust him to keep you safe?" I nodded once and Cail's wicked smile deepened. I attempted to move away from him again only to be stopped by the ever encroaching wall of people.

"He can't hide you from me forever." Edmund said and Cail smiled evilly, a small laugh escaping at his joy for whatever was to come. His eyes moved from mine to a spot beyond where Edmund stood against the trees, the wicked upturn on his lips growing.

"Besides, I have something you want." Edmund continued.

Something told me not to look, but I couldn't help myself. Through the trees I could now hear grunting and gasping, and the sound was getting closer. I waited in fear for some wild animal to burst through and attack me, but I knew better. My heart knew better. The pull of my magic told me I was right as well.

My eyes widened as I saw him being dragged into the clearing by his curls. Ryland fought the action, but his energy had been drained. I inhaled sharply, something that did not go unnoticed. Edmund turned to me with a joyful smirk, and I took a step back, careful to keep my emotions under control.

Seeing Ryland like that triggered an alarm in me. This wasn't right. I had felt it before, but now I knew it.

The dreams had always been distorted bits of a memory or expanded portions of my worst fears. They had never deviated from my expectations. There were always memories of Ryland, enacted horrors of his death, torture, and visions of my own impending death. But this was different. This was something new.

Nothing about Ryland being dragged into a forest was a memory. Cail's and Edmund's taunting of me, yes. But seeing Ryland the way he was in front of me right now held no past meaning. Ryland looked up to me, his bright blue eyes pouring into mine, and I stopped breathing.

"He remembers you, you know." I hadn't even noticed that Edmund had come up beside me. My whole existence had frozen at seeing Ryland, *my* Ryland, there. "After all of my hard work, he still remembers you."

"Jos..." Ryland gasped my name, his body barely strong enough to support himself when sitting. I breathed in a shaking breath, willing my feet to stay still.

"There is only one thing to do now, sir..." Cail's hand ran down my arm, but I barely noticed.

"I leave it to you, Cail."

"Jos, you need to run." Ryland whimpered as he spoke and I took a step forward, only to have my progress instantly halted by Cail's arms around my waist.

The contact broke me out of my shocked reverie. I turned to Cail, my face hard. This was wrong. Knowing the dream was wrong somehow, scared me; and my fear broke through my carefully crafted facade.

"Let me go." I controlled my voice carefully, trying to keep my emotions in check.

"Oh, no, no, no," Cail said, his face impossibly close to mine. "You see, I have a message from Edmund for you." I spun to where Edmund had stood a moment before to find the space empty. Cail smiled and I felt my insides freeze. Everything seemed too raw, too real. I turned to Cail, my head held high, not wanting to give away that I was scared.

"You see Ryland there? Alive? His memories returned? You have exactly one month to turn yourself in to us before we dispose of him."

"No!" I turned toward Ryland in a panic, but Cail's arms held me securely in place. I fought against him, though his grip was too strong, his hold brutal against me.

"Panicked now I see. A little worried?" He pressed his cheek against mine, his body moving with me as I fought his grip. "Well you should be."

"Joclyn, run!" Ryland screamed at me as the large man behind him produced a glimmering blade. The man didn't even hesitate, he just ran him through with the glowing red blade. Ryland screamed and fell to the ground, his body not even fighting its loss of life.

"No!"

"Now, now. Don't worry. This dream is only a shadow of what's to come after all. I'm sure you have realized by now that we can't really hurt you. Magic doesn't work here. We can only wake you up. The same has happened to him, although I would *like* to kill him." He said condescendingly, the terrible tones snaking around my insides like slime.

"Let me go!" I screamed. My thrashing pulled me away as Cail released me, and the extra force sent me hurling across the clearing toward Ryland's body. I grabbed him as I fell, knowing there was nothing else I could do.

I gasped his name, my heart breaking all over again as I held his lifeless body in my arms.

We were all shadows in a dream world. None of this was real. I repeated the fact to myself, trying to stop the heavy waves of emotions from overwhelming me. I felt my lungs reaching for breath and my heart's irregular beat speed up. I couldn't look away from him; his bright blue eyes still burned in my mind.

"Oh, and one more thing," Cail said from behind me, "if you don't come in one month, you can give up hope of ever seeing Wyn again, too. I will finish what I didn't before." He sliced his finger across his neck, his lips curled in a wicked sneer.

"You'll never find her." I tried to sound strong, but I knew the panic had seeped into my voice.

"Like I never found you? Ryland's bond with you was so weak we could barely track you across one little city, and if we were already in the city, what does that say about how safe you are? With or without Ryland, we can find you anywhere, Joclyn. It's all about who you know."

"Who do you know?" My voice echoed around the otherwise empty clearing. Cail only laughed.

"Really? You think I am going to give away information just because you ask? Tsk, tsk, that's not how it works, missy."

My magic surged uncomfortably under my skin thanks to the raw anger that coursed through me. I didn't second guess myself, I pulled the power together and shot it at him in a stream of fire powerful enough to do some real damage. Shock crossed Cail's face for a second before the attack hit him square in the chest.

Cail looked at the spot on his chest before he began to laugh, long and deep. "Oh, Edmund's going to be sad he missed this."

I clenched my teeth and raised my hands, ready to fire something at him again.

"Now you are going to fight me?" Cail said, "Sure why not! After all, magic doesn't work here the way you are thinking, you can't hurt a shadow."

I felt the blood leave my face and I looked at my hands.

"No," I said, dropping my hands to my sides.

"Yes." He pulled up his face into a half smile and I shied away from the wicked look.

"No!" I moved my hands behind me, making it obvious I wasn't going to fight him anymore.

"You're no fun," Cail pouted. "Kill her. I will tell my master it is done."

I didn't have time to register what he had said before I felt the blade plunge into my back. I could feel the cold metal separate my flesh and grind against bones as it moved deeper and deeper into me with the pain only a moment behind. I screamed in agony as my body fell on top of Ryland's lifeless corpse.

The pain lasted until I woke up in a panic, my terrified screams bouncing around our tiny space.

Ilyan's arms were already wrapping around me, his hand moving to cover my mouth. I didn't hear his comforting sounds, his song. I screamed into his hand, his warm skin muffling the sound.

I couldn't calm down. I couldn't shake the feeling of the dream. My mind kept replaying what Edmund had done, what Cail had said, and the feeling of Ryland's lifeless body.

Eventually, my screams died down, but my cries remained. Howls of despair broke from my chest as my breathing caught and shuddered. Ilyan held on until my sobs had stopped; his song finally seeping into my mind as he sang it over and over.

"It's okay, Joclyn. I'm here. The dream is gone." Ilyan's hand ran over my back, the touch triggering something in me. I pulled away from him in fear, wiping away the last of my tears. I looked beyond him to the large scorch mark in the wall and my insides turned to ice.

"They're not dreams," I gasped through the remnants of my sobs. "They are something far worse."

14

_____

ILYAN PRIED the memory of the dream out of my head and replayed it twice before I made him stop. I couldn't stand to see it anymore. I felt like my heart had been ripped open and filleted in front of me. Reliving every emotion with Ilyan to see had been brutal; he felt every pain, saw all of my reactions. In the end I had pulled his hand away and begged him to stop before collapsing on the bed, my head aching from the extended digging.

The exertion from the dream mixed with Ilyan's brain foraging had left me exhausted. I stared as Ilyan fidgeted in the small space, mumbling in Czech, his face twisted in anger and fear. I couldn't even find it in me to ask what was going on. I wasn't sure I wanted to know anyway. His reaction had made one thing very clear, Ryland remembered me, and I had one month to save him.

"Ilyan," I spoke quietly, hoping he would hear me, but he kept speaking to himself.

"Ilyan!" He stopped in his tracks and looked toward me, his long hair swirling to lay against his face. He fixed me with a stare that scared me. Not because I was frightened of him, but because *he* was scared.

"How is..." I stopped, I didn't want to know. "How do I keep them out of my dreams?"

"I'm not sure you can. I am not even sure how they are doing it. The only thing I can think of is that they are using Ryland somehow, but how..." he faded off, and I looked down to my feet. Great, my connection with Ryland was causing more misery. Everything felt numb inside of me—frozen in place—as my mind processed what was being said. I loved Ryland. I loved the person Ryland used to be. The way he held me, sheltered me, protected me. After the last few months, whenever I thought of him there was fear. I had yet to see the positive side to our bonding.

My pity party was cut short by Ilyan's finger dragging along the chain around my neck. I looked up, unsurprised to see him kneeling right in front of me.

"I need you to go to Ryland. See if the boy will tell you anything. If something is happening, he should know at least a part of it."

"But what if he doesn't tell me? What if he pushes me out like last time?"

Ilyan gathered my hands in his, looking sympathetic. I fought the urge to pull away.

"I need you to try, Silnỳ." I hesitated before nodding in agreement.

"Will you call Wyn while I am gone? Make sure she is okay? Tell her I will call her in a few hours." I pulled the chain out from under my shirt, letting the ruby settle on my palm.

"Of course. Tell Ryland his brother says hello." Ilyan smiled, but it was strained. I nodded my head once and settled back down into the bed before closing my eyes and walking into the Tòuha.

I opened my eyes to the kitchen of the LaRues' estate and gasped. It was the same kitchen my mother had worked in—the one I had first met Ryland in—except very little was recognizable about it. Yesterday's deteriorating expanse had been replaced by the kitchen, but the same rot had taken over the once familiar space. The counters were dark and slimy looking. The sink was filled with dirty dishes and molding food, and chunks of marble flooring were missing. The once pristine cabinet fronts were burnt, or rotting, or worse; many were covered in molding food and hanging off of their hinges. I jumped at the large rat that I glimpsed running from one food container to another.

I wanted to scream. This felt like a trick or a cruel joke, being stuck in the place where everything had started. A place that reminded me so much of my mother, Ry.

No one was in the kitchen, and I didn't hear any sounds. I looked hopelessly toward the door that would eventually lead me to Ryland's room. The front was grey and seemed to be covered by what I could only explain as rotting marshmallow. I took a step and stopped, hating how everything affected me. Without thinking, I turned toward the black door, the door that would make me wake up. Everything thumped inside of me, begging me to run through it, however I squared my shoulders and ignored my fears; I needed to find out what was going on.

I had been told that Ryland remembered me. I just needed the boy to remember me, too. I needed him to tell me what was going on. I walked across the kitchen and swung the marshmallow covered door open wide to reveal the little five year old boy I had grown to love on the other side. The hallway behind him was just as deteriorated and neglected as the space I stood in.

He looked up at me with dark blue eyes and a hard set jaw. I had never seen any child look so angry.

"You can't have him," he said, stronger than I would have expected him to.

"Have who?"

"Your friend. The one you are looking for. The man told me you knew he was here, but you can't have him. I won't let you."

"My friend," I couldn't ignore the overdrive my heart was experiencing right now. "He's here?"

"You can't have him," Ryland spat, his little voice laced with hate.

"Why... why not? Ryland, you have to tell me..." I kneeled down to get close to him and froze, hate and anger the only emotions that looked back at me.

"You can't have him. If I give him to you, then I die." His eyes grew wide when he said the last word. It looked more like he enjoyed it than he was scared of it.

"Who told you that?"

"The man."

"What man?" My nerves jumped once, something inside triggering me to run.

"The man with the black eyes. He told me you wanted me dead. That's why you want your friend. Because you hate me."

"I don't hate..."

"LIAR!" His yell rocked the air and I lost my balance, toppling backward into the kitchen. "You hate me. And I hate you, too."

Ryland took one step forward and looked down at me. I cringed away from him, seeing what he was planning a second before he did it. His little hand made contact with my cheek, the strike hard against my skin. I closed my eyes and turned away from him, knowing instantly that Ryland had pushed me out of our Töuha.

I opened my eyes to dim light seeping through the blackout curtain that covered the tiny window. I could tell I had only been gone a matter of minutes because the light hadn't changed. I could feel Ilyan's weight on the bed and heard him talking on the phone.

"Tell no one where we are, Talon. You cannot tell Wyn or Ovailia. This information is for you alone."

I twisted on the bed to face Ilyan who sat with his back to me. He turned at my movement, his expression dropping at the look on my face, which I was certain told the story of what had happened.

"We will be here a week, then we will be moving." Ilyan's eyes dug into me as he silently asked me what had happened. "I will tell you our next location when we get there, Talon. The less information you have the better."

Ilyan reached out with his free hand and moved some hair that had fallen over my face, his hand resting against my cheek for a moment before he turned back to his phone call.

"I don't care how much damage she causes, she is officially out of the loop, Talon. She cannot be Ochrana on this. Call me if you find anything out. I don't care what time it is, just let me know."

Talon spoke for a few minutes before Ilyan clicked the phone shut and turned to face me. I stared at him, unsure of what I was going to say.

"How bad was it?" he asked, softly.

"Bad." I pushed myself to sitting, cursing this tiny space and wishing I could escape it. I looked away from Ilyan before I began to explain it to him, not trusting myself enough to look at him.

By the end of it, Ilyan had frozen in place. I could feel the waves of his energy ripple around the room, the kinetic anger of it scaring me.

"First my dreams, and now the Tǒuha? I'm not... I'm not safe anywhere. How am I supposed to save Ryland and be of any use to anyone if I am a danger to them? How is he doing it, Ilyan?"

"I don't think the question is how, I think the question is with who."

"Who?" I asked. I didn't like how he had phrased that. "What do you mean?"

"Ryland has made it quite clear he would rather die than hurt you, so I don't see him letting them use the connection much. Cail made that clear in the dream. He believes Ryland's bond is weak, but I have seen how strong it still is. Ryland is masking it somehow on his end, which means they would need a blood connection to increase its strength."

Ilyan paced as he spoke, his jittery movements making me feel more on edge than I already was.

"What do you mean, 'a blood connection'?" My stomach flipped. I wasn't sure I wanted to know exactly what this could mean. Visions of severed hands filled my mind and I cringed.

"You're an only child, right?"

"Yes," I said, my eyebrows rising in confusion.

"And you are sure your mother is dead?"

My insides froze at his question; I brushed away the pit of loss before answering him.

"She was crushed by a refrigerator and didn't flinch, Ilyan. I'm positive that she's gone." Ilyan sat down next to me on the bed, his hand reaching to rest on my knee. I reluctantly looked at him, knowing he would wait until I acknowledged him to continue. His eyes were apologetic, but not for what he had said, it was also for what was to come. My insides seized.

"What?"

"They have your father." I narrowed my eyes at Ilyan, waiting for something worse, but there was nothing. My father. The man had barely been part of my life.

"My father? But how..." I stopped and exhaled, trying to find the right words to fit my confusion. "He disappeared before they even knew about my mark. How could they have him?"

"I am afraid they have him for a completely different reason, Joclyn. How they found out he was your father, though, I have no idea. I worried about what had happened after he disappeared, but I never imagined..."

"What are you talking about?" I interrupted his rambling. "What would Edmund want with my dad?" Ilyan's eyes locked with mine for a moment before looking away, his hand moving to drag through his hair. I reached out instinctively and grabbed his wrist, stopping him before he avoided me.

"No, Ilyan. You have to tell me now. I don't care if you don't tell me everything, but you have to tell me about my dad. You have to tell me this."

The pause between us was deafening. It dragged on and on as Ilyan looked deeply into me. The blue of his eyes was shocking. I could see each fleck of gold move as he contemplated what to tell me. I kept my hand firm on his wrist, my resolve strengthening. I knew I wouldn't want to hear what was to come, but I needed to.

"Please, Ilyan." I was surprised when my voice broke.

Ilyan nodded once before turning away from me, his phone moving to his ear. He hadn't even dialed. I saw the screen flick white as a call was connected, the system being overridden by Ilyan's magic.

"Thom." Where had I heard that name before? "They have Sain. I need to tell the Silnỳ. Tell Dramin of our arrival. We will be there in two days."

Ilyan dropped the phone without even waiting for a response, the screen flashed white before returning to its screen saver. I looked from the phone to Ilyan, more confused than before. My body froze at the look Ilyan was giving me—bright and fearful—and the strength that was radiating off of him.

"Thom?" I asked, still trying to place the name in my memory.

"Thomas. He is my brother."

My jaw must have dropped a visible inch. Wyn had told me of him, of how he went missing years ago.

"But I thought he was missing, I thought..."

"I hid Thom after Cail found out where he was hiding. I couldn't trust anyone with the knowledge of his survival, it was easier to have them believe he was dead."

The explanation of Thom made sense, however it still left me confused, "What does Thom have to do with my father?"

"Thom had been your father's bodyguard for four hundred years until twenty-five years ago when they were found at a University in Ohio. Thom was able to wipe your father's memory and put him into hiding before he, himself had to run in order to pull Edmund off of your father's trail. We never thought your father would fall in love, let alone have a child. So when he found me in Prague with no memory of who he was, you can imagine my surprise. I almost told him of his past right then, but I could already see bits of the magic breaking away; parts of his memories seeping through. It was how he knew to find me; how he knew that something was wrong with your mark. I needed to break the truth of his past to him gently, and right then we didn't have the time. I needed to get to you first."

Ilyan ran his hand heavily through his hair in agitation. I couldn't piece any of it together in my mind. I tried to sit and listen, waiting for Ilyan to finish, but my disjointed questions kept flowing of their own accord.

"Wipe his memories?" I repeated, "Why would Thom do that?"

"It was necessary. Thom knew he could get Edmund's men to follow him, but your father had to stay behind. Your father's memories are more of a curse. It was essential to displace them in the chance that Thom failed and your father was found."

"But he..." I tried to form a question, but it didn't come. After all, I didn't want to hear this. What he was saying couldn't be true. There wasn't any way it could be.

"You're wrong, Ilyan. You have to be. I mean, I have grandparents, and uncles, and cousins!"

"The Despains lost a son, Jeffrey, in a car accident. Thom put your father in his place, replacing their grief with a surrogate son." My mouth dropped open in horror. So much of my life was a mystery, a lie. I felt so empty.

"But why..." I broke off, not sure what I wanted to know.

"I will not tell you everything, Joclyn, because not all of it needs to come from me. I will tell you this, however, by blending the blood of your father with the magic of your mate, Edmund has found a way to torture you, to infiltrate you from a distance. To try to stop you from what destiny has planned for you." Ilyan's strong voice ricocheted around the space, the power behind it seeping into me uncomfortably.

"But... my father?" I asked, still waiting for clarity. Everything was a jumbled mess in my head.

"His name is not Jeffery, it's Sain. He was bred from the mud to be one of the first of the carriers of magic. He was the first of the Drak."

I gasped, the quick intake of breath trapped inside of me as I froze in place. The Drak. The beings who possessed the gift of sight. The magical creatures who had been massacred at the hands of Edmund LaRue. Well, not completely; my father was still alive. The last one.

My head reeled like I was inside an old cartoon, my eyes bugging out of my head unnaturally. I knew this was huge, and scary, but I didn't quite understand how it had happened or even what it all meant.

"So, if my father was the first of the Drak, does that mean I am a Drak, too?"

"No, you bear the kiss of a Vilỳ. You are one of The Chosen, nothing more." Ilyan placed his hand softly on my neck, his whole hand covering my mark. I looked up to him, my wide eyes reflected back at me through his own.

"Then why does Edmund want him so much? What was so important that he had to have his memories erased?"

"He is not just any Drak, Joclyn. Not only is he the first of his kind, he is the one who saw a child come forth to defeat an opposing power. He was also tortured at the hands of my father so that he could convince his own daughter to work for him."

"You're not saying..." I stopped as his meaning caught up with me. I wasn't panicked. I wasn't scared. I was in shock.

Ilyan nodded as I pieced the last of it together. I remembered this story. Edmund had tortured Ovailia's mate to get her to work for him. Sain, my father. My father had been Ovailia's mate. He was the one she had double-crossed in her rise to a supposed power. No wonder he wanted his memories erased.

"But I thought he was dead."

"Edmund weakened their Zĕlství to convince her of that. Ovailia, believing him to be dead, broke their bond. Then for hundreds of years my father kept Sain hidden as he forced information of the future out of him until the day that Sain escaped with his memory mostly gone and his powers greatly weakened. I stopped Edmund's Vymãzat and put him into hiding. He was too hurt—too ashamed—to ever see my sister again. Ovailia still believes him dead and I will do everything in my power to keep the truth from her."

"So Ovailia doesn't know?" My stress lessened a bit, though not a lot. I knew I should be reacting more—crying, yelling, screaming—but nothing came. What Ilyan had said hadn't sunk in yet.

"No. She doesn't know he is alive. It is best kept that way."

"So, what my father saw... about the child... It's about me, isn't it?" My pulse thumped in my ears in fear of the answer I knew was coming.

"Joclyn, it is not my place to say..."

"Then don't tell me everything, Ilyan. Don't tell me what he saw. Don't tell me how, or why. Just say yes or no!" I moved to stand in front of him, making it clear I wasn't going to let him off the hook. He hesitated for a moment before answering, his eyes large and softer than usual.

"Yes."

I hung my head, my jaw tightening.

"I cannot tell you all, Joclyn, not yet. But soon. We are going to see Thom and Dramin in two days, and then you will know everything. And when they tell you... Joclyn, when they do, please do not hate me."

"Ilyan?"

"Know I am here to protect you as I was born to do; as I have promised you." He reached up and softly traced my skin from my jaw to the mark and back again, his eyes never leaving mine. I couldn't move. I didn't register the shiver that moved through me at his touch, either. I merely stood still, waiting for everything I had been told to settle into an understanding.

"I will do whatever I must to keep you safe." He smiled and my breath caught, which only seemed to increase his happiness. I stepped away, suddenly feeling uncomfortable before Ilyan moved toward the window, the pane opening as he approached it.

"Ilyan?" I wasn't sure what was happening.

"I am going to go get some food. I won't be long. Promise me you will stay inside these walls."

I nodded and he began to move, however I knew I couldn't let him leave without knowing one last thing. He wouldn't tell me everything, but I knew this one thing he could.

"Ilyan?" I asked again. This time he turned his body, hesitant.

"What does Silnỳ really mean?"

His answer came without hesitation; two words spoken before he exited the space, leaving me alone with a bit of his warm magic shielding me from the inside.

"Most powerful."

15

Most powerful.

I stared at the window where the last light of day was seeping in. My body was exhausted, but all the new information had left me feeling jittery and wide awake. Or maybe I was just stressed. I plopped down onto the bed, Ilyan's cell phone bouncing around next to me.

I grabbed it without thinking, flipping it open and staring at the screen saver. I missed my phone. I missed all the pictures of Ryland and me. I ran my fingers over the screen repeating his number in my head as I traced it.

What I wouldn't give to be able to call him, to hear his goofy voice as he taunted me, or to feel his hand against my skin as he comforted me. I closed my eyes, willing an imaginary phone call; bringing his voice so strongly to the forefront of my mind that I could almost hear it. I could feel the leather seats of his Lotus as we talked about everything... anything. We could talk about my father, about what I...

I pushed the phone away and dropped my head in my hands. The stress at what Ilyan had said was growing, but so was my irritation at continuously not being told everything.

"So, Dad," I sighed aloud to the empty space. "You cursed me, and you didn't even know it. You keep getting better and better."

I pulled up the blanket that I lay on, needing some comfort since my hoodies were probably gone forever. As the blanket moved, Ilyan's cell phone fell back onto my stomach. I grabbed it, making sure to keep the blanket around me, then held down the number three and waited impatiently for Wyn to pick up the phone.

"Jos!" She yelled the second she picked up. "Oh, please tell me you are okay! I've been so worried since Talon told me what happened, and then you didn't call me at all yesterday. I knew I should have gone with you! This never would have happened if I had—"

"It would have happened either way, Wyn." I cut her off, worried she would run out to find us right now. "If you were here you would have gotten hurt, too."

"Too? You got hurt?" she asked, alarmed. I rolled my eyes.

"Nothing a little magic can't fix." I heard her exhale through the line.

"I can still come out if you want; an extra pair of hands doesn't hurt."

"No!" I sat upright, the blanket falling off me as I moved. The last thing I needed was Wyn anywhere near me. "Stay where you are. You'll only get hurt if you get too close to me."

"Joclyn?" Wyn's voice broke a bit over the line, "What are you saying? I'm not going to get hurt."

"I don't want to risk anything. People seem to get hurt around me." I said and fell back down on the bed, cursing the tiny space. There wasn't even anywhere to hide around here.

"Is Ilyan okay?" she asked, alarmed.

"He's fine," I felt his magic pulse in my shoulder, and I instantly became worried he could feel my anxiety.

"Are you sure you don't want me to come out?" she asked again, her voice gaining back some of its normal, playful quality.

"I'm sure, but can you do something for me?" It was a silly idea, but I needed some of Wyn's silliness right now.

"Sure! What's up?"

"Sing me a Styx song." I smiled as she laughed, her voice echoing through the phone.

"You're a dork," she giggled.

"I can't help it, you've got me addicted."

"Addicted to Styx?" I could hear her disbelief, and I only smiled more.

"Yep." I rolled onto my side, bringing the blanket with me

"Alright then, when was their first album released?" I paused, leave it to Wyn to see through my little lie.

"1840." I said as confidently as I could, causing her to laugh harder at me.

"Liar." She obviously wasn't going to sing anything for me.

"Come on, Wyn, just sing me one of their stupid songs." Her loud gasp came through the line. I could almost see her offended face, dark scars and all.

"I thought you said you liked them?" Her voice was hard. Leave it to me to piss her off by offending her precious Styx.

"Please, Wyn." I let a little bit of whine seep into my voice. I didn't want to have to explain.

"I'm sailing away," she sang, "I've got to be free..." I

smiled. Her choice of song seemed a little bit too perfect given the current situation.

She sang and sang, and I let the lyrics wash over me, their meaning becoming deeper the more I heard.

Her song faded away, although I knew it wasn't over, somehow the words had helped; the edge of my anxiety had dulled and I felt a bit more relieved. I was glad I had Wyn, I just wished she was closer. I wished my existence hadn't put her in danger, too. I cringed and sat up, the blanket falling away from me.

"Thanks, Wyn."

"No problem. Are you okay?" she asked, her voice heavy.

"I'm better now." I spun around, looking at the window. I needed to get out of here.

"Good, I've gotta go find my husband now, okay? I'll call you in few hours."

"Sounds good, Wyn." I heard the phone click and I shut Ilyan's and placed it in my pocket, my eyes still focused on the window.

I knew Ilyan had asked me to stay in the room, but I needed fresh air. I had been trapped inside for two days, stuck in the same clothes I had been attacked in. My hair was gross, and I was sure I was beginning to stink. Besides, I had his shield around me, not around the room. I could go anywhere. I shuffled my feet as I rationalized, hoping this wasn't going to end up being one of my stupidest decisions ever.

The crisp air of dusk filtered into the room as I opened the window, and I breathed it in, letting its heavy energy fill me. The chill undertone of it reminded me of home. I opened the window a bit more and stuck my head out, a slight evening breeze tugging at my hair.

I could feel the steady warmth of Ilyan's magic surge

through me. I focused on it as I pulled my body out of the window, moving to sit on the small eave right next to the casement.

The main street of the small town was directly below me. Most of it was occupied by houses and small businesses. I could see a small restaurant and a gas station, and I thought I could make out about three hardware stores.

I curled my legs into my chest, cursing the breeze and my lack of hoodie for giving me goosebumps up and down my arms. Even with the chill, though, it still felt nice. I felt the heavy reality of what had happened sinking into me. Ryland was alive, Wyn was being threatened, my dreams and my Tõuha were both essentially controlled nightmares, and my dad... my dad...

I laid my head back against the siding of the house. It was almost too much for me to handle, and what was worse, there was more that I hadn't been told yet. I mentally pushed everything around trying to find a free path through it all. I could do this, I was strong enough. Slowly, the numbness I had been shielding my emotions with began to recede. My panic over everything began creeping in, but only enough to keep me aware.

"I thought I told you to stay inside?" Ilyan's voice wasn't mad; he was more amused than anything.

I didn't even open my eyes.

"I knew you would keep me safe," I said, patting my shoulder.

"Well, I am glad you have so much trust in me," Ilyan said as he sat down next to me, "but next time wait until I get back. You are lucky I was paying attention or someone would have seen you."

I blushed and looked at him. I was glad he wasn't mad at me, but I felt bad for not listening to him.

"I couldn't stay in there any longer. I felt like I was going to collapse in on myself."

"I guess I did leave you at a bad time, but I couldn't..." Ilyan stuttered to a stop, something I had never known him to do before. I looked to him curiously. His head was leaning back against the house, and as he turned to look at me, his long hair glistened in the setting sun.

"I'm sorry," he said through the night air. "I never should have left you right then." He paused and exhaled, his hand reaching around me to rub the goosebumps on my arm away. I leaned into him, part of me cringing against the contact while the other part desperately needed it and the warmth it gave me.

"It's okay, Ilyan." His hand continued to move up and down my arm, his magic warming me from the inside out.

"How are you coping with everything?"

"I don't know." I sighed and Ilyan squeezed me against him. "I'm not sure I understand everything, especially everything about my dad. It still doesn't make much sense."

Ilyan rested his head on top of mine, the weight awkward, though also strangely comfortable.

"It will in a few days, and then if you have any questions, I will answer them. I promise."

"I'm not sure I want to know, Ilyan, not anymore."

"I know. Just remember that I am here to help. I will keep you safe and help you through anything." Ilyan said, his hand continuing to run up and down the skin of my arms.

"My Protector." I spoke it like the term had become revered.

"Yes." Ilyan moved me closer into him, giving me a squeeze before he moved away. "Well, your Protector has broken a cardinal rule and brought you back a greasy, meaty, nothing-in-it that's-good-for-you sandwich for dinner."

I jumped away from him as he produced a brown paper bag from a fast food chain I knew all too well. I couldn't help the smile that broke across my face. There wouldn't be a dandelion leaf in the bag. I opened it greedily inhaling the smell of grease.

"Oh, I could kiss you!" I said, holding the bag against my chest.

"Um, no thank you," Ilyan responded a bit too quickly, his words morphing into an uncomfortable laugh.

I looked at him wide eyed. I didn't know why his quick shut down of my offhand comment hurt, but it did. I sighed and looked back to my cheeseburger, my stomach swimming uncomfortably.

"Unless you were talking to the cheeseburger, in which case, I will leave you alone." Ilyan laughed, my reaction obviously having gone unnoticed. Thank goodness.

I pulled the bag open and removed the haphazardly wrapped burger, silently thanking Ilyan for keeping it warm. The smell of meat, cheese, and mayonnaise wafted up to me. Right now I didn't care that my last cheeseburger had been the night I had to run from Ryland. I was happy for what could only be described as comfort food.

I took a bite and savored it, letting everything roll around in my mouth. I groaned and let my head fall back against the house in appreciation.

"Fat, burned meat, and dead veggies... and they get that kind of reaction?" Ilyan said, disgusted.

"Leave me alone, Ilyan, me and my cheeseburger are having a moment." I took another bite, ignoring the fact that he was staring at me.

"Do you want some?" I asked, waving the burger in his face. He cringed away from me, his face disgusted.

"No."

I laughed and moved closer, waving the smell toward him.

"That is far worse than mac and cheese and Vienna sausages."

"You know you want some," I teased, enjoying the fact that I could make him smile.

"I haven't eaten meat in five hundred years, Joclyn. I am not about to break that trend now."

"Don't sound like an old man, Ilyan." I smiled broadly at him before taking another bite of the cheeseburger, rolling my eyes back in slightly exaggerated joy.

Ilyan laughed at me as his phone in my pocket rang. I pulled it out and handed it to him, but he only turned it around to show me Wyn's name on the caller I.D.

"Speaker phone," I said through a full mouth, covering my face politely.

Ilyan laughed and rolled his eyes before answering the call, hitting speakerphone as he did. He didn't even get to say hello before the sound from the phone hit our ears.

Ilyan's face lost its smile and my cheeseburger lost all flavor as screams, yelling, and explosions filtered from the phone's speaker. Part of me wished that it was only a movie —that the sound wasn't real—but I knew better.

"Jos! Jos, pick up the phone!" Wyn's screech was loud above the screams, panic and tears lining her voice heavily.

I swallowed deeply, the cheeseburger feeling like lead going down my throat. Ilyan stood in a panic, holding the phone in front of him as he yelled into it.

"Wynifred! What's going on?" Ilyan's voice was

commanding and powerful, the waves of it spreading out from him.

"Ilyan? Oh, thank heavens!" There was a pause and more screams, Wyn panted through the mouthpiece.

I stood, my body tense as I leaned into Ilyan, trying to see the phone as if the screen would show me a play by play as to what was going on. Ilyan's arm wrapped around me, his muscles tense as he held me around my waist tightly. I had the distinct impression he might launch us into the air at any moment.

"Wynifred?" Ilyan asked, his powerful voice shaking through my rib cage. "Where is Talon?"

"They got him, Ilyan. They took him. I think..."

Another pause and more screams. I swear I could hear Wyn whimper and scream in the background. I clutched Ilyan, my fist wrapping around the fabric of his black polo shirt. When Wyn spoke again, it was clear she wasn't talking to us; her voice seemed farther away as if she had dropped her phone somewhere.

"No! Please don't!" I cringed as she screamed, her voice cracking and breaking. Other voices yelled in the background, yet I couldn't make anything out. Ilyan's knuckles went white as he clutched his phone, his arm tightening around me.

"Father! Please don't! Don't let them hurt me!" I listened to her plead with her father. The thought that Timothy could be there in Prague was terrifying.

Wyn screamed again, her voice breaking and crackling though the phone's speaker. I turned my head into Ilyan's chest, not wanting to hear anymore.

"Ilyan!" Wyn screamed, her voice losing strength. "Run!"

She hadn't even gotten the full word out before the line went dead. I peeked out from behind Ilyan's shirt, not wanting to see. His knuckles remained white and hard against the phone, his jaw clenching below his ice-like eyes.

"Ilyan?"

He didn't respond to me. He stared at the phone as the screen flashed white and Ovailia's name popped up as he placed the call. It rang once, twice, and then a third time. We stayed frozen against each other until she answered, the same screams and explosions sounding in the background.

"Ilyan?" Her voice was frazzled and scared. I had never heard her sound so raw before. "Ilyan, where are you? Please tell me you are all right."

"We are fine, Ovailia. What is going on? Wyn called..."

"They took her," Ovailia cut him off, panting as she moved through whatever destruction was tearing through the space. "They took Talon, too. I don't know where he is, but Timothy dragged Wyn off."

"Who's they?" Ilyan's voice was hard as he spoke through his tightened jaw.

"Father. Timothy. There are hundreds of them." I cringed. I didn't need her to elaborate; I knew who they were now, Edmund's hundreds of Trpaslíks.

"I don't know how they got in. Our whole city... I don't know how many are going to make it out."

"Get out as many as you can, Ovailia. Meet me in Isola Santa in five days. Can you do that?"

There was a break as Ovailia panted from running, and more explosions filled the air that was already rent with screams. The phone's speaker vibrated at its exertion.

"I can try."

Neither Ovailia nor Ilyan said anything as more screams filled the space and more explosions, crying, and pleading sounded around them. I moved my head back into him in an attempt to block it out.

"Be safe, Ovailia."

"And you, Ilyan."

The line went dead for the second time and Ilyan's other arm came to wrap around me. I could feel his heart hammer through his chest, his anger pulsing his magic through his veins, and in turn, through my shoulder. I was beginning to understand what Wyn had said about Ilyan's temper.

Wyn.

"Ilyan?"

"I know, Jos." I flinched at the use of my nickname. He had never used it before. "I will keep you safe, I promise."

"And how do you plan on doing that?" I jumped at Cail's voice, a hundred volts of emotion plunging through me. I clung tighter to Ilyan as I moved my head away from his chest to face the two still figures that stood in the street below us.

"I told you I could find you," Cail sneered through the dark at the same time that I could feel Ryland's black eyes on me as he stood next to the tormentor from my nightmares.

16

I STARED at the two immobile figures, they didn't deviate even a millimeter from where they stood. They merely looked up at us as Ilyan and I looked down on them. Ilyan's arms never moved away. If anything, they only increased their strength against me. I felt his magic flare, his shield around me growing. Even with Ryland right there, I couldn't feel the pull of his magic through the shield. Which meant Ryland couldn't feel it either.

My eyes fluttered between Cail and Ryland, my heart beating stronger the more I looked. The last I had seen of Ryland had been in the dream, and in the dream he had been himself with his memories back. The man before me, however, looked up with black eyes and a menacing snarl as he plotted all the ways he could hurt me.

They both laughed menacingly at us, and Ilyan's arms pulled me closer to him. I knew why. After what we had heard, neither of us was sure what to expect. I was scared, and by the erratic pulse of Ilyan's heart, I was aware he was as well. One of his arms moved away from me, his hand gently facing the two figures below us.

"Relax," Cail drawled in a falsely bored voice, "we are not here to kill you, at least not yet." He smiled as his teeth flashed in the dim light.

I could feel Ilyan's magic swirl angrily under his skin, the power of it growing hot in my shoulder.

"Then what do you want?" Ilyan yelled down to them, yet neither of them flinched.

"To give you a message. You must have heard by now that your precious safe house in Prague is gone. The wells of Imdalind are now ours. Imagine what we can do with all that power! And you, the last of the true Skřítek, have failed in protecting it." Cail laughed as Ilyan's muscles tightened even further. Ryland's musical chuckle joined in and I felt the chill of ice run over my skin. That laugh was almost identical to how it used to be. I pushed myself into Ilyan's side, repeating to myself that it wasn't Ryland down there.

It isn't him.

I looked to where Ryland stood, his hair falling over his head the way it always did. I couldn't help thinking that Ryland was still there. I wished I knew a way to pry him out of his prison. I stepped toward him, moving back when his black eyes met mine.

It isn't him.

"Then what is your message?" I heard the strength in Ilyan's voice rumble through his chest.

"It is for Joclyn," Cail said, and I reluctantly looked over to him. "We have found you, as I told you I would, and we have your little friend locked up where you will never find her."

"No!" I called out without meaning to. It was just like in the dreams, I knew I shouldn't show him my weakness—I needed to keep how scared I was inside—but this time I had failed. Cail smiled at my loss of control, his eyes dancing in pleasure.

"Oh yes, and you still have one month. Twenty-nine days to be exact, or your little friend is gone along with the love of your life." He stopped as he placed a hand on Ryland's shoulder. My insides froze, terrified as to what he was going to do.

"Unless you don't need him anymore," Cail finished, his head turning to Ryland. "Look how cozy they are up there, Ry." As Ryland turned his head to face me, I almost expected blue eyes, instead I only saw the black. "It almost looks like she doesn't need you anymore, don't you think?"

"You're right," Ryland said. I tried to pull away from Ilyan when I heard Ryland, but Ilyan's strong arms kept me there. "Have you told her then brother? Have you told her of her true purpose and what she is to you?"

Ilyan said nothing. I stayed frozen against him, not wanting to hear anymore. My heart still called down to Ryland, but I clung to Ilyan out of necessity and security.

"Well then," Ryland said, "if you have, I suppose you won't be needing me."

In a flash of blue I saw a spark of light bounce off a golden sword that had appeared in Ryland's hands. He spun it once before swinging it violently through the air to plunge it into himself. Ryland didn't even flinch as the air streaked with gold as it flew toward him.

"No!" I screamed louder than before as I fought against Ilyan's arms. That time he let me move, but still not enough to fly to Ryland's aid. Despite my reaction, I was thankful for his impeding arms. If I had gone down there, Cail would have killed me easily. Part of me knew that was the whole point of this demonstration.

My body went limp as Ryland moved the sword, having

stopped it millimeters from his body. Ilyan then gathered me up and pulled me back into him.

"Hmmm, I don't think he has," Cail said, his voice sad.

"I take it Sain has told you then?" Ilyan asked.

"Oh! Bravo! You figured it out. You will make your father so proud. He was beginning to think you had lost your touch. I sure hope it didn't take you the full three months to realize that we were controlling her dreams?" Cail took a step forward, his hands moving as he spoke. I couldn't take my eyes off of them, terrified he would attack at any moment.

"Not even close," Ilyan laughed humorlessly through his lie. "See, I know the full story, and no matter what you have done to Sain, I doubt you have managed to get it all."

"Sain may not have told us everything, but he has been a wealth of information both now and before. We have been waiting for her to make an appearance as long as you have, and we are willing to wait just as long to find the secret of how to destroy her. Another month or so and we will crack the lock you put on his mind. Then we will know everything."

"I wish you luck with that," Ilyan laughed, his deep joy rolling through the main road.

"At least you continue to make this whole game more interesting," Cail said.

"It's not a game," I yelled down to him, interrupting their banter.

"Oh, really?" Cail sneered, "I think it's a game. Ryland thinks it a game. Edmund *knows* it is a game. Your *Protector* up there, seeing as he hasn't told you everything, he must be playing the game as well."

Ilyan pulled me back against him and my insides went numb. Cail's loud voice boomed as he laughed and the yard to the house suddenly lit up with artificial light as a door was opened. Cail's attention turned to a man in the doorway, his laughter stopping as his face went hard.

"What's going on out here?" I heard the old man yell shakily through the yard, Cail having obviously scared him.

"Nothing that concerns you, old man." I realized what was going to happen a moment before it did. Cail raised his hand and placed his palm toward the old man then, as he had with me the first time, he let the power grow. His amusement at scaring his target was stronger than his intent to kill. In that next instant, Ilyan left my side to intercept the ball of energy Cail sent toward the old man. Ilyan's powerful energy redirected the fire toward a field of trees off to the side of the house with only a thought. Cail's red light connected with the trunk of a tree, sending it into a roaring inferno that spread inhumanly fast to the other trees in the small grove, the magical fire gladly accepting the timber.

The man yelled out in fear and the door closed, the yellow glow leaving the yard with the click of the door as the flickering light from the fire began to take over.

Ilyan stood before Cail, his tall frame towering over him while I turned to see the family coming out of the other side of the house and running away from whatever altercation was about to take place. I calmed a bit, hoping they would get away from this.

"Do you wish to fight me, Ilyan? I told you we were not here to hurt you. Not today." Cail's voice was strong, but I heard the fear that lay behind it.

"Then do not attack the innocent," Ilyan said, his magic growing and spreading through me from the Štít as his shield encompassed me.

Ilyan took off into the sky, presumably back to my side,

before his body was pulled back down to the ground and restrained against the damp grass by Cail's magic.

"I will attack any that get in the way of my job for my master," Cail said.

"You serve the wrong man, Cail." Ilyan's body seemed to glow with golden light before he burst into the sky, Cail's magical restraints flying off him. When he had moved enough to put himself between me and the two men on the ground, Ilyan flexed his fingers, electricity crackling between his knuckles.

"I guess that is a matter of opinion." I froze as Cail raised his hand toward Ilyan. Ilyan did nothing, though. He simply stood there as his hair danced in the wind, his muscular body lit by the firelight, and I felt his magic surge through me.

Light exploded out of Cail's hand, and a half-second later, Ilyan sliced his hand to the side, sending Cail's magic uselessly into the already blazing trees. Ilyan flexed his hand as the ground exploded around Cail, showering the yard with dirt and rocks.

I shielded my face from the onslaught of dirt, only to come face to face with Ryland when I emerged. I didn't wait; I raised my hand to attack; but before I could do anything, his hand wrapped around my neck and forced me against the house.

"Now, now," he said, his wicked voice cutting into me. "You know your magic has no effect on me, and as fun as a scuffle with you would be, my job is not to attack you. My job is to keep you here."

He snarled at me and increased his hold, and my vision popped and swayed from the lack of oxygen. I grasped at his hands, my magic not responding to my mind's weak calls.

"Oh, sorry," he said, although I heard no sympathy. "I

guess it would be better not to kill you yet. It was nice of Ilyan to leave you here for me to play with. I guess his desire to kill Cail is greater than his need to protect you."

He smiled as I squirmed underneath his hold. I wanted to yell at him that he was wrong—that Ilyan was helping everyone—but I couldn't get Ryland's words out of my head. I knew he was manipulating me like his father did in my dreams, however I couldn't get enough oxygen to even attempt to rebut him.

When Ryland released his hold enough to give me breath, though not enough to move, I let my magic swell at my increased freedom, only to have Ryland amplify his hold again. I groaned as he slammed my head into the house, the impact ricocheting through my skull. He smirked at me and my heart thumped. The look was the same one he had made when he had been teasing me, but there wasn't any love for me in him anymore; not in his eyes, nowhere.

"Stop trying to fight me," he snarled, slamming my head against the house again. "After all, there is nothing you can do. You see there?" Ryland decreased his hold on me again. My head was spinning from lack of oxygen and the aggressive impact as he then forced me to look toward the side of the house where four Trpaslíks had gathered in the shadows out of Ilyan's sight, their hands against the house.

"And there," he moved me roughly, this time to the other side of the house where even more Trpaslíks stood.

"They are going to blow you and this house clear into the sky while your dear Protector is in battle, too busy trying to kill Cail to save you." Ryland said, his black eyes shining. I stared at him, my jaw working independently of my mind. It was as if it was trying to bite the oxygen out of the air around me.

I could feel the house shudder under me, the joined

magic of those below congregating beneath us. The vibrating house continued to shake as he held me against the side of it, my body barely getting enough oxygen into my lungs. I gasped for a desperate breath in my attempts to yell, to scream, to fight him. My voice was caught, though; my magic a limp spark. It wasn't enough.

"Oh, and I have a riddle for you. Straight from Sain's own mouth." I froze. My father?

"'Two brothers stand beside you, both know of your true fate. They each have love in their hearts, but different needs to gain. One seeks power, the other light. The one with light in his heart may love you more, but he is the foolish one, the one who will die first.' I will give you one guess as to who that one could be," he said, releasing my throat as the vibrating reached its peak.

I gasped for breath again, trying to regain use of my magic, knowing there was only a matter of seconds before the house exploded.

"Ilyan!" I screamed with all the air I could gather, hoping that he would hear my call or feel my pain in his magic that pulsed through me. What I didn't expect was Ryland's answer.

"Correct." My eyes widened as Ryland's smirk increased. I didn't get a chance to ask him what he meant before Ryland pushed away from me to escape the impending blast.

I fell to my knees as the house begin to collapse in on itself and tried to push myself into the air, my body too weak to answer my call. Seconds later, I felt Ilyan's arms wrapping around me as the house imploded below me. The heat of the explosion on my feet burned as the blast grew, the sound of destruction ringing in my ears. I looked back and knew we couldn't escape it.

"Hold on to me, Silný, and whatever you do, don't let go." I looked up at Ilyan's face as his hold on me increased.

He wrapped his body around mine, his hold tight as I felt his magic rush into me with more pressure than he had ever used before. The pressure broke through my barrier, but instead of making me feel as if I was going to explode, I experienced the exact opposite. My body was squished even further against Ilyan as the pressure melded us together. The air was pushed out of my lungs, and my body felt as if I was being forced through a toilet paper roll. I tried to scream, but no sound came out while the last of my air left my already deprived lungs.

I could feel everything. I was convinced that the blast had found us until, suddenly, the sensation left. My body crashed against Ilyan's as we fell to the ground, his arms going limp and falling away from me.

Frigid air swirled around me, snowflakes flying around while my hair and clothes were whipped through the winter storm.

I sat up, my body beginning to shake in the cold air, and looked around in a panic, confused at the mountain landscape I was surrounded by.

"Ilyan?" I asked, my body beginning to shake with cold. "Where are we?"

I looked at the tall, snow-covered peak that towered over us, my eyes scanning for some form of shelter. I turned toward Ilyan when he didn't respond. My stomach immediately dropped into the icy landscape I was surrounded by.

Ilyan lay still, his body surrounded by snow while his blond hair whirled in the air, but he didn't move. His lips and eyelids were tinged with a sickly shade of blue, his body limp and still. I began to shake in fear as I saw him there.

"Ilyan?" I couldn't stop the panic that seeped into my voice. I pressed my hand against his cold cheek, surprised not to feel the warmth that usually lay right below his skin.

I moved my hand to my shoulder, trying to focus on his magic inside of me, but all I felt was a weak and dying pulse of latent energy. I pressed my hands against his skin, pulsing my magic into him, trying desperately to figure out how to help him, how to heal him.

"Ilyan!" I yelled, frantic to get his attention. "Ilyan, wake up. Please. Ilyan, please don't leave me." I continued to yell at him, my fear having turned into a full blown panic. Ilyan was the last person I had. Ryland's mind was still trapped, my mother was dead, and Wyn had been captured and taken who knew where. I screamed as the reality of what was happening hit me and everything came crashing down around me.

"Ilyan please!" The wind howled around me as I yelled, taking my voice with it.

I pressed my hands against his skin, pulsing my magic into him in desperation to awaken him—to heal him—but not knowing how. I looked around, knowing that my search for shelter, for help, would be in vain.

"You can't leave me!"

I didn't know where we were, or how we got here. I didn't even know what was going on.

"Help!" I yelled into the snow, my body shaking uncontrollably now, the cold freezing me down to my bones. I clung to Ilyan, my magic surging as I attempted to keep both of us warm, but I couldn't focus enough to keep the flow of magic going.

"Anyone! Help."

I turned back to him, my hands touching and pressing against his skin, desperate for any response.

"Ilyan!" I couldn't keep the hopelessness out of my voice. Everything was an impossible web of danger and fear, and I was trapped in the center of it.

My life was repeating itself, over and over. Somewhere deep inside I wished this to be a dream, whether or not it was controlled by Edmund. I wished that all of this was a fabricated nightmare. But I knew it wasn't.

I lay down next to Ilyan, my skin freezing against the snow and my arms clinging to his still body.

"Ilyan..." I pleaded, unable to deny the ache I felt for him. "Don't leave me..."

I had barely gotten the words out before I saw a dark figure moving toward us.

The shape was huge. I cringed against Ilyan's still form, fear of the unknown shape gripping me. I pulled my magic up to the center of me, dreading having to attack some monster. As it got closer, I could barely make out the shape of a man as he lumbered toward me. I sat up, not daring to hope, but terrified all the same. The figure yelled out something into the storm, his voice carried away by the wind.

Soon, the shape towered over me, his sharp green eyes digging into mine. He was an absolutely hulking figure, mostly caused by layer after layer of large fur coats. He pulled down his scarf to reveal a cleanly shaven face.

"Silnỳ! What are you doing here? What happened?" The man was panicked. He reached out and grabbed my shoulders with his heavily gloved hands, bringing me up to eye level.

I stared at him, unsure of what to say. I didn't know who this man was, and his voice and manner were scaring me.

"Tell me! You are in safe hands, but I must know!"

"Thom?" I asked, hoping beyond hope that Ilyan had gotten us to safety.

"No," he said, his voice strained. "He is coming, though. Now, tell me, what has happened? Is everyone safe?"

He continued to look into me, and I felt my heart fall. No, no one was okay. Ilyan was hurt. Wyn was gone. Prague...

"Prague. They found them," I stuttered, trying to find the right words. "They found us. Ilyan..." My voice broke and I looked toward Ilyan's still form, scrambling out of the man's hold and back to Ilyan's side.

"So it has happened." I barely registered that the man had spoken, my focus back on Ilyan again.

"Ilyan is hurt," I said, pulling the man's attention away from his reverie, desperate for help.

"Do not worry over your Protector, Silnỳ, his energy was spent in getting you here. He will be well in a few days." He smiled, his face lighting up.

"Thom!" he yelled into the blizzard that surrounded us before turning back and grunting a bit. "The poor lad moves slowly in the snow. My name is Dramin, by the way, but you can call me Uncle."

17

I LEANED my body over Ilyan's protectively while Dramin smiled at me as if he was amused.

"Uncle?" I asked, my voice shaking as my body convulsed in the cold.

"Yes, didn't Ilyan tell you?" He leaned over me, and I moved away instinctively.

"Ilyan didn't tell me anything." I grabbed Ilyan's hand, my heart plunging at his lack of response.

"I told you, Dramin. Ilyan wouldn't do anything he didn't need to, especially when it comes to her." I turned my body toward the gruff voice, surprised at the other large shape that had appeared out of the snow. He was tall and appeared twice as wide as I was sure he was thanks to all the coats he wore. I could just make out a long, dirty brown dreadlock protruding from underneath his woolen hat.

"Put that on," the second man said, dropping a huge fur coat in front of me. "You don't want to freeze to death."

He leaned over me and I caught a glimpse of deep blue eyes as he shooed me out of the way. He then picked up Ilyan's limp and unresponsive body with one big jolt. I called out as he moved Ilyan over his shoulder and covered him with a shaggy fur. The man turned to me, his stare piercing me even through the blinding snow.

"You look just like your father," he said before turning away and walking into the snow storm. I jumped up, moving to run after him, but my red shoes slipped in the snow, filling them with wetness. I grabbed the coat and attempted to put it on, moving after them as quickly as I could.

"Slow down, child," Dramin said from beside me. "You will be going nowhere fast if you continue at that pace."

I glared daggers at Dramin and ignored his warning before continuing my trudge after Ilyan and the man I could only assume to be Thom. I could see Ilyan's blonde hair swinging beneath the heavy fur that Thom had covered him with, the snowstorm threatening to swallow them up. I continued to slip and slide through the snow and wind, desperation filling me as they vanished.

"Wait," I yelled, knowing my voice would be swallowed up by the storm.

"Don't worry, child, Thom is taking him to our shelter," Dramin said.

I continued to move stubbornly forward, though I could no longer feel my toes. I had only made it a few steps before Dramin came up beside me and lifted me into his arms. I yelled and struggled away from him, only to land on my back in the snow.

"Don't touch me!" I yelled as I pulled myself up, the bulky fur coat making my movements clumsy.

"I'm just going to carry you, Silnỳ. Nothing more." He waved his hands in front of me as if to show me he was safe. I shied away from him.

"I've got to get to Ilyan. He has to be okay. He needs to shield me so they can't find me."

"Ilyan? He won't be helping you for a few days yet." My mouth opened in terror.

"No! I need him..."

"You've come farther along than I assumed." Dramin said, but I barely heard him.

Only one thing on my mind; I was completely unprotected. My mind swam around fuzzily, terror at being found again mixing with my loss and fear over Ilyan. He had saved me as I had known he would. No matter what Cail and Ryland had said. I needed to get to him; I needed to make sure he was alright.

"You have to do it!" I yelled as things clicked together. "You've got to shield me or else they are going to find me!"

"Don't worry. You are safe. Ilyan is safe. No one can track you here." I locked eyes with him for a moment, my teeth chattering, before looking toward where Thom had disappeared with Ilyan's body. I could see nothing except snow. My body sagged, collapsing in on itself, as I convulsed in the cold.

"Ilyan," I whispered. I felt so lost without him, he had been so constant over the past few months, and now... I watched the space he had been carried into, growing more desperate with every frantic beat of my heart.

Not long after, I felt Dramin's hand come to rest against my shoulder, his weight pushing me further into the cold snow. I shifted away from his contact, wrapping my arms tighter around me in an attempt to get warm.

"Do not worry. His mind will awaken when you call for him in your most hopeless state." His voice had taken on a dead quality that chilled me further, if that was even possible. My head snapped up to look at him, and I inhaled sharply. His eyes were fully encompassed in black, the centers glowing like the ember of a flame, staring off into the distance."

"It will happen after the sun has risen three times, after your heart has broken twice."

Slowly the blackness left his eyes, but I stayed still in the snow, feeling my magic attempt to heal my frostbitten extremities.

"You're a Drak." He smiled at my realization, his face lowering to mine, his eyes back to their bright green color.

"Ah-ha. So, Ilyan *has* taught you something." Dramin smiled wider, but I screwed my face up in confusion. How could he be a Drak? I had been told they were all dead... and my father...

"You're a Drak," I repeated.

"Yes, so now you can be calm that your Protector will live. Although I am sorry about the heartbreak part. I can't often control these things."

He smiled at me, but I only stared at him, my confusion growing.

"Hmmm, I can see the gears turning in your mind. You are wondering how I could be a Drak if your father was the one born from the mud, the first of his kind, and without any children except you of course." He continued to smile, but I did not know how to respond.

"I will make you a deal. Let me carry you and then I will tell you everything. I will answer every question that is burning inside that little brain of yours. Stay here, or worse, attempt to walk on your own, and I guarantee that you will lose a leg by morning." He said happily. I could already tell he knew what I was going to say.

I nodded once and he swept me up, cradling me like a baby. I cringed at the contact, trying to keep as much of my body away from him as possible.

"Nice shoes. Did Ilyan make them for you?" He asked; I glared at him, having no interest in answering him.

He said nothing more as he raced through the snow, the cold air brushing past my face and making my eyes sting. Reluctantly, I glanced toward my feet, wincing to see them as red as the delicate shoes I still wore.

Dramin continued to run as we approached a large cliff with a small opening in the center. Disappearing through the opening was the dark mass that was Thom and Ilyan. Dramin followed right behind them, carrying me through a dark cavern.

"Well, Thom, you got your wish. She is just as stubborn as her father." Dramin said as he came side by side with his friend. I looked around Dramin's arms to see Ilyan's head swinging as Thom walked, his eyelids still tinged with a deathly blue.

"Well at least she is not my responsibility this time," he grunted before moving off to the side, taking Ilyan away from me again.

Dramin kept walking as he moved us into a large, rounded cavern. The space had obviously been carved magically because each curve of the rock was smooth and perfect. Light that filtered in through enormous, ornate sky lights reflected off of bits of mirror and glass that were suspended in obscure places across the ceiling. What could instantly be dismissed as trash was turned beautiful by the light and gave an insane amount of character to the space. The light shone brightly, glimmering off of faded paintings that I could tell had once been masterpieces. Dramin set me down in a large, squishy arm chair as a fire was lit in the middle of the large space.

The whole cave had been set up like the spokes of a wheel. In the center was the large fire, and surrounding that a circle of chairs and couches, beyond that was a space that was raised up a bit from the sunken centers, which held about twenty bunks carved into the stone walls. Each had a mattress and a shelf. One was hidden behind a gold inlaid dressing partition and another had an ornately woven blanket. The rest were bare. I could almost guess which one belonged to Dramin and which to Thom. Thom didn't seem the type for inlaid gold.

I looked around until I found Thom gently laying Ilyan in one of the bunks. I watched as he carefully stripped off Ilyan's shirt before covering him with blanket after blanket of thick animal fur and placing his hands firmly on his face. I moved in an attempt to get up and go over to him, but Dramin stood right in front of me, placing a steaming cup of some foul smelling liquid in my hands.

"Thom will take care of him, don't you worry."

"I have to help him. He needs me," I said, shock filling me at my own words. It would have been natural to be concerned, however this level of worry was shocking to me. I shoved aside my doubt of my own emotions as I attempted to stand and move around Dramin, but he only pushed my shoulders back into the chair, his hand wrapping around the cup to ensure I didn't spill any.

"You need to sit right there, drink that, and let your magic heal your feet before you lose them."

Dramin placed a blanket over me, I could feel my magic moving sluggishly around my body, congregating in my feet and toes as it attempted to heal me. I let it flow freely, even though I couldn't stop my eyes from drifting to where Thom was healing Ilyan, my mind continually checked the Štít in my shoulder for any change.

"What happened to him?" I asked, trying to keep the

fear out of my voice without daring to look away from where Ilyan lay. It was hard to believe that Ilyan could get hurt.

"He's exhausted," Dramin said and began shedding his many coats, laying them gently in one of the many chairs that surrounded the fire. The more he shed, the smaller he got until he was nothing more than a tall, wiry man with square shoulders. His hair was a tangle of long brown strands, his green eyes looking into me sharply as he smiled. He looked vaguely familiar. Not like I had seen him somewhere before, but as if I had *known* him. I was aware that it wasn't possible, though. He appeared to be a few years older than me, whatever that was worth given how magical people seemed to age.

Dramin sat down in the armchair next to me, his hand patting my knee. "Ilyan is one of only a handful of Skřítek who can perform a Stutter. It is draining enough with one person, I have never known it to be done with two people before."

"A Stutter?" I pulled my eyes away from Ilyan to look at Dramin.

"Yes, a tri-dimensional move from any given point to another. It happens in the blink of an eye." Dramin took a drink from another mug filled with the same foul smelling liquid I still held in my hands.

"You mean, he instantly moved us from farmland in Ohio to..."

"High in the Alps, near a peak known as the Pizzo delle Saette." My eyes bugged out of my head and Dramin chuckled at me lightly before taking another drink.

I looked away from Dramin to Ilyan; I had no idea anything like that was possible.

"It takes a spectacular amount of power to accomplish. Most people do not have enough magic to transport themselves let alone another. I am surprised the effort did not kill him, but then, Ilyan is one of a kind. His heart is good, child. Without that goodness and light, he may not have been able to save you tonight."

"'One seeks power, the other light.'" I mumbled to myself.

"I'm sorry?" Dramin asked, but I only shook my head at him.

I didn't want to think of Ryland's words on the roof. I didn't want to consider the possibility of Ilyan thinking about me that way, or even Ryland using me. The thought gave me a jittery, butterfly feeling I wasn't very appreciative of. Ilyan had saved me. He was my Protector and that was what he had done.

"And you're sure he is going to be all right?" I desperately wanted to run over to him and somehow help Thom, but I could still feel the tingling of magic in my toes, and I wasn't sure I could stand on my feet yet.

"Never doubt the word of a Drak, child. He is resting. You will see him in a few days' time."

"After my heart has broken twice," I repeated. I turned to face him, unsurprised to see him staring at me. I shifted my weight in the chair, the look he was giving me making me uncomfortable.

"I am still very sorry about that, but don't worry. It will be for a good cause." He lifted his glass to me as if to tap it with mine, but I stayed still.

"So, you are a Drak, then?"

"Yes," he said. "Didn't we establish this already? Oh, wait, you are wondering how I can be alive, or even be here considering the position of your father."

"Yes, but you promised answers."

Dramin looked at me for a moment, his gaze making my

inside squirm. I felt like he was looking into my future; which given his magic, he possibly could be. I wasn't sure I wanted anyone looking into my future, so I shied away from him, squishing my back further into the chair.

"Are you going to drink that?" he asked, gesturing toward the still full mug of steaming, dark-brown fluid he had given me. I swirled the mug around a bit, the thick fluid not moving around much.

"Probably not. The smell is making me a bit sick." I tried to move it away from me, but Dramin only smiled.

"It tastes better than it smells, and it is the best thing for awakening magic. If you drink that, I will tell you everything."

I pulled the cup toward me before looking at him, one eyebrow raised in accusation, "I thought our deal was you get to carry me here, and in return, you tell me everything."

"This is a new deal." He smiled and I scowled back at him. I didn't like being tricked.

I locked eyes with him for a moment, hoping to stare him down, however he only grinned at me and leaned forward, giving me the same look he had before. My insides squirmed again and I shrunk away. I didn't like the way he looked at me, the way he seemed to see through me. I pulled the mug to my lips, cringing at the smell of the fluid before the sweet honey flavor hit my tongue. The second I swallowed I could feel everything inside of me speed up. My magic warmed and moved faster. I hadn't felt the current inside of me feel so alive since the morning after Ilyan had first centered me.

"Talk," I said, not willing to admit that the drink actually did taste good.

Dramin smiled widely before sitting back in his chair, his legs crossing to face the fire. The light flickered around the space, ricocheting off of the pieces of metal and glass that hung from the ceiling and giving the whole space a glittery feeling.

"In the beginning, the four types of magic were born from the mud, the magical well of Imdalind that sits far below Prague: Rinax, the Vilỳ; Chyline the Trpaslíks; Frain the Skřítek; and Sain the Drak. From the beginning they knew of their abilities, knew of the magic that flowed through their veins. They used it in the ways that their souls dictated of them; for good, for love, and for assistance to others. Magic was good in the world. Three went into the world, were married and bonded, and carried on their seed. So the magic grew; each mate—each child—bringing their own magic into the world, yet one, Sain, was alone. He walked the earth desperate to find someone that his soul would call to and bond with, but none came."

He paused, and I took another drink, worried he would stop if I didn't. Even though some of this I already knew, I had the distinct impression that this was how Dramin operated, from the beginning. He smiled at me, a look I didn't return.

"In his loneliness, Sain went to the mud and begged for companionship. He cried into the well and from a slice in his finger, added two drops of blood. The well blessed the world with another Drak, but still Sain's soul did not sing. He took me from the mud, named me, and raised me as he would a son."

"You?" I asked, confused. I guess it made sense that he looked familiar.

"Yes, so you see. I am your uncle." He smiled brightly, and I almost choked on the dark liquid.

"Wouldn't that make you my brother?" Dramin laughed at my question.

"I am a bit old to be your brother, child," he said with a smirk.

"And Sain is a little too old to be my father," I replied, a little angry. Dramin chuckled and rested against the back of his chair, his feet lifting onto a large ottoman.

"Touché."

I ignored him and took another drink of whatever he had given me. It was delightfully warming, and oddly enough, the smell was growing on me.

"So, if he was all alone, how did he end up with Ovailia?" I cringed at my words. I wasn't sure I wanted to know. This was possibly the largest piece of my past—of my father's past—that I still couldn't quite make myself believe.

"Sain wasn't alone. He wasn't complete, but he wasn't alone. He thrived as the head of the Drak, the race surviving through my progeny. It wasn't until the day Ovailia was born —when he went to visit the newborn daughter of the King —that his soul finally sang. He held that child in his arms, and before the day had ended, was telling everyone that he had found his mate; that he would bond himself to her when the time was right. Ovailia resisted him at first, but after sixty years she finally consented to a bonding. Everyone was so happy for Sain—for both of them—but after the bonding, something changed. No one was sure what until the day that Ovailia betrayed him."

"Betrayed him?" I said, "But, I thought..." My voice faded off as Dramin shook his head, his eyes looking sadly away from me.

"That Edmund almost tortured him to death? That Ovailia made a pact with her father in an attempt to save him? It is all true, but her betrayal began before that.

"She delivered what little she knew about Sain's sight about you to her father. When Edmund heard it, he demanded to know who had spoken it, however Ovailia only knew that a girl would be born who could defeat an opposing power, nothing more. She didn't know when, she didn't even know who the opposing power was. Edmund needed the seeing Drak, so he could glean more information, and Ovailia eagerly sacrificed her mate for what she believed to be a greater good. It wasn't until Edmund began to torture him that she began to second guess her decision."

"It was too late." A deep, gruff voice spoke up from across the large space.

I looked up as Thom joined us, his long dreads swinging as he sat across the fire from me on a large, brown couch. I wouldn't have even recognized him if it hadn't been for the dreads. He was short and stocky, and his brown dreads looked out of place with his clean-shaven, boyish face. He swung his mukluk covered feet onto the couch and looked away from me, closing his eyes.

I looked toward the bunk where Ilyan had been laid, his body still with only his head visible from underneath the large amount of furs. I went to move, but one grunt from Thom stopped my progression.

"He's fine. You can go fawn over him after your feet are better." I turned hastily toward Thom, my forehead furled in a scowl.

"I wasn't going to *fawn* over him," I said a little too acidly; Thom only snorted at me.

"You sure she doesn't know, Dramin?" Thom asked, his eyes still closed.

"I'm sure." Dramin smiled and refilled his mug with a wave of his hand. "Now, where were we? Oh, yes, Ovailia broke the bond."

"How could they survive?" I asked the question more to

myself than to him. I still remembered the pain, the way my body had attempted to rot from inside out after my bond with Ryland had been cracked, and the way it would now protest every time I stayed away from the Tŏuha for too long.

"It is the one who breaks the bond that walks away unscathed while the one who is broken will suffer and die. It was Sain who suffered to the point that he appeared dead. Ovailia was unscathed because she broke the bond and because she no longer loved him."

I looked down into my glass, hurting for my father, although I still struggled to think of Sain in that way. He had waited all his life to love, and the person he chose had somehow chosen not to love him back. I exhaled and drank deeply. At least my mother had loved him until the day she had been killed.

"In his anger Edmund massacred all of my posterity; my sons and daughters, thousands of my grandchildren and beyond, all murdered. All while Edmund kept Sain imprisoned, hidden from Ovailia, trying to glean more information about the sight. Sain never gave it to him no matter how much he was tortured, though. They never found out more than what Ovailia had told them. Which is why they never identified you until Ryland found your mark. For centuries Edmund used Sain's abilities for his profit. He kept him under a Vymàzat so strict that, while it never completed, it was enough to keep control over him. He wouldn't let him near the Black Water that the Drak rely on, and so he weakened further." Dramin spoke quietly and I could tell how much he was affected by what he was saying. He closed his eyes and leaned back against the chair, his hands still grasping his mug.

"For centuries he was only given an opportunity to drink

the Black Water when Edmund needed the use of his sight. He was as weak as a human, his ability becoming so reliant on the Black Water that he could no longer control the visions or interpret what he would see, however Edmund had learned to do all that for him. Sain's body slowly learned to rely more on human food than his own resources. In many ways, the Drak in him died." Dramin spoke into his mug heavily, his knuckles white against the pottery in his hands. I couldn't help but feel sick to my stomach at this new bit of information.

"How did he get out?" I asked quietly, my voice awed like I was being told a bedtime story and not the history of my father.

"I got him out," Thom said from across the fire, though his body did not deviate from its relaxed position. "I grabbed him, knocked my father unconscious, broke Timothy's arm, and made a run for it. It took me quite some time to get any information out of Sain as to where we were supposed to go."

Thom scowled darkly and moved his hands behind his head, his eyes moving to look at me.

"Worst mistake of my life." Thom said, "I should have left him there. Having to spend the next three hundred years in hiding, trying to get your best friend back from the mess your father had created of him, only to see him end up captured with no memory is not something I would like to repeat."

"Tell me about it," I groaned unhappily. I wound my hands together in my lap, wishing that everyone would be okay. Wyn, Talon, Ryland, and now Ilyan were on top of that list. I sighed and slammed my back into the chair. Dramin reached over and patted my leg like a comforting grandfather, the action awakening something in me as I forced back a smile.

"So you were in hiding?" I asked. After all, I could relate.

"I'm still in hiding," Thom grumbled, "My existence as well as Sain's had to be kept as much of a secret as possible. If Ovailia found out about us, there is no telling what she would do, and while Ilyan has his suspicions, none of us want to find out what Edmund would do with us."

"How did they find you?" I asked, not wanting to dwell on all the negative that had happened in the past few hours.

"We were in college, pretending to be Seniors, and we were bored out of our minds. Then, one day, we saw him— Cail." I visibly froze and Thom stopped briefly. He turned toward me, his eyes narrowing a bit. "I hid Sain with a human family and erased his memory in case he was found then pulled Cail off his trail. I was only able to return when I knew it was safe, which was about ten years later, yet without a true memory of his past, he had married. I stayed nearby, but I couldn't see any signs of magic from you, so I left. Content to give him a normal life and return when the time was right."

I wasn't sure what to say. I ran through the story, the fact that my life had been a giant sham becoming more of an irritating reality. I shook my head and tried to bring forward any amount of strength or confidence I could find. It wasn't much, though.

"How did you know Edmund had found you simply because you saw Cail?" I asked.

"When you see Cail, Edmund and Timothy are not far behind. Even if you don't see them, they are always there."

"Why?" I shook my head trying, to clear the image and the memory of Cail and Ilyan fighting out of my mind. "How do you know that?"

Thom sat up all the way and leaned forward. His blue eyes shimmered in the firelight as he looked toward me. "When Cail was born, it was decided that Edmund needed a new bodyguard. So Edmund and Timothy both infused the infant with a Štít of their magic however Edmund also placed his there to give Cail power. You see, Edmund placed his Štít right inside Cail's heart. From birth, Edmund's wicked power has influenced him, and from birth, Cail has been taught how to use Edmund's power as his own. All with the knowledge that if he steps one toe out of line, Edmund can kill him no matter where he is."

I gasped, my hand subconsciously moving to my shoulder where Ilyan's weak tendrils still swirled within me.

"Yes," Thom nodded, "I know that Ilyan has done something similar to you." I saw Dramin's head spin toward me at Thom's words, but I ignored it.

"I will admit I was shocked when I was healing him and suddenly my energy moved across the room, but Ilyan's Štít in you is different than what resides in Cail's body. Ilyan has placed his there to protect you. Besides, I doubt you could use his magic to your benefit. Even trying to hold Ilyan's magic inside of you would kill you."

After Thom laughed as if he had told a great joke and lay back against the couch again, I let my eyes flow away from him to Ilyan's still body.

But I had held Ilyan's magic. He had accidently pushed too much within me when setting up the Štít, and I had survived. I was sure he had done it again when using the Stutter to get us here, too. I shook my head and looked away.

"So Cail can use Edmund's magic?" I asked before drinking the last of the liquid from my mug.

"Yes," Dramin answered, "although I don't think he does

very often. I am not sure he can without Edmund's express permission."

I nodded and looked away from him into my empty cup. I knew exactly when Cail was using Edmund's magic with his permission—every night when he haunted my dreams. I didn't dare look over to Ilyan. I wished I could talk to him, tell him I had figured it out. Even though I am sure he already knew, I needed to tell him... needed someone to understand. I shook my head and looked up, cringing a bit to see Dramin staring at me.

"What is it?" I wasn't sure if he didn't know or was just being polite in asking, but either way, I still didn't want to answer. After all they would both find out tonight when I woke up screaming with no one there to calm me.

"Ummm..." I asked the first thing that came to my mind, lifting the empty mug to make my intent clear. "Can I have some more?"

"I'll get it," Thom grunted from the other side of the fire, as he lifted himself up to a sitting position.

"Don't bother," Dramin said as he waved his hand, the mug filling with the dark brown fluid.

I smiled appreciatively and took a big swallow, loving how it was energizing my body.

"No," I turned toward Thom, surprised at how his voice had changed from before. He stood in front of the fire, his startled eyes jumping between me and Dramin.

"What?" I asked, looking around, worried something was coming up behind me.

"You didn't?" Thom yelled at Dramin.

"I did. You can imagine my own surprise when my sight showed me what would come if I did." Dramin's voice was calm against Thom's outburst while I continued to look back and forth between them, my confusion growing.

"You could have killed her, Dramin!" I jumped at Thom's shout, my heart thumping at his words.

"I wouldn't have done it if I hadn't been shown that it was the right path, Thom. Besides, she just needed to be woken up," Dramin said. "At least now we know and can work with it."

"Know what?" I practically shouted. I needed to know what was going on.

"He gave you some of the Black Water to drink," Thom said, his voice strained. "Your father's blood flows strongly in your veins."

18

———

"WAIT, WHAT?" I looked between the two men, from Thom's panicked face to Dramin's gleeful grin. They seemed to be waiting for me to do something. I looked directly at Thom, deciding that his anger might prompt him to tell me the truth a bit faster.

"You," I said as sternly as I could, my panic seeping out anyway. "Tell me what he did."

Thom's eyes narrowed at me as he grunted in disapproval. Normally I would have apologized for my rudeness, but right then I didn't care. I glared at him for a moment longer before he grunted again and sat back down on his couch.

"The Black Water is the water that the Drak use to cultivate the magic of sight. It is their main food source, and essentially the very core of their power. The water can only be held in a mug made from the mud of the outer rim of the Wells of Imdalind. It's why your father became so weak when Edmund kept it from him. If you keep the mugs away, you keep the Water away. The water is poison to any being other than the Drak. By giving it to you to drink, he could have very easily killed you." Thom huffed before looking away from me, his continued frustration at the situation evident.

"But I didn't die, so what does that mean?" I looked between the two men, waiting for answers.

"You are one of The Chosen, correct?" Dramin asked calmly before sipping from his cup.

"Yes." I nodded my head, waiting for him to continue. That in itself was a reason none of this made sense.

"And you have a mark?" He smiled at me from behind his cup. I nodded at him. "Can I see it?"

I looked at him for a moment before exhaling. I didn't see any reason why I shouldn't other than that I didn't want to, and that wasn't a very good reason. I closed my eyes before lifting my hair to reveal the small mark on my neck. Dramin exhaled sharply, which I wasn't prepared for, but I still kept my eyes closed.

"Look Thom, it's a dragon. How interesting." His tone made it sound like it was far more than just interesting. It made my skin crawl. I dropped my hair and opened my eyes, turning to face the two, only to be shocked at Thom's open-mouthed stare.

"What?" I asked, affronted. "Does that mean something?"

"Hmmm?" Dramin studied me and I got the same feeling as before, like he was looking inside of me. "Not yet, I think."

I narrowed my eyes at him in confusion and he laughed at me.

"The important thing here, Silnỳ, is that you are in fact a Chosen Child, and yet you can hold the Black Water within your body."

I waited, but Dramin said nothing more, he only smiled.

Thom grunted from the other side of the fire, making me more upset; at least I had gotten answers from him.

"Which means..." I prompted him.

"Which means that you not only have the powers that the Skřítek and Trpaslíks carry—which were awakened within you when the Vilỳ kissed your skin—but also those of the Drak as well." Dramin smiled like I was the most amazing thing in the world, but my stomach tied itself in knots of confusion.

"So... I can, like, see the future?" I asked, the disbelief heavy in my voice.

"Ohhh... I know you can do much more than that." Dramin's smile increased. Thom sat up again, swinging his legs to face us, the same disgruntled look on his face.

"What are you getting at, Dramin?" Thom asked, obviously irritated.

"Tell me, Silnỳ, what does the Black Water make you feel like? What does it do to your magic, your body, when you drink it?"

I shifted my weight, hating the intense stares that both men were giving me. I looked for something to do and instinctively took a drink from the mug in my hands. I regretted it immediately. Both their eyes were on me waiting for an answer. I swallowed the mouthful of Water and I suddenly knew what to tell them.

"It makes me feel warm, stronger somehow. My magic feels a little more alive, a little looser." I looked up to find Dramin smiling more, if that was possible. The man seemed to be smiling all the time. "Is that good?" I asked, worried that I had said the wrong thing.

"Oh, that's very good." Dramin stood and threw the heavy furs off of my lap. I sat there, staring at him, wishing I could put the blankets back on. My feet were now a normal color and I could feel all my extremities, but the cave was still cold.

"Come along, Silnỳ. I want to try something." Dramin pulled me up, carefully taking my mug from me as he did.

Carrying my mug in front of him, he began pulling me along behind him. I was secretly thankful that my feet seemed to be working the right way.

"Where are we going?" I asked when I realized he was dragging me toward the dark tunnel we had entered the cavern through. I looked back to Ilyan, nervous that I was being pulled away from him. The longing I felt scared me, though, so I shoved it away.

"I want to try something," Dramin repeated.

"Yes, I heard that the first time," I snapped while he continued to drag me forward. I looked back to see Thom standing near the fire, his arms folded, having no intention of following us. He smiled at my panic stricken face.

"I'll stay here," he called after us rigidly, "and watch over sleeping beauty." Thom batted a hand at us before turning toward his own bunk, but I didn't see anything else as Dramin dragged me not into the dark tunnel that led outside, but into another round cavern that was connected to the first.

This one was not as nice. In fact, it was bare. The large dome of the rock spread high above us, yet there were no paintings or dancing bits of reflection; it was only stone and a hundred blue, glittery orbs that Dramin had sent to the ceiling when we arrived in order to give us light.

I stepped away from him to look at the large space. While bare, it was still impressive.

"What is this place?" I asked, one magically assisted cave I could accept, but two perfectly rounded caverns?

I turned to Dramin, surprised to find his smile faded.

"This was to be a home for one of my posterity, a young lady named Delia and her mate Chandle. They were killed in the massacre. Thom and I stay here because no one except Ilyan and I know of this cave's existence. Ilyan helped me to build it. It was to be a surprise." He smiled sadly, and I didn't know what to say so I turned away from him, trying to keep my own sense of loss at bay.

"The room we came from is the living quarters, this is the practice hall, and through that door there," he pointed toward a small opening on the opposite edge of the space, "is the Hall of Sight. It is a sacred room where the Drak can see and record their visions."

I looked toward the room with interest, but I knew I didn't want to go in there. I was afraid that if I did Dramin would expect me to do something I wasn't prepared for.

"So what are we doing here?" I worded my question carefully, hoping to take his attention off of the Hall of Sight.

"Did you know, Silnỳ, that only one magic can exist in a soul at one time? A Vilỳ can only ever be a Vilỳ, a Skřítek a Skřítek, a Drak a Drak. If the love is strong enough they can mesh; it has been done in the past, but I am not sure Ovailia ever loved Sain. That was one of the reasons Sain and Ovailia's bond never held; their magic could never truly be one. The only form of magic that can intermingle is that of a Chosen child, but to have two types of magic in one person prior to a Zělství has never happened. It would be too much. The body, the soul, could not contain it. And yet, here you are. You have the magic of a Trpaslík and a Skřítek, as caused by the bite of a Vilỳ and the magic of the Drak from your father. All that, in one little body."

I stepped away from him, instantly feeling awkward. I didn't like the way he was insinuating that I was some super powerful being.

"The Silnỳ," he said as if on cue. Most Powerful. I shook my head and moved away further.

"Too much magic. Are you saying I might be like Ilyan, like how he can't use the whole of his magic on one person?" Dramin's eyes narrowed at me as he began to move around me. I held still, even though I wanted to move away from his hawk like stare.

"No, not yet," he said. I could tell it was more to himself than to me, but it still peaked my interest.

"What do you mean, 'not yet'?"

"You are not yet ready to see all that you must see." He smiled again as he stopped in front of me, his body far too close for comfort.

I stepped away, my insides tensing when he smiled again. He pushed the mug back into my hands, the warm Black Water still swirling heavily inside.

"The Drak drink the Black Water from birth. It is part of our very nature, part of who we are. You have had two mugs. It is the start of your new life. You will find in a matter of days that you will no longer desire human food. You will not need to sleep as much. You will only need the Black Water to sustain you."

I looked into the mug uneasily. I already wanted to take another drink and that alone was worrisome.

"Now, let's conduct a little experiment. I will shoot a target into the air for you. I want you to drink of the Black Water and then fire your magic at the target. Aim to kill." I nodded once. That sounded easy enough, if only my stomach would stop flipping from nerves.

I lifted the mug to my lips and drank greedily, loving the way the liquid filled me up. Dramin smiled as I downed it. I lowered the mug as he fired a dark, heavy shape from his hands across the large space. It appeared more cumbersome than the magic I had learned to control, it almost looked... weak. I lifted my hand, surprised by the response my magic had to that simple thought. Without even having to focus the way I always had, a ripple of brilliant violet flew from the palm of my hand faster than I had ever seen to intercept Dramin's dark target. The two collided heavily in the air, a purple shower filling the room as my magic destroyed the target.

I didn't move. I didn't dare. I stared at the now dark intersection, the impact replaying in my mind. Ilyan had been training me in combat for months and I had never been able to obtain that kind of power, even after I had been able to shield myself from the drain caused by the necklace. Ilyan had always said how strong my magic was, but it had never responded. Not like that.

"Wonderful!" Dramin shouted as he clapped his hands enthusiastically. "Did you know that the Drak carry no defensive magic? So the fact that you can do that, and so well, is amazing."

I stared at him.

"Would you care to try it again?" Dramin waved his hand over my mug, the liquid instantly refilling.

I looked at the Black Water for a moment before nodding my head and emptying the mug with one gulp. Dramin laughed as he sent another target for me. This time I released the mug into the air where it floated before me as I sent a strong impulse from both hands. The energy wave moved away from me, disintegrating the target and leaving a long divot in the rock. I reached out and grabbed the mug from where it still hovered in the air, my hands wrapping around the smooth ceramic as if I was afraid I would drop it.

"Amazing," Dramin whispered beside me.

"How is that possible?" I asked, looking at my hand. "I have never been able to... I mean, I..."

"It appears the Black Water has opened up your true potential, Silnỳ."

I turned to him, my hair flying as I moved, and stared at him wide eyed, hoping he would answer my unasked question since I wasn't sure how to phrase it. He met my gaze, his eyes shining as they searched through me, though I wasn't certain for what.

"No, not yet."

"Then when?" I demanded, suddenly worried I would not get the answers I desperately needed.

"When you have accepted who you truly are." His answer was simple, yet it seemed so impossible. Especially considering that I didn't even know *what* I truly was. I looked at my free hand, my eyes trailing back to the large dent that had rent the smooth surface of the stone.

"I am a Drak," I said. I could still feel the Black Water buzzing through my veins. The feeling was definitely addicting.

"Yes."

"But I am also one of The Chosen." My fingers grazed over the seldom touched skin of my mark, as if I needed concrete proof.

"Yes."

"But the two cannot exist together. Different magic cannot exist in one being without a bonding."

My statement was simple, confident. He had already told me the answer, had already given me that much of my fate.

"It seems," Dramin said, "that now they can, Silnỳ. In you, all things are possible."

19

THE FOREST. I cringed when I saw it, my heart falling to my feet in terror. I fought the urge to curl into a ball in expectation of what awaited me. These weren't just nightmares anymore, they were real. With nightmares you could at least count on waking, but with these dreams I was not so sure anymore. I couldn't even defend myself in them without the risk of hurting someone else.

I began to run into the forest, darting through trees and jumping over rocks, my breath coming in sharp bursts as I exerted myself. I had reached about two hundred yards from where I started when I heard it; the growling, the laughing, and the panting. It all flooded over me and I picked up my pace.

My running took me straight into a large hedge. I jumped swiftly over it only to land right back in the middle of the clearing, face to face with Cail who stood in the center inspecting his fingernails as if he was bored. Edmund stood behind him, but he was faded somehow, as if he was shrouded in fog.

"Tsk. Tsk. Running from me, Joclyn? Really? Are you

that scared?" Cail mocked me, and I took half a step back before bringing my feet together again. I stood straight in front of him, chin held high.

"No." I let enough magic stream through my fingers to let the electricity crackle between them. Cail smiled at my taunt, excited at the prospect of a fight.

"Really? I mean, you should be. You haven't made us very happy, you know? Escaping from Edmund's trap yet again, surviving no matter how hard we try to kill you. It's not fair."

Cail gestured toward Edmund who smiled slightly.

"Make it good, Cail."

"Of course, master."

Both men sneered before Edmund's shape shimmered and disappeared from view. I flinched as a jolt of fear lodged itself in my chest. I clenched my jaw and ignored it.

Cail circled around me as he spoke, his eyes never leaving me. When his hand reached out and glided down my long hair, I pulled away from the touch, but he only smiled more.

"Did you come bringing another message, Cail, or is this the only way you can even get close to a woman?" my voice was hard as I looked away from him, locking my jaw in defiance.

Cail laughed a bit, pulling my hair up to his nose. He inhaled the scent as I moved away from him, the strands falling from his grasp. He kept his hand against his nose as he looked up at me, his intense gaze causing me to shrink away.

"Hmmm, no message. I just enjoy spending time with you." I laughed at him, the hollow sound giving my nerves away.

"Yeah right," I scoffed. "You only like spending time with me if it involves attempted murder."

Cail smiled wider at my voice, his body moving closer to mine.

"Or torture," he added, his smile growing. I stepped away again, hating how insecure I was feeling.

"Is that what Edmund told you to do, Cail; to torture me?" He didn't answer. He just continued his advance into my personal space.

"Ryland tells me you now know that Ilyan loves you. Is that true?"

"Ilyan doesn't love me," I shot back, side stepping him to move across the clearing. I didn't like how this was going. There was always more than this. More screaming, more crying, more pain. "Not in that way."

"Oh, so he hasn't told you. Could it be that I know more than you at this point in time? Oooh, I would love to see your face when you figure everything out; what Ryland did, what Ilyan is keeping from you. This game gets more and more exciting." He clapped his hands, his eyes dancing in a way that made my insides squirm.

"This isn't a game!" I yelled at him, making my voice ricochet off the trees and reverberating through the clearing.

He froze, his face blank for a moment before the grin returned.

"Not a game you say? Well, what do you say we turn it into a game?" He came up behind me quicker than I had expected him to, his hands wrapping around me and holding me in place. He rested his chin against my shoulder, my insides squirming at the unwelcome contact.

"Why don't we see who has the upper hand?" His voice

was soft in my ear, I moved my head away from him, but he followed, keeping his cheek against mine.

"Bring them out!" he yelled. I cringed against the sound, but his arms still held me against him.

I felt my fingers crackle; my magic was surging in expectation of an attack, but I pushed it away. It wouldn't work here anyway.

I watched as dark shapes began to form in front of me. They were not the regular shapes of Edmund's henchmen, they were rounded balls that were accompanied by the grunts, groans, and screams of injured people being forced to move. My mouth opened in a silent scream as I saw the forms break between the trees. One after another they came, each of their broken bodies framed by two of Edmund's men. I looked to each of them, Ryland and Wyn fighting weakly against their captors, Talon weak and still on the ground, and a man I didn't recognize. The man lifted his gaze to mine and I knew at once who he was.

My father.

He looked the same as I had always remembered him, the imprint of his features still strong in my mind. His hair, as black as mine, was longer than I remembered. It made him look older and more travel worn. He looked up to me with his rounded face, his strong jaw tight and defiant as he fought against the men who held him. His eyes were as green as mine were before they changed, my breath catching at how much I looked like him. The resemblance that would never have been recognized in a child was now obvious in his teenager. Thom had been right, I looked just like him.

He blinked at seeing me there, his eyes instantly glossing over with unshed tears. I could see the confusion and heartbreak that must have been tearing him up inside.

I could only stare at him, though. I wasn't sure what to say or how to react to this man. He was my father. My heart beat heavily against my chest as it screamed at me to run to him. Part of me wanted to, yet another part was too hurt to care.

We stared at each other while a million words, thoughts, and purposes flowed between us before Cail cut off our individualized reveries.

"We hold in our possession two of your friends, your lover, and even your father. And who do you still have? A 'Protector'. Someone who hasn't even told you the truth yet."

I looked between them all, my heart breaking at seeing them there. I had to remind myself that this was only a dream. They weren't really here. I could not save them. Most importantly, however, I reminded myself that I could not tell Cail of Ilyan's current state. I swallowed the giant lump in my throat and looked away from them, trying to keep my confidence high.

"Let them go," I snarled.

"Why? We have the upper hand. We. Are. Winning. And you, you don't even know what's going on." He smiled and I pushed against his strong arms.

"Now, now, don't go anywhere yet. We still haven't gotten to our game! You see, we have four people in front of us and you can pick one. One that you will not have to watch die right now. The others we will kill before you. You will not have to see the last die, but here is the clincher. Whoever you choose will have to watch you die before we will release them from this nightmare, and let them wake up."

I fought against him, not wanting to hear anymore; not wanting to play his game.

"Who do you choose, Joclyn? Who do you want to watch you die?"

I looked at each of them as they fought their captors. Each one had fought for me, and I for them. I fought the burning emotions behind my eyes as I looked between them, my vision stopping at my father. He didn't fight against those who held him. He met my eyes, nodding his head once in understanding. I inhaled deeply.

"My father," I said. "I choose my dad."

He nodded to me once more, my mouth forming the words 'I'm sorry', hoping desperately that he would understand.

"It's okay, Joclyn." A million childhood memories flooded me with his voice.

"Wonderful!" Cail sneered, his hold on me tightening. "She's made her choice. Dispose of the rest."

I tried to look away, but Cail held my head as three swords plunged through the chests of my friends. In sync, each screamed and gargled as the life left their bodies. As Wyn's hand extended helplessly toward Talon, I tried not to cry. I tried to convince myself that they were not hurt—that it was only a dream—but the tears dripped down my cheeks anyway.

"No!" I yelled the word even though I didn't want to, even though I knew it was useless.

Cail laughed at me, holding my head in place for a moment longer as I watched their lifeless bodies fall to the forest floor.

Cail, thankfully, didn't let my eyes linger long before turning me to face my father, the men behind him holding him in place and forcing his eyes open so he didn't miss a thing. An instant later, I saw the flash of the blade to my side, praying that whatever Cail was going to do would happen quickly.

"I'm sorry, Daddy." I closed my eyes as I spoke, not wanting to know what was going to happen.

I felt the flow of the air as the sword moved, and then the pain filled me. I screamed at the impact, at the intensity of the agony. I continued screaming as Cail's arm around me disintegrated and the rough sheet of my bunk took its place. Then I continued to shriek and writhe at the memory of the pain, waiting for the arm to wrap around me that would never come. I cried, and howled, and yelled in panic while, somewhere in the back of my mind, I knew that Thom and Dramin could hear me.

I screamed Ilyan's name until I had gained a little bit of control over myself. Still shaken, I replaced his name with his song. My shaky voice was louder than usual, the song ricocheting around the stone walls that threatened to swallow me whole. I sang Ilyan's song over and over until my voice became a whisper and then faded to nothing.

I didn't dare move. I faced the cave wall with no desire to know if Thom or Dramin had witnessed my episode. I held still for much longer than necessary, not daring to go back to sleep no matter how much my exhausted body begged me to. When I was sure that enough time had passed, I turned, thankful to find no one except Ilyan's still body that lay in the bunk across the common area from me.

I couldn't take my eyes from him. I stood, my stocking-covered feet hitting the stone of the floor then grabbed one of my heavy fur blankets and ran across the space, prancing lightly from level to level until I stood before him. I had checked on him before I went to bed, but after the terror of my nightmare, I ached for him.

I hadn't realized how much I had come to rely on him—

how much I needed him—especially in times like these. I hadn't realized how much he had come to mean to me.

And it scared me.

I climbed onto the bunk, worming my way behind him, making sure not to step on his feet. I curled myself into a ball, wrapping the blanket around me and leaned my back, staring at his calm face, the blue tint still prevalent. Sighing, I folded my arms over my knees in frustration.

He was calm, resting. In some way I was glad that he was free from everything that faced me, but in another way—the terrible selfish way—I wished he would wake up and hold me.

"So, Cail is using you against me now," I whispered to him, even though he couldn't hear me. "I can't say I'm surprised. It was going to happen eventually, right?" I tried to laugh, but the sound came out strained.

"Ryland told me some stupid riddle about love and seeking power or light. He said it was about you." I lay my head against the stone wall, not daring enough to look away from Ilyan.

I didn't know what else to say. I didn't even know why I was talking to him. This stupid game that Cail was playing with my heart had me in knots. I knew it wasn't true, it couldn't be. Cail had spoken about love like I was being fought over and spoke of death like it was joyous; it made my insides squirm. I didn't like that Cail had dragged Ilyan into this whole mess or that he had become a weapon to be used against me, too. I knew I was being manipulated, but the thing that bothered me the most was that what he had said had somehow crawled under my skin. I shook my head and swallowed, trying to find some stability.

"I wish I was stronger, Ilyan. I wish I could face the

nightmares alone, but I can't. I think I can, but I still wake up screaming anyway."

I pulled the blanket over my head, fighting the tears, pushing the weakness away from me. I couldn't just wish to be stronger. I needed to *be* stronger. The problem was, I didn't know how to do that. I had gained some strength—I was a million times more capable than I had been a few months before—but I needed to be able to face everything and not be scared.

I looked back to Ilyan. Ilyan was brave. He was confident. He was capable. But right then I couldn't help seeing how defenseless he was, how weak, and perhaps, even human he appeared. I closed my eyes at the confusion. The odd pulls and jerks that drew me toward Ilyan were making me uncomfortable.

I brushed away the emotion. Ilyan wasn't weak; he wasn't defenseless. I didn't need to protect him, no matter how strongly I felt that I did right then. Ilyan was the strongest person I had ever met.

I did need him. More than I had ever thought I would, but I didn't need him to do everything for me. I was strong, too, and Ilyan had made me that way. He hadn't told me I couldn't. He had shown me how I could. He made me stronger because he believed in me.

I moved, letting my hand brush his cheek, his weak magic swirling beneath the surface of his skin as it did inside of me.

"I saw my dad. He looked exactly the same. It was weird." I leaned my head against my knees, the pain from the nightmare still heavy inside of me. I left my hand against his skin for a moment longer before bringing it back inside the warmth of the fur blanket.

"You know, when he left I shut everything inside, and

then Wyn asked me not to do that anymore. She asked me why I was throwing everything away..." I exhaled and looked away from him, my eyes scanning the large cave without really seeing anything.

"It was then that I decided not to. I'd always let Ryland in, but after that I *really* let him in. I gave him my heart. I gave him my magic, even though I didn't know it at the time." I dragged my eyes back to Ilyan's pale face, my finger moving to touch the dim blue of his eyelid without my even knowing.

"I let Wyn in, and I actually started to feel like I had a friend. I mean, even though she didn't understand me all the way—even though she didn't really know me—I felt like she could. Like she wanted to. Like I mattered to her." Everything had come out in a rush. I stopped abruptly, my voice catching on my last words while I sank back into the wall, my head hitting hard against the stone.

"And I let you in, Ilyan. First as a teacher, someone I could trust, and then, over the last three months, you became more than that. You have become my friend. Someone that... I mean... I could..." I stopped as my heart thudded, my eyes burning. I didn't know exactly what I wanted to say. I didn't know how to word it properly because everything was jumbled inside of me. Cail's manipulative taunts still fresh in my mind.

"I hope you can't hear me, or else you're going to think I sound like a lunatic." I inhaled again, my nose sniffing loudly.

"I loved Ryland and they took him. I mean, I might be able to get him back, but what if I'm not strong enough? What if I can't get there in time?" I buried my head in my hands, cursing the tears that had finally broken through.

"I trusted Wyn, and they got to her, too. They took her,

too." I wiped at the weak tears that rolled down my cheeks with the back of my hand, wishing I had been strong enough to keep them away in the first place.

"And I..." I stopped, searching for the right words, but I wasn't finding them. "Ilyan, Thom says you're going to get better." I pressed my hand to my shoulder from within the warmth of my blanket, wishing his magic was stronger. "And I want to believe them, but there is so much that I don't understand, so much that I don't get. I am scared that everyone I care for is being taken from me."

I looked away from him again, my eyes moving somewhere, anywhere, at the same time that I tried to wade through the tangle of emotions inside of me.

"It's my turn to protect you now, Ilyan. It's my turn to be strong for you. I need you to wake up. I need you to come back. I... I need you." I stopped, trying not to give life to my nightmares; to Cail's taunts.

"I... I don't know how else to say it..." I think I did know how to say it, though. I wanted to say I loved him, however it wasn't the same love as I had for Ryland. It was the love of a friend—of a companion—and saying it would make my nightmares real. I couldn't let that happen.

"Don't die, okay?" I said as I moved to lie beside him, squeezing my body against his unresponsive one. I pulled the fur over me and snuggled into his neck. I knew I shouldn't be here. I knew I should be able to be stronger.

Yet right then I wasn't, and right then I could accept that.

"Goodnight, Ilyan,"

20

" WAKE UP, Silnỳ, you are in the way."

My eyes fluttered open at Thom's gruff voice. I knew at once why he had spoken, too. I was still lying in Ilyan's bunk with my arm draped over his torso. Two nights ago I had awakened uncomfortable with Ilyan's proximity, now I was doing the same to him. Great.

I sat up, my head buzzing a bit at the movement, but Thom wasn't even looking at me. He was already moving blankets, his hands pressed against Ilyan's skin as he checked on him. I pushed a hand against my shoulder, saddened to find the same weak magic flowing through me.

"He's still the same?" I asked as I moved to the foot of the bed. Cramming my body into the corner of the bunk, I tried to keep myself covered with the heavy fur while Thom shook his head and kept working.

My body had that heavy, dizzy feeling it always had when I had stayed away from Ryland too long. I was surprised it wasn't worse given that yesterday's visit had definitely not been long enough to fully rejuvenate me. I leaned my head against the cold stone, letting the cool temperature take away some of the dizziness. I had forgotten how fast and strong these sensations came on. I knew it had been more than a day and that I needed to go see him, but I didn't want to. I traced the tip of my finger along the silver chain and sunk into the stone work.

Having to endure the aftermath of the nightmare on my own had weakened me both emotionally and physically. With Cail gloating over his control of my subconscious, I was afraid of what I would find if I went into the Tŏuha. What once had been an amazing place for Ryland and me to share had become just another potential torture chamber.

I might be able to go in and come out in a matter of minutes, however I knew it wouldn't be enough. Or worse, what if something happened while I was in there? Ilyan wouldn't be here to pick up the pieces. I could already tell Thom wasn't the type to be willing to do that.

"Are you okay?" I looked up from my daydreams to see Ilyan was covered again, and Thom was staring me down.

"Yeah, I'm tired; that's all." Thom narrowed his eyes at me for a moment.

"Here," he said, pulling over one of the large, ceramic mugs from last night. "Dramin left this for you."

I took the mug from Thom and smelled the Black Water. It almost smelled appealing to me now.

"Thank you," I said before draining the mug in one large gulp. The Black Water moved into me and I began to feel better. I still felt the body aches from my separation with Ryland, but they weren't as sharp and my head didn't feel as fuzzy. I sighed and leaned against the rock wall.

"Where is Dramin?" I asked, wishing I already had more of the Black Water.

"Shopping," Thom said, although I could tell it was

more than that. He leaned forward a bit and looked into the mug, his eyebrows rising to see the contents gone. "Does that stuff taste good?"

"Yes," I said, placing the mug on the shelf above Ilyan's feet. "It smells a bit funny at first, but the taste is nice."

"Well, I am glad it didn't kill you," Thom said gruffly before leaning against the side of Ilyan's bunk. He narrowed his eyes at me and I jumped a bit. I knew that look; I had grown up with that look. It was the look every kid had given me when they were trying to figure out what was wrong with me.

"What?" I asked, feeling uncomfortable.

"You are very interesting," he said. I waited a moment for him to elaborate, yet he never did.

"I'm aware of that," I said before turning away.

"You're nothing like your father. There is a lot of bitterness in your heart."

"Well that's what happens when said father abandons you, I suppose."

"Not all fathers abandon their children on purpose. Your father didn't abandon you," Thom spat, causing me to jump a bit at his bitterness.

"Well he certainly wasn't there." My hackles were up, his tone setting me on the defensive.

"Sain only left you to do what was best for you."

"Oh, how would you know? You're not a dad."

"Not anymore." Thom whispered.

He didn't need to say any more. I could see the pain in his eyes, and I immediately hurt for him.

I kept my glance off to the side, staring into the nothingness of the cavern, not wanting to make eye contact, while I contemplated where to go, or what to do. Ultimately, though I didn't want to be anywhere else. I didn't want to leave Ilyan's side.

"Did you know I lived with my father for two hundred years before I left?" I heard his feet shuffle, but I still didn't look at him.

"No."

"Yes, I had seen many of my siblings go off and fight against Ilyan, leave to fight against my father, go back and forth until they would find their death, however I stayed on my father's side. I trusted him beyond anything. I didn't see a reason not to. I *knew* he was right. He was my father."

I looked toward Thom, surprised to hear him say so much.

"Your father showed me how wrong I was. That's why I helped him escape. I would have never pegged Ilyan for a good guy until the day I met him. I watched him heal Sain without question, and then he held me like a brother..."

He stopped for a moment, his eyes lingering on Ilyan. I followed his gaze, almost hoping Ilyan would be sitting there listening.

"I'm glad to return the favor," Thom said, more to Ilyan than to me before placing his palm against Ilyan's forehead.

"He's going to be alright then?"

"You can check for yourself, Silnỳ." He waved his hand over Ilyan's body as if in invitation, but I shook my head no.

"I don't know how." Thom's face was pure shock for a moment before turning into an awkward looking smile. "We mostly focused on defensive magic." I answered his unasked question, yet Thom didn't seem to notice.

"Place your hand on his cheek then," Thom said as he gestured over Ilyan's body.

"Excuse me?" I didn't know what Thom was getting at,

but I didn't want to learn healing magic on Ilyan. I shook my head, hoping to get my point across.

"Most powerful, my ass." Thom grumbled as he roughly pulled my hand out of the warm fur I had curled myself into. When he stretched my hand away from me to rest on Ilyan's cheek, I was forced to shuffle forward to keep from falling on top of Ilyan.

"You do know something about human anatomy, correct?"

"Yes," I raised an eyebrow at him, worried about where this was going.

"Good. Now, push your magic into him." This I had done before, so I obeyed while looking to Thom for instruction about what to do next.

"Think of his body as a body."

I stared at him.

"You know," he continued, irritated, "with a heart, and lungs, and bones, and muscles. Now use your magic to find his heart."

I looked at Thom for a minute, waiting for him to elaborate without actually expecting him to. When it became obvious that he wasn't going to help me anymore, I pushed my magic through Ilyan, trying to focus on where it was in relationship to his body. I felt my magic flow through him slowly, nothing really defined. Discouraged, I pulled my magic away. I could make giant gashes in rock walls after the Black Water, but healing was probably not going to happen. I began to shake my head and move away, but Thom's hands moved over mine, keeping them in place.

"You have to actually try, Silnỳ." His voice was stern. I looked away from him, closing my eyes in an attempt to focus.

Okay, so in Thom's world I hadn't been trying. I cinched

my eyes together tighter and tried harder. I pushed more magic into Ilyan and let it flow right to the spot where I hoped his heart would be. It took me a minute, but before long, I could feel it. My eyes snapped open to meet Thom's. His eyes shining at my obvious success even though he did not smile in encouragement.

"Now, close your eyes," he instructed, "and use the interior eye of your magic to see his heart."

My lip curled in disgust, this was pushing an envelope. Why would I want to see a beating heart inside someone's body? My stomach turned at the thought.

"Gross."

"You will not actually see his heart, Silnỳ. Have you ever seen the Matrix?" Of course I had seen the Matrix, but the fact that he had seen it was a little odd.

"I'm going to see computer code?"

"No," Thom said, his patience wavering. "It's different for everyone, but it won't be a real picture."

I looked at him for a moment longer before closing my eyes to focus. Slowly, the red mass of what I could only assume to be Ilyan's heart came into view. It looked smooth and abstract, like a water color painting.

"Now, find the problem." Thom's gruff voice broke through the silence.

"What will that look like?"

"It's different for everyone."

Great. Why was he so little help? I searched with my mind's sight before seeing a dark spot near the base. It wasn't as smooth as the rest of Ilyan's heart and looked like a burn. I opened my eyes, surprised when the image of Ilyan's heart stayed before my eyes for a moment longer.

"What's the black part?" I asked, surprised when Thom's eyebrow raised.

"That's the whole of our problem. When you arrived, his whole heart was covered, the exhaustion from your journey had burned him from the inside. I have taken away most of it. Once the last of it is gone, he should awaken within a few days." Thom moved a bit closer, his hand resting on Ilyan's forehead again.

"What can I do to help?" I felt more of my magic flow into Ilyan of its own accord.

"You can do nothing. In fact, it would probably be best if you didn't let so much of your magic mingle with his." Thom said harshly and I withdrew quickly, moving my hand away from Ilyan's cheek.

"Why?"

"Well, first, because of what you are, and second, because of who you are."

I sat up straight at Thom's words, my head almost hitting the shelf inside of Ilyan's bunk. I wasn't sure if I should be offended or hurt at Thom's words, but my pride bristled a bit.

"What do you mean what I am?" I spat, the term made it sound like I was poison.

"You are one of the Drak, Silný. The Drak do not normally heal those with different magic." I glowered at him for a minute, hating the limit that my supposed new species was placing on me.

"But, I am also one of The Chosen."

"Yes."

"So I should be able to heal others as well," I countered softly.

Thom looked away from me for a minute before coming to a decision. He placed the palm of his hand against the stone wall and pulled down, pressing hard against the surface. He brought his palm back to me, revealing a few shallow scrapes, one of them bleeding.

"Then heal me, and let us see if it works or not."

Reluctantly, I placed my hand underneath Thom's. I didn't like physical contact with other people, especially with people I barely knew, but Thom seemed to be the same way, so I tried to swallow my pride.

I pushed my magic into him, surprised at how quickly it flowed. I closed my eyes and searched through his hand for the cuts, smiling when I found the dark black amongst the pink watercolor strokes of his skin.

"Now what do I do?" I kept my eyes closed, not wanting to lose the shapes and colors of his injury.

"Think about how your body heals you, about how you can feel it knit your skin back together, and about how it straightens and repairs. Use your mind and your magic to do the same to me."

I nodded once even though I didn't quite understand what he was saying. I tried to focus on the colors and my magic that moved so close to them within Thom's body. He had said to think about how my magic knit me back together. That seemed to make the most sense so I focused on it, thrusting my magic into the black mass of his injury. I pushed the skin back together, laying it end to end before driving even more in the hopes of eliminating the wound all together.

"Incredible." I opened my eyes to Thom's hand, shocked to see that not only had the blood flow stopped, but the skin had completely put itself back together. I couldn't even see so much as a scar.

"I have never seen that work quite so fast before," his voice was awed, yet for once I wasn't uncomfortable. Instead, I felt a bit proud.

I couldn't help smiling at my accomplishment and how quickly I had managed it. Although it was still weird to be referred to as a Drak, the Black Water had undeniably unlocked my ability.

"Now I can heal Ilyan?" I asked, leaning away from Thom to sit next to Ilyan.

"No, Silnÿ, it is still not a good idea." I froze at his words, his tone making it obvious what this was about.

"It's because of what my dad saw, isn't it? Because of who I am?"

"Yes."

"And, you're not going to...."

"No," Thom cut me off. "Dramin will decide when you are ready."

I leaned over Ilyan, letting my eyes linger on his dull blue lids before moving back to sit by his feet. As I crawled back across the bunk my body began to ache again. I shoved the pain to the back of my mind, determined not to go inside the Tÿuha yet.

"Do you normally sleep with Ilyan? We have some double bunks if it will help you to sleep better—"

"No!" I interrupted him loudly, Thom stopped midsentence his face tensing in confusion. "I don't sleep with Ilyan. I kind of sleep next to him for half the night after... after..." I let my words drift away as Thom continued to glare, aware that I had begun to ramble. I turned away from him, ashamed.

"After your nightmares," he finished for me. I turned toward him, my head nodding in agreement. I wasn't sure what made me open up even a little bit to him—maybe it was the fact that he had heard my screams—but it made me uncomfortable.

"Do they happen every night?"

"Yes," I whispered. I didn't know how much I wanted to tell him.

"Dramin told me. He said that you would wail, but the only one who was to help you was Ilyan." I looked away from him. I was grateful neither of them had tried to help. I had fought Ilyan when he had first tried, and my exertion against him had made it worse. Yet the only one who could help me was asleep for at least a few more days.

"And there is nothing you can do to stop them, a tea maybe?"

I looked to him and shook my head. Ilyan had tried everything in the beginning, but nothing had worked. Now I understood why.

"Cail controls my dreams." I said, my eyes looking back to Ilyan again. I wiggled my feet a bit until they were right up against his leg. I needed the reminder that I wasn't facing this alone.

"Cail?" His voice was scared, and I didn't blame him. He had every right to be. I was.

"Yes, he uses them to taunt me, to hurt me..." I rested my head on my knees, my eyes unfocused on the blanket in front of me. "I'm scared to go to sleep anymore, and now, without Ilyan..." I exhaled and stopped, not wanting to elaborate anymore.

Thom didn't say anything. He looked at me intently before pulling up a tall chair and sitting next to me. He didn't get too close. He didn't reach out to touch me. He just sat, looking around for a few minutes. Surprisingly, it wasn't uncomfortable. We both sat thinking about our own vices for a moment before Thom spoke.

"Have you ever seen the statue of the Greek Titan, Atlas, who holds the world upon his shoulders?"

I looked to him, confused as to where this could be

coming from; his comment was so out of the blue. I raced the story of Atlas through my brain. I knew it, however I couldn't find any similarities with what we had been talking about.

"Yes," I said.

"My father had that statue in our home when I was with him. He used to say that it was there to remind him of the best way to defeat your enemies. Those who hold the world can do nothing except struggle and cry."

"So you're saying that Edmund is doing this to weaken me, to keep me from whatever it is I am supposed to do?"

"Exactly." Thom's eyes shone, and I groaned as I rested my head on my shoulders.

"Well, he is succeeding," I mumbled to myself.

"If you think like that, then you have already lost." I snapped my head up to Thom and fought the urge to yell at him.

"He has taken everything from me, Thom; forced me into this life with its pain, and fear, and secrets. And I still don't even know all of it yet, in case you have forgotten." I was a little bitter, and I knew it, especially since Thom was trying to give me words of wisdom.

"You need to find someone to help you carry your load. That is where Atlas failed. He tried to trick others into taking it from him instead of asking for help."

"How can I lighten my load if he has taken away everything that's ever been a support to me?" I had calmed down, but I still felt my anger surge.

"You are speaking of your friends? Of your father?" Thom leaned forward in his chair.

"Yes."

"What of Ilyan?" Thom asked.

"He's kind of busy at the moment, isn't he?" I said.

"You never know who may be supporting you from behind the scenes, Silnỳ. Even though Ilyan is ill, he is still with you. He has the strength to carry the weight of the world for you, and he has that strength for a reason. When he wakes, he will be there to help you hold it, and hold you up along with it if needed."

Ilyan had told me several times he would be there to support me, to help me and lighten my load. I knew he would be. I knew I could trust him. I just wasn't certain I wanted him to. Ryland's riddle was still too fresh in my mind.

"I think I see what you're saying," I admitted. Thom said nothing, he only grabbed his chair, and walked away.

I slid off Ilyan's bed, my body aching at the movement, then moved to Ilyan's head and smoothed his long hair. Thom had said that Ilyan had his strength for a reason. I couldn't rely on him carrying all of my worries for me—I didn't want him to—but I didn't know if I had enough strength of my own. I didn't know which I wanted to be; strong on my own; or strong enough to ask for help.

I didn't know which I was supposed to be.

21

_____

I CLUTCHED the mug of Black Water and pressed it to my lips, a soft groan escaping as I felt the liquid flow through me. I tried to ignore Dramin's happy chuckle from behind me and let myself enjoy the way the Black Water made me feel. It was better than a cheeseburger.

Dramin had been supplying me with the drink since he had returned earlier that morning. Although it had been weird to only eat a small amount of rice and vegetables for lunch, my body didn't want food anymore, and I didn't care. The Black Water was all I needed. Dramin had been right.

"Do you need more?" Dramin asked.

"Not yet. It's good this is just water, Uncle, or I might be worried I was turning into an alcoholic." Dramin chuckled, and I heard Thom grunt loudly from beside me.

"Poisonous water," Thom amended, which only caused Dramin to chuckle more.

A grunt and a chuckle. I couldn't think of anything else that could explain the two men better.

"Well, if you don't need more," Dramin said, "let's get back to work, shall we?"

I took another drink and let the warm energy pulse through me. So far it was taking away all my aches from having avoided the Tòuha today. I enjoyed the feeling, but what I loved even more was that the Water had fully unlocked my abilities.

I had sparred with Thom this morning, and even through my sore and rigid body, I was able to beat him in three matches. I could tell he wasn't as powerful as Ilyan, yet I had never beaten anyone before—without cheating of course. It made me excited while it only made Thom surly.

I sat on the floor of the large training hall, a giant fur cloak draped around me. It was there not only for warmth, but also for some semblance of decency. I hadn't had a chance to change clothes, or even take a shower, since before the fight in Santa Fe. So, thanks to last night's nightmares and today's sparing matches, I was sweatier and more ratty than usual. I had tried to smooth my hair, but had given up when I realized I was fighting a losing battle. I would have to look a little bit derelict until I located a shower and a clothing store; both of which I had been informed the cave did not have.

Dramin stood about ten feet behind me and Thom slightly to my left. Even with my eyes closed I could see them. I had opened up my internal vision to include the whole room, much to Thom's dismay. He could only manage about a ten foot circle, and even though I could see the whole cave, I was sure I could manage even more if I focused.

"Ready," I called out. Thom stretched his fingers before he began to shoot objects away from him; real, magical, and conjured. I caught the real objects with my mind, only to set them down by the entrance where they had begun. I shattered the conjured objects with a pulse from my own magic, and intercepted each of the magical attacks with either an attack of my own or a wave of negative movement.

The room exploded with color and action for the brief time it took me to do away with each of Thom's potential weapons. The ribbons of color snaked down to the ground last, only to fall in pools of glittering power before they disappeared back into the stone. Through it all, I didn't move my hands an inch.

"Six seconds!" Dramin called out. I saw him running toward me, so I opened my eyes, stiffly moving to my feet again.

"How many was that, Thom?" Dramin asked as he came up beside me, his eyes eager.

"Twenty real, ten conjured, and five attacks." He didn't seem too pleased, although after our talk this morning I was realizing that Thom was not one to show his emotions in public.

"You probably could have gone faster," Thom grunted.

"Thanks for the vote of confidence, Thom," I said a bit sarcastically. Thom only rolled his eyes and moved away from us.

"Do you think you could do more, Silnỳ?" Dramin asked as he bounced on his heels. He took my hand in his, but I pulled away, fighting the urge to ask him not to touch me. He looked a little shocked, so I grabbed my mug, drained it, and shoved it into his chest.

"More items or more magic?" I asked, not understanding.

"Both," Dramin's voice was so eager, he reminded me of a five year old being offered ice cream.

"Well," Thom yelled from across the large space, "if you don't need me, I am going to go check on our invalid."

"Thom!" Dramin yelled after him, but Thom only waved his hand in farewell.

"Thom!" Dramin tried again, but Thom didn't even turn to look back. "You great lazy oaf! Get back here!" Dramin yelled loudly, but Thom had already disappeared back into the main room where I was sure he was going to take a nap by the fire.

I smiled a bit and Dramin turned to me, joining in before returning my now filled mug to me.

"Well, what are we going to do now?" I asked, before taking a nice long sip of the Black Water. Yep, I was definitely becoming addicted.

"How about we test your sight?" I looked at him out of the corner of my eye. I knew what he was talking about, and honestly, I wasn't interested.

"It's twenty-twenty thank you very much." I spoke as brightly as I could before smiling and strolling away, following after Thom. I may have Drak blood, but I didn't want to see any of the things the sight could give me.

"What's twenty-twenty?" Dramin asked obviously not getting the reference.

"My vision." I provided, but Dramin sighed, his regular smile disappearing a bit.

"I am talking about your sight, Silný. Not your vision. There is no reason to be scared."

I froze, but didn't turn to face him. Instead, I looked up to the large gash I had placed in the stone dome the day before, not wanting to give him an answer. Of course I was scared. I had no interest in reliving my past, let alone seeing the future.

"There is no reason to be scared," Dramin repeated. "This is simply another step in the process. Without using your sight, you will not be able to summon the Black Water for yourself, and I will not be able to show you the sight that told of your true purpose."

"That's not a problem," I said, turning toward him. "You can come with me and Ilyan, and you can tell me what was said rather than show me." I smiled brightly, happy when he chuckled. My thoughts of compromise were dashed when he began to shake his head.

"I cannot follow you all around the earth while you fight Edmund, Silnỳ. I am also not going to travel with you on your honeymoon, or always be there when you are injured."

"Honeymoon?" I said, interrupting him. "Who said anything about a honeymoon?"

"You must call the Black Water on your own," Dramin continued as if I hadn't said anything. "And as for the sight, I have to show you."

"You don't *have* to," I countered, folding my arms and bringing the fur cloak closer around me. I still missed my hoodie.

"I do. I have seen it, Silnỳ."

I knew he had me there, and I hated it. I needed the Black Water. I could already feel my body calling for more, and as much as I didn't want to admit it, I needed to know what had been foreseen about me. I turned toward him, keeping the cloak around me tightly.

"Fine," I said grumpily. "Show me the way."

Dramin bounced once before turning and walking toward the large opening he had shown me the day before. I followed after him, my body hurting the more I moved. I took a drink as I walked, the Black Water taking away the ache for the moment.

I followed Dramin into the adjoining chamber, this one different from the others. It was the same dome shape, the same raised stone work circling the walls, but there were no bunks or benches lining the platform. Instead, there were odd rune shapes carved into the stone and a portion of the circular room was sunken, however you wouldn't be able to tell without looking closely. The sunken area was filled right to the top with an unmoving liquid that I could easily recognize as Black Water. Somehow, even though the water did not move, the room was filled with the rippling reflections of waves on a pond.

The rippling light hit against the far wall revealing more carvings, more runes, and delicate glass work that revealed the outside where the blizzard still reigned. The light of day that managed to make it through the blizzard filtered into the space, mixing with the magical shimmers.

I stepped around Dramin to walk around the large cavern. The light ran over my face as I traced the rough carvings with my fingers. I didn't feel any peaks of my magic or strong sensations of what was going to happen, but I felt comfortable. The terror at seeing into the past or future had ebbed, leaving me with a jittery excitement.

I continued to walk, letting my fingers trace the shapes. I had all but forgotten that Dramin still stood behind me until he spoke.

"The Hall of Sight. This was the last one built and one of the only ones that remain. They can only be built in select places on earth where the magic seeps to the surface, the Black Water bubbling up for our use. While we can use the Black Water at any time because the Water resides within us, the larger, more important queries always require our sight to be used within this hall, and many times, more than one Drak must be present."

I barely heard him. My blood seemed to hum the more I was in the room, reminding me of when Ilyan had centered my magic.

"It has been many years since I have used my sight beyond the mundane. I miss the power very much. Someday perhaps I will be able to see with others again."

"Is it hard to do?" I asked, the question more to myself than to Dramin, my nerves having almost left.

"It is as easy as breathing, Silnỳ. The magic already resides inside of you. Once you have unlocked the door, the rest of your abilities will open to you." He said reverently. I could feel his excitement at what was about to happen.

"What abilities?" I turned from the runes to face him. He stood right by the water, the still surface reflecting nothing.

"The ability to recall previous sights, provide yourself with the nourishment you need, and most importantly, to use your sight at will. After you experience your first sight, the Black Water will become a part of you."

I swallowed heavily, my feet moving me toward him. He held his hand out to me, but I didn't take it. I stood next to him, looking into the smooth reflection-less surface of the water. I could feel my body pull me toward the surface, willing me to join it somehow. I took a step forward before moving back again, fighting my need to touch the water.

"Does it hurt?" It was a child's question, but I needed to know. My life had been full of so much pain; so much loss.

"No, child, but your first sight will be the strongest you will ever experience on your own." I looked toward the water, my uneasiness growing again.

"As the water moves into you and becomes part of you, you will see the past, present, and future for yourself and those you hold in your heart," Dramin whispered. "It will come in a web, and likely nothing will make sense. It is only after, when you learn to recall your sight, that you will be able to make sense of the confusion."

My desire for the water was thrumming steadily in my

veins, calling me to it. I fought the strong craving to jump in and shuffled my feet.

"Are you ready?" he asked, his eager anticipation bleeding through him.

"Yes." My answer was instant. I still could not take my eyes off of the water.

"Then place your hand in the water."

"That's it?" I asked, turning toward him for the first time.

"Yes. For those who are not among the Drak the water will burn their skin, but to touch the water is essential for the Drak."

"Will it burn me?" I asked, even though my desire overpowered my worry.

"No, Silnỳ. You are one of the Drak. Just place your hand in the water."

I looked away from him, unable to ignore the pull from my blood any longer. The prickling of my skin grew as I fell to my knees, the heavy fur cloak falling off of my shoulders. I reached toward the water, my hand hesitating for a moment before I pushed it beyond the surface.

I had barely registered the warmth of the water before my vision faded to black. A bright red ember, like the flame that I had seen in Dramin's eyes that first day, followed the darkness almost instantly. My head felt light and airy, as though it had been inflated with helium and was trying to fly away. None of it was uncomfortable, however; it felt natural.

I looked into the burning red color for a moment before my sight changed again. Shadows twirled and danced before me as an image of an infant being placed into my mother's arms began to form. The vision changed to a flash of blonde hair running down a hall I had never seen before as screams filled the air. The hair stayed before me for a second before it changed to a flash of me crying in my bed as my parents fought. A moment later, a vision of Edmund choking Talon against a wall came into view, Talon's face battered.

"Give me what I need, Talon," Edmund's voice rang out like an echo in my ears.

"You better make it look good, Edmund." Talon let out a deep chuckle.

I saw Edmund's hand move back in preparation for a strike before the colors washed away to be replaced by me running through the trees. Ryland's hand hovered over the ground as he formed a perfect ring of Pansies, which disappeared as soon as they grew, changing into Wyn and my father running through a dark cave, a man falling to the ground in agony before them.

"Was that really necessary?" my father asked, his voice tense and scared.

"He would have done the same to us," Wyn hissed without looking away from the body in front of her. "Don't like it, don't travel with a trained killer."

"As long as that assassin doesn't turn her skill on me, I think I will be happy." Sain laughed humorously as the vision changed to Ryland as a child, speaking to his mother through the bars of a cell, their hands intertwined.

"Don't cry, my little love, you are stronger than your father will ever be." Her voice echoed around the space as Ryland cried.

The sight changed again to Cail crying in the dark and Wyn wrapping her arms around him in an attempt to comfort him, a ripped t-shirt hanging off her shoulders. A flash of fire met my eyes before it faded again to me crying on a bed, older this time, screaming for help as Ryland moved toward me, his eyes gentle and blue.

"Jos?" Ryland said softly, "I'm not going to hurt you, honey."

"Go... Away!"

A quick change showed me an image of Ilyan running down a stone hallway, his hair short and dark with his face covered in blood and bruises. My heart ached for a reason I couldn't place. My head began to pound as the speed of my sight increased, some images barely registering, the voices beginning to overrun one another.

"Take him and use him for your benefit; maybe that will give you the upper hand." Edmund said as he spoke to someone I couldn't see, his hands pushing Ryland's weak body away from him.

It flashed again to Cail lying in a chair, Edmund and Timothy around him. "Make her break the bond, Cail, then the sight can never be."

The colors washed away to something else before Edmund had even finished speaking.

"If you touch her, father, I swear I will end you," Ryland was firm, but Edmund only laughed before they continued to spar in the basement of their estate.

The image of them sparring changed to Ilyan holding me against a wall, a building burning around us, his hand soft against my face. I could just make out tears flowing down each of our cheeks before it changed again to Ilyan walking into a large stone hall that I had never seen before, his hair short against his head. It then flashed one last time, a man's scream echoing in my head as it followed me back into reality.

My knees ached from being pressed against the cold stone floor while I panted heavily as the vision left me, everything that I saw combined into a jumbled mass. One thing stood out, though. One thing was crystal clear to me.

I felt Dramin's arms come around me as he replaced the cloak, my breathing slowing down.

"It's okay, Silnỳ," he said softly. "It's over now."

I continued to gasp as I reached for Dramin, holding onto his wrist tightly.

"Dramin," I gasped, "I saw your death... I saw..."

I felt my head go light, my vision blacking out as the sight showed me his death again. He moved in front of what I could only guess was Ryland, a bright light shattering into the space around him. As I watched the scene unfold, my voice spoke in an oddly dark and monotone way. I should have been scared, but my heart rate never increased, my mind accepting my new power.

"Betrayed by your brother in the last hour of light, you will save one who has lost more than you. It will come at the dusk of a powerful death before the blood red moon will herald a birth."

My voice faded out as my vision returned, Dramin's surprised face coming back into focus.

"Uncle?" I asked, alarmed at having seen his death.

I expected him to be more concerned, for panic to spill out, but instead he only nodded.

"I know."

22

I CLUTCHED the mug between my hands and sat back in the large, squishy armchair, letting my magic pull the fur tighter around me. I kept the fire strong, the eerie, orange light casting odd shadows around the empty chamber. The only noise was the howl of the wind from the long tunnel that led to the blizzard outside, the sound deep and relaxing as I sunk further into the chair, willing myself to stay awake.

Dramin had carried me back to the main hall after my first sight because I had been too weak to get there on my own. He had draped me in blankets and talked on and on about the significance of what had just happened, and what I might have seen. He had taught me to use recall for my sight, but I had been so weak that I hadn't been able to sustain it for long.

He told me about the subtle changes for sights of the past; the dirty quality of the image as well as the tinny distanced voice of the subjects. My tired body was unable to remember much, though.

The image of Wyn comforting her Brother upset me the

most. That was obviously not a sight from the past, and it made me anxious to know what it could mean.

Dramin had tried for about an hour to get me to use my recall to view the sight again and in further detail, or to even be able to call the Black Water myself, but it was no use. I was too tired and my mind too unfocused.

I knew why. I had a feeling that Dramin also knew, but I wasn't going to say it out loud, nor was I going to visit the Tŏuha to remedy the matter.

I was scared.

I was as scared of the Tŏuha as I had become of my nightmares. I looked toward Ilyan against my better judgment. I needed to be strong, and pining over the current disposition of my Protector wasn't going to help me much.

My Protector. It was odd to think of all that the words had come to mean to me; all that he had come to mean to me.

I wiped the thoughts from my head, not wanting to dwell on something that would ultimately lead me to replay my nightmares and riddles. I didn't want to think about it.

I sighed, knowing I couldn't avoid sleep any longer, my eyes had already started drooping. I drained the last of the cup and walked to my bunk, my body groaning and my head spinning.

My feet had barely carried me across the space before I collapsed on my bunk, the impact ricocheting through my body.

"Be strong, Joclyn," I moaned to myself, the sound echoing around the tiny alcove my bed sat in. A few days ago I had been desperate for my own bed, and now I wanted anything but.

I heaved myself under the blankets and closed my eyes.

It only took a matter of seconds for sleep to overtake me and the dream to come.

I stood in the middle of the clearing as always, the eerie branches stretching and swaying around me.

"We've been waiting for you, Joclyn." Cail's voice was loud and right behind me. I fought the desire to spin around to face him, instead keeping my body still and stubbornly looking toward the trees.

"I take it you thought that if you stayed awake you could avoid me?" He ran his hand down my hair, the weight pulling at the long strands.

"It was worth a shot," I said a little too honestly. I attempted to keep my voice light and airy, but my fear was too severe.

Instead of replying, however, Cail laughed. The sound bounced around the clearing and reverberated inside my head.

"Oh, Joclyn. Sweet Joclyn." His words were endearments, but his voice was like ice. It ran up my spine and sent an unpleasant shiver through my shoulders.

He had come around to face me, his dark eyes appearing even darker in the dim light as the red of his hair disappeared in the night. He looked at me with his wicked smile, his hand coming to wrap tightly around my wrist. I felt pain shoot up my arm as he squeezed.

"You should know better than that," he said as he increased the pressure then yanked my arm and pulled my torso into him. "You can't escape me, and you can't beat me." He laughed like it was a joke. I pulled my arm away sharply, my magic boiling through me.

"You wanna bet?" I spat. I took one step back before he could stop me, turning around to hit my hands hard against his chest. Even though my magic surged with the contact, the dream dampened it, making my power useless.

Cail looked shocked as he stumbled back to slam roughly into one of the trees. When he had steadied himself, I prepared myself for his attack, but he wasn't angry. He wasn't going to fight back. He simply laughed.

"It's a good thing your magic doesn't work here. With a temper like that, you'd be an awful lot of fun. I sure hope you don't throw magic at Ilyan, like that." He clicked his tongue at me while he walked closer, his strut making my stomach flip in disgust. "There he is, sleeping next to the one he loves, and you go ahead and kill him!"

Cail laughed with all the humor he could muster and my stomach tensed uncomfortably, my eyes narrowing.

"Ilyan doesn't love..." I began to say confidently, but Cail clamped his hand over my mouth and pinned me to his side, his eyes flashing dangerously.

"Don't say it. You're going to take away all of my fun, and we haven't even gotten to our little game yet."

My insides flipped at the mention of yet another game. I tried to get away from Cail's firm grip, but he increased his hold, his hand turning into a claw against my face.

"You see those trees?" He jutted his chin toward the line of trees directly in front of us. I followed his line of sight, my eyes widening to see two bright-red trunks creating a doorway into the shadowy forest behind them.

"I have hidden two very different things in there, and I am going to send you to find them." I tried to fight him, but his hold continued to increase, his grip plastering me against his body.

"One of them will kill you the second you are seen and the other will rejoice in your arrival. If you find the one who would kill you first, then the game is over and you will wake up. If you find the other, you have until I find you before your time here is over. So either way, it ends in your death." He spoke lightly, my stomach dropping at what he had implied. I couldn't take my eyes off of those trees.

"I am going to give you a ten minute head start." I swallowed hard as Cail released me from his grip, my body instinctively taking a step away from him.

"Go." He said the word behind me and I didn't wait. One of the surprises had to be Ryland. I ran into the trees, my heart racing at the thought of seeing him.

The forest was quiet, the silence making the dying landscape even more terrifying. Desperate to get away from Cail, I ran for a while before realizing that my hurried steps would give away my approach.

Magic may not work as a defensive tactic here, but it could work to my benefit. At least I hoped it would. I took off into the sky, thankful when my magic supported me as I sped through the trees.

It wasn't long before I caught a glimpse of something dark ahead of me and I slowed to a stop, my heart hammering in my chest as I hovered directly above Edmund. He stood tall in the middle of the forest, his dark curls slicked back. He didn't move, nor did his eyes waver from the direction I had just come from.

Seeing him stand there, I knew he was one of the surprises I was supposed to find. Cail had sent me into the trees on a direct route to Edmund, practically a guarantee that he would be able to torture me and send me back. I didn't doubt that Ryland would be here as well, but he would be hidden.

I found him about a hundred feet behind Edmund, his body limp and leaning against a tree. I dropped from the air, barely able to catch myself before I hit the ground.

I stood, coming to face Ryland. I wasn't even sure it was really him. This was a dream and not a Tòuha after all, but I couldn't ignore the fire that was steadily moving through my veins.

I moved toward him, stopping at the bright-blue eyes that met mine. He smiled at seeing me there, his hand coming up to rest against my face as I knelt beside him, his thumb lightly tracing my bottom lip.

"Is it you?" I whispered. I knew I should bask in the fact that he was here, but I had to know. I was terrified that this was just another trap.

"I don't know," Ryland's voice was forced, his tones strained. My heart dropped as I fought the need to run away.

"I think it is," he continued. "I remember a lot, but not everything. My brain's messed up. I..." He stopped as his eyes met mine, the blue looking deeply into me.

"It's okay." I said. I placed my hand on top of his, leaning into his touch. I didn't feel my magic pulling toward him as it always did, but part of me didn't care if it was him or just another way to torture me. I wanted to listen to the little voice that was begging me to give in to the simple joy that we were together. That was the part that won.

"I love you, Ry," I whispered. "I miss you so much."

"I miss you too, sweetheart." His weak body reached up and pulled me into him, his arms draping over me limply without the strength to hold me to him.

"I'm going to save you." I made my voice as powerful as I could make it. I wasn't foolish enough to tell him how strong I was now or where I was hiding, but I could tell him that I was going to save him.

"I wish you wouldn't." I sat up abruptly at his words, his weak arms falling to the side.

"What?"

"I don't think you can, Jos, and I don't want you to get hurt. Please, stay with Ilyan. He will protect you."

It was the rebuttal he had given me since the beginning, but it broke my heart to hear him say it again. Both of us had been through hell. If there was a chance I could save him, I was going to take it. Especially since Edmund and Cail were using him to manipulate and torture me every chance they got.

"I can save you. I can't let them hurt you anymore."

"While they what? Give you beautiful dreams and magical fantasies in our Tŏuha? I won't let you go through it anymore. I'm going to break the Zĕlství. I am going to break our bond." Ryland's voice had gained some confidence, but his body was weak. I didn't know what was involved in breaking a connection, but I knew he didn't have the strength to do it.

"No, Ryland, I can't let you do that. If you do, you will kill me. Do you understand that?" He balked a bit at my words before sitting himself up, his hand reaching forward to grab mine.

"Not if we do it at the same time."

"No." I pulled my hand away, disgusted with what he was saying.

"It's the only way to save you, Joclyn. I have to do it. They are going to keep torturing you, can't you see?"

I stood up and moved away from him, shuffling my feet into the ground. This couldn't be him. Ryland had sacrificed everything to complete the connection. He would never suggest breaking it.

"No," I said. "This isn't you, Ry. This isn't..."

"Besides," Ryland interrupted me, his voice even stronger than before. "It probably won't even hurt you. You don't truly love me anymore. If I break the connection, it won't even affect you."

"What are you saying?" My voice was barely even above a whisper. "You can't be... Ryland!" I dropped to my knees feeling pain so strong I couldn't breathe. "Don't say that. I do love you. Why else would I have gone through all of this to get you back?"

Ryland stopped my rant as he pulled me against him, his arms gaining strength as he pressed his lips into my hair, kissing me softly. I moved at his touch, desperate to feel his lips against mine at least one more time. He looked at me right before he kissed me, seeming to decide if I wanted him to or not. I waited, my breath caught in my chest for the moment before our lips met.

This was not a Tŏuha, it was only a dream. There was no electric connection, yet my heart still stuttered with the feeling of ecstasy that washed through me. I clenched my hand around his shirt, pulling him closer to me, and inhaled deeply as his tongue wiped against my lower lip, the sensation strong and desirable. I groaned and leaned into him further. My body was begging him to deepen the kiss, but instead of answering my need, he pulled away, his eyes boring into me.

"It's okay if you don't love me anymore, Jos. I don't blame you. Our connection has done nothing except cause you pain and misery."

My jaw dropped at his words. Hadn't I just proved that I still did? The pain returned as the fears I had been hiding for the past few days were spoken aloud by someone who was supposed to love me no matter what. But, no. He didn't love me because he wasn't Ryland.

"No!" I yelled, desperate to counter his words.

"Oh, yes." I froze at the voice.

Edmund snaked his arm around my neck and pulled me against him, his strong arm cutting off my air supply. I gathered my strength and produced a large chain to wrap around him, but the magic turned to smoke in my fingers.

I heard him laugh in my ear as I sputtered, his strong arm causing my vision to pop much faster than I would have expected.

"Watch your mate die, my son," he said, his voice deep. "Oh, no, Joclyn. It doesn't seem like he is too concerned."

I looked to Ryland, gasping out his name with my last breath, but he didn't move. He just sat there, his body too weak to do anything, his eyes dim and unfocused.

I woke up in a start, gasping for breath while the panic at what had happened worked me up into a terrified state. I wasn't screaming as I had been before, this time it was a howling depression. The sounds I made were those of heartbreak.

I cried and called out to Ilyan, to Ryland, to anyone that would help me, but no one came. No one was there. I wasn't sure if I was upset that no one came or glad that I had been ignored. I couldn't have Ilyan or Ryland, and there was no one else I wanted to calm me.

I turned in my bunk, my body calling out in pain as I moved to face Ilyan's bunk where he continued to lay in his dimly lit space, his hair fanning over the edge of his bed. I looked at him until my howls had died down into gentle sobs. I desperately wanted to go to him, but one move of my arm told me how impossible that was. Pain shot through my shoulder and my back, eventually traveling into my head. I gasped through the tears at the new pain.

I was alone. Ryland, if that had really been him, was pushing me away. Wyn was gone. My parents were gone. Ilyan... I was too afraid to think about. I was supposed to be the most powerful of all, destined to do something huge that I didn't even understand. It was as Thom said, I was like Atlas, holding the world on my shoulders, and try as I might, I would never be strong enough.

I stopped; my pity-party halting in its tracks. Atlas. I had missed the whole lesson behind what Thom had tried to tell me. I had been too caught up in my pity—in my desperation—to have fully taken in what he said. Atlas had possessed plenty of strength. He had just been too proud to ask for help when he had needed it. It wasn't strength that I lacked, it was pride that I had too much of.

I didn't need to be strong all the time. I needed to get over my insecurities and start to have faith in someone else to help me through it. I needed to stop hiding silently behind my pain and throw the emotional hoodie away.

I was strong.

I looked at Ilyan. He might be the one who could help me do that. At the very least, he was definitely the one I wanted.

23

I KNEW the moment I sat up the next morning that I was in trouble. My back ached and my head spun, causing me to fall back against the bed with a groan. I couldn't wait any longer. I reached for the chain and pulled the necklace out, letting it rest in my palm.

My life felt like an endless stream of torture. First the nightmares and then the Tòuha. I may not be strong, but I did have help. I looked briefly toward where Ilyan still lay, reminding myself I was not alone before plunging my magic into the necklace and closing my eyes.

I opened them again to the same disgusting kitchen as last time, everything rotting and falling to pieces. I regretted coming here so soon after my last traumatizing nightmare, but I had been given no choice.

The memories this kitchen induced and what the destruction seemed to mean felt like another knife to the heart. If the trend of my last few trips to the Tòuha held true, Ryland would show up and push me out of the space. So I held still, hoping to make my time in here last as long as possible and rejuvenate my body as much as I could.

I couldn't silence that tiny voice in the back of my head that was nagging me to break the connection, though. I closed my eyes and shook my head roughly, opening my eyes again to a very small, very angry Ryland.

"I told you not to come back," he spat, his little voice dripping with hatred.

"You know I can't do that, Ry." I tried to keep my voice level in an attempt to calm him and hopefully lengthen the Tòuha, but I could tell it was a pointless effort.

"I don't care about you anymore!" he yelled before shoving me abruptly. I let him. I didn't know how to fight him, and even if I did, the very idea of fighting to stay in such a terrifying place did not interest me.

I opened my eyes to the carved stone roof of my bunk. The light that was reflecting through the chamber seemed brighter than before, but I knew I couldn't have been gone long considering I hadn't been in the Tòuha for more than a few minutes. I certainly hadn't been gone long enough to repair me completely because everything still felt heavy and painful, just not quite as bad as it had been before.

I clenched the blankets in my hands, reminding myself that a little strength would go a long way.

"Good morning!" Dramin's bright, sing-song voice echoed around me.

I sat up to face him, happy the worst of my aches had disappeared while still wishing that all of them could have left. Dramin stood in front of me with two mugs in his hands. He held one out for me, and I took it gladly, grateful for the Black Water that would take away the last of the pains.

"Thank you, Dramin." I sighed as the water buzzed through me.

"You seem to be doing better today," he said. "How is your mate?"

I attempted to hide my shock at his knowledge, though I wasn't sure I had succeeded. Of course he knew. I shouldn't have been surprised.

"He's fine," I lied, which probably wasn't a good idea, but I didn't know how to explain all that was going on.

"Hmmm." Dramin's comment was obviously to himself, so I chose to ignore him by draining my cup of Black Water.

It flowed through me and I wiggled my toes, relishing the sensation. Dramin leaned over to look inside my cup, chuckling to see it already empty.

"You have the appetite of a child," he said, smiling. "It's quite refreshing."

I smiled back at him, handing over my cup. My body was already calling for more.

"Oh, no," Dramin smiled. "Not anymore, your body is healed. You can do this on your own."

He grabbed my hand and placed it firmly over the top of the mug.

"Think of the water and how you would like to see it; warm, cold, or maybe iced. Now pulse that thought into the cup."

I raised an eyebrow at him, looking more confused than I felt, however he merely continued to laugh at me.

"It's easier than it sounds. It is second nature. Give it a shot." He smiled and I nodded my head at him before closing my eyes.

I followed his instructions to a T and was surprised when my body seemed to respond instinctively. I felt warmth fill my hand for a moment before opening my eyes to look at the cup, the steaming liquid filling it right to the rim.

"Good job! Now, if you will go into your Tǒuha every day, you will continue to have the energy to sustain yourself." Dramin took a drink right after he spoke, his eyes digging into me from over his mug. I felt a blush rise to my cheeks then lowered my mug.

"How *did* you know?" I asked softly before taking another sip.

"The question is not how I knew, child—for that should be obvious—but, why are you avoiding your mate?"

I couldn't look at Dramin so I chose to look at the thick contents that swirled slightly inside my cup instead. I guess if I had to confide in someone while Ilyan was indisposed, I should. Besides, I had started opening up to Thom, and that had turned out well. I supposed I needed to be more trusting.

"Well, for one, Ryland keeps pushing me out. Two, I am pretty sure Cail is controlling them." I sounded so dejected, I tried not to cringe at the sound of it.

"You mean he is controlling the Tǒuha as well as your dreams?" I had been beginning to think there was nothing that would surprise Dramin, yet I couldn't miss his shocked tone.

"Yes." I was suddenly feeling very cramped in the tight bunk. I slipped off my bed and walked right past him, my mug still clasped between my hands.

I moved to the large chairs that surrounded the fire, trying to avoid looking at Thom who was busy healing Ilyan.

"But how do you know?" Dramin asked.

"Ilyan pieced most of it together, but what you said about Edmund's Štít inside Cail, it kind of fit it all together for me." I sat down in what had become my trademark chair, draping one of the many furs that were piled around the space over my legs.

"But what does he want from you? Does he know—" When Dramin finished abruptly, I lowered the mug from my lips to raise an eyebrow at him in question, but he didn't answer right away.

"Does he know that you are one of the Drak?" He finally finished, his voice oddly distant.

"No, I don't go screaming out random bits of information for them to hear. I am a bit smarter than that." I spat the words out a bit icily, but good grief, someone needed to have faith in me.

"Mostly, Cail enjoys messing with my mind." I tried to keep the tone of the conversation light, but I could already feel the desperation creeping into my own voice. "He finds different ways to torture me. In the dreams he plays little games or makes me relive bad memories. In the Tŏuha he has been telling what is left of Ryland's mind to get rid of me. They are trying to get me to break the Zĕlství."

Dramin dropped his mug to the stone floor in surprise where it promptly shattered. I jumped at the noise, startling even more when I saw his face. For a moment I was worried he was lost in a sight.

"Who has told you this?" Dramin asked, panicked. His jaw was open and his eyes wide, the bright green thankfully still there.

"What?"

"Who asked you to break the connection?" I sunk away from his panic, keeping the mug tight in my grip. I didn't want mine to break.

"Ryland asked me in the dream last night, but I'm not sure it was him. There was something off about him."

Dramin nodded enthusiastically. "And in the Tŏuha?"

"What's left of Ryland's mind in the Tŏuha doesn't know enough, but I can tell someone is trying to break us apart. Ryland told me the man with the dark eyes told him to get rid of me."

"And you're sure he means Cail?" Dramin leaned forward eagerly, his eyes boring into mine.

"Either Cail or the Ryland that they are controlling."

"Or Edmund," Dramin provided, his voice oddly eager which sent a chill up my spine.

I nodded, not wanting to give him an answer. I emptied my cup and refilled it, hoping that Dramin's excitement would leave him.

"Are you going tell Ilyan of this?"

I glanced toward Ilyan's bunk at Dramin's words. Thom had disappeared somewhere, and my heart dropping a bit to see him still unconscious.

"Tell Ilyan, what?" I asked, unwilling to rip my eyes away.

"That someone is trying to convince you to break the connection between you and Ryland."

"I suppose I will. I tell Ilyan everything."

Dramin paused before speaking. "I am not sure that is the best idea in this instance."

I narrowed my eyes at him. I had decided I wouldn't be like Atlas. I would swallow my pride and ask for help, but Dramin sat there, telling me that it might not be the best idea to tell Ilyan something that was already eating at me.

"You will know why before the day is over, child."

My eyes bugged a bit, I knew what he was talking about. The sight. The sight concerning me. He was finally going to tell me.

"But not yet," he finished, and I leaned back into the chair. "You need to decide for yourself whether to tell him of what Ryland is telling you and if you decide to break the connection. I believe you will, but not until the time is right."

I wanted to scream at the thought of willingly breaking the Zělství. Somehow, though, even then, I knew the possibility of me doing that was high.

"And when is that?" I asked, curious.

"Your sight will lead the way."

He smiled and I returned the movement, although not as brightly.

I wasn't feeling as heavy as I had been, thanks to Dramin. My team seemed to be getting bigger. I hoped that someday soon I would have the support of Ryland, too. My Ryland, with his memories intact. I still had three weeks until Edmund's deadline. With my newly unlocked abilities and Ilyan at my side, I felt a bit unstoppable. Maybe it was the Black Water flowing through me, but I felt a bit cocky.

I was going to knock Edmund on the pavement.

I laughed at the thought, ignoring Dramin's raised eyebrow by taking another deep drink of the Black Water.

"Well," Thom announced as he approached the fire. "He should be awake in a few hours."

My back straightened, my eyes flying toward Ilyan's bunk in expectation.

"Relax, Silný, I said a few hours not a few minutes. It could still be tomorrow."

I exhaled heavily and sat back in the chair. Thom grunted at me in greeting before setting a blueberry muffin on my lap. It looked delicious, but I didn't want it. I eyed it for a moment before picking it up and setting it on the small side table next to me.

It seemed like such a simple act, but it had immediately caught the close attention of both men.

"Aren't you going to eat that?" Thom asked, alarmed.

I looked to the muffin and bit my lip, nervous about their sudden interest.

"No, I don't think I am." I didn't meet the eyes of either of them, although I knew they were both staring at me. Instead, I took another drink before placing my now empty mug next to the muffin.

"You are ready." I froze at Dramin's words, my hand coming back to rest in my lap.

I turned to him, nerves and excitement getting all jumbled up in my body.

"Are you going to show me now?" Dramin nodded his head once in response to my question.

"I'm not sure I am ready," I answered honestly, my voice quiet.

"You are, Silnỳ." I turned to Thom, his head nodding in encouragement.

"But... Ilyan said... Will I really hate him?"

Dramin smiled in response to my question, but his face was sad. "Ilyan has worried for the past eight hundred years if what he said in the Hall of Sight was the right thing. That is eight hundred years of nerves. Of course he is scared. But know this, all that you are about to see will happen; you cannot change it. You are ready to accept that, and that is why you are ready to see the sight."

Dramin stood right before me, his frame towering over me.

"But what if I am not ready, Uncle?" I sunk away from him, scared of what was about to happen.

"I am afraid, child, that you no longer have a choice."

Dramin placed his hand against my head. But instead of pulling out my memories as Ilyan had done, I felt my head go light and airy as this time he put them in.

24

I RECOGNIZED the room as a Hall of Sight the moment everything came into focus. This one was bigger and more ornate than the one in our cave, though. The same sunken pool of Black Water filled the center of the room, but instead of the raised shelf that surrounded it, a number of chairs and thrones had been carved out of wood and placed facing the pool. In each of the thrones a man or woman sat. They did not speak, they sat with their eyes closed, heads bowed with their features obscured by large, woolen cloaks. I knew what they were doing and it worried me.

I let my eyes wander away from them to linger on the carvings and beautiful stained glass windows that covered the space. I didn't know what I was doing here, and I was still shaky about the details of what Dramin had done to me and how he was showing me this. Even if I knew everything about the process, I didn't think I could shake the nerves connected with what I was about to see.

I tried to find comfort in the fact that I was about to learn everything, but I was still worried. Ilyan's begging me not to hate him continued to echo through my head. I thought of his sleeping body—of all he had done for me—and straightened a bit, aware that his sacrifices demanded more courage from me.

"He is coming, can you feel him?" I turned toward the voice, surprised to see that one of the still figures had stood. His head moved from his bowed position to one of strength. I must have audibly gasped, —though no one seemed to notice— I had come face to face with my father. His face and body seemed younger—if that was possible—and his hair was shorter. He was powerful and strong, so much more so than I ever remembered seeing him. The change was startling. I could tell he was the patriarch among them. He was respected and revered, his commanding voice guiding all of them.

"We can feel him." The remaining Drak in the hall stood in unison as they spoke as one, their voices echoing around me. I jumped a bit at the intensity of the sound.

"He wishes to know," Sain said, his voice deep and rumbling.

"Know of his future," said another.

"Know of his heart."

"Shall we tell him?"

"Shall we give him sight?"

"He is the only one who can see, the only one who understands."

"That is why he has come, come to see us."

I spun around as each voice spoke, their voices coming in quick succession. Each of the Drak stood still, their eyes black centered with glowing embers of color as they looked beyond their own sight and into the Black Water.

"He has come." I turned toward my father at his announcement as all of the Draks' eyes shifted from black to their normal, multi-colored array. I looked around them, unsurprised to see Dramin standing to the left of my father.

I waited, my nerves on edge, wondering what was happening—what they were talking about—however no one in the Hall of Sight moved. Their eyes merely remained focused on the door behind me, their gaze deep and unwavering. I heard the creak of the oversized door as it was opened, another gasp escaping me when Ilyan walked through.

Although he looked different, I knew it was him. I would recognize him anywhere. In my head I pieced together why this seemed so familiar; I had seen him walk into this room in my first sight.

His hair was short and cut above his ears, the blonde strands darker and waved slightly against his head. I had seen his hair short once before, but somehow this look was different. The change was becoming, his features more defined, and dare I say it, he looked... gorgeous.

He walked in quickly, his eyes appearing both strong and yet nervous. He wore the same clothing I had seen him wear for council; the long tunic, high boots, and ornate jewels all firmly in place. Yet I had the distinct impression that this was not some special attire, this was the clothing of the time.

Dramin's words of Ilyan having waited eight hundred years echoed through my head. My jaw dropped as the numbers sprang to life in my mind; eight hundred years ago would make it around the year 1200, and Ilyan would be a little over two hundred years old.

Ilyan marched in before falling to one knee, his head bowed against his hand as he said nothing. He stayed like that while all of the Drak looked at him. I was frozen in place, my eyes glued to Ilyan's back, waiting for something to happen. Finally, after a few minutes, Sain stepped off of his throne and approached Ilyan, who remained still.

"Welcome, My Lord." Sain greeted him warmly, his pleasure at seeing him echoing around the large cavern. Ilyan rose at Sain's words, and I was surprised to find his eyes bloodshot.

"You know why I have come?" Ilyan asked, his head rising about a foot above Sain's.

"How could I not?" Sain smiled sadly and took Ilyan's hand, leading him toward the pool of Black Water that stood in the middle of the hall. I reluctantly followed, my skin prickling with nerves.

"Tell me, how did you survive for so long?" Ilyan's voice was so pained that it cut straight into me. Sain patted his hand softly with the same sad smile in place.

"You of all people know that I did not manage it easily. If I had then we would not have my lovely Dramin, and I would not be bonded to your sister. My life is full now, but only after many centuries of waiting." Sain's voice was not sad as it echoed around the stone chamber, if anything it was full of acceptance and comfort. It was a voice from my childhood; I had heard it with every scraped knee or tumble. The tone of his voice reminded me of home.

"I know, but still..." Ilyan trailed off and hung his head, looking into the still water that did not show him his reflection. None of the other Drak moved, their eyes remaining focused on Ilyan and Sain.

"You are lonely," Sain finished for him confidently. Ilyan nodded once, his eyes glistening with tears, which he tried in vain to hold back.

"I feel lost. My heart breaks for someone I have never even met, someone who may never exist. I cannot weave my magic with someone without causing them injury. I am beginning to believe that the joy of a Zĕlství will never be in my future."

I took a step toward him, wishing I could console him somehow until I reminded myself that this was a memory. Ilyan wiped the tears from his face before raising his head to Sain, who wrapped his arms around him comfortingly.

"Would it help you to know that I have felt your pain?"

"That is why I have come to you. I knew you would understand." Ilyan clapped my father on the shoulder hard, causing him to lose his balance, both men chuckling at the stumble.

"And yet you still wish to use the sight to see into your future?" Sain asked, his tone curious and worried.

I found myself growing concerned about what exactly I was about to see. I had been told this was the sight about my true purpose, but Ilyan was asking about his love life. Cail's words about Ilyan's feelings for me shot through me, my body freezing in fear that the two things might be connected.

"Yes. I would gladly wait until the end of days if only I knew that she would be waiting for me, that someday I would be with her."

"The future does not always hold hope, Ilyan. What would you do if no one ever came into this world for you?" Sain moved away from Ilyan and around the pool before facing Ilyan from the other side. The Water began to ripple between them, and yet, their reflections still did not shine on the dark surface.

"I would do what I have been doing, Sain. I will continue my work with Man, but at least I will know to stop looking."

Sain studied him for a moment before coming to a decision. He nodded once and moved back to place his cloak on the throne he had originally come from. Returning to the pool, he knelt next to the water.

"Bare your chest Ilyan. This is a matter of the heart, and not one that the Black Water will take lightly. My soul tells me that this is more than it seems." Sain spoke loudly as he leaned over the water, each of the Drak kneeling in unison as he did.

Ilyan did not hesitate before removing his tunic, the fabric falling into a heap on the ground near his feet. He moved to the center of the room wearing only the thick tights of the time and high leather boots. His chest was smooth and scar free. I had grown so used to seeing the scars that seeing him without them was odd.

"Do you wish to use my sight to know the matters of your heart, Ilyan, son of Edmund, heir to the throne of our King?" Sain's voice was loud. It had taken on that strange dead quality I had heard in my voice when I used my sight.

"I do."

"Then show him," the voices of every Drak in the hall spoke at the same time, their voices hollow as well.

"Tell me of what you desire." Sain extended his hand until it hovered right above the Black Water, his fingers barely skimming the surface.

I inhaled sharply, my stress at what all this could mean growing.

"I wish to know if the fates have designed a mate for me —be it now, or in the future. I must know if one will be born who is strong enough to hold my magic." Ilyan's voice ricocheted around the space, growing louder as he spoke. My neck muscles stiffened, my body reacting to what I knew was to come. What I didn't want to hear.

"So let it be." All the Drak spoke together as Sain plunged his hand into the water.

The moment his hand was submerged, the water seemed to come to life. The gentle ripples of before became a torrent as they bubbled over the surface in an angry pattern. The bubbles continued to grow until the water sprouted vertically into a pillar of thick darkness. I could no longer see my father as he knelt beside the pool. The only thing left visible to me was Ilyan's back as he stood before it, his muscles flexing in anticipation.

Once the Black Water had grown to a height above his head, Ilyan called out in pain, his yells loud as they cut through me. I ran over to him in a panic, needing to help him even though I knew this was only a memory. I stopped in place as I saw what was happening; streams of Water flowed away from the pillar to drag themselves along Ilyan's chest. I inhaled sharply, remembering what Dramin and Thom had told me; Black Water was poisonous to any other than the Drak, but contact with it was necessary for the Drak to use their sights for others.

Ilyan yelled out, his voice restrained enough that I could tell he was trying to hide how much agony it was causing. He clenched his jaw as tongue after tongue of roving water dragged itself over his chest. His flesh bubbled and turned an angry red as it sliced through him, over and over. He yelled and screamed, but he did not call for them to stop. I could see the determination in his eyes, his fervent desire to know guiding him.

It took far too long for the Black Water to stop slicing away at Ilyan's flesh. His screams died as his magic healed him, his power taking away the pain. Ilyan squared his shoulders and looked straight ahead as the Drak began to mumble, their voices overriding one another until they began to join together.

The sound was both deafening and terrifying. I cringed

into myself as the sound grew in strength and in caliber. It ricocheted off of the walls and around my head until it became one voice, and as it did, the water exploded even further, the pillar extending violently up to the ceiling.

The Black Water began to swirl and ripple as colors passed over it, the sights from the Drak reflecting onto the water so that Ilyan could see them. Flashes of red began to move together before forming a tangible image of fire, of destruction.

"There is one among us..."

The Drak spoke together, their voices so precise it sounded like one loud voice. The power of it filled me. Even though I knew this was a memory, I could feel my own Drak blood calling to them.

"...who seeks to change the magic. Someone who seeks to kill the magic."

As the Drak spoke, the fire in the vision was joined by the faint sounds of screaming, the image within the pillar changing to running feet, explosions, and above all, Edmund's laugh.

"He seeks to kill the magic for his own personal gain. We see him as he fights, as he sheds the blood of us, as he sheds the blood of others. We see him as he stops the reign of magic, as he stops the time of ours."

As the Drak spoke, more sights of the early destruction caused by Edmund flashed through the water. The screams of children and families rang out around us as the flashes of misery continued. I cringed away from them all, I had seen enough of what Edmund was capable of in my own life.

"Is this now?" Ilyan asked, his voice raised above the constant noise that filled the chamber.

"The time is now, My Lord," The Drak said together.

"You alone will be brave enough to fight him. Where others will lose their lives, you will prevail."

More sights flashed before us as the Drak continued to mumble. Ilyan and I looked at the pillar as images of him fighting against unknown foes were replaced by his stripped body strung up on a tree as he was beaten, and then it returned to a sight of Ilyan and his strength. I looked to Ilyan curiously, surprised to see his shoulders squared and jaw set, almost as if he was ready to plunge into battle at any moment.

Looking at him right then, I could understand why he always fought; why he relished battle. It wasn't a thirst for blood as Edmund would have me believe, though. It was a pure desire to help, to be good, and to protect. It was light.

"In a time far ahead, near the end of the world..." Flashes of war after war, all raged by man, filled the pillar of Black Water. I ached at seeing all the destruction humans had waged in such a raw way.

"...in a time when everything is changing and everything is new..."

The water showed us visions of my time and I watched Ilyan's eyes bug out of his head at the sights of high-rise buildings, cars, and the everyday modern life he was being shown.

"...there will come a child."

The same sight from my own vision flashed on the water; that of my mother being handed an infant, me. My heart beat rapidly as I began to put it all together.

"A child, an infant, a child that we see. We see her when she's born. We see her when she's grown. We see her now, and we see her then."

Visions of my childhood flashed through the water in quick succession, I recognized moments of triumph sprinkled through the many images of loss, pain, and anger that made up my childhood. Ilyan clutched his heart, his sadness at my life evident on his face. I had to look away as the images continued, each heartbreaking memory hurting more. Then they began to change. I was smiling more. I was laughing. And I knew why. Each of these sights were when I had been with Ryland. Even though he was never shown, I knew without a doubt he was there. My spirits soared thinking about him as he used to be; before the pain of his insistence that I break the Zělství had crushed my joy. I shook off the feeling, focusing on the smile that filled the water before it too began to fade.

"She is of The Chosen. Marked by the sign of the creature of fire, she has smoke in her eyes."

More visions flashed by quickly, showing us snippets of when I received my mark, my eyes before and after, and of how I had tried to hide the mark over the years. I reached up and covered my neck, suddenly feeling very self-conscious.

"A Chosen-Child just for you." Their voices reverberated through my head as the pillar showed a sight of Ilyan and me. His arms were entwined around me, his body soft against mine, his lips pressed firmly against my own.

"No," I gasped silently. My stomach turning at the sight I was seeing. I had known from the beginning what was going to happen, yet I didn't want to see it. I didn't want to accept what Cail and Ryland had said as truth.

The vision continued and I looked toward Ilyan, his hand extended longingly toward the passionate kiss we shared. I could see all the longing in his eyes. He had waited so long. This wasn't supposed to happen, it wouldn't happen; I wouldn't let it. Yet I was pained for him.

"For in this child is power, power beyond belief."

The sight of our kiss faded to an image of me, strong magic flowing as I fought several Trpaslíks at the same time. I was shocked to see that I was winning.

"She is the most powerful. She will be The Silný, the one who protects us all."

The sights continued—one after another—of me fighting, my power prevailing. More often than not, Ilyan was by my side, his magic battling right beside me. The visions continued before ending with Ilyan defeating an unseen assailant, his arm wrapped around me securely. I recognized that one because it had already happened. It was from the night we had fled the LaRues' mansion, the night we had failed to rescue Ryland.

"Her life is nothing other than misery, for everything she touches is ash and in her heart is only pain."

More images of my childhood. My heartbreak as my father left. My pain as I was bullied through every year of school. My misery at finding my mother dead, only to be thrown out of a window. I gasped as I saw my fall, the impact never shown, though the pain on my face was heartbreaking.

"Only you can help her and fill her heart with love."

They spoke as more sights flew through the water. I looked, expecting to see some startling way that Ilyan would make me love him, but all of these had already happened. I felt my heart loosening toward him in that moment just as it had then. They showed Ilyan caring for me as I pined, holding me as I was minutes from death, tenderly making shoes for me, and holding me every night as I cried. Seeing it from this angle—watching his actions as I slept and screamed—changed my perspective. I saw the tears I never knew he had shed over me, and the love he had kept hidden.

"Only you can save her and keep her for her true purpose."

A sight formed again, this time of Ilyan gently laying me on the bed in the attic, his finger running along my jaw as I fell asleep. It showed him then lean down to kiss me. A forbidden kiss; a kiss I had never felt. I gasped as I saw the action. I was angry that he had kissed me, and yet... and yet...

"For you were born and you were bred only to protect her."

More images of Ilyan and I floated past, his arms always around me, his body protecting me from those who would hurt me. Some I had lived through and some I had yet to experience.

"It is your future, Ilyan. Now is your time to see her. Then your place will be near her. It is your purpose to protect her. But beware, even as your heart longs for her, she will love another."

My heart clenched as the sight replayed my first kiss with Ryland, our magic exploding as Ryland sealed himself to me, completing the Zĕlství. This time it was not my turn for heartbreak. This time Ilyan reached longingly out, his voice calling out in disbelief. I could hear his heart break and it fractured something inside of me as well. I shook my head, basking in the memory of the kiss instead of the trauma I had been facing.

"Your heart will long for her, but she may not be yours to take."

More sights of Ilyan; more visions of secret kisses, intimate moments when we sat with our arms around each other, as we laughed and joked. Finally, when he had attempted to teach me to Salsa dance. I couldn't help but smile at the memory. Even though I didn't want to accept all that was being shown, I couldn't keep out the joy that tried to seep its way into me.

"You must find your strength to protect her—to be near her—for it is only by your side that she can find her true purpose; that she will find the strength to kill those that would end the magic of the world."

The images in the water changed again, this time to show Ilyan standing by me as I fought, his presence strong as he supported me from a distance. I could tell what was happening. I was using his magic. The knowledge of that rocked through me and my jaw dropped. There were only two ways in which that could happen, through a bonding, or through the Štít. I clutched my hand to my shoulder. He had known.

I understood the look now, the look he gave me when I spoke of the Štít for the first time. It was heartbreak. His heart had broken because he had known that he could never have me and that the Štít was the only way he could be close to me. Then, when I had held his magic, all of it, he knew that a bonding truly was possible, but also that it would never happen.

I had come to love Ilyan, maybe more than I could ever fully accept. I felt my soul rent with the realization of his pain and heartbreak. I longed to help him—to protect him, to make it okay—yet I knew I couldn't. I was bonded to Ryland, and Ryland had protected me, too. Ryland loved me, too. And even though Ryland's protection might end by a severing of our bond, I didn't know if I could ever move beyond that.

"It is only when she is with you that she will be able to accomplish all that she must. It is your place to protect her until the day that she passes from this world and into the next."

"No." Ilyan and I said together at the vision of him holding my body, his arms wrapped tightly around me as he howled and cried in agony, explosions filling the space surrounding us.

"This child is power." Sain spoke alone, his voice loud and powerful. "Power that is strong enough for you."

More flashes of my ability raced across the pillar. I couldn't tear my eyes away from them. I couldn't comprehend that I could be so strong.

"For you," the Drak repeated together, "for you, for you."

Their voices reverberated eerily as image after image of Ilyan and I together filled the space. Sights of intimate kisses, intertwined bodies, beach houses, and children flashed one right after another. They came faster and faster until they were a blur which continued for a moment before the water went black, the pillar falling into the pool again. I ran to it, gasping at the smooth surface and the reflection of myself that was now staring back at me.

"You will love her," Sain said with the deep, deadpan voice of a sight. I looked up to him, unsurprised to see him standing, his eyes covered with blackness and lit only by the glowing embers the Black Water gave him.

"But you cannot have her." The Drak spoke as one, each of their eyes also covered. They stared out, unseeing, the glossy blackness calling to me.

"You will protect her," Sain said.

"But you will fail," the Drak continued, their voices coming in quick succession.

"The one bred to change the world of magic," Sain lifted his hands as if he was seeing something, but the hall stayed still.

"The one bred to die." I froze at the words of the Drak.

"What?" I said aloud to the empty space, even though I knew no one could hear me.

"She is the only one who will come to this world," they continued together, "the only one your heart can hold."

"The only one?" Ilyan asked, my insides tightening to hear how defeated he sounded.

"She is here," Sain announced, his voice deep and reverent.

"Do you feel her?" They all spoke together again, the addition of Sain's voice doubling their intensity. "Do you see her?"

"I do." Ilyan's voice was right in my ear right before his arms came around from behind me and pulled me into his newly scarred chest.

25

I FROZE at the contact so foreign and yet so welcome. My heart thumped in my chest at what I had heard. It screamed for Ryland. It screamed for me to run away from Ilyan, but even here, he comforted me.

Somehow I had crossed over from being inside of a memory to being a part of it.

Ilyan's arms tightened as he pressed his cheek softly against mine. I did not lean into his touch, though neither did I shy away. I stayed still, trying to make sense of everything that had happened; everything I had heard.

"Do not be afraid, mi lasko." I relaxed at Ilyan's voice, so soft and familiar in my ear. "I know you have seen everything, and I know you are scared, but do not be. I can feel you inside of me; I can feel your soul inside of mine. Know that I am here to protect you, to save you, and to love you. Even if you will never love me, I will still be here, right by your side."

He turned me in his arms, his hands pulling me gently around, his arms still holding me against him. I looked up to him; he was so different, and yet so much the same.

"You're beautiful." He sighed the words like a prayer, his fingers coming up to trace the lines of my face.

He leaned down and my heart froze, but instead of kissing me, he pressed his lips against the Vilỳ's kiss on my neck, his lips soft and gentle.

The touch of his lips against my mark sent a jolt through my whole body. I had only felt that electric response to Ryland before; it was the jolt that preceded bonding. He sighed as he felt it as well, his heart rejoicing at feeling something he had been longing for.

My breathing accelerated into a panic. What did this mean?

"I love you." He said softly, his words true and honest. I could tell he meant what he said, but I didn't shy away from it, either—not as much as I should have—and it scared me.

"No!" I yelled out in a panic. My voice echoed around the great stone chamber as I pushed my hands against Ilyan's chest, pushing myself out of the memory and into my usual chair in the cave.

It was obvious that a whole day had passed; the light from the skylights in the ceiling was coming from an angle that suggested it was already night. Thom's partially eaten lunch still lay on his couch, but neither Thom nor Dramin were anywhere to be seen. Even though I had done nothing but sit all day, I could feel the exhaustion of a full day seeping into my body, begging me to sleep.

I exhaled deeply, my chest shaking a bit before I reluctantly looked toward where Ilyan lay. I was glad Thom and Dramin had left me to myself for the moment. Although I was worried about where they had gone to, and even about being alone, I knew I needed the time. Dramin must have known, too. After all, he had known from the beginning all that had been said; all that had been seen.

Ilyan had known, too.

Ilyan had known for eight hundred years about me; he had known my face, known some semblance of a future. And yet, he had said nothing. Even when I had struggled and pined for Ryland—even as he had trained me—he'd said nothing of the future he longed to have; the future he dreamed of with me. He had never tried to talk me out of it. He had never tried to place himself in a better position. He had let me do what I had longed for.

Suddenly, the look that Ilyan had possessed the very first day I had seen him standing against the wall in English class made sense; his intense gaze, his look of frightening awe. After eight hundred years of waiting, I had been sitting right before him. I cannot imagine the heartbreak he must have felt, or how the knowledge that he could never have me must have eaten him up inside.

I stood to face where he lay, still and calm on the bunk, his long hair falling gently over the side. I couldn't decide if I was angry with him, agreed with him, or accepted what he had done. Everything lay numbly inside of me as I stood staring at him.

My Protector.

He had been born to protect me—born with magic strong enough to do so—and yet, too strong to give him companionship. He had borne it willingly, his actions showing his strength. Although he loved me more than he could ever love any other, he had held his tongue and let me follow my own path.

He was truly a better man than I would have guessed. How could he ever worry that I would hate him? I shook my head before walking toward him, my steps slow and controlled. Thom's words of his imminent awakening sounded in my head. Right then was not a time I needed him to awaken, though. For that moment, I needed to think. I needed to figure out what was going on.

I had been born to defeat Edmund—born to usher in a new age of magic— while Ilyan had been born to protect me and bring me to serve my true purpose, even if it ended with my death. An image of him from the pillar, his heartbreak as he held my dead body, entered my mind and I stopped a few steps away from him.

I clutched my hand to my chest as the pressure in it built. I knew the second heartbreak was coming and I knew why. I had fallen in love with Ilyan, but the love was wrong. It was a love and devotion in and of itself, but beyond that...

"I'm sorry, Ilyan," I whispered to his sleeping body, my voice catching on my tears, "but I can't give you what you want."

I turned and ran before I had finished speaking. My feet stumbled as I tore across the large space in tears, only to lunge myself into my bunk. I covered myself with as many of the large furs as I could, hoping to dampen the sound I knew was coming before it escaped my lips.

I felt my chest tightening as I fought against it, however I knew it was no use. The tears had reached a peak, and my body curled inwards as I screamed within the shelter of my blankets. I writhed with the overwhelming pain of my emotions, with heartbreak, and with loss.

The sight had said that everything that I touched would turn to ash, and this seemed to be no exception. I was in love with and bonded to my best friend. A man who had been tortured by his father for loving me, who may or may not remember me, and whose very bond with me terrorized my waking and non-waking existence. Ryland meant the world to me, and yet he had begun to actively attempt to break our bond. Even thinking about his words, about his promise to sever the Zělství, sent more panic through me. I screamed again, desperate to get the emotions out of me.

Nothing about my bond with Ryland brought joy, and that in itself was painful for me. I longed for him while, at the same time, I was scared of him.

I screamed in an attempt to release my fear and my pain, shoving the blankets into my mouth as I did, hoping to muffle the sound.

The scream opened up a further chasm in my heart. It rent open the feelings I had been hiding even from myself. The feelings I now knew Ilyan shared.

Everything around me was crumbling again, the weight on my shoulders too much to bear. Bred to die, born to fight, raised to be broken, and always the cause of pain for those I cared about most in the world.

I howled as it all came crashing down on me. I could no longer do it on my own.

"Ilyan!" I called his name as I had become accustomed to doing. I needed his strength, his song. I needed someone to tell me it was going to be okay. Feeling like this, he was the one my heart called to. I don't know if it was because he was the only one that was left or because he was the only one I felt could truly help me, yet he was my Protector, and right then, that was what I needed.

"Ilyan!" I wailed his name, knowing he would not come. Knowing that even if he did, I could not give him what he truly wanted.

I wailed louder, his name mixing with my tears, my sobs becoming an uncontrollable monster inside my chest. It clenched, and clawed, and burrowed into me, increasing my howls and my pain.

Everything inside of me was breaking. It was not fair for

me to feel so much pain. Not when so much had already been placed upon me.

I writhed my body in the foolish hope of getting rid of the pain, but it didn't help. I could find no comfort. The blankets of security I had placed around me had become a prison.

I had not even felt the covers lift when long, sinewy arms I knew all too well wrapped around me, a strong chest coming to rest against my back.

I turned in his arms, my tears changing from those of despair to some of hope. Ilyan lay right next to me, his arms wrapped around me tightly, his magic flaring through me as he calmed me. I looked into his bright eyes, my heart beating much faster than it had ever done before.

He smiled as he carefully moved my tangled hair out of my face, his eyes never leaving mine. They had that look I had seen during the sight; a burning love that incapacitated me.

My tears had slowed to nothing as I reached up, carefully placing my hand against his face, touching him in a way I had never done before. His skin was soft and smooth.

"You're all right," I gasped out, the words almost washed away with my tears.

"I am all right," he affirmed, his accent thicker than I had ever heard it. Ilyan pulled me to him, his lips pressing roughly against my forehead before he buried me into his chest. The scarred chest.

"I will never leave you, Silný." His voice caught and I could tell he was crying, too.

We stayed like that, my tears falling over his chest while his mingled into my hair, our joy at seeing one another again settling in.

Slowly I began to come back to myself, the rough scars on his chest coming into my line of sight.

I reached up to trace the lines with my fingertips, my heart unsure about such close and intimate contact. The white scars zigzagged over his chest, no longer as angry as the red they had originally been.

"I'm sorry that the water hurt you." I continued to trace the raised scars, the skin rough under my fingertips. He stiffened at my words.

"So they showed you then?" His voice was taut and I could hear the fear behind it. I didn't want him to be scared. I pushed my head against his chest, the wild thumping of his heart fluttering in my ear.

"Yes."

His heart continued to pound as he hesitated; as he decided what to say to me.

"I am glad I have them, the scars. They have always been a reminder of what I may someday have."

"I know." My voice was soft.

"And... you are not mad at me?"

I hesitated. I wasn't sure how to phrase this; how to say what needed to be said. I pulled away from him, my eyes meeting his as he searched mine for any signs of what was to come. I reached up—my fingers hesitant to touch his face, to trace his features—before withdrawing again, leaving him untouched.

"I'm not mad," I said simply.

"But why not?" I could understand his confusion, however there was something very important that I needed him to understand.

"Because I love you too, Ilyan." His face lit up at my words, yet my heart only cinched tighter at what I was about to say. "But it doesn't change anything. We can never be together."

I thought for sure I would have shattered his heart. Instead, the radical light that seemed to be emanating off of him grew, his magic flaring within me until I could feel it push against my barrier. His smile grew and he pulled me back into him, his arms wrapping me tightly to him.

"I know, Joclyn. I know it doesn't change anything. I know I can never have you. I am all right with that. I expect nothing from you, but hearing you say it, even if it is only this once, that is enough for me. I can live the rest of my life knowing that you love me, even if nothing else will come of it."

Ilyan sighed heavily and I felt his tears fall against my skin, my own not far behind. I could still vividly recall his heartbreak as he had talked to my father, his longing as he had watched the images of us; the images that would never be. I wanted to soothe him, my soul longing to heal those pains.

"You are not alone, Ilyan," I whispered. "Not anymore."

"Thank you, Joclyn." I buried my face into his chest, his warmth and his heartbeat surrounding me.

My heart swelled at the comfort he gave me. Thom had been right, I needed someone to help me to hold the weight, and there, in Ilyan's arms, I actually felt stronger—like I could accomplish anything. Besides, even though nothing could ever happen between us, I knew the devotion we held for each other would be enough.

Until the day I died.

Ilyan did not move from my side all night. We simply lay

in each other's arms until we drifted off to sleep. Ilyan was there when I awoke from yet another of my nightmares, his song softly lulling me back to sleep.

As I woke the next morning with his arms around me, our legs intertwined comfortably, I knew I should move away. I knew it was wrong for us to be lying like this, but I didn't care.

I looked over at Ilyan's still sleeping body and smiled at the serenity that encompassed him. I could feel his magic's strong presence in my shoulder, the gentle lull of it as small tendrils weaved throughout my body. I knew that he was there for me no matter what. If the sight had not given me enough proof, what I was feeling now was more than enough

I sighed heavily and shifted a bit, cursing my sore joints that creaked and fought me. I hadn't entered the Tòuha yesterday because of the sight, so today would be a miserable day. Unless... I was stronger now; I could face it.

I pulled the necklace out from underneath my torn shirt and let it rest in my hands. I knew whatever I found inside would not be pleasant, but even a quick trip would help my body and then I may not have to worry about it for a few days.

I grasped Ilyan's hand tightly in my own and leaned into him again before I pushed my magic into the necklace, closing my eyes to enter the Tòuha.

It was all the same; the same kitchen, the same mold, the same deathly silent space. My heart beat erratically as I stood alone in the middle of it, suddenly terrified about what was going to happen. I didn't know if Ryland would do something to shove me out or if 'the dark-eyed man' that Ryland had told me about could find me there. Either way, I needed as much time as possible in that wretched place.

I moved further into the kitchen before ducking down and sliding myself underneath the counter by the bar stools. My knees slipped on rotting food and a couple of small mice scurried away, but I barely took notice.

Had it come to this? Had the Tŏuha really become nothing more than a vessel for energy? Ryland's voice echoed in my head, his promise to break the Zĕlství; his gentle words begging me to do the same.

And yet here I sat, hiding from him underneath a counter amongst garbage, terrified about what was going to happen in this place that joined me to my mate, just so I could keep the connection without wasting away. It seemed ridiculous even to me. What was I doing? I felt my eyes burn with the threat of tears. My emotions were too close to the surface after last night.

"I thought I told you not to come!" Ryland yelled.

I could only see his foot as he attempted to kick me. I was sure the contact would send me back so I dodged it, scrambling through rotten food and broken glass, sending barstools side-long into the kitchen.

"Get out of here!" he yelled as he chased after me.

"Please leave me alone, Ryland. I will leave in a minute," I begged as I continued to crawl away, my hands and knees covered with filth and dirt.

"No one wants you here anymore!" Ryland yelled again. I looked back to him as I reached the end of the counter, my stomach dropping to see his angry little body swinging a bar stool right toward my face.

It made contact and I howled out in pain, the impact sending me right out of the Tŏuha. I sat up automatically, my hand flying to my nose. Pain had never followed me like this before, not like it did with the nightmares. Even with the nightmares I was never truly injured. In the Tȯuha, however, it seemed that I could be.

I lifted my hand to my nose, hoping to add some pressure to my magic in order to help the injury heal faster. I froze when my fingers touched the warm wetness of my own blood, which seeped from the gash in my face. I stared at the blood on my fingers, my breath coming faster than usual.

"Joclyn?" Ilyan asked softly. My panic had obviously woken him up. He placed his hand on my back, rubbing up and down my spine in a comforting way. "Are you okay?"

"I'm bleeding." I spoke like it barely even mattered, my shock still seeping in.

Ilyan was up in a flash, one arm wrapped around me while the other held my hand before moving to inspect my face. His fingers pushed softly against the skin, his face filled with deep worry lines.

"What happened?" Ilyan asked.

"Ryland threw a chair at me."

Ilyan froze, his hand still pressed against my face. I felt his other hand tighten against my hip, his magic swelling in frustration.

"In the Tȯuha?" The heavy restraint he placed on his words made me tense.

"He has become very aggressive in getting me out of them." I said and looked away from him.

"But... to hurt you?" Ilyan's fingers pressed against the bridge of my nose, his magic healing me quicker than I could heal myself.

"I'm not sure it's coming from him." I looked up at Ilyan as I felt the skin knit back together, the red tips of his fingers moving away from the tender skin as he raised his eyebrow at me, prompting me to continue. I swallowed hard, worried as to how he would respond.

"Cail made it very obvious that he is in control of my dreams. I think he is manipulating the Tòuha as well." I picked at the hairs of the furs we were covered with, uninterested in looking at him.

"What!" Ilyan's voice echoed around the cave. I cringed a bit and moved away from him, however he only moved me back against him. "Has he hurt you?" His magic surged strongly into me as if expecting hundreds of broken bones.

"No, he likes to mess with my head, but I don't know what else to do. I have to go into the Tòuha, and I can't control if the dreams come or not."

Ilyan's body stiffened, his panic seeping into me. I could tell that my new injury, mixed with the fact that Cail was controlling my dreams, was terrifying to him. I had been worried before, but hearing his shallow breathing against my hair, the worry was building into fear.

"I only went in once while you were gone," I said as I pulled away from him, desperate to calm him down.

"How long was I gone?" he asked, his voice soft.

"Three days." Ilyan's hand moved down my face to lift my chin up to look at him.

"And the nightmares?" I looked away from him, not wanting to be reminded of the horrors I had been faced with. "I will fix this. I will make the Tòuha safe for you to go into. I will never let it happen again."

I pulled his hand away from my face, holding onto his fingers tightly. I still couldn't believe that he was all right, that he was awake.

"Thank you," I said. "I can't do this without you."

Ilyan pulled me against him, his hand still wrapped around mine. "I know."

He held me against him, his heart beating in my ear while I traced his scars with my free hand, his grip pressing me against his chest.

"I will never leave you," he whispered in my ear before he kissed my mark. The jolt I had felt only twice before shot through my body. I stiffened at the sensation, looking up to Ilyan in a panic.

"You feel it, too?" His voice was awed, which somehow made me worry more.

"Yes. I felt it before when you... in the sight, I mean..." I let my voice trail off uncomfortably, unsure of how to phrase it.

"You felt it then?" Ilyan's voice was quiet and unsure. I had never heard him without his confidence, it was somewhat endearing. "I have always wondered—since that day all those centuries ago—I always wondered if you felt it, too. If you heard what I said."

I nodded once, his face relaxing, his confidence almost instantly returning. It was interesting, every time I saw that hidden side of him, it was like I was seeing the real him.

"I did. I heard every word." He smiled again and I looked away, unsure if I wanted to talk about this.

"I meant every word," he whispered. "I will always love you, but I will never force you to be with me. I will never stop you from being with Ryland. He is your mate, Joclyn. I will always respect that."

Ilyan gently placed his hand against my face, and lifted me to meet his gaze. He looked at me softly, his eyes full of the golden specks of light I had seen before.

"Thank you."

"Of course," Ilyan let his finger trail up my jaw to rest on the mark on my neck, the jolt shooting through my body again. Ilyan smiled; I am not sure he could help it.

"Ilyan, what does it mean?" He only shook his head, his face confused and yet so hopeful.

"It means," Dramin began from behind us, his voice making me jump, "that the Silnỳ has come to accept what you mean to her, My Lord."

Ilyan turned at Dramin's arrival, his face breaking out into a wide smile. Dramin returned the smile as he set down a heavily laden breakfast tray before embracing him.

"Welcome back, my old friend," Dramin said. "It is so nice to see you alive and well. You had us worried."

"I highly doubt that," Ilyan chuckled, "but thank you for taking care of me and Joclyn. I cannot thank you enough."

He clapped Dramin heavily on the shoulder, however Dramin only looked at me curiously.

"So, Joclyn, is it? That is a very pretty name." He smiled and I instantly felt awkward. I hadn't realized I never told them my name.

Ilyan looked at me, his eyebrows raising in confusion.

"They never asked." I reached out to grab a mug out of Dramin's hands in an attempt to ignore the look he was giving me.

The cup had made it only half way to my lips before Ilyan hollered out and hit the cup hard. It sped away from me, spilling the delicious Black Water all over the floor.

"Stop! Joclyn! Do you know what that is?" I turned to Ilyan, my stomach tensing in realization. There was something he didn't know after all.

"Oh," I said, nerves wiggling into me. I turned to Dramin who nodded to me once in encouragement.

I said nothing as I grabbed the empty mug off of the floor and placed my hand over the rim. I felt it fill instantly. I took a deep breath before removing my hand; I knew there would be no easy way to tell him.

"Yes, Ilyan, I know exactly what it is." I spoke as plainly as I could, trying to ignore the nerves that filled me and the terrified look on Ilyan's face as I took a drink from the rich Black Water. I felt it move into me, tingling me to the very core. I sighed appreciatively and turned back to Ilyan, smiling shyly.

He looked at me with his mouth open, gawking at me with a heavy, new found appreciation. I felt my insides loosen. I was afraid he would react like Thom, or worse.

"You're amazing," he said, his hand moving softly up my arm.

"If you think that's amazing," Dramin chuckled, "wait until you see what else she can do."

26

I STOOD in the middle of the training hall, the three men facing me. Dramin bounced on his toes in eager anticipation, Thom stared off into space looking bored, and Ilyan looked into me with a deep-rooted mix of confusion and anticipation. I shrunk into myself again, feeling uncomfortable, before consciously shaking off of the sensation.

I firmed my feet against the ground, took another deep drink of the Black Water, and prepared myself.

"Now, Ilyan," Dramin said, "remember, you cannot help her. As much as your body calls for you to do so, she will not be able to show you all that she has accomplished if you do."

Ilyan nodded once before turning back to me, the intensity of his gaze increasing somewhat. I felt my pulse quicken.

"Great, Dramin!" I yelled back to him. "Now if I mess up who is going to come to my rescue?"

Dramin laughed and I felt my nerves jump.

"What's the score again?" Thom asked as he flexed his

fingers and shook his head, his dreadlocks swinging clumsily.

"Six seconds for thirty-five attacks," Dramin said with a hint of pride. I let out a deep breath and took another drink.

"Sounds good. You ready?"

I nodded in response to Thom's question and closed my eyes. My mind opened up completely, letting my mind's eye see the room in detail. The second I closed my eyes, Ilyan shifted his feet. I could tell he was getting nervous.

"Go!" Dramin's voice rang out in my ears and Thom rained hell in my direction.

Rather than send things flying around me as we had done in the past, he sent each and every object flying directly toward me. I hesitated for less than a breath before clapping my hands together and forming a large orb around me. The objects began to hit my shield and the fireworks started. The magical arsenals hit the barrier with an explosion, conjured objects vanished, and with one flick of my mind, I sent each of the furniture pieces back to line up along the side of the room.

"Joclyn!" Ilyan's voice was panicked, but I stayed still, waiting for the smoke to clear. My eyes still closed, I saw Ilyan barreling through the mess to try to reach me. His magic was flaring through my shoulder as he desperately checked for injuries. The second he broke through the smoke, he stopped, his eyes practically bugging out of his head at seeing me standing there unharmed.

"Four seconds!" Dramin yelled, his excitement evident. I heard Thom swear loudly, however I couldn't take my eyes off of Ilyan.

He walked toward me slowly, like I was going to go wild and attack him.

"Don't look at me like that, Ilyan. You're making me feel like I am going to sprout an extra head."

He stopped his slow advance, his face breaking out into a smile rather than the oddly reverent face he had before.

"You're amazing."

"So I've heard," I said a little too bitterly.

"I'm not sure you need me anymore." He spoke lightly as he came up beside me, but his words made my stomach drop to my toes.

"Don't say that, Ilyan. It's not true. I may have power, but I do not have strength. Do not forget, I have seen the sight. I know what was said, what you said." He blanched at my bluntness, we had yet to discuss all of what I had seen and what it would mean to either of us.

I stepped forward and grabbed his hand, pressing it between mine. I hoped he understood what I was saying. I knew he wasn't being serious before, but I needed him to understand.

"I know, mi lasko." Ilyan said, his finger tracing to my mark. The jolt moved through me again and I shivered.

"I heard you. The night you came to me while I slept," he said softly. "I heard you."

I blushed and moved away as Dramin came bounding up, grinning from ear to ear.

"See, Ilyan, I told you. Turn the girl into a Drak and suddenly the world opens up to her."

Dramin grinned at me, but I turned away from him still waiting for the blush to go down in my cheeks.

"It's a little weird, I must admit," Ilyan said, "the fact that she can see into my future, although the extra power is nice. It makes my job a little easier."

Ilyan smiled widely and rubbed his fingernails against his black polo like he had just taken credit for something spectacular. I glared at him and smacked his arm, which only caused him to smile more.

"Well, what do you say? Do you want to fight her?" Dramin's eyes sparkled as his voice bounced through the cave.

"I'm not sure," Ilyan said, looking me over. "Are you ready to lose, Jos?" I flinched at my nickname, but tried not to let it show. That made two times he had used it. I let my nerves melt, bringing a smile to my face.

I had beat Thom twice before. While I was sure Ilyan would be much more of a challenge, I was kind of up for it. I knew I would at least be able to mark him without cheating, and that in itself would be a miracle.

I swiped my hand through the air. A large, ornate sword appeared, only to fall gracefully into my hand. Ilyan's eyes popped a bit before settling into an impressed smile.

"I'm sorry, what where you saying about losing?" I knew my attempt to trash talk him was useless, yet I didn't care. It was kind of fun to do.

Ilyan smiled at me before producing his own sword and swinging it through the air. I rolled my eyes at him.

"Magic and conjured weapons, first person to five wins unless I take you down first." I announced confidently.

"Wait. Magic and conjured weapons, Joclyn? Are you sure?" I could see the worry behind Ilyan's eyes, but it just made me more excited to show him what I could do.

"I'm sure. Will you keep score Thom?" I yelled back to him, but he only grunted in reply. I took that to mean yes and squared my shoulders once before attacking Ilyan. I wasn't going to hold back.

I swung my sword wide while simultaneously shooting a wave of fire toward him from the other angle. Ilyan swore loudly as he turned to stop the magical attack, my sword hitting his arm.

"My point." I jumped back, spinning through the air to land twenty feet away from him. I held my sword up in front of me, my head low in preparation for what was to come.

Ilyan froze and stared at me in awe before his jaw set and his eyes lit up in eager anticipation. I watched as he processed my new abilities and I winked before exploding into the air. He jumped at the same time, meeting me mid-air where our swords clanged, the force of our collision sending me away from him. I could see that Ilyan was content to glide back down to the ground, so I quickly changed direction, shooting myself toward him. I met him as he landed. My sword moved fast, his moving only slightly faster.

I closed my eyes and continued to fight him, my mind seeing more than my eyes. My action offset him and he lost his nerve for a moment, but it was enough. I swung wide, sending a strong burst of wind into him that knocked him into my sword before he was slammed into the wall with a dull thud.

"Two points," I said as I smiled at him. He returned my smile and lunged at me, his eyes determined and dangerous.

"You're going to keep trying, Ilyan?" I asked as he swung wide, his attack blocked not by my sword but by my magic.

He didn't acknowledge the block. He continued to move, going from one attack to another as he got into his stride. I knew I was only going to have enough in me to barely match him, even with my new found power.

I sent another attack toward him and he spun away from me, the movement of his hair revealing tiny drops of sweat near his hairline. He was working hard in order to match me, and I was barely exerting myself. The thought made me laugh out loud, my hand swiping toward him and sending him off balance as I flew through the air away from him.

"You're looking a little tired, Ilyan? You doing okay?" I asked lightly. I was shocked when he scowled at me.

I should have known what was coming, but his move blindsided me as he came behind me, his arm wrapping around my waist to bring me flat against him.

"Did I ever tell you how beautiful you are?" he said softly in my ear. He released me and I spun away from him, my feet faltering. He took advantage of my stumble and hit my leg with the flat side of his sword. "My point."

"Once," I replied, not going to give him the credit of admitting his dirty trick had worked. "Several hundred years ago. You were very sweet about it, too." I gave him a saccharin smile as I moved carefully around him, watching my steps.

"Of course I was sweet. My mind was filled with images of kissing this beautiful girl I had been told I could never have." He smirked and I balked again. My jaw dropped and my hand flew to my mouth in horror. Saying it like that made everything much more real.

He took advantage, swinging his sword toward me, but he was not fast enough. I jumped and swerved, my body moving faster than I had ever been able to accomplish before.

"You're right," I taunted him, trying to ignore the kicking in my chest. "You can't have her."

"Yet."

I balked in confusion at his one simple word. "What do you mean, 'yet'?"

Ilyan only smiled wider.

"I'll tell you in a hundred years or so."

"Not fair." I pouted and pushed two waves at him from

opposing sides. He grabbed me and shot us up into the air, his instincts to protect me kicking in.

"You don't need to protect me here, Ilyan." I smiled before kicking hard off of his chest and sending him flying back into the wall. I spun and flipped to land carefully on the ground of the cave.

"My point," I said as I carefully watched to make sure he was okay.

Ilyan jumped up and sped toward me, his body like a bullet through the space. I threw my sword to the side, the conjured weapon vanishing into the air at one simple thought, and jumped right before he met me, my arms wrapping tightly around his neck.

"Sorry, Ilyan," I whispered in his ear. I kissed his cheek before spinning us around and pinning him to the ground, my sword appearing in my hand pointed right at his heart.

"I win." We stared at each other for a moment longer, his eyes holding that same fiery look of desire that I had seen before.

Finally, I could take no more. I moved away from him, sending the sword back into the air.

"That was amazing, Joclyn!" Ilyan exclaimed as he jumped up. Who knew he would be so happy to lose? He hugged me tightly before stepping away, making it obvious he was giving me space.

"Of course; you always knew she would be, Ilyan," Dramin laughed as he walked up, a reluctant Thom following him over to us. "You did see her in the sight after all, and a sight is never wrong."

He smiled and looked between us, and I knew what he was getting at, all those images of Ilyan and me.

"What do you mean, 'a sight is never wrong'?" I asked, alarm alighting comfortably into my voice.

Dramin's eyebrows arched precariously high, Ilyan looked worried, and Thom looked as though he was preparing to settle in for a show.

"A sight is never wrong, Silnỳ." Dramin's voice was placating, like he was herding baby tigers.

"Now, that's a matter of opinion, Dramin." Thom interjected, his voice hard.

"Not in the opinion of the Drak, Thom." Dramin glared sternly at Thom as he spoke.

Both men stared each other down, jaws and fists clenching. Ilyan's hand snaked around my waist protectively as he pulled me against him.

"He understands that, my friend," Ilyan said, Thom's scowl increasing as the tension built, "he is only talking about the few times where sights have never seen fruition."

"You are talking about the zlomenỳ." Dramin snapped.

"That is exactly what I am speaking of," Thom spat, "sights which never came to pass."

"It is hard for a sight to be infallible when the one who gives it is being tortured," Dramin said, his face inching closer to Thom's.

"And what about the one who was tortured after? What about her?" I had only seen Thom mad once—when Dramin had given me the Black Water for the first time— and that outburst had been nothing compared to this. The air around him seemed to ripple, his dreadlocks shook, and his fists were clenched firmly by his sides.

I looked between them, their faces tight with nerves and frustration. I felt my shoulders knit together as their anger seeped into me.

"That is not the fault of the Drak."

"I suppose that is a matter of opinion, Dramin," Thom spat angrily.

"I'd take the word of a Drak over a stubborn Prince any day," Dramin jibed.

"I'm not a prince anymore, Dramin," Thom yelled.

"And my sight is never wrong." Dramin tried to smile, but it was strained.

"Well, I hope you're right, Dramin." Ilyan interjected in an obvious attempt to break the tension. "Because tomorrow we will find out exactly what we are facing." Ilyan said as he moved back into a protective position.

"What happens tomorrow?" Thom asked; his anger only barely masked.

"Well," Ilyan said. "I've been told I was asleep for three days. And if my sister has made it out of the onslaught in Prague, she will be meeting us in Isola Santa tomorrow."

"What!" Thom bellowed, his anger quickly returning. "For what purpose? So that she can come here for a happy family reunion?"

Ilyan looked toward him, his face making it obvious that he was willing to stand his ground. Dramin, on the other hand, looked on the point of tears.

"You would bring her to our door? You would meet with her?" Thom shouted, his voice threatening fire and his fingers twitching with static magic. "After what she has done to me, to Dramin? She destroyed my best friend and betrayed her love. She is single handedly responsible for the murder of every last member of Dramin's family, of Joclyn's family!" The tone of Thom's voice scared me and I moved up behind Ilyan, his arm wrapping around my waist the second I made contact with him. I felt his magic surge through my shoulder, a shield rippling out around us. I looked up at him, concerned. I hadn't thought we were in that much danger, but now I was worried.

"You know she was tricked. She was used." Ilyan spat. "It

was not in her full control."

"To what extent, Ilyan?" Dramin spoke, his voice strained as he tried to keep it level. "Even after everything, she still fought with him for hundreds of years."

"As did Thom," Ilyan yelled, his patience gone. He roared and I cringed into myself unsure of where to hide. Ilyan must have sensed my discomfort because his hold on me increased as his magic filled me, his breathing leveling out as he gained control. "She came to me beaten and bleeding. Her heart has been in the right place for the past four hundred years. She has proven that to me."

"Then why don't you trust her, Ilyan?" Dramin asked, the tone of his voice controlled.

"I trust her."

"Not completely." Thom's loud voice ricocheted around the cavern and I cringed.

"I have forgiven her the same way I have forgiven Thom. I must trust that." Ilyan's voice had almost taken on a pleading edge. He had told me himself that he wasn't sure if he could trust Ovailia.

"And yet, you still dare to bring her here?"

"She is our sister, Thom, and I must trust her." The powerful quality of Ilyan's voice had returned, his tone loud and commanding.

"Then you are a fool." It was not Thom but Dramin who spoke, his voice like venom.

"How can you say such things, Dramin?"

"You have sentenced us to death," Thom snapped as he stepped closer, his blue eyes flashing red.

"Do not say such things!" Ilyan roared. Again I cringed, my torso moving into his. He sensed his mistake and calmed, his tight muscles loosening and his breathing slowing.

"I must say such things. Ovailia would happily see us dead; you have hidden our existence from her for centuries because you yourself do not trust her, and now, you would bring her into the one place on earth we have to hide, the one place in the world that is a sanctuary. When she turns this information over to your father then where do we hide? Where do we go?"

No one spoke. I looked between the three men, my nerves accelerated as my breathing increased into a panic. No, it wasn't a panic. It was me. I felt my head grow light, my vision blur, and I knew I shouldn't fight it. I clung to Ilyan's shirt as the Black Water took over, the sight filling my mind and my eyes burning with the embers within me.

I gasped as I saw her, Ovailia carrying Ryland out of the LaRue estate. She did not fight. She simply walked past those who should attack her. She moved quickly as she dragged him, her head held high, her nose crinkled as if she was carrying out the trash.

My voice came in a wave, the monotone sounds rippling through the cave.

"A tryst has been set in motion, one you cannot ignore. The father of the four is using his seed, one against another, and in the end none will fall until two lives are lost. It cannot be stopped. Beware where your trust lies."

I looked up to Ilyan, his mouth open in wonder. I reached up and placed my hand against his jaw, needing him now more than ever to trust me. Even though this sight may mean I never get to see Ryland again.

"You can't trust her, Ilyan. Do this for me." Ilyan gazed into my eyes questioningly. His jaw worked soundlessly once before he nodded, his resolve weakened at my request.

"Okay, mi lasko. Anything for you."

27

I YAWNED and took another long drink from my mug of Black Water. It had been hours since my sight and still they had not come to a decision. The bickering had gone on and on. Part of me wished I could use my sight and then tell them what to do, but Dramin had informed me that it didn't work that way.

So I sat and drank deeply of what was now my only food source, letting their conversation roll around me as I avoided sleep, yet again.

"I'm telling you Dramin," Thom snapped, "if she shows up in Isola Santa and no one is there, she is going to think both of them have died."

"I don't see the problem with that," Dramin countered, his usual chuckle strained.

"There are two problems with that, old man. First, Edmund has control of the wells of Imdalind. If he thinks the Silnỳ is dead, he will do whatever he wishes with the power without fear of repercussions. I don't fancy trying to clean up that mess, do you? And second, if Ovailia is working with them she knows every secret Ilyan has trusted her with. We don't want Edmund knowing where we are, he has been after our heads for centuries." Thom said emphatically from his white couch, his dread locks swinging wildly.

"She knows about Sain at this point, that's the problem," Dramin countered. He gestured wildly and spilled some Black Water which Thom glared at evilly.

"Only if she is working with my father," Ilyan countered, his words seemingly going unnoticed.

"So she knows about Sain," Thom said, calming down a bit. "If she knows about Sain, then obviously she is going to go above and beyond the things she would normally do for Edmund, just to spite us."

"And with Ovailia that is the issue," Dramin said.

I knew exactly what he was talking about. Ovailia on a regular day was a pill. I would hate to see her unleashed. I took a sip of my Water and sat back, knowing that ignoring them was going to be impossible. Their voices kept getting louder and louder.

"You understand now. We are all in trouble!" Thom yelled, his dreads whipping around frantically.

"We? Us? Why are you including me in this? I am not even sure she has 'crossed over' as you two so eloquently put it." Ilyan's voice roared to life and I flinched automatically at the close proximity of the noise.

They were talking in circles; they had, yet again, gotten themselves off topic and were focusing more on mud-slinging than the actual problem. This fight was not helping anyone.

"Of course I am including you in this, Ilyan," Thom snapped. "You're the one who kept Sain from her for hundreds of years. If it wasn't for you then this whole mess may not have happened!"

"Oh, placing blame, are we? Don't even get me started on your little debacle at the university!"

"At least I was able—" Thom began

"Will you guys shut up?" I yelled loudly, stopping Thom in his tracks. They all looked at me for a moment as I glared them down. Someone needed to stop them and get them back on topic, all this bickering was driving me bonkers.

"Listen, what if we gave her a job? Something to do. Then she wouldn't realize that we know... might know that she is a traitor, and then, if she doesn't know we know, she wouldn't go out of the way to do anything. Besides, if she has a job, maybe we can use it to our benefit."

"What are you saying, Joclyn?" Dramin asked, his eyes narrowing into that look I knew all too well. I returned it for a moment before looking back at the other two.

"Well," I said, "in the sight she was carrying Ryland down the hall in the LaRue estate, no one was stopping her."

"Yes, yes, you told us this," Ilyan said. I turned to him. His face was worried. He didn't like the idea of Ovailia having turned on him again.

"Well, if she is working for them and we give her a job, say... getting Ryland out of the estate," I said strongly, hoping my conviction would give them all something to talk about instead of yelling, "then not only can she bring Ryland to us so we don't have to worry about rescuing him on our own, but she is proving to us that she is on our side, even though we know she really isn't. She will think that we believe she is, so she will also think we trust her, and then..."

I stopped; they were all looking at me like I had cats growing out of my head.

"Well, that's a brain twister if I have ever heard one," Dramin chuckled after a moment.

"Cool it, Dramin," I said a little icily before running my hand through my gross, greasy hair. What a stupid habit to have picked up from Ilyan.

"Look," I continued, "if she gets Ryland out, I won't have a deadline anymore. That's one less stress I would have to deal with."

"You don't have to deal with any stress, Joclyn." Ilyan said as he took my hand. I smiled at him but ignored the sentiment.

"If she gets Ryland out, that's one less thing to worry about. We get what we want, and she thinks she gets what she wants. Everyone is happy; some more the others," I added softly, knowing what it would mean for Ilyan to have me back with my mate again. Not to mention the fact that Ovailia would get nothing other than double-crossed in this plan.

"It could work," Ilyan said softly, his hand squeezing mine.

"Thank you, Ilyan." I sat back in my chair and recovered my hand, content to lose myself in my Black Water some more.

"Joclyn and I will go to Isola Santa tomorrow to meet with Ovailia. We will instruct her to get Ryland and tell her where we are going..." Ilyan stood up as he spoke and began to pace.

"Why does she need to know where we are going?" Thom jumped to his feet, alarmed. I put down my mug on the side table; so much for calming everyone down.

"Well, if she gets Ryland, she has to be able to bring him somewhere," Ilyan argued. Thom just continued to fume.

"It's risky," Dramin said. He stayed sitting, but I could hear the uneasiness in his voice.

"Of course it's risky! Having Ovailia anywhere near us is risky! She is going to kill us!" Thom spat, the fire growing abruptly as his magic surged, causing everyone to jump.

"Tomorrow we will go to Isola Santa, we will find Ovailia, tell her to get Ryland, and tell her where we are going to meet her. We will all go there, all four of us. After all, she will soon find out you are alive anyway."

"I don't want to go anywhere; I would prefer to stay here. It's nice, warm, and claustrophobic. It suits me here." Thom sat down as he spoke, his body language practically closing the deal.

"Thom," Ilyan whispered. "Please, I may need you."

"Not right now you don't." Thom snapped, jumping up again. "But when you do, you know how to contact me, and when you call me, I'll come running to your rescue. Right now, however, I am fine here." He sat down and turned away, his eyes closed.

"Thom."

"I have spoken my peace, Ilyan. I am staying here."

"Dramin?" As Ilyan turned to his old friend—hopeful—I felt my insides clench, I didn't want to witness Ilyan being undermined by two people in one night. I was surprised he hadn't pulled out his 'king' voice yet.

Dramin didn't answer right away; he took a long drink before lifting his eyes to meet mine, then turning to Ilyan.

"I will come with you because she will need me." His voice was darker than usual and I felt my magic spark up my spine in warning.

"Dramin, what aren't you saying?" I could tell this was more than a hunch. Dramin had seen something, and he wasn't making it sound positive. I waited for him to respond, yet he simply continued to drink from his mug, his unfocused eyes looking at the fire. My uneasiness grew.

"What have you seen?" I clarified after it became obvious he wasn't going to answer.

"Ah, child, sometimes one's sight is for personal use alone." Dramin spoke softly before waving his hand and refilling my mug from across the room.

"I don't like how that sounds," I sulked as I threw myself back in my chair, stubbornly leaving the newly filled mug on the side table.

"Well, at least now we have a plan." Ilyan sighed before he too moved to sit back down. At least everyone had finally seemed to calm down.

"Worst case scenario, Ovailia doesn't bring Ryland, betrays us all, and we are dead by morning." Ilyan mused humorously. "Best case scenario, she brings Ryland, isn't a traitor, and everyone lives happily ever after."

While I was happy that we were finally going to have a chance of getting Ryland back, I couldn't help feeling a sense of loss at what we were going to be leaving behind.

"What will happen to Wyn if we take Ryland?" I asked, everything clicking together. "She was their bargaining chip. You don't think they'll...?"

"They have Wynifred?" I jumped at the startling panic in Thom's voice.

My head jerked over to him, my eyes narrowing in confusion.

"Thom, we can talk about this later," Ilyan said, that thick royal tone streaming into his voice.

"But, she said..." Thom pleaded.

"I know Thom."

Their eyes locked daggers. I looked between the two of them before looking to Dramin for answers, but he wouldn't even meet my eyes.

"They will not hurt Wyn," Ilyan stated firmly, and I wasn't certain if he was assuring me or Thom. "They will still need a bargaining chip to get you to turn yourself in. Without Ryland, Wyn is the best they have."

Thom nodded and sat down, Ilyan followed suit as he grabbed my hand. I looked at him in confusion—Wyn had told me that she'd never met Thom—but he shook his head. I brushed it off, I would get answers later, besides it wasn't just Wyn they were holding captive.

"And what about Talon and my dad?"

"One thing at a time, child," Dramin said, his voice low and comforting. "You saw her carry Ryland, so we know she will bring him. Maybe the others will be mentioned tomorrow, but at least we know of one who will be returned to us."

"I understand." I said and grabbed the warm mug without thinking. This was war; there were always casualties in war. I already knew I was going to be one of them. My anxiety peaked at the thought, Ilyan's magic instantly moving to calm me. He looked at me out of the corner of his eye, but I ignored the fact that I could see him.

"We will get them back, Joclyn," Ilyan said when it was obvious I wasn't going to acknowledge him. "But if we don't, please do not forget what you and I have seen. No matter what happens, I will always be there for you." Ilyan leaned forward, his voice low and meant only for me. I knew the others could still hear him, but I didn't care. I was grateful for his comfort, his support.

"Well then," Dramin interrupted loudly, "if that's all settled, I am going to bed. I have been awake for seventy-eight hours, and my body is a little tired. Seeing as Joclyn's eyes are dragging, I don't think she is ready to face a full two days without sleep."

Dramin stood and began to make his exit, his long black bathrobe dragging on the stone floor.

"More water, child, more water!" he called as he walked away toward his bunk.

"Good night, Dramin," I called before taking an obligatory sip.

"Well, if Dramin's leaving then I sure as hell don't have to be here to watch this gush fest." Thom didn't wait for anyone to say anything more. He stood and strode away; his hands plunged into his pockets.

"Goodnight, Thom," I called, although I knew he wouldn't care either way.

"Whatever." He grunted as he disappeared behind the blanket he had hung over his bunk.

I watched the blanket for a moment before turning back to my Black Water, letting it warm me.

Ilyan sat silently next to me, watching me as I took sip after sip. After a few minutes, I began to feel uncomfortable. Mostly because I knew he was aware of what I was doing. I took another long drink, staring him right in the eye.

"Are you ready?" he asked, softly.

Honestly, I would never be ready. I looked, back to the fire and set my mug down with a gentle clink.

"You know, with everything that has happened, you think I would be more ready," I whispered, not wanting anyone but Ilyan to hear. "You would think that I could plunge into the nightmares and know exactly what's going on and there wouldn't be a worry or a stress about it."

I hesitated and pulled my blanket up to my neck, trying to fight the desire to hide. Instead I watched the fire, the magical flames burning and crackling in a rainbow of colors. I kept my focus on the flame, not knowing if I wanted to meet Ilyan's eyes.

"But every time I close my eyes, I am scared of what Cail is going to do to me. I'm scared of what he is going to make me witness. It's the same with the Tòuha. I'm scared of it, too. I never know what Ryland will do to me the next time or how long he will let me stay in."

When I turned to him and extended my hand, he grabbed it eagerly, wrapping my hand in his. He leaned forward, his torso close to me as he absorbed my words.

"My body gets weaker and weaker." Ilyan's magic surged through my shoulder and I smiled. "I can't control when the nightmares come, but I can control when to face the Tòuha. I can't do it tonight. I can't do it tomorrow."

"I understand, Joclyn, and when you wake tonight and your heart is aching and your mind is screaming, I will still be here." I leaned toward him and wrapped my arms around him, the chair awkward in between us.

"I know, Ilyan. I can't do it without you," I whispered in his ear, surprised when he lifted me up and swung my legs up over his other arm.

He held me against him as he moved, carrying me to my bunk where he sat me down softly, his hand sliding up to rest against my neck. His finger touched my mark and the now familiar jolt shot through me. I closed my eyes at the touch, my heart hammering, unsure of what I felt or what I wanted to feel.

"That is why I am here," Ilyan whispered, his lips millimeters from my face. "That's why I was born. I have waited the last thousand years so I could protect you."

I closed my eyes and exhaled softly, his proximity making it hard for me to focus.

"Someone has to help me hold up the world." I spoke softly, more to myself than to Ilyan, however Ilyan smiled anyway.

"Ah, you've been talking to Thom." He smiled and moved to sit on the side of bunk. He pulled the heavy blankets over me, his hand resting softly on my knee.

"It took some doing to get it out of him, I'll admit."

"He is a very smart man. He just has a lot of pain in his heart – a lot of regret."

"How does he know Wyn?" I asked.

"He doesn't," He said, his voice strained, "He knew her mother."

"Oh." I guess that made sense, but that had been quite the reaction he had produced earlier for someone he didn't even know.

Ilyan looked at me, my eyes drooping further the longer he stared at me. Finally he shook his head and gently helped me to lie down, his hand smoothing over my hair. I was suddenly very worried that he was about to leave me.

"Sleep well, Jos." I smiled at his use of my nickname before panic set in.

"Ilyan." My hand shot out to grab his, desperate to stop him from leaving. "Will you stay with me, just for tonight? I don't mean... but I need..."

I stuttered to a stop as Ilyan came back, his fingertip tracing the lines of my face.

"I know."

My eyes began to droop again at his touch; at the gentle magical pulses that he weaved through my body. His finger left my face as he moved, my eyes opening as I watched him shift to the foot of the bunk, his strong arms hoisting him up to settle near my feet.

"I will stay here, Joclyn. I want you to go to sleep now."

I felt his magic grow in my shoulder, the strong energy moving through me as he put me to sleep. I tried to fight him for a moment before I gave in, letting the world of sleep and the horrors that it held take me.

"Good night, my love."

28

Isola Santa was a small tourist trap of a village in the high Alps of Italy. It consisted of one restaurant, a small hotel, and a few homes of those who worked in and ran the small businesses. Each house was made of grey brick with the trademark alleys and small walkways that were the signature of the renaissance. The whole thing was nestled up against a beautiful lake, the high mountains surrounding us on all sides.

It was exquisite. I looked around in wonder as I sat in one of the many outdoor tables of the town's café and forced down my perfectly sautéed mushrooms, the crisp mountain air breezing through my hair, moving the clumps around awkwardly. I just hoped I didn't smell too bad, I didn't need many more of the tourists cringing in my direction. I had already had a few.

Ilyan looked around uneasily before his magic surged through me strongly. Even though I could now easily manage my own shield, Ilyan didn't want to take the risk. I was grateful for it anyway. I could already feel my body ache from being outside the Tŏuha so long. I should have been calm and collected in this beautiful place, but instead I was so on edge that I could barely function.

Ilyan looked as he had that night in Santa Fe. His hair was pulled back in a braid and he had aviator sunglasses on. Although his jeans were a little ripped and dirty, it was nothing compared to the disarray I was in. My clothes were filthy, my hair greasy and matted, and I was certain that I looked like a messy beggar that Ilyan had picked up along the way.

I kept placing the Ilyan in front of me against the image of him from the sight. With short hair, his jaw line popped more.

Ilyan caught me looking at him and I looked away quickly, causing him to laugh.

"What?" he asked, his accent rolling.

I looked back to him, narrowing my eyes as I contemplated what to say. "I think I like you better with short hair."

I spoke my mind and instantly regretted it. His eyes widened and a smirk played on his lips as he connected where my comment was stemming from.

"Not like before, not dark. You didn't look good with dark hair."

"But short..." he interrupted me, "like in the sight."

I nodded and looked away. I didn't know why the conversation was making me uncomfortable, but it was.

"Maybe I will cut it for you," he mused.

I ignored him and went back to staring at my mushrooms, contemplating if it was worth it to try and eat another. It had been decided that morning that it was imperative that Ovailia not find out that I was a Drak, which meant that I needed to at least attempt to force down normal food. But the taste was so bitter and the texture so gritty that I was having trouble making it look like I was enjoying it.

"Are you okay?" Ilyan asked from beside me. He sat back in his chair sipping at his wine, his eyebrows arched in question.

"I'm swell," I grumbled, poking at a mushroom. "You know, I am just chilling in a beautiful Italian village, dressed like a hobo, forcing down strange food, and waiting for your sister—who is, in a strange way, my step-mother—with the hopes of begging her to go save my boyfriend." Ilyan's smile at my discomfort grew, I scowled and decided to ignore him.

"How did I ever eat this stuff?" I asked a little grumpily, but Ilyan only laughed deeper.

"I think they are delicious." Ilyan leaned over the table and plucked one of the perfectly golden mushrooms from my plate. He plopped it in his mouth and smiled heavily as he leaned back in his chair.

"Better than a hamburger," Ilyan said with a smile.

"Ew." I cringed at the thought and Ilyan laughed harder. I rolled my eyes at him and forced another mushroom into my mouth.

"It is kind of endearing, this new side of you." Ilyan swirled the wine in his glass alluringly as he leaned in, his back arching him forward.

"Why? Because I don't eat meat now?"

"Well, there is that. It is everything, though; all of it. How strong you are, how confident, and how powerful." I cringed. "You're amazing, Joclyn." My heart thumped into a restart, however I ignored it.

"At least you don't think it's creepy. The last thing I need is for you to think I'm some kind of freak."

Ilyan reached forward and grabbed my hand, his thumb rubbing over the ridges on the back.

"Never, Joclyn."

"Well, aren't you two cozy." I jumped at Ovailia's voice, my aches surging through me.

Ilyan stood at her arrival, his arms wrapping around her without question.

Ovailia looked the same; perfectly poised, not a hair on her head out of place. She embraced Ilyan awkwardly, looking thoroughly out of place in jeans and a silk top.

"Ovailia!" Ilyan finally released her, but he kept a hold on her shoulders. "I'm so glad you are okay!"

Ilyan's voice was so pained, so relieved. I felt bad. Especially given what the situation was. The planned double-crossing suddenly felt like acid on my tongue.

"You, too, Ilyan. You have no idea. When I saw them... in Prague..." Ovailia broke off, and I was suddenly worried we were going to hear a play by play of what had happened. I wasn't sure I was ready for that. I didn't want to hear traumatizing accounts of what had happened to my best friend and what she had gone through because of me.

Ilyan pulled away from her and brought up a chair, prompting her to sit down. The waiter approached and Ilyan ordered something in Italian before sitting. The entire time, Ovailia kept her face down in an emotionless mask. I couldn't take my eyes off of her, the sight of her carrying Ryland down the hall still fresh in my mind.

"Ovailia," Ilyan said as he sat down. "I need to know what happened. You have to tell me who betrayed us."

Ilyan's voice boomed with his normal, regal air; a sound I hadn't heard in quite some time. It was obvious he was putting on the front with Ovailia in an attempt to get the information he needed from her. I tensed as I turned toward her, my body stiffening in expectation of whatever truth or lie was going to spew out of her mouth

"It was Talon." I gasped at her words, her head whipping around to glare at me.

"Talon?" Ilyan asked, his voice just as stunned as I was.

"Yes," she said, her voice strained. "I don't know how and I don't know why, but he was leading them down the hall. There were so many. I don't know if anyone else escaped, Ilyan. I couldn't find anyone else."

"No one else got out?" Ilyan asked, his voice loud in his heightened fear. The waiter jumped a bit as she came up behind him, placing another glass of wine and another plate of mushrooms on the table. Ilyan apologized in Italian before turning back to Ovailia.

"No one?" He repeated, his voice catching as the emotion of this new reality pushed its way up. I reached my leg out toward him from underneath the table, pressing my calf to his. He looked up to me gratefully, his eyes shining.

"I couldn't find anyone. I was too scared to stay. Father was there and I... I..." Her voice tensed to a stop and Ilyan reached out gently to take her hand.

"Why would Talon do that, Ilyan?" I asked softly, "It doesn't make sense. Why would he do that to Wyn?"

"She was screaming to her father when we last spoke with her, it must have been his call. Besides, I don't see Talon allowing them to kill her. She had to have been taken." Ilyan's logic made sense, but something still did not fit.

"But Ilyan, I saw..." I stopped myself, having been about to reveal something I had seen during my first sight.

"Oh, what would you know about it?" Ovailia snapped, her icy blue eyes digging aggressively into me. "And what in the world gives you the right to call him by his given name?"

I opened my mouth to reply, but then closed it quickly. I needed Ovailia to believe me weak and incapable still.

"Ovailia," Ilyan scolded soundly, "Joclyn is as much of a piece of the puzzle as we are now. I do not keep anything from her anymore, and as for the name, she is free to call me anything she chooses."

He smiled at me and I looked away, placing another of the gritty mushrooms in my mouth. My body was angry with me, it needed Black Water.

"So, you have told her everything, then?" Ovailia asked, her voice awed. I kept my gaze away from her, fully aware that her eyes were boring into me.

"I have."

"Odd. She doesn't seem worried, and you don't seem to be as hands on as I thought you would be." I kept my head down. I did not appreciate this reminder as to why I did not enjoy Ovailia's company.

"Unless that is due to her hygiene. I had assumed you knew how to take better care of yourself, Joclyn. Though this look does suit you, it's disgusting."

I flinched at her words and sunk into the chair, my body aching as I looked away from both of them and toward the café.

"Be polite, Ovailia," Ilyan scolded her loudly his leg moving against mine more. It was my turn to look toward him, grateful for the contact. "We've been hiding in terrible places since someone ratted us out in Santa Fe. There hasn't exactly been a shower available."

"And yet, you stay perfectly poised."

I fought the urge to yell at her. To tell her that Ilyan had been unconscious for three days whereas I had been working and training almost nonstop. I hung my head forward and let the clumps of hair fall around me. I was beginning to realize why Thom had kept his hair in dreads.

Ilyan and Ovailia spoke in Czech, their tones quick and

irritated, before I felt Ilyan's hand on my chin. He lifted my head and I closed my eyes, not wanting to be looked at.

"I think she is beautiful."

His chosen words in front of Ovailia caught me off guard and I opened my eyes.

"Not now" I reminded him, my voice caught between pleading, worry, and joy.

"Not yet," he replied, his hand dropping back down to the table.

"And speaking of that," Ilyan mused, turning back to his sister who was looking at us with a mixture of disgust and irritation. "I need you to go and get Ryland."

"What?" Ovailia burst to her feet. The table shifted with her movement, causing most of the remaining wine to spill from the impact. Heads turned toward us at the sound and I shrunk away, hating the way people were wrinkling their noses at me.

"Sit down," Ilyan hissed, yanking her arm back down toward the table.

I felt his magic flare in me abruptly, his power pressing right up against my barrier, then turned his head slightly to either side as if looking for something. I closed my eyes and expanded my vision, but I didn't see anything out of the ordinary.

Ovailia sat down with a pout, her descent making almost as much noise as her outburst.

"Get Ryland?" she hissed. "Why in the world would I want to do that?"

"Because our father has given Joclyn a one week window to save him, but she is too weak to do anything, and because I am commanding you to do it." Ilyan's voice was authoritative and far too loud. Multiple heads in the tiny café turned to us. I hoped they didn't understand English.

I saw Ovailia calculate things in her mind. Her eyes narrowed toward her brother before darting to me and back again.

"The last thing you commanded me to do, you ended up handing over your most valuable piece of information to a traitor. Why should I trust you Ilyan? How do I know you're not feeding me to the wolves?"

The two locked eyes, their blue gazes so different, yet so similar. I couldn't breathe as I waited for her answer. I knew she would do it, but at the same time, I couldn't help thinking that I was signing Wyn's death certificate.

"Let Joclyn come with me," Ovailia said.

Ilyan's magic flared and I gasped as it pushed roughly against my barrier, though Ilyan didn't seem to notice. He was staring right into Ovailia, his eyes narrowed and angry.

"Why would I let you do that? Not only is she mine to protect, but I told you she is too weak to fight." Not to mention that she hated me—probably more than ever if she knew about Sain—but I wasn't going to bring that up now. In fact, I was quite content to sit and let the two of them duke it out.

"She knows the interior of the mansion better than anyone. Not to mention, I am going to need her there to get Ryland to cooperate." She spoke as if it was the plainest thing, but I saw her flaw immediately. My head spun to Ilyan in the hope that he had seen it as well, however his jaw stayed tight and firm, and his gaze never left Ovailia.

"Ilyan?" I asked; ignoring the glare Ovailia gave me at using his name.

I felt his leg press against mine and I held my tongue.

"Ryland's mind is erased, Ovailia. How would Joclyn be able to help?"

"If Ryland's mind is erased, then why does Joclyn want

him back so much?"

The two continued to stare hard at each other, neither of them spoke and I got the feeling they were very carefully dancing around each other in a game of chess. Each one was plotting their next move. Each one was tracking the movements of the other and waiting for a misstep.

"I have my reasons," Ilyan said. "I need a pawn to play with as well. They have Wyn and Talon. I want Ryland on my side."

"That boy would kill everyone the first chance he got, including her," she said as she pointed toward me absently, her eyes never leaving Ilyan's.

"I can handle it," Ilyan said.

"Have a death wish do we?" Ovailia spoke slowly, her long fingernail pushing around one of the mushrooms delicately.

"Most definitely." Ovailia raised an eyebrow at Ilyan's affirmation, the mushroom sliding away from her touch. Ovailia seemed to make her decision and stood as Ilyan placed a small envelope on the table.

"Our next location. Bring him there." Ilyan said, his eyes turning away from Ovailia to face me.

"Stay safe, brother," Ovailia said as she picked up the envelope, placing it in her back pocket without even looking at it.

"And you."

Ovailia turned away from us and began walking down the small alley, her hair swinging as she moved.

"Oh, and Ovailia," Ilyan called out, his eyes not leaving mine. "Don't do anything that you will regret in the morning."

"Same to you," Ovailia said as she turned away from us and continued down the street. Ilyan's eyes finally left mine as he covered his face, leaning his head over the table. I let him stay like that for a moment, not knowing how to react, or what to say to him.

"Ilyan?" I whispered his name after a moment, reaching over the table to grab his hand from off his face. He looked up at me, his eyes glistening.

"You were right, Joclyn. She simply can't be trusted."

"So you think she is working with Edmund then?" I asked as I put the mushroom I had picked up back on the plate.

"I am fairly certain of it. Just once I would like one of my siblings to stand by me. I want them to believe in something good and not to be taken in by his lies. My father only leads to hate and heartbreak." He was so sad. He had held out hope until the end, only to have his faith in his sister completely dashed.

I reached across the table and grabbed his hand, instinctively pushing my magic into him in an effort to calm him, I could feel his heart stutter and pulse as my energy wrapped around it, his muscles relaxing as extra oxygen flew to them. My actions must have caught him off guard because he looked up to me with wide eyes, his expression startled. The look made me uncomfortable so I quickly pulled away.

"Sorry," I said softly, dearly hoping he wouldn't make me elaborate or say something gushy.

"Don't be. No one has ever done that to me. Not since my mother anyway." His voice was so soft that I barely heard him.

"Healed you?" I asked, confused. After all, Thom had been pushing his magic into him all last week.

"Comforted me," he clarified, his eyes boring into me. I looked away, my heart pumping much quicker than normal.

29

I WALKED into the cave late the next day feeling clean and refreshed, if not a little awkward. In four months I had been through hell and back, chased, beaten, and attacked. So, when Ilyan had taken me to a nice hotel after our unfortunate encounter with Ovailia I hadn't known what to expect. It had been amazing to have running water and cotton sheets, but my life wasn't normal anymore; it didn't seem right to have normal things.

While there, I had taken a two hour shower that cleaned the obscene amount of dirt off of me, only to get out of the shower to a perfectly folded pile of clothes. I had breathed in the fresh smell and rubbed the cotton against my skin, thankful for something clean to wear. Who would have guessed that I would ever feel so much joy over a simple pair of khaki pants and a blue t-shirt?

I put them on and ran out to thank Ilyan who then convinced me to let him braid my hair. He had done it so gently, his finger rubbing over my mark frequently, each time sending a jolt up my spine.

So when I walked into the cave, my hair was pulled away

from my face, my mark revealed, and Ilyan's hand was wrapped firmly around mine. The contact as well as his magic had been taking away the overwhelming aches I was feeling from my absence from the Tòuha.

We walked in to find Dramin holding two large mugs. He handed one to me and I grabbed it greedily, thankful for his preparedness.

"You wouldn't be so needy if you would go into your Tòuha when you are supposed to." Dramin said, his scold lost amongst his chuckle.

"Don't judge me, Uncle," I growled between gulps.

"Next time you take her anywhere, Ilyan, remember a mug. This poor girl is ravenous."

I moved the mug away from me to scowl at him, but Dramin only chuckled more while Ilyan smiled down at me before placing his arm around my waist and leading me right to the same squishy arm chair I had been using for the past few days.

"Ah!" Thom yelled at us as he came around his bunk's partition. "You're back and alone I see."

"Were you worried, Thom?" Ilyan asked as he covered me in several furs before turning to his brother and embracing him in a slightly awkward way.

"I was."

"Well," Ilyan announced as he pulled away and moved to a large table laden with fruits and leaves, "you didn't need to be. You were right."

Thom stopped, hovering in mid-sit right before he fell onto his couch in shock.

"So she is a traitor then?" Thom said excitedly.

"I am still not convinced about that," Ilyan said, causing Thom's excited face to drop dramatically. Ilyan hadn't said anything about this to me last night.

"But you just said I was right." The disbelief in Thom's voice was clear, but Ilyan disregarded it.

"And you were. She can't be trusted. I am sure she is working with our father." Ilyan's voice was heavy, his heartbreak at the news still evident.

"But not a traitor?" Dramin spoke, putting words to the confusion we all felt.

I looked up at Ilyan, my eyebrows raised nervously; I had a feeling about where this was going, and I didn't like it.

"No," Ilyan said, his eyes meeting mine with deeper sorrow.

"Joclyn, you told me you saw my father with Talon in your first sight." My heart plunged to my toes, I didn't want to accept this.

"She wasn't telling the truth, Ilyan. She was lying to you to throw you off the trail." I pleaded with Ilyan as he returned to the fire with a small stone plate covered with what I could only assume to be dandelion leaves.

"I'm not so sure of that." I could hear the regal tone creep into his voice, but I disregarded it.

"You have to be. Talon had nothing to do with this." I begged him to understand. I had already lost Wyn, and Talon couldn't be responsible for that. He wouldn't have done that to Wyn.

"Talon?" Dramin and Thom's voices blended together in alarm. I ignored them, desperate to get my point across.

"There is no reason for him to side with Edmund, Ilyan." I reached for his hand, plunging my magic into him. I wanted to believe he was blaming Talon to try and take the blame off of Ovailia, yet I knew it was deeper than that.

"The Silnỳ is right, Ilyan. Talon has no reason to double-cross you." Dramin said, but I wasn't sure Ilyan even heard him. His eyes never wavered a millimeter from my own.

"The sight, Joclyn. Show me the sight."

I sighed dejectedly before closing my eyes and pushing that portion of the vision into his mind.

Edmund held Talon against the wall, his hand tight around his throat. Talon's face was bloodied and battered.

"Give me what I need, Talon," Edmund's voice rang out like an echo in my ears just as it had last time, though this time it had a longer, tinny sound that signified a sight of the past.

"You better make it look good, Edmund," Talon let out a deep chuckle, which echoed around my head.

I pulled the vision back, not wanting Ilyan to see too much. Ilyan's face swam back into view, his jaw set hard.

"You don't think..." I couldn't finish. I knew what it looked like; I had known from the beginning. I had always assumed that it was just Talon egging him on because it had seemed like something he would do. At least I thought it was.

"I do." The look of ultimate betrayal on Ilyan's face mixed with furious anger in a way that terrified me.

"Wait," Thom said loudly, "Talon is the traitor?"

Ilyan nodded once. "How is that even possible?" Dramin said. It was obvious no one except Ilyan believed this line of thinking.

"I'm not sure, but I will figure it out," Ilyan replied.

"I can't believe it; he wouldn't do that to Wyn," Thom began, his body leaning forward as his dreads shook. "Talon doesn't make any sense. Ovailia, however, does."

"I will give you that, Thom. If it is not Talon, then it is Ovailia."

"Really?" I didn't expect Thom to sound quite so surprised. He had been hell bent on how evil Ovailia was a few days before. Ilyan obviously didn't expect it, either. He chuckled lightly, yet the sound was strained.

"Now you're surprised. You were sure of her guilt forty-eight hours ago," Ilyan laughed.

"Oh, you misunderstand, Ilyan. I am not surprised she is a traitor. I am surprised that you are admitting it."

"Only partially," he said.

"So did she agree to it?" Dramin asked, heading off the bickering.

"She did," Ilyan said confidently. "Not without revealing her true nature, but she agreed to do it."

"So she's a traitor," Thom said happily.

"We've covered this already," Ilyan said as he popped a few of his favorite dandelion covered berries into his mouth. He must have known I was watching him because he turned to me and winked. I looked away, unwilling to accept the mix of nerves I was filled with.

"So she knows about Sain?" Dramin asked, his intent to stop any argument obvious.

"Without a doubt. If she is working for Edmund, then he has shown her. Especially if he is hoping it will fuel the fire of her anger against me." Ilyan's voice was firm.

"Oh, she must hate you," Thom taunted, his feet moving back and forth in joy.

"And yet, you do not think she is the one who betrayed you?" Dramin asked, his eyebrow raising as he ignored Thom.

"You have seen Joclyn's sight, Dramin. You know what it looks like." Ilyan's voice was tight and strained. He leaned forward in the chair as he pleaded angrily.

"I have." Dramin said calmly as he sipped at his Black Water. "But sometimes things are not what they seem. You know this better than anyone."

Ilyan exhaled deeply and sat back against the chair, his jaw tight. I had never seen Ilyan like this. He was so angry and betrayed. I reached out awkwardly and placed my hand against his cheek briefly.

"So," Dramin spoke loudly in an attempt to offset the tension. "Where is she bringing him?"

"The Rioseco Abbey."

"In Spain? The same one..."

"Yes." Ilyan cut him off in an obvious attempt to stop him from saying something.

I looked at Ilyan curiously, begging him to elaborate, however Ilyan only shook his head. Unfortunately, the exchange did not go unnoticed.

"Tell her, Ilyan," Thom moaned as he sat up on his couch. "Deep inside she wants to kiss you anyway, so you might as well let her know when and where it's going to happen."

I froze, an onslaught of images from the sight ramming into my brain. Not yet, maybe not ever. I repeated it to myself, although I couldn't ignore the excited heart slamming I was experiencing. My breathing picked up before Ilyan's magic surged into me, calming me almost instantly.

"Not yet." Ilyan spoke quietly in an effort to calm me. It worked until Thom spoke again.

"Get it over with, brother! Kiss her!"

"You're right, Thom," Ilyan said, his voice light. I froze. "Would you care to practice with me?"

Both men laughed in a way that said they were going to keep the bashing comments going for a while, something I wasn't looking forward to.

I wasn't the only one.

"Now, now boys," Dramin said with a smile. "You can

battle it out in the hall in a little while, goodness knows you need a bit of a testosterone release, but now is not the time."

Thom huffed and put his feet back on the couch, his hand moving to rest behind his head.

"If you do, I want to watch," I said, the thought of them battling out their manhood was almost too good to pass up.

"You can join in, too, Joclyn," Ilyan teased as he popped a berry into his mouth.

"No, thank you," I laughed.

"Why not," Thom said, sitting up. "You can be on my side. Together we can take him."

Thom rammed his fist into his open palm and I almost choked on the Black Water I had just swallowed.

"Number one," I sputtered as I tried to clear my throat, "I am not a man. And number two, I can probably take both of you with my eyes closed, thank you very much."

Both Ilyan and Thom stared at me open-mouthed for a minute as if I had seriously undermined their manhood while Dramin only laughed.

"Of course you can take them with your eyes closed, your mind's sight is better than your vision."

"Is that a challenge?" Thom said, standing up as if Dramin hadn't even spoken. "Ilyan and I can beat you!"

"I'm not joining in on this," Ilyan said, but no one seemed to hear him. I locked eyes with Thom, trying to determine why he had gotten so upset, before shaking my head and turning away from him.

"Maybe tomorrow," I said.

"Tomorrow? I say now!"

I jumped a bit at Thom's tone, Ilyan jumping into Protector-position automatically. Thom had obviously been a little too cooped up in here.

"I'll spar you tomorrow, Thom," I said from behind, Ilyan. "I'm too weak today."

Ilyan turned, his body dropping to my level, his face instantly concerned.

"Is it too much? We can do it today." I smiled at how he instantly knew what I was talking about and at his willingness to fix it. I felt his magic surge as he tried to repair any current damage that was being done to my body.

"Not today," I cringed. "I can wait one more day."

"Are you sure? It's already been two days." Ilyan asked, his finger tracing down my neck. I jumped involuntarily when the shock sped down my spine at Ilyan's contact with my mark.

"Yes," I said somewhat breathlessly. Ilyan smiled at my reaction.

"Let me know if you change your mind."

"Ugh!" Thom groaned loudly as he flailed around on his couch in obvious discomfort. "Will you two get a room? With a door?"

I blushed and looked away, suddenly feeling very uncomfortable. Ilyan stood and moved away from me to stand before Thom, the two beginning to fist fight each other playfully. Dramin took a long drink of his Black Water while I did the same as I sighed and sunk into the chair.

I watched the two men fight, their odd banter bouncing back and forth as they jumped around the large space. Dramin chuckled at their play. I sunk back further, and before I knew it, I had fallen asleep.

My eyes opened to Ryland standing alone in the middle of the clearing.

"Jos." He whispered my name before running to me, his body strangely strong and whole again. His dark curls bounced as he came to me, his bright blue eyes cutting into my soul.

"Ryland?" I didn't dare hope, but right then I was so happy to see him after everything that he had said before that I needed to know.

I opened my mouth to ask if it was really him, but I never even got one word out. His lips covered mine as he pressed into me, his hands and mouth encompassing me with a kiss I could have never imagined would come from him. It was deep and needy in a way that made my toes shake. I sighed as a spot deep inside my belly spun with joy.

He pulled away, his eyes gazing deeply into mine. His look was suddenly desperate and panicked.

"Ryland?" I asked, growing worried.

"You know I love you, right?" he asked, his eyes darting frantically over my face. "More than anything?"

"Yes," I answered breathlessly.

"And you know I would do anything to save you, to protect you. Right?" My veins turned to ice. I didn't like where this was going.

"Ryland?" I asked, not willing to give him the answer to his question.

"Break the connection, Joclyn. Now. Have Ilyan show you how. Do it the second you wake up." He grabbed my hands tightly and pulled me down to the forest floor, my knees crunching against the dead leaves.

"Ryland, why are you asking me to do this?" I could barely get the words out, my throat felt so tight.

"It's the only way to keep you safe, Jos. I should have never completed the Zělství. I thought I was strong enough, I thought I could..." He shook his head and looked away from me.

339

"I can't. Ryland... I can't." I clung to his hands tighter, pulling him into me. "I need you."

"No, you don't!" he yelled loudly, his voice reverberating off the trees. "I can't save you. I can't protect you. Not anymore!"

"Ryland," my voice was a squeak, my heart thumping wildly in my chest.

"You have to break..." He stopped and his eyes went wide as his gaze strayed somewhere beyond me, the panic evident on his face. I went to turn, terrified at what I might see, yet Ryland forced me back to look at him. Quick footsteps were coming up behind me; a hand grabbed my hair and pulled me to standing.

"Break the connection, and don't go in..." Ryland's voice was silenced in my ears as I felt a body behind me at the same time a knife was thrust against my throat. Cail's wicked laugh echoed through my head before I woke up clutching my neck. My breathing came in sharp, panicked spurts, but I did not scream.

I stared at the roof of the bunk I had obviously been moved to as I waited for my breathing to calm, my mind playing Ilyan's song for me inside my head. I listened to it until the panic was gone, most of the vivid images of the nightmare fading into the netherworld that existed between sleep and waking. I curled into Ilyan's chest—partially wondering why he was already in my bed—before I drifted off to sleep again.

30

_____

I WOKE up the next morning and almost yelled out with my first movement. My body was filled with the aches of having avoided the Tŏuha for so long. I shifted my weight in Ilyan's arms and my back seized, the muscles calling out in protest.

I knew I couldn't wait any longer to go into the Tŏuha, but I was still scared; more so after last night's dream. Dramin had told me to wait to talk to Ilyan about breaking the bond until after I had decided what course to take, but I didn't know how much more time I could wait. I needed to talk to someone.

It scared me the way Ryland had begged me to break the Zĕlství, begged for me to do it right then, and then there was Cail.

Cail lived off of his taunts—his torture—yet he hadn't even hesitated before killing me. The lack of his usual games made my teeth clench.

I shuddered at the memory, my heart rate accelerating in an unhealthy way.

I rolled over again, turning to face Ilyan. I moved the

hair that had fallen over his face, his mouth slightly open in his sleep as usual.

I knew what I had to do as much as I didn't want to. As much as it hurt, I needed to break the connection. I needed Ryland; at least I thought I did. Ryland had protected me as I grown up. He had loved me and taught me how to love when I hadn't been sure I knew how to anymore. He had protected me from his father and used his body to shield me, and now he was trying to protect me by breaking the connection.

I loved him more than I ever thought I could love someone. That's why it hurt so much every time he asked me to break the connection. I didn't want to lose that. I didn't want to lose the last normal thing from my old life.

But I wasn't normal anymore, and I had changed. I had grown stronger and more confident than I had ever felt.

I think I knew I had to break the last connection to the old me, no matter how much it hurt to say it. Besides, once that connection was broken, I would be free. Free from the torment. Free to become what I was born to be.

The Silnỳ.

"For it is only by your side that she can find her true purpose, that she will find the strength to kill those that would end the magic of the world." I whispered the words of the sight to myself; the sight that told of me and what I had been born to do.

I knew it was true, and although part of me shattered at the thought, I knew it needed to be done.

I needed to break the connection.

"Ilyan," I said his name loud enough for him to hear me, my hand still on his bare chest.

His eyes opened sleepily, blinking a few times before he fully registered where he was.

"Jos," he sighed, his voice heavy. He reached up and placed his hand over mine pushing it into his scarred chest.

"No nightmares?" He was so hopeful, I only smiled and shook my head. After all, that would be the last one.

"I am so glad." He freed my hand from his chest to pull me into him. I cringed at the pain the movement and pressure caused me. He stopped immediately, his magic flaring abruptly as he searched through my body. He looked at me alarmed and I knew he had found something.

"I'm scared, Ilyan," I whispered, my voice as weak as my body felt.

He leaned over to me and gently kissed my forehead, his lips soft against my skin.

"I will be here the entire time, Joclyn. Be quick." I smiled at him and nodded. When I got back I would tell him. I would need strength to break the Zělství anyway.

I pulled the necklace out from under my shirt and pushed my magic into it before leaning into Ilyan's chest and letting his arms wrap around me.

I closed my eyes only to open them to the same dilapidated kitchen and instantly started hyperventilating. Cail stood right before me. His face was pulled into a wicked grin, his eyes blacker than I had ever seen them.

The dark eyed man.

"Why hello, Joclyn," he said. "You don't seem happy to see me."

I stared at him, unsure of what to say.

"What are you doing here?" His twisted joy grew at my fear.

"Why, Joclyn, isn't it obvious? I've been here all along." He smirked and stepped forward, causing me to step back instinctively. My foot hit the table leg and I stopped, trapped, as he continued to move forward.

"I was here when Ryland showed you the Vilỳ, I was the one who told him that you didn't want him, and I was the one that took away the pretty overcoat Ryland had given this place." He gestured around him to the rotting kitchen, but I couldn't take my eyes off of him.

"For the last three months I have slowly brought you into Ryland's mind. This is what your mate's mind truly looks like; destroyed, rotten, forgotten. There is no love here, which is why you don't belong here."

He continued to move toward me, but I couldn't move. The memories and fear of every encounter with him weighed me down.

"You're the one who has been telling him to force me out." I gasped, letting the fact free from my fears.

"Now, that's an interesting thing. I actually have not been telling him to do that. It would ruin my fun, after all. Ryland's mind is an interesting place, though. Not only does he remember enough about you to realize you're in danger, but he also brought himself into your dream last night. He was desperate to get you to break the bond to keep you from this mess. Thankfully, you didn't listen."

Cail emphasized his last words, each syllable shooting through me like I had been slapped. Ryland had been trying to protect me all this time. I felt the wind suck out of my lungs.

"And, now," Cail continued, "here you are. Trapped."

"Trapped?" I repeated the little air that I could hold in my lungs gasping out.

I spun around to look for the black door that I had always been able to exit through. My heart dropped to see a tall man standing in front of it, his eyes boring into me dangerously.

I took a step forward, my hands raising toward the tall

guard, I was getting out of here. I felt my magic crackle between my fingers, it felt more alive than in the nightmares; more powerful.

"I wouldn't do that if I were you," Cail taunted, freezing me in place. "Everything you do here, you do in the waking world. You attack him, or me, and you will throw that weapon at Ilyan. I bet he sleeps right beside you, holding you. Protecting you. It would be a shame if you killed him. An absolute shame."

Cail came up behind me, his hands moving to rest on the table on either side of me, pinning me in place.

"Now, I bet you are thinking," he began, his voice wickedly soft in my ear, "that you could just find a way to fight him and leave, but then, Ryland hit you with that barstool last time, and I bet when you woke up you were bleeding."

He let his words drift off, his hand moving to trail up my arm. The touch shot through me and I spun around, grabbing his arm and twisting it awkwardly into the table. He yelled out as my strength pinned him down. His discomfort lasted barely a minute before I felt his magic surge and a conjured knife appeared in the palm of his free hand as he motioned me away from him. I gasped and jumped away, the memory from my last dream still fresh. My movement only caused Cail's joy to increase, his smile widening.

"Did Ilyan heal you when you woke up? Do you think he could heal you if you didn't wake up?"

I looked toward the man who stood in front of the door, his eyes following me greedily as he flexed his fingers, red energy crackling between his knuckles.

"What are you saying?" I immediately regretted asking,

but I couldn't help it. I silently prayed he wasn't saying what I knew he was.

"This is not like your dreams, Joclyn. You attack me here, you attack Ilyan there. You conjure weapons here, you do the same there. You will not wake in the arms of your true love if you die here, you will simply die."

I gasped and he smiled more. He grabbed a rotten apple and balanced its weight in his hand for a moment before throwing it against one of the teetering cabinet doors. The door fell to the ground as the apple exploded.

"Boom!" Cail yelled joyfully, causing me to jump. "Dead. Gone! Which in all honesty is how we want you. But I figure, and Edmund agrees with me, why not have a little fun first? Why not play a little game?"

"No," I gasped in panicked desperation. I clutched my shoulder where Ilyan's Štít lay, yet I felt nothing.

"Oh, yes." He smiled and my breathing picked up. "If you try to get through that door," he pointed to my normal exit, "he will kill you. Which means the only way out of this room is through that door."

Cail grabbed my shoulders and moved me to face the door that led into the mansion.

"Now through that door are the depths of Ryland's mind. In there, he may remember you, he may not, or he may hate you enough to kill you himself. But do not fear, I am not sending you in there after him, I am sending you in there away from me. And when I find you, I will do away with you in the most painful way I can think of."

I cringed as he produced his knife and rested the blade against my chest. I tried to move away from him, but he held me tighter.

"Don't worry, I will give you a head start. It's only fair after all." He dug his fingers into my shoulders, causing me to gasp at the pain. "But don't forget, whatever magic you do here, you do in the real world. Though if I do my job right, in a matter of hours you won't even remember you have magic inside of you."

"Let me go," I snarled as he continued to hold me. I stumbled when he released me with a little push, surprised he had done it so quickly.

"If you insist," Cail said. "But you'd better run, your ten minute head start begins now."

I spun around to face him, Cail stood with his face screwed up in manic excitement.

Cail had trapped me in here with the full intention of torturing me in a way that would only end in my death. I needed to get out of here. I knew there had to be a way. I could already feel my soul call to it, a promise of showing me a way out that would not end in my death.

My eyes darted to the guard who stood in front of the black door, blocking my exit. I knew I could defeat him easily, but I also knew that Ilyan still lay right beside me, his arms wrapped around me. Anything I would do in a fight, would go right into Ilyan.

Cail caught my eye, his lip curling as he interpreted my thoughts, knowing his plan was working.

"Run." Cail said, and I didn't wait. I turned and ran into the pits of the house, which was all that was left of Ryland's mind, tears already streaming down my face.

31

I RAN into the mansion without looking back. I knew Cail was serious. I needed to get away from him as fast as possible and figure out a way to get out of here before Cail found and killed me.

A few steps into the house, I tripped on broken bits of carpet that had been pulled up, burned away, or maybe eaten by some form of rodent. I caught myself, picking my feet up in my run and quickening my pace. Without thinking about it, I sped through the house, taking the path I had traveled almost every day of my life until last May; the path that would take me to Ryland's room.

My heart thumped loudly as something told me to stop, my breath catching at the overwhelming sensation. I stopped dead, clutching my shoulder, hoping to find Ilyan's warmth inside of me but still finding nothing. I kept my hand there as I thought through what I was doing, what I was going to do, something unsettling deep in my gut telling me to hide.

I had gone right to where Cail would expect me to go;

into what I could only assume to be a trap. I needed to figure out what to do before I came face to face with him.

I stopped before opening the door to Ryland's hall and instead sunk into what I knew would be a supply closet. Cail had given me a ten minute head start, surely five of that had already past. I had five extra minutes to hide or five minutes to find my way out. That was, if Cail chose to wait the full ten, which I doubted.

I closed the door to the closet behind me as softly as I could. I would know in a few minutes if Cail would come right here in his attempt to track me down or if he would begin his search elsewhere. It all came down to how well he knew me.

I needed to be smart about how I handled this, the faster I got out of here the better. Without being able to use magic to defend myself, though, I was limited as to what I could do and how fast I could leave. If it was an option, I would blast right through the man blocking my exit, but Ilyan was lying right next to me. The risk of killing him was too great.

My eyes were trained on the dim light that was filtering in through the crease in the door while I attempted to keep my mind off the scurrying feet and other noises that were filling the small room. I had only waited a minute before heavy footfalls filled the air, the impact of them rattling bins and boxes of who knows what in my hiding space. The sound grew louder as Cail ran down the hall, tracing my exact steps. I slunk away from the door, holding my breath in terror that he would find me. My back hit against a shelf, causing moldy towels and mouse feces to fall over my head. My mouth opened in expectation of a scream, but I shoved my fist heavily into it, desperate to keep myself quiet.

If I was going to fight, I needed surprise on my side.

I heard his footsteps stop, and I knew I had made too

much noise. As quietly as I could, I shoved myself into a corner, placing my body as much behind one of the large shelving units as possible. I cringed as my foot stepped on something soft, closing my eyes as I shut my mind off, not wanting to think about what it could be.

As soon as I had moved myself into the corner, the door flew open. I flattened my body even further against the soft, damp wall, hoping that I was back enough that he wouldn't see me. The light from the open door caught the eyes of more than a dozen large rats, each lifting their head in expectation.

The light illuminated the stacks of molding towels along with mildewed sheets that were dotted with feces and cleaning supplies which had rusted through their containers leaving glistening patches of dried chemicals underneath them. Everything lit up dimly as Cail stood with the door open, his breath flowing through the room in silent puffs.

I kept my breath trapped inside me, focusing on random objects around me so as not to think about the pain that was beginning to seep through my chest. My eyes widened when they came to rest on a long, rusty length of pipe hidden in the piles of rot.

I kept my eyes on the pipe as I listened to Cail's breathing, trying to ignore the earsplitting pressure from my lungs. My mind screamed at me for air, and I screamed back that he would kill me.

The door slowly closed, the sound of the hinge grinding through my brain and making the movement feel even slower. I waited to breathe, but his footsteps did not retreat. He was standing right on the other side of the door waiting for me. He knew I was in here.

Cail was playing his game.

Everything inside of me was begging for air. I took a step forward, my feet soft against the floor, then reached out and wrapped my hands around the pipe, the metal cold and slimy underneath my fingers. I gripped it firmly, moving it up like a bat as I surged my magic through it. If I couldn't use my ability as a weapon against him, then I would use it to increase the power of a weapon.

I closed my eyes. Please don't let Ilyan still be next to me. Please don't let this actually move through into the real world.

My breath released as I swung the pipe forward, aiming it where Cail would be standing on the other side of the door. My magic filled the metal, making it grow red as it prepared to explode through the door and hopefully Cail.

I saw the shadow of Cail's feet shift as the pipe made contact with the door, the rotted wood falling away from the impact. I had expected to hit Cail, but instead the pipe sliced through empty air. My eyes widened in confusion before a long-fingered hand wrapped around the pipe, and with one pull, yanked it through the door, my body following as I futilely held on.

I stumbled through the shards of wood, my feet barely keeping me upright before the hand moved from the pipe to my arm, the grip digging into my skin as Cail pulled me against him.

"Joclyn, Joclyn, Joclyn. You are going to make this far too fun, aren't you?" I cringed away from Cail's brittle breath in my nostrils.

"I wouldn't call this fun, but if that's the word you choose..." I gritted my teeth and moved closer to him, hoping to catch him off guard.

Cail's eyes widened in excitement before I slammed my knee in between his legs, his body toppling over me before I grabbed the pipe and hit the metal against his back with as much force as I could muster.

I didn't wait to see if I had done any damage. I turned and ran from him, the pipe in front of me like a sword. I had just begun turning a corner when I felt Cail's magic wrap around me, his power dragging me back and slamming me against a wall.

I cringed as Cail limped up to me, a string of profanity flowing from him as he rubbed his neck. His magic held me tightly against the wall, rendering my pipe useless. I racked my brain for options as he moved toward me. I had already been trapped inside of the Tòuha for the last twenty minutes by my best guess, meaning it had only been a few minutes in the real world if my math was right. Ilyan would still be laying right up against me. I couldn't risk using any magic yet.

Cail came up beside me, his one hand resting against the wall by my head while the other massaged his neck where the pipe had made contact.

"You naughty little girl," he said, his lip turned up a wicked grin. "Now I see what Ryland was talking about."

"What? That I am strong enough to defeat you?" I raised my eyebrow hoping to sound confident while knowing that the shake of fear in my voice gave me away.

What little bravado I had used for my façade faded away as Cail began to laugh, his loud voice ricocheting around the hallway.

"No," he taunted, my muscles tensing, "that you need to be trained."

I didn't have time to think about what was going to happen before the pipe collided with my stomach. The impact raced through my body, vibrating up my spine and ricocheting through my skull. I screamed out at the impact as Cail's binds left me, my body collapsing to the ground.

I didn't have time to run or even move before the pipe impacted my spine. Once. Twice. It sent me sprawling to the ground. I screamed out and little flecks of blood flew from my mouth, splattering the ground with glistening red droplets.

"Will you look at that?" Cail mused as he kneeled beside me. "Blood. I bet Ilyan is having a conniption. I can almost hear him, 'Oh, my love! Why are you bleeding!'" Cail's voice went high as he mocked Ilyan, however I barely heard him. If I was bleeding in real life, Ilyan wouldn't be by me. Ilyan would be running for Dramin.

At least, I hoped he would.

I didn't wait to think. I focused my magic on the floor right below Cail, sending a pulse directly at it. The floor exploded at the impact, sending him hurtling through the fissure I had managed to open.

I watched the hole in the floor for a moment before crawling away, my body slow and sluggish as it healed itself. I moved as quickly as I could toward Ryland's room, terrified that Cail would return before I could get behind the door; terrified that I had injured Ilyan in some way.

I pulled my way through the door to hide in the shattered remains of Ryland's kitchenette. Once inside, I felt my organs knit themselves back together as I sat hiding behind a displaced cabinet.

So, fighting him may not have been such a good idea. While I was more than powerful enough to do away with Cail, I could not guarantee I wouldn't hurt someone in the cave or collapse the cave itself. While part of me hoped Ilyan would place me somewhere logical, chances were higher that he would be so worried that he wouldn't leave my side. His instincts as my Protector wouldn't let him. So if I couldn't fight, then I had only one option, hide and find a way out...

"What are you doing here?" My head snapped up at the voice, relaxing to see Ryland's frame towering over me.

"Ryland?" Everything in me relaxed until I registered the panic on his face and the anger lines on his forehead.

"You've got to get out of here." He grabbed my hand and pulled me up, not saying anything before dragging me behind him and out the door.

We moved back toward the main kitchen, our feet slipping and catching on debris. Before we had gotten too close to the kitchen, Ryland deviated, pulling us out of the servants' quarters and into the main living space.

Large, rumbling bangs sounded through the house as we moved. It reminded me of when we had fled this place leaving Ryland behind during the battle. I had just caught sight of the main ballroom before Ryland dragged me into a large office, shutting the door behind us.

The door had barely clicked shut before he turned back to me, the anger on his face now mixed with fear.

"What are you doing here? I told you to break the bond." Ryland's hand shook as he moved hair away from my face, his eyes staying on mine for a moment before darting around the room. The movement of his eyes and the shake of his hand put me one edge, his paranoia contagious.

"What do you mean?" I asked. Where was our happy reunion?

"I told you not to come back." His hands dug into me, his grip pushing me against the wall.

"I know, I needed to see you..." I reached up to touch his face, my hand stopping halfway at the look in his eyes.

"Why didn't you break the bond?"

"I was going to, after..."

"You waited, and now it's too late. He's going to kill you, Jos! Do you know what I risked to warn you? What they did to me? To Wyn? To your dad? We risked it all and you didn't listen." His anger cut through me. I could only stare at him wide-eyed as I tried to make sense of what he was saying.

"I know! I'm sorry, alright," I stammered.

"Being sorry means nothing!" he yelled, slamming his fist into the wall by my head.

I jumped and tried to move away from him, but his hands kept me restrained.

"What do you want from me, Ry? I'm trying, okay?" I couldn't help but yell. The anger and fear inside of me bubbled out, directing itself at Ryland.

"Trying to what, Jos? Not Listen? I'm trying to save you and you can't even let me do that. Why did I even bond myself to you?" His words were loud and echoed around the empty room. I wanted to sink away into nothing. I had asked myself the same thing a million times because of the doubt that I had felt, the hopelessness that the Zělství had caused me... us. Because of the pain, the torture; I had felt it all and asked the same question, however hearing it from him still hurt.

"Why did you?" I asked, my voice soft.

"Because I can't live without you! I couldn't see you with someone else, ever. I was hoping I could take Ilyan's place if I sealed myself to you!"

"Take his place?"

"You can't love him, Jos. He's not the one for you. I am."

I stared at him, my mouth hanging open. I loved Ryland, but he stood there admitting that he had known what I had been born for. He had known what the mark meant, and he had still bonded himself to me. I didn't know if he had done it because he wanted to protect me, or because he really did love me, or because he wanted the power.

"*I* love you," he said, his hands strong against my forearms.

"Love me? Then why did you do it? You knew what I was. You knew I was meant for Ilyan. What did you have to gain?" My words trailed off at the memory of the riddle Ryland's possessed body had told me on a roof top. It couldn't be...

"No!" I yelled, pushing him away from me.

Ryland couldn't have bonded himself to me for his own gain.

I repeated it to myself, almost willing the words to be true.

"Leave me alone!" I yelled as I turned away from him, his fingers curling around my forearm like a vice and stopping me in my tracks.

"Is that what you want? For me to leave you alone?"

"Yes!" I spat, ignoring the knife-like stab in my heart.

"Wish granted!" He pushed me away from him as I stumbled, my head spinning as the room shook. As another explosion sounded, this one closer and more aggressive than the last, Ryland swore loudly before grabbing my arm and dragging me through the manor.

We didn't get far before he shoved me into a closet just as footsteps approached. I moved my body into the corner as Cail yelled out, his voice loud in the tiny space.

"No!"

"Yes," Ryland taunted him, his voice deep and menacing.

"How did you get here?" The level of fear in Cail's voice was shocking to me. Why did Ryland's presence scare him so much?

I felt the small paw of a rodent press against my

shoulder before the full weight of the creature transferred onto my collar bone. I opened my mouth in horror, not daring to move, while my body unwillingly took in a shaky breath that I prayed was not audible.

"It is my mind, Cail." Ryland said, the smile evident in his voice.

Everything froze as the rat walked across my back, his body tangling itself in my hair. I tried to keep my panic under control and another shaky inhale silent as he made his passage.

"Not for long."

The tiny closet shook as an explosion rattled the space sending books and baskets onto me. I screamed and covered my head, hoping my voice was not heard through the fight that was being waged right outside the door.

My breathing picked up into a pant as I began to panic. The explosions grew in number at the same time that they moved further down the hall, Ryland leading Cail away from me and giving me a chance to escape. I wiped away the invisible tracks of the rat, my shoulders shuddering in disgust. Then, without thinking, I broke out of the closet and took off back the way I had come. I turned into a hallway I had never entered before, hoping the two locked in battle had not seen me flee.

I was at a disadvantage here. I only knew parts of this mansion. I knew how to get to Ryland's room and most of the servants corridors of the upper levels, but the main living space and all the lower rooms were foreign to me. If I was going to get the upper hand, I wasn't going to find it here.

I continued to run down the hall, my feet slipping on decaying carpet at my increased speed.

I hadn't gone very far when a loud crash echoed in the

space around me causing light fixtures to shake and pieces of plaster to fall. I stopped in my tracks at the movement, my pulse surging heavily as I waited; as I tried to figure out what course to take. I could hear it pulse through my ear drums and feel it move through my fingers.

"Don't stop moving," I whispered aloud to myself, but I still couldn't move. Slowly I pried my feet off the floor and shifted into a run, knowing that a moving target was harder to catch. I kept going until I came to a split flight of stairs, one side leading back up to Ryland's room, the other side leading down to the unknown levels of the house. I stayed still for a second before moving to go down.

I picked up my pace as I headed down the stairs, my hand lightly grazing the dirt and mold covered railing for stability. I turned corner after corner as I descended, each level becoming more infested, more deteriorated, and more blood covered. Even though I knew that was what it was, I begged my mind to believe it to be paint. It was splattered everywhere.

The more I moved through the silence, the more I became aware of every noise and twitch of the air surrounding me. I jumped at every creak, at the steady thumping that came from somewhere around me. I would pass doors which lead to floors of the estate, sure I heard voices on the other side, only to stop and have those voices turn into the squeaking of mice or ripping of paper.

I stopped abruptly when I had moved down about six stories, my heart thumping wildly at the pool of red liquid that occupied the landing of the steps below me. The smooth, red fluid swirled aggressively as if it was being disturbed; as if something around the next turn was moving through it.

I gasped as my muscles tensed, my panic growing. I

turned as quickly as I could, running back up the stairs, desperate to get away from whatever was deep within the pool of blood.

I had gone up far more floors than I had gone down when I realized that nothing was changing. I should have moved back into the manor by now, but the walls still remained red and glistening. My eyes darted around wildly before I turned to retrace my steps.

Two steps down, I howled in horror as my foot plunged into the warm pool of fluid. I looked at the bubbling pool of blood, fear pulsing through my ears. I had left this pool behind me, at least ten flights of stairs down, and yet, here it was.

As I watched, the liquid lurched, growing a step and splashing against my foot. I screamed and grasped the door knob to the nearest floor, flinging my body through the door, not bothering to check if anyone was waiting for me on the other side. My only thought was to get away from the pool of blood.

32

_____

I PRESSED my back against the door as it closed, my eyes widening as I came face to face with the longest hall I had ever seen. The walls were burnt and red while the floors were damp with large chunks missing from them. I almost expected Cail to come bursting through any of the many doors.

I tried to control my panic, but I knew it was no use. Cail had trapped me in the worst nightmare I had ever experienced. This was a million times worse than every time he had chased me through the manor, hunted me through the forest, or murdered me into waking. I could feel my neck twitch in fear as I fought the urge to collapse into myself.

Instinctively, I began to sing Ilyan's song in my head, the notes playing loudly as I walked down the hall and into the unknown realm I had entered.

I moved as silently as I could, jumping over the open gaps and tiptoeing around small animal carcasses as I moved. Every other step would trigger a sound far down the hall and I would freeze, staring at the floor, not willing to look up and face whatever might be before me. Praying that nothing was there. I kept moving, my pace slow as I trudged forward in desperation, my heart calling for a way out.

A way out?

That was what I was down there for, right?

Everything was fuzzy, like the recall in my mind had been broken.

Two hours in the Tŏuha for every twenty minutes in the waking world. I wanted to say it had already been two hours, but it was hard to tell. Somewhere in the back of my mind I wondered if Ilyan might know how to pull me out of here, but I knew he wouldn't. After all, Edmund and Cail wouldn't even be playing this little game if there was a way for him to do that.

But still, I had to hope.

My thoughts were cut off as heavy footsteps began to sound behind me. These weren't like the other sounds, these were rough and heavy. The gait was familiar in my memory. I stopped for a moment before picking up the pace, my panic moving deeper into me. My fear was becoming part of me, a tangible thing that was weaving itself into my soul.

I jumped over open caverns, moved around bones and feces, only to have the vibration increase, the sound grow louder. I took one last leap before fiddling with the knob of one of the many doors along the hall. It swung wide and I jumped inside, slamming it loudly behind me before turning to face the room. But it wasn't a room. It was yet another long hallway with more blood, more bones, and more pits into an endless abyss below.

Even though I had escaped one hallway, the rattling footsteps of the last seemed to follow me here. I couldn't suppress the feeling that whoever it was stood right on the other side of the door.

I immediately began opening doors, the thought of escape consuming me. I moved from one hallway to another, my feet running without thinking. The only things I could focus on were the footsteps and the drumming of blood through my eardrums.

Doors.

One of them had to lead somewhere I would recognize. One of them had to lead to... to...

Where was I going?

I stopped as I moved through the fifth door in the third hallway and looked around. This hallway looked like all the others. Was there something there I was trying to find?

Yes.

But what?

I closed my eyes, racking my brain and trying to replay the last few minutes.

The way out.

I was looking for a way out.

This space was messing with my mind. I immediately turned around and went back through the door I had entered, back into another identical hallway when I froze.

Doors.

I had no way of knowing which one I had come through. I was so concerned with getting away from whatever was following me, that I had gotten myself lost; lost in the house that was Ryland's mind.

I sunk down to the ground. Tears burned my face as they trailed down my cheeks, I tried to restrain the noise, unsure if Cail was down here or if he was even still trying to find me. I sucked in my tears, letting Ilyan's lullaby take their place. I sang the song aloud, whispering the words in the desperate hope that no one would hear me while still needing the comfort.

Slowly my pulse began to slow. My breathing evened out, and I let the song fizzle away. I wasn't comforted. I wasn't safe. I was still trapped in this hell that Cail had designed for me, but things didn't seem so desperate. I needed to find...

What was it again?

That was right.

Home. I needed to go home.

I stood and walked across the hall, my hand reaching for yet another doorknob. I froze, my hand still poised over the knob.

There were voices on the other side of this door.

The voices seemed familiar, but I couldn't place them.

"It's been hours. How is the progress?" The older man's voice boomed. He almost sounded bored, as though he was looking over paperwork.

"It is coming, Master. I have guided her to where we want her and begun the process as you have asked."

Master? Why did that phrase sound so familiar?

Suddenly the voice of the younger, scared man clicked into place—Cail. Which would make the older man Edmund. I shook my head in an attempt to clear the fog. How could I have forgotten them?

"Have you? Already?" Edmund sounded shocked now, pleased.

"Yes."

"Very nice, Cail. I'm impressed," Edmund said, "They have already begun to break their bond, I will continue the process before she finds her way back. Without the path back to her own mind, she will be trapped here."

Break the bond? That sounded familiar. I moved one step closer to the door, pressing my eyes against the small opening, desperate to see. Cail stood before Edmund, who sat in a large ornate chair with his legs crossed as he played with an elaborate ring on his finger. Edmund looked wrong somehow, though; almost like he was faded or covered in wax paper.

"Do you think that is possible?" Cail said, his voice breaking with tension. "I have set a web to trap her inside my mind. There is no way to find a way through it without guidance." Edmund didn't even look at him.

I stepped away from the door to look around me. Cail's mind. He had told me it was Ryland's mind.

Ryland.

The bond.

"She has been brought here through the bond, meaning Ryland could find his way inside and lead her out. Break the bond and I destroy the path that got her here. She would be trapped, her mind lost inside of yours with no way out."

Everything clicked together and I covered my mouth. Something in me was screaming trap, danger, warning; but I still couldn't quite remember why they would do all this to me.

"Are you sure you are up for the challenge, Cail?" Edmund asked, yet Cail only laughed in response.

"I am sure, Master. She is putting up quite an enjoyable fight."

"You better give me a good show, Cail. Otherwise I will unbind that little curse you put on your sister."

I pressed my eyes against the opening again at the mention of Wyn, surprised that the recollection of her name had come so swiftly. I didn't like how fuzzy this place was making my brain. I needed to get out of here.

"No!" Cail's voice was loud, panicked, and unexpected. I would never have expected such terror to come out of him.

Cail had taken a desperate step forward, the action causing Edmund to look up.

"Oh, yes, imagine all that poison weaving itself away from her skin and into her blood stream..."

"Master, you..." Cail began to interrupt him but was silenced with one look from Edmund. Cail's hand flew to his heart in panic.

"Cail." The strict tone of Edmund's voice was like ice down my spine.

"Yes, Master." Cail spoke quietly—dejectedly—before his back straightened and his head turned to look right at me. This time I was sure he had seen me.

"Yes, Master," He said again as his lip curled. "Let the games begin."

"Oh, good. I will give you one month, Cail." I barely heard Edmund's voice over the heavy thumping of my heart. Cail turned and was walking right toward me, his eyes looking into mine. I couldn't move. I had frozen in place, my hand still clinging to the doorknob.

I knew I should be looking around for some form of weapon or trying to get away, but I couldn't tear my eyes from his black stare or the sneer on his lips.

"Run, Joclyn." I barely registered that someone had spoken before a hand wrapped around mine, another person dragging me down the hall.

I stumbled along for a few steps before turning toward whoever was pulling me away. My heart jumpstarted at the mop of dark curls bouncing in front of me.

Ryland led me from hall to hall, the long passageways changing to smaller rooms, and even apartments complete with kitchens. Everything about the space we now moved through was familiar, like a place I had lived in or visited once. I looked at them all in brief intervals, unwilling to take my eyes off of my savior for long.

Ryland could get me out of here.

Couldn't he?

But what had Cail said about Ryland's memory, or was it his mind?

I couldn't remember.

Everything was tangling together again.

Finally Ryland came to a stop, his large hand pressing me against a damp wall as he looked around the corner we had just travelled around, obviously worried we had been followed.

I clutched his hand, wanting to cling to him—to apologize—but I couldn't think of why I needed to apologize. Had something happened?

"I think we're okay," his voice was relieved, yet when he turned to face me, I audibly gasped.

It was Ryland, but something about him was off. His eyes weren't as blue, or maybe his forehead was higher. I couldn't place exactly what was wrong, however it was possible that I just wasn't remembering him right.

That must have been it. I sighed and pushed myself into him, my body relaxing as his arms wrapped around me.

"Oh, Jos. You have no idea how happy I am to have found you." His hold increased, it was almost like he couldn't get close enough, a sensation I could relate to.

"I know," I said, my body shaking much more than I would have expected. "I thought Cail was..."

My voice cut off as Ryland's grip got tighter again, choking the air from me.

"I thought I would never see you again." He said deeply, his tone becoming monotone while his grip continued to increase.

I gasped and sputtered at the sensation. I hit him and pounded at his back, but he didn't respond until the last possible minute when his hold loosened and his eyes lowered to look right at me.

"I'm sorry, Jos. I got scared."

I looked in his eyes, desperately trying to figure out if it was him or not. All the times in the Tòuha, all the dreams as well as every encounter with Ryland's possessed body had made it so I couldn't tell the real Ryland from the fake Ryland anymore. I didn't know if this Ryland would hurt me or protect me. The old Ryland—my Ryland—was now becoming a fuzzy memory of someone I wasn't even sure existed. I didn't trust the Ryland that held me. I didn't want to be near him.

With that one thought, everything that I had felt before was shattered. I didn't feel the love I had once felt for him and it scared me.

"It's okay," I said, my words stopping as the heavy footsteps from earlier filled the space, the cabinets and bottles in our current refuge rattling with each impact.

Ryland clutched me to him, his nails digging into me at each beat. I barely noticed. My muscles jumped at each footfall right along with them.

Before I knew what had happened, Ryland had grabbed my body and thrown it across the room. I sped through the air, screaming at the unprovoked action, before slamming into an empty book case. The second my body made contact with the moldy shelves, the thumping stopped.

"You brought them to me!" Ryland yelled, his voice echoing around me.

I picked myself up to face him, my body aching from the impact. His eyes were wide and his fists balled at his sides. I stared as he yelled at me before hunching his shoulders and charging at me.

"You cursed me!"

He had made it about halfway across the room before I picked myself up and ran through the first door I could find, Ryland still yelling behind me. I swung the door shut, though I did not halt my progression. I ran from door to door, hallway to hallway, until I thought that I had put enough space between us.

I looked wildly around the room I had entered to see cabinets, a hospital bed, a dresser, and a filthy toilet. I recognized this place, but like all the other rooms, nothing made sense. The walls that had once been solid had deteriorated enough that you could see through them in many areas, but only enough to see what was coming.

It was a lookout.

A hiding place.

I ran over to the toilet and wedged myself between the filthy bowl and what was left of one of the walls, the hospital bed perfectly placed to block me from view.

I moved my legs into my chest and clung to them, my eyes wide as I looked around and tried to figure out my next move.

Next move?

Why was I here anyway?

Did I live here?

No.

That wasn't right.

I clung tighter to my legs, rested my head on my knees and tried to ignore the smell of the toilet, the scurrying feet of large pests, and the

drip

drip

drip

of water that was falling on my head.

A strange heat slowly began to spread through me. It began in my shoulder and soon reached every part of me. I screamed and jumped up, expecting to see blood trickling over my skin, but I found nothing. I looked around in a panic, knowing my yell had given away my location and that Ryland would be right behind me.

I ran my eyes over my skin, still looking for some form of injury, however nothing was there even though the warmth stayed with me.

The warmth seemed familiar, but I didn't know why.

I had the distinct impression I was forgetting something.

Or was it someone?

33

THE WORDS WERE FUNNY, but they calmed me. The strange words belonged to a song, a beautiful song that warmed my heart. I sang the song, the melody one that still lived somewhere deep inside me. I sang it to put myself to sleep every night in the only place I knew. In this room, against the toilet; I stayed here because I could see when they were coming for me. It was the only safe place in this terrifying space.

Ryland was hunting me.

He was determined to kill me. He tried to every day. Every day for forty-two days, I had made marks on the floor by the toilet to track the days, all the days he hunted me. The lines of my blood told me how many days he had hurt me. Forty-two days.

Forty-two days of Cail taunting me before Ryland came. Ryland hurts. Cail didn't hurt; Cail warned.

Cail came first.

Cail always came first.

I felt the drip, drip, drip, against my neck, and that strange warmth flared again. I clawed at it, the same way I had for weeks, the skin now raw and broken in places. I scratched again, trying to get it out of me, but only my own blood ever came.

Blood wasn't comforting. Ryland showed me that every day.

But this warmth was supposed to be comforting. I knew that somewhere deep inside of me.

I knew.

It was like the song; the one with the funny words. I knew they were the same. I knew because of how the song made me feel; how fear slowed when I heard it. I knew the warmth was supposed to be the same.

I knew I was missing something.

If only I could figure out what it was, then I could get out of here.

Go...

CLUNK

I FROZE.

He always tried to find me at night, but he hadn't found this place. Not yet. The only place I was safe was in here. I had hidden here every night during the times I should have been sleeping. Nights, I sat. Days, I ran.

Forty-two days.

Like the marks on the floor.

I had forgotten why I was keeping track. Why did the days matter? I had forgotten what the lines meant, yet still I marked them. Every day a new line. Every day a new mark. I was sure they were supposed to mean something, but I had forgotten.

I forgot everything.

Except the song.

CLUNK

I KNEW HE WAS CLOSE. THE CLUNK WAS CLOSER. I HAD TO move. If he found me here, I would have nowhere to hide.

I stood and ran, not willing to see if he had found me. My foot dragged. It didn't work right after encountering Ryland yesterday. I held onto walls, keeping myself steady, and moved as fast as I could.

I ran from the safe place, through the hall of doors, through the door that led me to what looked like a school, and beyond that a library. The biggest one I had ever seen. I could be safe in the library, but I kept going.

I jumped at all the noises. I cringed away from the rats that watched me run. But I kept going until I reached the room where the desk was. I hid underneath it, hoping it was far enough.

My heart beat loudly, and my breath came hard. I couldn't stop the pounding in my ears. I knew Cail was right behind me.

The door opened before I could stand and find another spot. Cail's heavy footfalls entered. I hid behind the desk, trying to ignore the deafening sound of my pulse in my ears.

He had found me.

I tried to keep my breathing even, yet I knew it was no use. He was looking right at me. I stood slowly, my hand slipping against the side of the desk.

"Y...y...you ca...can't have m...me." I stuttered the words out slowly. It only increased his smile. He shook his head at me dejectedly, looking at me like I was the disgusting filth I knew he saw me as.

I moved my chin toward my collar bone, my nerves catching at his stare, my eyes not quite willing to leave him. I began to twitch and his smile grew.

"Oh, Joclyn," he mocked. I had to remind myself that he was using my name.

"Don't you think this has gone on long enough? Can't you give in? It's already been a week."

I twitched at his words, my eyes darting around. A week? Wasn't it longer? It felt longer, much longer. Forty-two marks, weren't those the days? I looked at Cail questioningly, but he only smiled more.

"No one is coming for you, Joclyn. It's time to end the game."

Was I expecting someone? I couldn't remember. The warmth in my shoulder grew again, and I instinctively moved to scratch at it.

"Wh...wh...who?" I managed to get the one word out, but I could instantly tell that Cail was playing with me. There was no one there to help me, there never was.

"You can't even remember? I wonder what you *can* remember. I wonder what you are holding onto." He looked at me again, and I twitched away.

CLUNK

I JUMPED AND CAIL SMILED AT MY MOVEMENT. MORE NOISES could only mean one thing. Ryland was coming. Ryland hurt. I knew nothing other than pain from Ryland. Somewhere deep inside me something yelled at me that there had once been more, but I couldn't remember what it was anymore. It had been forgotten like everything else. Only one thing mattered.

Ryland hurt.

I knew I needed to run. I moved out from behind the large desk, my eyes getting wider as the sound increased. I jumped at each thump, my eyes so wide they burned. My leg dragged from where they had caught it in the doorframe yesterday. I could see Cail smile when he saw it still hurt.

I didn't wait.

I just moved. I went through the door that would take me through the apartment, then the hall with the fingers. Cail watched me as I went. Cail never hurt.

He just came first.

34

I SCREAMED as the bone cracked.

It always cracked.

And then healed.

Always healed.

"COME BACK HERE! LET ME FINISH WHAT I STARTED!" RYLAND
was angry, always angry. Always hurting.

I dragged myself to the room with books. I could hide
there until it healed. I heard him behind me, he was too
close. He wanted to end it. He wanted me gone.

He had told me so.

He'd said it had been too long. Two weeks.

No, eighty days.

I had lost track, I didn't know which made sense.

Lots of lines on the floor.

Which day? How long?

I didn't know how long.

I clawed at the warmth in my shoulder, my fingers wet
with blood. The warmth was there all the time now. It was

nice; I liked it. If I got it out, I could see what caused it. I could hold it in my hands.

I got to the books and pulled myself into the corner where the rats lived. They let me in. They sat on my lap.

Song.

Song.

No more words.

Words were gone.

Only the song.

I rocked, the rocking helped. The rocking felt nice.

Like the warmth, the warmth so strong.

Song.

Song fading.

I was fading, too.

I could feel it.

"SNAP OUT OF IT, JOCLYN!"

THAT VOICE.

I knew it.

"MI LASKO! SNAP OUT OF IT! GET OUT OF THERE!" THE VOICE was close.

THE WARMTH WAS STRONG. SO STRONG IT HURT. I LOOKED UP to find the voice, yet it was not a voice. It was a girl on a bed. A man was kneeling over her. He was strong. His face was strong. He was tall with bright blue eyes and short blond hair. He was the one who was yelling, but he was not angry like Ryland, he was scared.

Seeing him scared me, too. I moved into the rats, but the rats were gone. They were scared.

"Joclyn! Come back to me!" he yelled again. I could tell he was crying. He placed his hands on the girl, but his hands didn't hurt. His hands were gentle.

I didn't know someone could be so nice.

The warmth inside me grew, but I didn't claw at it. I didn't think I was supposed to anymore.

I couldn't stop looking at the man. I knew this man.

"Joclyn!"

That was my name. He called the girl my name, but the girl was not me. This girl was clean. This girl was beautiful.

I moved to look at the girl.

"Dramin! Bring the Water!" he yelled. Another man entered. This one was tired, but he was kind, too.

"What in land's end is going on here?" The new man was worried.

I walked around them. I couldn't take my eyes off the sad one.

I knew him.

Something was familiar about him, but something was off.

He couldn't see me.

Why couldn't he see me?

"Ovailia has returned. It was just as Joclyn said.... Ryland's here. He's awake."

I spun in fear as the new one said his name, but he was not here. Pain was not here.

"What do you mean he is awake?" the sad one said. There was fear in his voice. He looked back to the girl.

"Joclyn!" he yelled again, but the girl did not respond.

"Ovailia brought him. He is fine, however the bond is gone. Edmund broke it weeks ago."

The sad one was still scared. The new one looked scared now, too.

The warmth. It grew again. It was hot now. It hurt.

"But she is still sleeping... She has been in the Töuha for two weeks. How can she be..." The sad one's voice was heavy. He placed his hand softly against her head.

They were both so nice. Could people be so nice?

"It's a Vymãzat."

"What?" The new man dropped a mug he was holding, the dark liquid seeping into the floor. "How did you miss that? You tried everything..."

"I didn't miss it. It was hidden."

The warmth was so hot it hurt. I clutched my shoulder, my teeth grinding with the pain.

"Ilyan, you can't possibly be saying what I think you are saying..."

Ilyan.

I knew him.

My Ilyan.

The song.

My song.

He sang me the song as I lay dying, when I woke from nightmares, and when I was sad.

I remembered.

Everything.

The sight. The sight of the Drak.

My sight. It must be how I was seeing this.

I looked to Ilyan as he continued to yell at the girl, no, to yell at me. Was this happening now, or had it already happened?

"Ilyan?" I yelled his name in a panic, words feeling

foreign on my tongue after not using them for so long, yet he didn't respond. He looked at the girl, his hair short on his head. I liked it. Now it was the way it had been in the vision. Was that why he cut it? Was it really him?

I waved my hand in front of his face, but he didn't turn. The warmth continued to grow. The warmth that was Ilyan's magic.

Magic.

I walked around them, watching their movements, trying to figure out what to do, and why I was seeing this. It had to be for a reason. It was my way out. I knew it.

My heart thumped at the possibility, my body twitching with overstimulation the way it had for however long I had been trapped in here. One hour to every ten minutes. Weeks. I twitched again. It had been so much longer to me.

I yelled to Ilyan, screaming at him as his panic grew; as he and the new one, Dramin, yelled back and forth. The room was full of sound as they yelled, each person's panic adding to the noise. Without thinking, I reached out to place my hand on Ilyan's arm.

My hand made contact, Ilyan's skin warm underneath my icy fingers. He looked up, and I was sure he could see me. His eyes widened in horror before moving back to the beautiful girl he still sat over.

Everything clicked together as Cail walked through the door, his wicked scowl fading at the scene before him.

And then it hit me.

I had magic.

I placed my hands firmly on Ilyan, shoving him out of the way and directly onto Dramin. Both men fell onto the floor in a heap as I raised my hands; the sleeping form of myself raising hers as well.

I could feel the crackle in my skin, the power

congregating before I released it right into Cail's chest. Cail screamed and jumped to the side, the powerful burst flying into the soft, blood soaked wall behind him.

"No!" I could only smile at his outburst, the fear in his voice making me feel more powerful.

"How do you remember?"

I looked at the group to my left. Cail obviously couldn't see the vision as I could. "I am stronger than you would have ever assumed, Cail. My father made me that way."

"No! It can't be!"

Cail moved to attack, but I stepped to the side, my brain able to determine the weakness of his weapon early on. I did not wait for him to regroup. I did not wait to find a weakness. I needed to get out of here, and Cail was keeping me trapped. I moved my energy seamlessly into him, the power burning him away.

His eyes grew wide at the first of the energy and at the pain my attack was causing him. Soon his legs gave way and he sunk to the ground; his life ebbing away.

"Wyn." His final word was a whisper of his sister's name. My best friend. I didn't have time to make sense of it. I didn't have time to rejoice.

It took only a moment for me to realize my mistake, though. I was trapped inside Cail's mind, a mind I had just destroyed.

Everything around me began to shift and fall as Cail's consciousness disintegrated into nothing. I screamed as the ceiling peeled away, the doors fell off of their hinges, and red liquid poured into the room from behind every new opening. I would drown in it. Drown here, in Cail's mind. There was no return path out of here. I would die here.

I turned to Ilyan, knowing this was the end.

My breath caught as Ilyan looked right into me, his eyes

seeing me as I stood in the melting room, the floor shifting as it attempted to give way.

"Goodbye." My voice caught as I reached toward him, my fingers twisting around his newly cut hair. I wished I could tell him that I liked it. I liked how young it made him look, how strong. I smiled, trying to ignore the tears on my cheeks.

"No!" I felt Ilyan's arms wrap around me, his body bridging the gap between worlds. His magic flared and filled me so quickly I couldn't stop it.

I screamed in fear at the pressure before I realized the change.

My body seemed more real, and my brain was clearer. Ilyan had somehow brought me back.

I looked around wildly not knowing what to expect. I was lying on a bed, my body twitching and my breathing ragged. I could barely make out Ilyan's voice while my mind tried desperately to focus on his magic.

"Joclyn?" Ilyan's voice was wild, his eyes wide at everything that had happened.

I didn't know how to respond to him. I didn't know if I could. I reached up and placed my hands on his face, my eyes boring into his. I had his eyes memorized; every speck of gold, every vein. Those memories came back stronger than I had ever experienced, and for one fleeting moment, I felt my heart calm.

It was him.

"Ilyan."

I pulled him to me, placing my forehead against his as I clung to him, basked in him.

And then everything changed.

The door to the room I had been placed in flew open

and Ryland walked in. His blue eyes were wide and scared as he searched for me, but it didn't matter.

He was pain.

I couldn't stop it.

My learned reflexes took over and my breathing picked up as my body moved into a panic. I pulled my head toward my left shoulder and tried to hide.

And then I remembered.

I had magic.

I lifted my hands as something deep inside of me yelled at me to stop. My brain screamed at me, but I couldn't focus through the fear. The response that I had been trained to display over the past two months had become far too strong in me now.

Somehow—in the recesses of my mind—I knew I had seen this scene before.

Still, I aimed to kill.

My magic flew away from me and Dramin stepped in front of Ryland as he did his best to shield him. I knew why my mind had been screaming.

I had seen this before.

And now I knew where.

The screaming of everyone in the room intensified as did Ilyan's magic running through me. I was able to glance once at Dramin's slow decent to the floor before Ilyan's magic put me to sleep.

35

I DIDN'T KNOW what had woken me. I didn't even know where I was. I heard the thump of a knock, the whisper of voices and my mind kicked into overdrive. I spun out of the bed, landing on the floor as quietly as I could, my eyes darting around the unfamiliar space.

Several large, stone arches sat to the left of the king-sized bed I had been lying in, each one opening to a beautiful, star-filled sky. I should have been able to bask in the beauty—the safety that this mysterious place was offering me—but I couldn't convince my mind of that.

My heart still beat erratically, my eyes darting around. This space was too open. I was too exposed here. Pain could find me.

There were two doors, both rounded arches covered by large, wooden slabs. I could hear voices behind one, so I moved to the other, holding my breath in case I was heard. I slipped behind the other door, my eyes burning at the dim blue light that filled the space.

Slowly my eyes adjusted to a modern bathroom built out of porcelain and glass which gleamed against the light. I looked around for another way out but found nothing. I was trapped in this mysterious room.

You're safe. Nothing is going to get you.

I tried to convince myself of it, even though I wasn't quite sure where it had come from. The blood-bathed rooms of Cail's mind were still so fresh in my consciousness. The torture, the running, the fear. Still, I could see Ilyan's face as he'd rescued me. And Dramin...

I slid myself between the toilet and the sink just before the door on the other side of the room creaked, the voices from the hall becoming audible.

"I can't do everything, Ilyan. Ovailia is already eyeing me, and I am not sure how much I can do for Dramin." Thom's voice was loud with desperation. The impact of the sound shook through me and I twitched, my hands flying up to tangle in my hair.

"We need him, Thom. The faster we know if he is going to pull through, the better. I cannot produce the Black Water and Joclyn will be needing some very soon..."

"But that's just it, Ilyan," Thom interrupted. "It's almost as if he saw this coming. His room is covered with at least fifty mugs, each filled to the brim with that poison."

"What?"

"I know, and if he saw that, then what else did he see? Especially with how Ovailia is acting."

"Is she still not letting our brother out of her sight?"

"No. I don't trust her, Ilyan." Thom's voice was heavy, hurt. I had never heard so much fear in him. I shook and sunk closer to the toilet.

"I don't trust her, eith—" Ilyan stopped talking suddenly and then swore loudly in Czech, the echoes bounding around me.

"Where did she go?" Thom asked, his question fading as Ilyan closed the door.

I didn't hear Ilyan's footsteps, I only felt his magic grow inside of me as he tracked me. His energy moved through me, strong and aggressive; the absence of my barrier giving his magic free rein. I gasped and moved closer against the wall, hoping to disappear behind the toilet.

It was only moments before the door to the bathroom opened a bit, Ilyan's magic lessening as he approached me. His body folded into a crouch in front of me. He had obviously been sleeping; his short hair was tousled, his chest bare. Ilyan's eyes were soft, wide, and shining. My heart rate settled somewhat at his gaze. It hadn't felt this normal in months; the pain from the incessant thudding lessened.

I stared into those eyes, relishing the steady beat, the calmness that he was bringing me. I hadn't even noticed his hand was moving until it came to rest against my cheek. I jumped at the unexpected contact before settling back, my shaky hands moving to cover his.

My hands clung to Ilyan. I held his magic deep within me as he healed me, comforted me. I refused to look away from him. Part of me was still scared he would disappear or that this was all a trick; that he would hurt me, too.

I leaned my head against the base of the sink—my hair falling over my face as I moved—Ilyan gently moved it away, his finger touching my mark as he placed the strands behind my ear. I jerked at the jolt that moved down my spine from Ilyan's touch, the single jerk morphing into a million twitches.

"Shhhh, mi lasko, shhhh." Ilyan attempted to move closer to me in an effort to comfort me, yet in the end, he gave up and magically slowed my heart rate instead.

"Is-is Dr...Dramin... d-d-dead?" I tried so hard to keep the stutter out of my voice, but it didn't work. It seemed to have followed me. Ilyan's eyes widened at my voice, and I realized I hadn't spoken more than his name since my return to this world.

"No, he had a shield around him, but your strength was still too much for him. He is alive, but we do not know for how much longer." He wrapped his hand around mine, his eyes refusing to leave mine in fear of my reaction.

My eyes widened at his words, my neck muscles twitching. I had seen Dramin's death in my sight, the unknown magic flying toward him. So to have seen it replayed in life, with my magic as the death blow, I knew what that meant; Dramin would not recover. I cringed, pushing my terror away as I clung to the cool porcelain.

"It's not your fault, Joclyn." I turned toward him, my eyes wide. I couldn't tell him how wrong he was. I may not have been in my right mind, but it would never be anything other than my fault.

"Ryland had a shield around him..." Ilyan's sentence was drowned out by my screams.

Just hearing his name brought every single memory that I had been trying to restrain to the surface. They cut into me like a blunted knife; tearing through me in slow agony. I cringed and howled, my eyes darting around for him, expecting pain to come through the door at any minute.

"N-n-no!" I howled. Ilyan's eyes widened as he tried to figure out what was going on; why I was reacting this way.

"H-he ca-can't f-find m-me." I clawed at the toilet in an attempt to push myself further back against the wall. My hands moved to claw at the warmth that was moving through me. I knew it was ridiculous, yet I couldn't help it. The action had become learned, almost comforting.

"Jos... love... calm down..." Ilyan's hands fluttered around me, the panic on his face growing.

"H-he wi-will hurt-t me." I grabbed his arms, desperate to make him understand the danger I was in. My twitches flowed freely even as I tried to control them.

My body was waging a battle with itself. One side desperately wanted to run, to hide. The other pleaded with me that I was safe, that Ilyan was here and the nightmares were gone.

"No, love, no," I focused on Ilyan's words as his magic flared, my heart rate slowing at his command. "He will never hurt you again. I will keep you safe."

He looked deeply into me, my insides continuing to unwind.

Safe. Ilyan would keep me safe. I knew it was true. I knew it deep within me. I focused on him as I willed the calm to overtake me, as I willed my brain to believe his words.

"What happened to you?" I could tell the question was more to himself than to me, but it still startled me. I didn't want to relive it all.

I looked at him—his magic moving through me, his hand wrapped around mine—and wished I could tell him everything, but I didn't want to see it. I didn't want to say it.

I uncurled my hand out from underneath the security of my body, the fingers stiff and bent. I stared at that hand, feeling the strength of my magic under my skin and the strength of Ilyan's magic that moved alongside mine. I knew what I wanted to do, but I didn't even know if it was possible.

I placed my hand against his forehead and let my magic surge into him, his eyes closing as I pushed the memory into him. For one sparkling second my body relaxed, the flinching stopped, and my heart rate normalized. As the memory left me to play inside of Ilyan's mind, I felt like myself again, like everything was okay.

But I knew it wouldn't last; this clarity. Finally I could see Ilyan and Ryland clearly. I could feel some of what I had once felt for Ryland; the feelings that months of torture at his hands had taken away from me.

Ilyan's eyes opened and the memory came flooding back into me, the twitches and fear returning with it. I moved further back against the toilet, the sudden return heightening the emotions.

"Mi lasko?" Ilyan said softly, but I could hear the heartbreak, the blame he was already placing on himself.

Ilyan didn't wait, he moved into me, his body wedging mine against the toilet. I tried to find comfort in his touch, but the fear was too raw. I cried out and sunk away, my panic increasing.

"You are safe, Joclyn." he said, his heavy voice right against my ear. "No one is going to hurt you, not anymore."

I wanted to believe him, I longed for it, but I couldn't make my reality calm down enough to do so.

"So you were trapped in Cail's mind?"

I stared at him from the security of my porcelain prison. I didn't want to say it, though I knew it was true.

"It makes sense. For two weeks I couldn't figure out what was going on. I couldn't get you back. I tried everything..." Ilyan dragged his hand through what was left of his hair, his eyes shining with the residual emotion of what he had gone through.

I looked at him, unsure what to contribute, knowing I didn't want to say anything. I wasn't even sure I wanted to hear what he had to say, yet I needed to. I needed to know that I was safe and why.

"It's no wonder I couldn't. They had taken you through the Tŏuha and into Cail's mind, leaving no trace. Your mind was disconnected from your body. It's a miracle I got you back... especially without the connection of a Zĕlství."

"Wh...what-t-t d-do y...you m-m-mean?" I struggled to get it out of me, my internal mind still screaming at me to run.

I'm okay here.

I repeated the words to myself, trying to keep my panic in check, however I already knew it wasn't working. I could feel the panic taking over.

"Edmund broke the Zĕlství between you and... and..." he hesitated and I knew he was trying to tiptoe around Ryland's name, "your mate, in an effort to trap you in Cail's mind."

I stared at him, not sure how I was supposed to feel. Strangely, I wasn't as sad or heartbroken as I probably should have been at hearing about the loss of my bond with Ry. I wasn't even sure what I felt. When I thought of him, instead of love, I only felt scared. I was still scared of Ryland coming to find me, scared of the pain, of how he would hurt me.

But more than that, I was relieved.

I was free.

No more nightmares. No more torture. No more.

I opened my mouth to say something when a knock on the bathroom door sent me jumping. Ilyan calmed me before opening the door just enough to look out while still keeping me out of sight.

"Yes?" Ilyan asked, his voice level.

"He said it took about a week to adjust, but he's not sure what was done, so it may take longer." Thom's voice was quiet on the other side of the door.

"Was it this bad?"

"No," Thom said, "but you know how Ryland was raised... she's not used to that."

I screamed, my eyes darting around at the mention of his name. My pulse picked up again and Ilyan's magic flared in an attempt to calm me.

"No," I moaned, "no, no, no."

"Jos," Ilyan soothed, "It's okay. He's not here."

"He...h...he's g...going t...to f-f-find me. Hurt, hurt, hurt me." I instinctively began clawing at my shoulder, the warmth of Ilyan's magic triggering my learned response.

"No, mi lasko, no. I'm not going to let that happen, remember? Remember it wasn't really Ryland in the Tõuha."

"I-i-it wa-was him. P-p-pain. No, no m-more."

Ilyan's magic flared aggressively, causing my consciousness to dip enough for me to get a grip on my panic then he grabbed my hand, holding tight as he rubbed his thumb over my skin.

I saw Ilyan's jaw clench. I tightened my shoulders, expecting Ryland to burst through the door.

"What else is it, Thom?"

"He's asking to see her again." Thom's voice was laced with more worry than I had ever heard.

"No." Ilyan said, his tone making it clear he did not want to elaborate.

"When?" Thom asked, although I was sure he didn't care.

"A week, a month, maybe never. I don't know. You heard what happened when you said his name. I'm not sure what I am looking at here yet." Ilyan looked at me and I glanced away.

"Well make it snappy, we spotted two more camps this morning...."

"I know, Thom," Ilyan interrupted, making it obvious he was hiding something. I simply didn't care.

"Are those for her?" Ilyan asked, gesturing to something that I couldn't see.

"Oh, yeah, I brought quite a few with me now, in case she breaks some." Thom brought a tray with about five mugs of Black Water into the room, Ilyan scowling at him as he looked toward me. His eyes widened at seeing me there, against the toilet.

"Hi, T...T...Thom." I tried to sound as normal as I could, but still couldn't keep the stutter out of my voice.

"Hey, Silnỳ," he said, a deep vein of pity lining his voice.

In his eagerness to spy, he dropped the tray a little fast and one of the corners snapped against the tile floor before Ilyan could catch it.

I jerked so fast my head slammed into the side of the sink, my hands coming up to cover my ears as I began to rock back and forth, Ilyan's song humming on my lips.

"Good Gravy!" I heard Thom exclaim, "What did he do to her?"

"Out, Thom!" Ilyan roared as Thom left, the door clicking a little too loudly behind him.

I groaned out my panic and pulled my head down into my knees. Ilyan's magic surging through me as he put me back to sleep.

36

I woke in Ilyan's arms, rejoicing at the return of something that could now be described as normal. I moved into him before the panic could start, pressing my face into his chest. His smell made me light headed in a pleasant, comforting way. I hadn't remembered Ilyan having a smell, especially one as strong as this; wildflowers and smoke. Was the smell new, or had I chosen not to acknowledge it until right then?

I pressed closer to him, my cheek resting against the scars that crisscrossed his skin. I breathed deeply, flinching when Ilyan's arms tightened around me. I tried to focus on staying still, on staying sane, but it didn't seem to be working.

His touch triggered my spasms, my fear. I knew it wasn't him, it was any touch. Anyone would give me the same reaction.

Ilyan seemed to sense my increased heart rate, his magic calming me instantly.

"Joclyn?" I leaned into him more, focusing on his magic, focusing on the calm I so desperately wanted.

"Are you okay?" His chin brushed against the hair on the top of my head, his arms holding me tighter.

I nodded my head in response, knowing that I would stutter if I talked and not wanting to. If only I could talk into his mind like I could send pictures. He must have accepted my answer, though, because his hand loosened its hold and moved to smooth my hair, sweeping rhythmically over my head. His song hummed against the top of my head where his lips pressed against my skin.

His song.

I sighed at the tune, sung by the person I wanted to hear it from more than anyone else in the world. I could feel his lips turn up in response to my reaction, but he did not move, his song remained strong and consistent.

We stayed like that for longer than could have been deemed normal, but I could have stayed there much longer. With his arms around me and the song replaying constantly, I could feel the feelings of panic and despair leaving me.

I could feel normal.

Almost.

Ilyan pulled away enough to look at me, the gold specks in his eyes reflecting the morning light right back at me. His soft hands moved my hair away from my face, his finger grazing against my mark. The jolt of magic shot down my spine and I knew it was now only Ilyan that could cause it. I fought the panic that tried to break free at the shock, my eyes glued to his as he smiled. His face was a mixture of pride, worry, and most of all, love.

I buried my head into his chest while his arms stayed strong around me as he moved his head down to whisper in my ear.

"I'm going to go get you some Black Water. I'll be right back." The heavy, wooden door opened and closed as he left, but I stayed still in the bed, hiding underneath the covers. I stretched my hand out over the cotton sheet, laying it flat on the warm part where his body had just been. My heart rate stayed steady even though he had gone; the warmth almost a promise of his return.

But I wasn't sure, and that worried me.

I didn't even have time to think about it before the door opened again, this time closing with a thunk before heavy footsteps moved toward me. I jumped at the noise, my body instantly rolling into a tight little ball. I tried to convince myself that it was just Ilyan coming back, but I knew better. I knew that gait. My brain had memorized that breathing. I peeked out from behind the covers, not wanting to see.

Ryland stood before the bed, his hands calmly at his sides, his dark curls falling over his bright blue eyes as they had always done, but my mind didn't see that.

My mind replaced the happy smile with a wicked grimace, dark curls with greasy strands, and even the wall behind him began to turn red in my panic.

My breathing picked up in a matter of seconds, my body moving away from him as I panicked and stuttered, his eyes growing wide at my reaction.

"Jos? Sweetheart? What's wrong?" His voice was kind and gentle, but I didn't trust it. He had played this game on me before, only to end up hurting me.

"G-go a...a...away." I tried to make my voice strong, knowing from the start that it wouldn't work.

"Jos? I'm not going to hurt you, honey." His voice was pleading, but I couldn't stop moving away from him. Ryland was now leaning against the foot of the bed, his body posed as he prepared to crawl towards me over the bed.

I howled as he moved onto the bed, my voice making

noises that had no recognition in any language in an attempt to get him away from me.

"It's okay, sweetheart. It's okay. I had to see you. I had to know you were all right. After everything that Cail did..."

"Go. Away!" I was surprised at my own voice, but tried hard not to let it show.

I balled my fingers into fists, grateful my fear kept me from attacking him, but not knowing if it was the right choice. I wanted to attack him.

"Jos! I'm not going to hurt you!" he yelled in frustration. He was practically on top of me now, my heart felt like it was going to beat right through me with how hard it was thumping in my chest.

We both stayed silent at his outburst; my breathing ragged, his heavy. He didn't remove his eyes from mine as I watched him calculate what to do with me. I tried to find the power to fight back, yet my fear kept me restricted. Then we both heard it, yelling voices in the hall.

I recognized them both immediately. I had heard them enough. Ilyan and Ovailia. My eyes widened as Ryland looked at me, a million different puzzle pieces clicking into place. But the picture still didn't make any sense.

"Ovi...Ovailia b-brought y-you hee...here?" I tried to speak beyond the panic, but I wasn't quite sure it was working. Ryland's eyes softened, as if he himself had made some great breakthrough.

"Yes. Ilyan wouldn't let me see you. I needed to see you, Jos. You are all I think about. One of the only memories I have left." I could see the heartbreak in his face, and for one moment, I almost pitied him. I almost understood him. But even if I had wanted to, I couldn't trust him. I still waited for him to hurt me at the same time that I continued to fight the desire to hurt him.

"Ilyan p-protec-cts me." I had wanted to explain to Ryland how safe Ilyan made me, that he was doing what I needed, but Ryland's face changed.

His eyes grew dark, and I watched his body shake. In turn, mine went into a further panic. What little calm I had been able to find was washed away.

"Ilyan hides you from me!" He rose up above me, his shoulders squaring dangerously.

"N-no!" I tried to move further away from him, but his legs had pinned me down. I was trapped.

"Yes! He wants you all to himself as he feeds you lies about how dangerous I am; how mean I am! Even though I would never hurt you. Ilyan made you break our Zělství!" Ryland's yell rose as I continued to panic.

"N-no!"

"Ovailia was right." He roared at me, and I almost missed what was coming. His fist pulled back as the skin of his hand glowed red, his magic fueling his anger as he moved to punch me.

I couldn't move. I couldn't make my magic respond. I stared at him, tears flowing down my cheeks. The part of me that had held out hope that this was not the Ryland who had hunted me died when he moved to do that which I had come to believe he always did. Hurt me.

His fist moved toward me at a speed I couldn't even comprehend, the knuckles making contact with the side of my face. I howled at the impact. My voice rising up as burning pain spread through my skull, as I fought to get away from what Ryland would do next. Before either of us could make another move, a gust of wind flew through the room and lifted Ryland off of me. I didn't look to see who had rushed in, I only howled as I rolled off the bed onto the ancient stone and slid myself underneath the heavy, wooden bed.

Hiding was my first defense now. It felt safe here. I could feel the pressure of both the bed and the floor pushing against me. I tried to keep my breathing and cries to a minimum in the hope of not being found, however I was not sure it mattered. Ilyan and Ovailia's raised voices had entered the room, the screaming match in Czech having only intensified at what they had found.

"But he didn't hurt her did he?" Ovailia yelled as she transitioned smoothly to English.

"Ovailia, he punched her when I came into the room!" I heard Ilyan's feet move toward me, his stocking feet coming into sight. I cringed at the possibility that he would pull me out, yet he stayed there, guarding my hiding place.

"I didn't see that." Ovailia lied, I heard Ryland chuckle next to her and my insides stiffened.

"He's going to lie anyway, Ovailia. He's been feeding her lies. Just as you said." I stuffed my fist in my mouth at the sound of Ryland's voice to keep from screaming.

"What lies have you been telling *him*, Ovailia?" Ilyan asked, the amount of fear in his voice alarming.

"Nothing much. Two can play at this game, Ilyan." Her voice was sweet as honey, but I knew better because this wasn't a game; no matter how many times Cail had told me that it was.

Cail.

Without warning I began to howl again. My safe place suddenly felt like a prison. I could hear Ovailia laughing beyond my screams.

"I want you out, Ovailia! Leave the Abbey and take your games with you," Ilyan roared above my yells. I could just make out Ovailia's laugh as Ilyan removed her and placed the door back in place.

It took a second before his face appeared in the gap under the bed, his hand reaching to help me out. I couldn't see through the fear enough to respond, though. I only howled more.

I felt Ilyan's magic flare inside of me, his warmth moving through me as he steadied my heartbeat. My voice died into nothing, my anxiety lessoning. Ilyan reached forward again, but I just looked at him, not quite willing to leave the security the bed provided me. Ilyan waited another moment before relaxing his hand, his body lowering as he lay down on the ground beside me. His body was stretched out on the floor while mine was crammed under the bed.

"I'm sorry, Jos." His voice was soft, and while I could feel some of my panic edge away, it wasn't quite enough. "I will make you safe. I will make you whole again."

I stared at him, my eyes wide. I tried to convince myself that what he said was true; that I was safe, that I would be whole again, and that I would no longer feel this panic and pain that controlled my body.

But I didn't know if I could believe him. I wasn't even sure if that was possible.

Ilyan began to wedge himself under the bed; his tall, wiry frame moving right up against me. I could feel the warmth radiating off of his skin.

Without thinking, I reached up and pulled at one of the short locks of hair that covered his head. He smiled at the action, his body moving closer as I brought my hand back.

"I cut it for you after what you said in Italy. When you couldn't wake up... I was..." his voice caught, and I could almost swim in the emotion that was emanating from him, the fear and the terror. I knew what he must have felt because I had felt it too when I had first been trapped in the Tŏuha.

I curled myself into him as he lay beside me, his body wrapping around me tightly. I laid my head against his chest as the space around us filled with his song. Ilyan whispered the words roughly, the sound surrounding me in comfort.

I stayed stiff in his grip as he sang, his hand rubbing over my back, his lips heavy against the skin on my temple. All the while, deep inside I was still waiting; waiting for someone to attack, waiting for blood to come. Waiting for Ryland to hurt me; Ryland, who wasn't even safe in the real world anymore. I knew that place was gone. I had made it out, right to where I wanted to be.

Where I yearned to be.

I was where I had held out hope that someday I would be again. It was the reason I had never forgotten his song. My heart had held onto him. As he clung to me, as he soothed me and held me, I felt everything begin to relax.

My heart opened me up, taking me away from the panic that still clung to my body and hid deep inside my muscle tissue. The panic, fear, and anxiety deep inside of me continued to be there. I knew it wasn't gone, yet somehow Ilyan made it better. He made my heart calm.

My heart.

Love.

It was so strong. It filled me, consumed me. If I focused on it, I could almost feel normal. Normal. No twitches, no stutters, no rats scurrying through my brain. I could easily remember every moment of my life, every heartbreak, every joy, and every fear. Every moment I'd shared with every person that ever meant anything to me. I saw it all with perfect clarity, the emotions sharper than I had ever remembered them previously. They weren't as raw as the terrors I had escaped from, they were just me, and with only those thoughts inside of me, I could just be me.

Just a girl in Ilyan's arms.

Slowly I uncoiled my body, my arms disentangling from against my chest to wrap them around Ilyan. My fingers dug into his shirt, wrapping the fabric around them. I pulled him close to me, and he enveloped my body with his own, keeping me close, keeping me safe.

Danger was everywhere. Heck, danger was now tucked deep inside my brain. I knew without a doubt I would be haunted by it for the rest of my life, but right there—right then—I was bigger than it. Ilyan made me bigger than it, made me stronger than it.

Ilyan made me stronger, and there in his arms, I felt everything open. Every magical vein in my body was alive, surging with fire—with power.

I wasn't as scared anymore. I wasn't as confused. I could do anything.

I was also certain of where I was going to start. I didn't know if it was based in fear, or pain, or revenge for what he had done to me, but one thing was clear...

I was going to start by killing Ryland LaRue.

ALSO BY REBECCA ETHINGTON

THE WORLD OF IMDALIND

THE CIRCUS OF SHIFTERS

Flame of the Phoenix, Book Four

The Dragon Queen Series

Rising Flame (coming March 2019)

Books 2-4 TBA

THE OTHER WORLDS

The Through Glass Series

Book One: The Dark

Book Two: The Blue

Book Three: The Rose

Book Four: The Cut

Book Five: The Light (Coming 2019)

Book Six: The Ascended (Coming 2019)

Of River and Raynn, The Series

The Catalyst: Act One (Rereleases 2019)

The Requisite: Act Two (Coming 2019)

ABOUT THE AUTHOR

Rebecca Ethington is an internationally bestselling author with almost 700,000 books sold. Her breakout debut, The Imdalind Series, has been featured on bestseller lists since its debut in 2012, reaching thousands of adoring fans worldwide and cited as "Interesting and Intense" by *USA Today's Happily Ever After Blog*.

From writing horror to romance and creating every sort of magical creature in between, Rebecca's imagination weaves vibrant worlds that transport readers into the pages of her books. Her writing has been described as fresh, original, and groundbreaking, with stories that bend genres and create fantastical worlds.

Born and raised under the lights of a stage, Rebecca has written stories by the ghost light, told them in whispers in dark corridors, and never stopped creating within the pages of a notebook.

Find me online
www.rebeccaethington.com
contact@rebeccaethington.com

ACKNOWLEDGMENTS

Who could have predicted the outpouring of love and support and kindness I have felt after Kiss of Fire made its debut. I certainly didn't! I have been overwhelmed by everything that has happened, and continues to happen. I cannot thank you (yes you!) enough for being part of that. Thank you for reading, for sharing, for loving, for reviewing, for your eager anticipation. Thank you for your support.
My fans have blown me away!
Thank you to my family who has stood by me, and cheered me on.
Thank you to Kim who stepped in to edit at the last minute and saved the day. Thank you to Sarah whose endless vision creates one amazing cover after another. Thank you to Crystal for the neck rub, and the final edit gloss over – you perfected this piece!
Thank you to my beta readers and anyone who stepped up with a smile and supported me.
Truly, you amaze me.

THE IMDALIND SERIES

CPSIA information can be obtained
at www.ICGtesting.com
Printed in the USA
JSHW031008130420
5066JS00001B/242